Flashman and the
Golden Sword

Robert Brightwell

This book is dedicated to my friend and weaponry expert, Garry James, whose help and advice was essential to the tale.

Published in 2018 by FeedARead.com Publishing

First Edition

A CIP catalogue record for this title is available from the British
Library.

Introduction

Of all the enemies that Thomas Flashman has shrunk away from, there was one he feared above them all. By his own admission they gave him nightmares into his dotage. It was not the French, the Spanish, the Americans or the Mexicans. It was not even the more exotic adversaries such as the Iroquois, Mahratta or Zulus. While they could all make his guts churn anxiously, the foe that really put him off his lunch were the Ashanti.

"You could not see them coming," he complained. "They were well armed, fought with cunning and above all, there were bloody thousands of the bastards."

This eighth packet in the Thomas Flashman memoirs details his misadventures on the Gold Coast in Africa. It was a time when the British lion discovered that instead of being the king of the jungle, it was in fact a crumb on the lip of a far more ferocious beast. Our 'hero' is at the heart of this revelation after he is shipwrecked on that hostile shore. While waiting for passage home, he is soon embroiled in the plans of a naïve British governor who has hopelessly underestimated his foe. When he is not impersonating a missionary or chasing the local women, Flashman finds himself being trapped by enemy armies, risking execution and the worst kind of 'dismemberment,' not to mention escaping prisons, spies, snakes, water horses (hippopotamus) and crocodiles.

It is another rip-roaring Thomas Flashman adventure, which tells the true story of an extraordinary time in Africa that is now almost entirely forgotten.

Check out the other books in the series and a gallery of some of the historical characters featured at www.robertbrightwell.com. As always, if you have not read the adventures of Thomas' more famous uncle, Harry Flashman, edited by George MacDonald Fraser, then these are strongly recommended.

Robert Brighwell

Chapter 1

I doubt you have ever found yourself in the death hut of the Fantee tribe in Africa, and you should give fervent thanks for that every day. The whitewashed mud walls were daubed with various signs and symbols in a dark reddish-brown paint that I strongly suspected was blood. I shuddered as I sat tied to the central post that held up the roof and wondered if the contents of my veins would soon add to the primitive mural before me. I could have wept, and possibly did, as I thought back on the appalling luck which had brought me to that place.

Readers of my last adventure will recall that it ended with me being pitched from an open boat, alone on an unknown African shore. I had planned to walk north along the coast until I found some sign of civilisation. But having been chased by an improbably huge and fast grey beast with big teeth in both jaws, I tried to make my way inland. Two days' struggling through the impenetrable jungle and I found myself back by the sea; scratched, stung, bitten, hungry and thirsty. I began to think that my game was up. I had not seen any sign of mankind since I had landed. I knew I needed help to survive. Then I had the first promising idea since I had beached on that hostile shore: I would let the locals come to me. Apart from the rags I stood in, my only other possession was my Collier revolver pistol. I used some of the powder in the cartridges and a spark from the flint to start a fire. I piled on kindling until I had a good blaze and then some large damp leaves, which soon had a dark column of smoke rising into the air. I sat back then, wondering what kind of visitor I might be summoning. Would they be some friendly tribe who would know of European missions or forts on the west coast of Africa; or alternatively some murderous savages, who would kill me on the spot and then possibly eat my remains.

Twice I nearly stamped out the fire as my imagination filled with thoughts of death by torture. Then, I wondered, if no one saw the smoke, whether I would just die a long and lingering death on the beach or be stamped on and gored by one of those vast grey creatures. Finally, just as I began to conclude that there might not be another living soul within a hundred miles, the drumming began. Perhaps it was my imagination, but it seemed a dark and sinister rhythm, a rapid tattoo of beats that were regularly repeated. Then the same staccato noises were replicated from a new direction in the jungle and later a third. I knew then that they would come for me, whether they be angels or demons.

I crept away from the fire that night and hid in the dunes down the beach, where I was half eaten by sand-flies as I watched for my visitors. I must have fallen into an exhausted sleep for at dawn I awoke to the low murmur of alien tongues. As I warily opened one eye I saw that I was surrounded by a forest of black legs. Their owners stood in a circle about me staring down at my prostrate form, more with expressions of disgust than any sign of aggression. As I stirred, two stepped back and wrinkled their noses in distaste, as though I was the town drunk rolling out of the church porch on a Sunday morning. I must have looked and smelt pretty foul. I had not been able to change my clothes or shave for nearly a month, after I had abandoned a sinking ship to find land in its longboat. I was covered in cuts and bites and my throat was dry, but I managed to croak, "Please, do any of you speak English?"

They stared at me blankly as I added somewhat desperately, "Do you know of any other white men like me?" I pointed at my skin, which was now more grey than white.

Surely some Europeans had come this way in the past, I thought, but then I realised that if they had, they were probably slavers who would not have endeared themselves to the local populace. Most of the men about me had long spears, but two had muskets, which were still slung on their shoulders. At least they had not butchered me on the spot, I thought, but then I began to wonder if they would help me at all. As I stared about me, looking for any sign of comprehension, two of them stepped back to make way for a beaming new arrival.

"Good morning, sir, I am Mr Fenwick."

I stared at the man in bewilderment as while he spoke in perfect English, he was dressed in just a loin cloth and a homespun tunic, like the others standing about me. Wait, though; while the others were as black as the ace of spades, this warrior clearly had some European among his recent ancestors, for his skin was brown. I realised that I was still gaping at the fellow and pulled myself together. "Er, Mr Fenwick, I am delighted to make your acquaintance," I gasped. "I have been shipwrecked here. Is there a British settlement nearby or someone who can help me get back home?"

Fenwick beamed back. "The British are at the Cape Coast Castle, but that is several days' march away. We have a white man in our village, would you like to meet him?"

I could have wept with relief; instead of being killed I was being helped. I could recover my strength at this village and then make my way to the British settlement. Once there it would only be a matter of time before a ship came to take me home. "That would be most agreeable," I replied, feeling a weight of worry lift from my shoulders.

I had long since learned not to take people at face value, for in my time I have met the most treacherous villains dressed as princes and some of the most generous appearing to have little to give. I'm not proud, I will take advantage of 'em all to get what I want, which is invariably a way back to a safe, warm bed in Leicestershire. My new friends gave me water and a grey paste to eat – it had a strangely fermented taste, but I was far too hungry to care. Then we set off back to their village.

They found paths and tracks through the jungle that I had missed and, in a few hours, we were approaching the outskirts of a settlement. It looked a poor place – two score of mud-walled huts with grass roofs. As we approached curious children stared at me from behind their mothers, the braver ones running alongside my escorts, shouting to announce our arrival. By the time we reached the little clearing in the middle of the village there must have been over a hundred people gathered there, the arrival of a dishevelled white stranger clearly being a rare occurrence. I stared around for the other white man that Fenwick had mentioned, but he was nowhere to be seen. There was a gnarled lump of wood in the centre of the clearing, covered with scraps of cloth, knotted leaves and some bloody pieces of flesh that were half covered in flies. I felt the first twinge of alarm as I looked about me and saw that many of the men present had brought spears or muskets. Why did they need those? Had they lured me here under false pretences?

I searched out Fenwick, "Where is this other white man?" I asked.

"He will be here soon, they are just getting him ready." Fenwick beamed a reassuring smile and gestured over my shoulder as a horn sounded nearby. I turned around to see a white man being carried into the clearing on a chair raised on the shoulders of four natives. I could tell he was white as I could see his calves, but his face was obscured by a large drooping parasol. The crowd had acclaimed his appearance, jumping up and down, shouting and waving weapons in the air. Whether they were cheering their white chief or threatening me it was hard to say. He was set down ten yards in front of me and Fenwick went forward to announce my arrival. I glanced again at the decorated lump of wood; perhaps it was my imagination, but the gnarled surface looked like the face of an angry man. I could not help but wonder at what awful sights it had scowled down on that had resulted in its bloody varnish. I remembered stories we had been taught at school of the ancient British druids making human sacrifices, but surely times had moved on. I tried to convince myself that no European would countenance such a thing. No, I thought, whoever this fellow was, he would welcome one who could share news and talk to him in his own tongue. I was no threat to him and he, in turn, could help me reach the British fort. I would leave him to rule his little kingdom.

Then Fenwick stood back and the parasol was raised. My jaw dropped in astonishment, while my bowels must have danced a polka in terror.

It was Jonah, the half-mad bastard who had tried to kill me as we had been shipwrecked on this coast. As readers of my previous adventures will know, I had last seen him as I had tightened a coil of rope around his ankles that was attached to an anchor embedded in the reef off shore. How in heaven's name he had got to land I could not say, but it had evidently not been easy as I now saw that he had a splinted and bandaged thigh. He must have dragged himself onto the beach while I was trying to find my way through the jungle.

If his appearance had shocked me, then certainly the reverse was true. Jonah gaped for a moment like a gaffed codfish. His mouth was working but no sound came out. He had drunk seawater on our voyage and consequently had lost at least half the wits he once possessed. But now his voice came back as he screeched and pointed an accusing finger.

"You foul and treacherous fiend. You tried to kill me, but God has spared me again. Now you will pay for your crimes. I will have you torn limb from limb!" He was raving now, spittle flying from his mouth, and he was positively shaking with fury. "Your entrails will be taken from you before your very eyes and your bones will be fed to the dogs. But wait…" He paused and stared up at the heavens for a moment as though seeking divine guidance. "No," he declared, "he has spoken to me. You will be burned, you will be consigned to the flames of hell." He turned to Fenwick and shouted, "Seize that villain. Tie him up to the post!" he cried pointing at the gnarled wood in the clearing, "and make a fire around him."

Fenwick stared open-mouthed at Jonah and then at me. He was clearly astonished at the violent reaction my appearance had generated. But there was confusion too on his face and I realised that as Jonah had been raving in Portuguese, the African had not understood a word of it. "Your chief is mad," I shouted at my interpreter. "He has drunk sea water and it has addled his wits."

Before I could say any more, Jonah also realised the problem and reached down to grab Fenwick by the arm. "He is a *diablo*, an amigo of the great Satan himself," he hissed in pidgin English, making a sign of the Devil's horns with his fingers. "He is enemy of Cristo, of Christ the Christian God, do you understand?"

Fenwick now looked even more bewildered as others about him shouted for him to translate what Jonah and I had been saying. He started to gabble the news in the local tongue and it caused a sensation. In a village where a goat with a boil probably had them talking for weeks, to have a personal friend of the Devil delivered to their doorstep unsurprisingly had them all screaming and shouting. There was only one sensible thing to do and I did it: I turned on my heel and ran for my life back the way I had come. I had only gone twenty yards when I was brought down by a crunching tackle that would have been worth house points at my old school.

"Get off me, you fool," I shouted as I tried to kick the fellow off, but he had a grip on my legs like a cooper's iron hoop. I felt something hard pressing into my side and remembered my Collier pistol was still tucked into my belt. But I had barely got my fingers around the hilt before I was rolled over and the weapon snatched from me. I tried to get to my knees but there was half a dozen of the shouting fiends around me, several with spears levelled. "He is mad," I protested, but they weren't listening as they pulled me to my feet and yanked my arms behind me, tying them with some rough cord. "Look, I am a Christian too," I babbled. "Baptised Church of England, go to church every Sunday when I'm home. I even give money to the collection."

It was no use, those holding me could not understand a word I said. I stared over their heads and could see Jonah shrieking in delight at my capture. He was pointing to the wooden post in the centre of the square and demanding that a fire be built at once. He could not wait to have me embraced by the flames. Fenwick was arguing with him that it would take some time to build a proper pyre, but Jonah was only half listening. He was also shrieking up into the heavens that God's unworthy enemy had at last been captured and would soon be consigned to hell.

I had been in some pickles in my time, but I was damned if I could see a way out of this one. Even if I could get away, I had no idea in which direction to run. It did not matter as I suspected that the villains who held me would be experts in tracking me down. It was a choice between being burned as a heretic, getting speared by some local or at best being killed and eaten by wild animals.

I struggled to take it all in; just five minutes ago I had expected to meet a white stranger, with every expectation that he would help me to the nearest British outpost. There would be no reasoning with Jonah, I knew that. The man was as mad as a March hare. As I was dragged back into the clearing, he giggled like a young girl at the sight of me still struggling with my captors. "Lock him away," he shouted

9

gleefully, "until we are ready to burn him." And that was how I came to be in this wretched death hut awaiting my grisly end.

Chapter 2

I must have been in that damned hut for a good couple of hours. I twisted around so that I could see through the low doorway. Two warriors now guarded the entrance, but they did not stop a succession of children and even some adults crouching down in the threshold to gawp at me as though I was a sideshow freak. Perhaps to them I was, although their viewing time was set to be limited, as over their heads I could see a crowd of villagers industriously building a large pile of tree branches.

"Mr Flashman," called a cheery voice and a new pair of legs appeared in the hut entrance. "I have come to see how you are."

As the native I knew as Mr Fenwick ducked down to enter I stared at him in bewilderment. "How I am?" I repeated incredulously. "I am about to be burned alive on the orders of a raving lunatic. How the bloody hell do you think I am?" I took a deep breath to calm myself. Fenwick was my only hope and it would not serve to upset him. "You must tell the elders that…" My words trailed away as a new figure entered the hut. I was to learn that every time I thought Africa had no more horrors to offer, it would prove me wrong – and this one was a corker.

He was a creature of your worst nightmares. Wearing a cloak and headdress made of grass and leaves, he scuttled sideways into the hut like a crab, rattling some gourd in one hand and loudly sniffing the air with an expression of distaste. He only had one eye, but it wasn't that which drew your attention. Nor was it the grotesque false eye which had been painted on his cheek below the sunken empty socket in his face. No, what drew your gaze was the object hanging around his neck on a long cord: a severed human hand clenched into a fist. At first, I could not take my eyes away from the grisly thing. It had shrivelled in age and glistened with some varnish that presumably helped to hold it together as it decayed. Not entirely successfully, though, for as this new arrival scampered around the hut muttering incantations, I saw that the end of one of the fingers had broken off with the white end of a bone visible.

"May I have the pleasure of introducing you to Banutu," said Fenwick calmly as though he were introducing a fellow member of a London club. He smiled at me encouragingly as I twisted my head around the central pole in the hut to keep an eye on the fiend as he danced around me. "He is, I suppose, what you would call our priest," continued my guide as the capering creature continued to circle me.

The last vestige of hope that I could still talk myself out of this, melted at that moment. If this was an example of their village headmen, then in comparison, Jonah probably did seem perfectly sane. "Forgive me if I do not shake hands," I muttered sardonically while tugging again at my bonds. "But then if the last proffered hand is the one hanging around his neck, perhaps that is just as well."

"No, no," Fenwick laughed politely at my attempt at gallows humour. "That hand was taken from someone who tried to steal his daughter. You are quite safe."

"Not for long," I insisted, gesturing at the growing pyre visible through the door. "Look, if he is here to administer the last rites, then I would really prefer him not to bother."

"So, you are not a follower of the Christian god, then?" Mr Fenwick pounced on my words. I was about to reply when Banutu finally spoke in a deep gravelly growl. "He wants to know," continued Fenwick, "if it is true that Jonah's name is in the Christian Book and if he is a friend of Jesus."

"Of course he is not a friend of Jesus!" I exploded. "Jesus lived nearly two thousand years ago. This fool is a Portuguese sailor who went mad after drinking sea water when we were lost together in an open boat."

Fenwick hurriedly translated my words for this nightmare cleric, who stared at me impassively with his one remaining eye. He gave a grunt in response and reached out his arm towards my chest. I tried to move back to avoid him, but as I was still tied to the central pole this was impossible. His thumb pressed me on the breastbone. It seemed improbably cold, almost icy, and I felt a chill move into my chest.

"Hey, what is he doing?" I shouted as the strange sensation spread across my torso. I did not want some damn local warlock spreading his magic into me. I tried to twist away but he kept me pinned to the pole like some wretched specimen. This Banutu ignored my protests, but the sensation did not get any worse and he continued to examine me. You could not look him in the eye, you found your gaze drawn by the false one painted on his cheek and I did not want to look down at the hideous severed hand dangling just a few inches away from me. In the end I stared at his bare chest at roughly the same point he was touching mine. I saw that his skin had various tattoos that were barely visible on his dark skin. One was vaguely familiar; it was a rough diamond inside a circle, but the top of the diamond had a narrower angle and thinner inked lines than the bottom half.

Banutu at last said something in his rumbling voice. He talked for a while and Fenwick listened closely before he started to translate. "He does not think you are a good man," Fenwick spoke in almost a whisper. "He feels your hatred for Jonah and thinks that you have tried to kill him already." For a moment I was shocked as I had told no one that, but then I realised that Jonah had probably peached on me in his mad ravings to this so-called priest. Fenwick looked at me sadly as he continued, "He knows Jonah's name is in the Christian Book, I have seen it myself, and he thinks that Jonah is a powerful spirit for the Christian god."

"Nonsense," I protested. I had almost resigned myself to my fate now, but I would not go quietly. "That was a different Jonah who died a long time ago. Your new king is nothing more than a mad sailor who hates me because I know the truth about him."

"He is not our king," said Fenwick, his brow creasing in puzzlement that I could come to such a conclusion.

"But you carry him around on a throne and you are obeying his orders to burn me to death."

"We carry him because he has an injured leg," started Fenwick, but he got no further as Banutu wanted to know what we were talking about. Fenwick started to translate but then the priest asked more questions and for the first time a smile crossed his lopsided features. While the painted eye bore into me I looked again at the mark on his chest and I remembered where I had seen something similar before.

13

When I was in Rio, I had been in a brothel after a masonic gathering and I was sure that amongst the banners they were taking down, was one with a symbol very like the mark on the priest's chest.

"Not king," Banutu now barked at me directly while pointing out through the hut door in the direction Jonah had been taken. Then he pointed at himself and announced, "King."

"But I thought you said he was the village priest?" I asked Fenwick.

"He is that too," said Fenwick simply. "We worship Nyame and the king is also the priest. He serves the local spirit, the carving in the centre of the square." I looked through the doorway and saw again the strangely twisted wooden tree stump. Only now did I realise that they had not built the pyre against it as Jonah had instructed, but some distance away.

Now I was more confused than ever. "But then why do you want to burn me to death?"

"The Christians try to make people worship their God and so the Christian god is an enemy of Nyame. Banutu thinks that you are a bad Christian because Jonah hates you."

"Oh I am," I prattled, seeing a glimmer of hope after all. "I am a very bad Christian indeed, I regularly take a piss in the font. You don't want to waste that big pile of logs on me. No, just give me some directions and I will take myself off to the English fort and never bother you or your gods again."

Fenwick smiled at me, "The pile of branches is not for you. Now Banutu has examined your soul, there is no danger for you." As proof of his words, he leaned forward and tugged on my bindings and in a moment my hands were free. I felt a wave of relief come over me as I sagged down against the central pole, rubbing my wrists as my hands tingled with renewed circulation.

"You bad," stated Banutu, clearly a man of few words. He treated me to another of his lopsided grins, which suddenly looked a lot less intimidating, now I knew I was not about to be roasted. I smiled back and then looked again at the strange mark on his chest.

"I say," I started, thinking as I spoke that what I was about to ask was an absurd question. "That mark on his chest, he is not a mason, is he?"

Fenwick's face lit up. "Yes he is, and my father was a mason too. Are you of the brotherhood?"

My jaw must have dropped in astonishment. I knew nothing about masonic rites, but it must have been a deuced queer lodge if the likes of Banutu was a member. But I was not fool enough to admit my ignorance. All I remembered about masons was that they looked after each other and if there was one thing I needed right then, it was some help. "Yes, I am a mason."

Fenwick beamed with delight at this news but as he translated for Banutu, the chief looked more than a bit suspicious. He pointed at my chest and his voice rumbled a question.

"He says that you do not have the masonic mark," pointed out Fenwick as he gestured to the unblemished skin visible through the open top of my tattered shirt.

"Ah, well, no," I admitted. I had no idea what masons did in England, but I had never seen such a mark on anyone there. "We had badges," I lied, "but mine was stolen while I was in Brazil."

When this was translated, Banutu shook his head in dismay at the perfidy of the Brazilian thieves. Doubtless there would be a hand or two missing if he had a say on things. Then he burrowed into a pouch hanging around his waist and pulled out a pierced metal disc. It looked to be made of gold and was beautifully engraved, showing clearly the compass and set square that made up the masonic symbol within the circle. Then he gestured for me to remove my shirt.

"He says you must lie down while he gives you the mark," said Fenwick. It would not do to upset my new friend and so I pulled the shirt over my head. I heard them both exclaim as they saw the old musket ball scar in the middle of my chest. Fenwick was sent off to get some supplies from the chief's tent while the old man stared at me with his good eye. After a while he pointed to my chest and mimed firing a musket. I nodded and turned to show him the smaller entry wound on my back and through hand gestures explained that the other was the exit scar. He sat and chanted for a moment – whether he was praying for me I could not say – and then Fenwick returned with several earthen ware pots. I lay down and Banutu smeared some green paste from one of the pots in a circle towards the top of my chest. Then, with some more incantations he laid the gold disc on top. Finally, he picked up a wooden tool that had a sharp thorn on the end and dipped the point in a pot of ink. I realised with alarm that he was planning to tattoo the mark onto my skin, but I was in no position to protest. I braced myself for the pain, but strangely I felt nothing as he started to mark out the shape using the golden template.

I have no idea what was in that green paste, but it would be worth its weight in gold to a surgeon as I had no pain at all while the chief gradually inked in the masonic crest. In fact, whether it was due to the paste or exhaustion from the previous trying days, but I fell asleep while he worked. I woke up to find myself alone in the hut with my shirt folded neatly by my side and my Collier pistol lying on the top. There was a steadily growing chant coming from the square outside and I guessed that it was this noise that had brought me from my slumber. I stuck the pistol back in my belt and pulled the shirt up over my head. Looking down, I could see the glistening black shape of the tattoo and pulled the shirt back to keep it on display. It would do no harm to show that I had the same mark as their chief.

I crawled out of the hut and stood up. There were no guards now and several villagers who saw me emerge just watched me curiously, making no effort to stop me. The sun was low in the western sky, it would soon be dark. Banutu and several others were making incantations in front of the gnarled wood that Fenwick had told me was their spirit and most of the other villagers were watching them. Several though, I was slightly alarmed to discover, were adding logs to the wood pile that was also still in the clearing. I felt a chill of unease at the sight of that but before I could consider it further, Fenwick saw me and came across.

"Why are they still building the pyre?" I asked.

"Because Jonah told them too," he replied.

"But he also told you to burn me on it," I queried taking a step back and wondering if I had dreamt the conversation in the hut.

"Do not worry," said Fenwick, grinning. "You will not be harmed now." The words were barely out of his mouth before a horn sounded from somewhere behind the huts on the far side of the square. Cheering and spear-waving broke out once more among the masses as between the huts my old shipmate appeared, carried aloft again on his wooden chair. He was oblivious to any danger and you can hardly blame him, for the reaction of the people did not seem a whit different to when I thought that they were planning to burn me. They set him down in the middle of the square and nearly tipped him out of his chair in the process. I watched as he surveyed the crowd, looking for me. He did not seem to notice as two warriors passed around his chest a rope made of plaited creeper stems that tied him firmly to his seat. Still not entirely convinced of my own safety, I looked around to check that no warriors were waiting to pounce on me and bind me at the last minute, but they all were giving me a wide berth.

"There he is!" shrieked Jonah as he picked me out in the mass of people. "Seize him and set him on the pyre. Let him suffer the fires of hell!" Then as he saw Banutu walking towards me, he must have thought that his orders were about to be obeyed, for he started laughing. As the chief reached me, the noise from the crowd died away until there was silence broken only by Jonah's maniacal cackle. There was a tension in the air now that made the hair on the back of my neck stand up. In the next few moments one of the two white men in the clearing, or possibly both, was about to be horribly disabused.

Banutu stood beside me and started to shout to the crowd. I could not understand a word but then he reached towards me and pulled my shirt wide open to show my new tattoo and then pointed to his own. I finally felt a surge of relief. It was clear that he was indicating that I was now a player on the home team. There was another roar of acclaim from the crowd and Jonah's throne was hauled once more up into the air. Only then did he seem to realise that something was wrong.

17

"Seize him," he shouted down from his chair while pointing at me. Still oblivious to his own predicament he yelled, "Don't let him get away!"

Now I knew I was going to live, I felt that familiar surge of bravado at escaping death once more and instead of moving away I stepped up in front of his throne, forcing his bearers to stop. I pointed at the tattoo and spoke to him in Portuguese so that only he would understand what I was saying. "The Devil has saved me again," I crowed. "Now you will pay for killing João and for trying to kill me. I'll see you in hell." I stepped back then and watched as his throne went past towards the log pile. Jonah was properly raving then. He was yelling for God to smite us all down and send us to the fiery pit. He did not seem to notice when his throne was set down on the heap of lumber.

It was only when two torches were lit that he finally seemed to appreciate his own fate. "Noooo, Noooo!" he yelled as they came closer, but Banutu gave an order and the burning brands were tossed onto the bottom of the pile.

Until that moment I think I had been happy to see Jonah burn. He had after all tried to kill me twice, once on the boat as we came ashore and again in the village. But as the kindling began to crackle and the flames started to leap up the pyre, I had a feeling of revulsion. Perhaps it was because until a few hours ago, I was convinced that it would be me tied to the top of this bonfire. But as Jonah began to thrash about in his bonds and call out for more divine assistance, I knew that I could not let him die by fire. You would not do that to a mad dog, never mind a lunatic. While the old English queen Bloody Mary and the Spanish Inquisition might disagree, I could not see a man consigned to the flames. I reached into my belt and pulled out my Collier pistol. I rotated the chambers so that some powder fell in the priming pan and hoped that it would not be too damp to fire.

"Don't kill him," shouted Fenwick. "If you do, the Christian god will take his revenge on you."

I rather thought that the reverse might be the case should I ever reach the pearly gates, which was unlikely. I ignored him and took careful aim. The flames were licking around Jonah's legs now and he was writhing and screaming in either pain or fury, it was hard to tell. I slowly squeezed the trigger and as the pistol kicked in my hand, I saw his chest slammed back in the chair by the impact of the ball. Through the heat haze I watched his head fall forward onto his chest and he was finally at peace.

Chapter 3

I was pleasantly surprised that Banutu and the rest of the village were not cross with me for putting Jonah out of his misery. Instead, they viewed me as some sort of hero as I had saved their spirit from the retribution of the Christian god. As my old shipmate's corpse was slowly cremated in the centre of the clearing, food and drink were produced and an impromptu feast began. I had not eaten properly for days and gorged myself on various mysterious meats and vegetables, washing it all down with a milky liquid called palm wine. I was beginning to feel I had landed on my feet again.

Instead of the death hut, I spent the night in a lodge on a comfortable bed made of wood, ropes and an animal skin. I slept until well past dawn. To add to my good humour my breakfast was delivered that morning by a pretty young woman wearing nothing above the waist but some strings of beads. Now there is a custom we should start at home, I thought. A pair of bouncers like that made a boiled egg and a flatbread look far more appetising.

I could not remember when I had last laid eyes on such a bounteous vision and growled my appreciation as I sprang up to welcome this handmaiden into my humble abode. I even managed to cup one of them in my hand, feeling a pang of familiar desire course through me as she put my breakfast down. She twisted away but did not seem the least offended as she giggled and backed demurely out of the hut.

"Come back," I called after her. "You can help me dip my soldier," I added, and I was not referring to a strip of flatbread in the egg. I laughed at the thought, for suddenly the world was a much brighter place. That sensation lasted just a few seconds, though, as a moment later Fenwick entered the hut.

"You must not touch that girl, Mr Flashman. She is Banutu's daughter and he is very protective of her."

"Oh Christ," I muttered as my imagination was filled with the gruesome image of a new white hand hanging around the chief's neck to match the black one he already had. I looked down at my offending digits and asked, "You don't think she will tell him, do you?"

20

"It does not matter. He has asked me to take you to the British at Cape Coast Castle. We will leave as soon as you have finished your breakfast."

I don't think I have ever bolted down an egg and bread so fast. I have encountered enough protective fathers in my time to know that it does not pay to outstay your welcome. I well remembered an angry blacksmith in Spain, who had wanted to pound my manhood flat on his anvil after I had dallied with his daughter. Yes, possessive fathers could be most unreasonable creatures and I felt a sense of relief as we set off down the jungle path.

There were four other warriors with us, armed with long blades to cut through the thick jungle where necessary. For the first mile we were able to walk two abreast, but then the paths began to narrow and we travelled in single file. The warriors took turns to be point man, swinging their knives to clear foliage that was quick to encroach on the track. We crossed a river using a wide fallen tree trunk as a bridge; Fenwick explained that as well as the big grey beasts they called water horses I had already seen, there were crocodiles in the rivers too. The jungle was a dangerous place for the unwary traveller.

While we walked, I found out more about my guide. As I had suspected, his father had been a slave ship captain who had sired several children from his cargo. But Fenwick felt no resentment at his parentage. With a note of pride, he explained how his father had brought his mother back to Africa when he discovered that she was carrying his child.

"He did not sell my mother again until I was five," he boasted, as though this was some exceptional kindness. By then she had borne him at least one other son and when they were old enough, Captain Fenwick had sent the brothers to a missionary school at Cape Coast Castle. There they had learned to read and write as well as speak perfect English, while also studying how to calculate numbers in a ledger. It seemed it was his father's plan to use his sons as clerks to help him conduct his trade on the coast, but the doting paternal intentions were thwarted when Britain outlawed the slave trade.

"We thought he might take us to England," said Fenwick sadly, "but we never saw him again after that. I heard that he did at least one more slave run from a Danish camp down the coast, but then he disappeared. My mother was a Fantee and so we went back to her people and that is how I ended up in the village."

We pressed on. It was hot and humid and I was soon tired even though I had not taken a turn swinging the machete to clear our path. My legs were still weak after so long in that wretched open boat and several times we had to stop so that I could regain my strength. Towards dusk another village appeared through the jungle, but I quickly saw that it had been abandoned. Only one hut had a roof and the rest had been torched, with black scorch marks showing on the walls. The central clearing was now overgrown, but a long mound was still visible between the plants. The end near me had been dug out by animals and I could make out several old bones that looked distinctly human.

"What happened here?" I asked.

"Ashanti," said Fenwick simply as though that explained everything.

"What is that? Some kind of disease like the plague?"

Fenwick gaped at me in disbelief. "You must have heard of the Ashanti? Even you British pay them tribute to recognise their dominance over you."

"We do?" I queried. I admit that my ignorance of happenings in West Africa was almost complete. I was aware that the Royal Navy sent ships this way to dissuade slavers from their trade, but beyond that I knew nothing. Yet I do not feel any great guilt for that. Why even now if you stopped ten people in London and asked them to tell you about the Ashanti, I would bet a guinea to a farthing that none could. For despite everything that follows in this tale, those who survived have little reason to boast of their accomplishments. Most like me slunk away, vowing never to return to this dark and pestilent shore.

"The Ashanti dominate all of this land," explained Fenwick. "Some years ago, the Fantee refused to pay them tribute and they came through our territory like a horde of termites. They killed all who stood against them, captured all the men, women and children they could find as slaves and destroyed all our villages. When their old king died three thousand were sacrificed at his funeral rites, including two thousand Fantee prisoners. One of them was probably my brother," he added sadly.

"Three thousand sacrifices," I repeated in awe. I could not imagine such a slaughter; there must have been literal rivers of blood. "But if they killed that many and captured even more, how large is the Ashanti army?"

"They are numberless like the termites they imitate. They make their prisoners fight for them too and so now some Fantees are fighting in their army. They get weapons by trading gold, slaves and goods from the interior so they all have muskets and plenty of ammunition."

"Are they nearby?" I asked, staring into the forest as though a horde of the murdering fiends could appear at any moment.

Fenwick laughed. "No, their capital, Coomassie, is nearly one hundred miles away. But from what we hear, they are again demanding tribute from all the surrounding tribes, including the British. They killed a British sergeant last year and there is talk of war."

I tried to reassure myself that the situation was not as dire as Fenwick described. Many a time in my career, I had seen enemies underestimate the resilience of a line of redcoats. In India I had watched experienced British troops and Indian sepoy soldiers defeat Mahratta armies several times their size. I struggled to believe that some wild African tribesmen would stand up against well-drilled volley fire and a bayonet charge. Perhaps the British had artillery too. If Napoleon had managed to defeat the Paris mob with 'a whiff of grapeshot,' then surely, we could do the same to the Ashanti with some well-aimed blasts of cannister. But whatever happened, I intended to be long gone by then. As long as marauding bands of these Ashanti were not at large in the forest now, I would have time to get to Cape Coast Castle and then board a ship home.

We spent the night in the only hut to retain a roof and in the morning, set off again. By the end of the second day we emerged once more on the coast, further west than where they had found me. Seeing the ocean again made me feel a little closer to home and walking along the damp sand was thankfully a lot easier than hacking our way through the jungle. On the morning of the third day I finally got my first glimpse of Cape Coast Castle: I was very impressed. I was half expecting a wooden palisade affair, but it looked as secure as the Tower of London and about the same size too. There was a mud brick wall encircling the town that had built up around the castle, complete with loopholes for muskets. But beyond that we could see the castle itself, a very stoutly built stone affair. It had a row of cannon in the battlements, with the guns all facing out to sea. But the finest sight, anchored out beyond the breakers, was the sweetest little schooner you ever did see. A vessel I desperately hoped would soon be homeward bound.

A small stone tower marked the seaward end of the mud wall and as we walked towards it, a young British ensign, followed by two redcoats, stepped out of its doorway. The soldiers looked a miserable pair, their faces flushed with the heat, and they were still pulling on their uniform jackets. They might not have been happy to be there, but they reminded me of all the times I had stood in their ranks. I felt a wave of relief wash over me at the sight of them. They gave a sense of familiarity, security and home, which contrasted strongly with the tropical beach they stood on.

"What is your business here?" demanded the young ensign.

"By Christ, am I pleased to see you," I replied cheerily. "My name is Flashman. I was shipwrecked up the coast some days back and these fellows," I gestured at my escort, "have guided me here."

"Shipwrecked?" repeated the ensign. "We have not heard of any vessels foundering on the coast. What ship was she, sir, and are there other survivors?"

"There are no other survivors," I admitted. There was no point in telling them about the one who had just been burned to ash. "The ship sank out at sea and I was the only survivor of an open boat that came ashore east of here."

The ensign's eyes narrowed in suspicion as he gazed on a stranger who had appeared from nowhere with a fairly implausible story. The soldiers were also staring at me with hard faces and one snorted in derision. "He is a bleedin' slaver who has upset one of the local tribes. Now he's come running to us for protection."

Well that was just too much. I had not expected to be welcomed like the prodigal son, but I was damned if I was going to be treated like some common felon. "How dare you speak to me like that, you impertinent dog," I fumed. "I was formerly Major Thomas Flashman and I served on General Wellington's staff for much of the Peninsular campaign as well as at Waterloo."

The young officer pulled himself to attention and introduced himself, "Ensign Wetherell, sir." But the truculent soldier still showed no sign of backing down.

"If you were in Spain, what battles were you at?" he challenged.

I glared at the young ensign, expecting him to reprimand the soldier, but the boy just shrugged. "It is an unusual tale, sir. Gentlemen do not normally end up on these shores."

"Very well," I agreed testily. "I was at Talavera, Busaco, Badajoz and Albuera." I fixed my gaze on the soldier, "Were you at any of those?"

"Busaco, sir," said the soldier, now shifting uncomfortably.

I noticed that he was at least now calling me 'sir' and so I continued. "Well if you were there you will know that Picton was commanding the right of our line and for some reason he chose to fight while still wearing his nightshirt."

The soldier finally stood to attention. He turned to the ensign and confirmed, "That is correct, sir," before turning to me and saying, "Apologies, Major, but we 'ave had some right rum sorts in 'ere lately."

The soldier had a point, I could not imagine why anyone would come here willingly. "Well now you are satisfied as to my *bona fides*," I told them, "perhaps you could direct my companions to somewhere they can get some food and point me in the direction of whoever owns that ship."

"That is the governor's schooner," said Wetherell. "He only got back yesterday from Sierra Leone. I had better take you to him and we can drop your companions off at the cook house on the way." Leaving the soldiers in the tower, the young ensign led our party further along the beach and through the ramshackle shanty town that surrounded the castle. Most of the buildings were circular huts with grass roofs similar to those that I had seen in the Fantee village, but I noticed a small church, some European style houses and a variety of market stalls selling everything from muskets to what appeared to be dead mice. We stopped there briefly while Wetherell arranged some food for my companions and I gave Fenwick my heartfelt thanks for his assistance. The ensign told them to stay in the town as he was sure that the governor would provide a more tangible reward for their help to a lost British officer.

Wetherell and I moved on into the town centre. Twice we passed more white soldiers but none of them bothered to salute the junior officer.

"You seem to have a pretty slack command here," I said pointing at a soldier lounging in a hammock with his musket leaning up against one of the supporting trees.

"Well things are a bit different here than in Spain, sir," said Wetherell defensively. "Almost all of our men have only accepted a transfer to the Royal African Corps as an alternative to punishment. Most have been court martialled for desertion, theft and drunkenness and some for all three. Many would still prefer to be flogged than come here. They know that up to half of our replacements are likely to be killed by fever in their first year. It is hard to impose strict discipline on soldiers who think they will die anyway."

"Good god," I exclaimed. I had thought I had been given some rough postings, such as when I was first sent to the Iroquois, but nothing like this. "What were *you* court martialled for?" I asked. "Surely you did not come here voluntarily?"

"I did, sir," grinned Wetherell. "It was a free commission and if you survive the first year's fever season then you can stay here with much less risk of harm. The governor has been in Africa for ten years now."

"Who is your governor?" I asked, wondering if it was someone I had heard of.

"Sir Charles McCarthy. He has had several roles in the region, but this territory was made a crown colony two years ago. It was previously overseen by a trading company that was not doing enough to abolish slavery. Sir Charles is our first governor and I think you will find he is a good man, sir."

"Is he Irish?" I asked guessing from the name.

"His parents were French, sir, and he first served in the French Royal Army. He fought for the royalists in the Revolution before fighting for us."

By now we were approaching the main gates of the fort and there at least the sentries did salute as we went passed. "It is a huge castle," I said staring around at a large central courtyard. "Much bigger than I was expecting."

"In the old days it was used to keep captured slaves before they were shipped to the Americas," explained Wetherell. "There are big dungeons beneath us that could hold hundreds of them, enough to fill a ship or two. The Dutch have a similar fort just a few miles up the coast at Elmina and the Swedes and Danes have settlements to the south."

"But they are not still trading in slaves, surely?" I asked. I knew from my recent adventures in Brazil that the Brazilians and Portuguese were still making shipments of slaves to their South American plantations. But the British had outlawed the slave trade back in 1807. I had been in London for a while back then and well remembered the campaigning marches for and mostly against slavery.

"Not from here they aren't and we have a naval squadron looking to seize ships involved in the trade. But it is a lucrative business. There are some captains of fast ships who still think it is worth the risk."

I heard some children chanting the alphabet and looked around to find a class of young black boys being taught in the shade of a canvas awning by the fort wall. But it was not the lads that drew my attention;

it was their teacher. She was the first white woman I had seen in the settlement, or indeed anywhere for well over a month and what a magnificent specimen. Tall, slim, blonde and I guessed in her mid-twenties. Now there is one I would not mind seeing in the traditional bead attire of Fantee women, I thought. As my eyes devoured her, I noticed that the humidity had caused her linen blouse to begin to cling to the curves of her perfectly formed breasts.

"Who is that?" I gasped, noticing that my voice had gone hoarse with desire.

"That is the wife of Reverend Bracegirdle, one of the missionaries here," answered Wetherell. As he spoke, the delightful Mrs Bracegirdle sensed my attention. She turned and appraised me coolly before moving her gaze across the courtyard where two more soldiers were leaning against a rail and ogling her with barely disguised lust. The object of our longing returned her attention to her charges, but I noticed she straightened her back almost imperceptibly, pushing her breasts tighter into the surrounding cloth, while brushing a strand of hair behind her ear. By George, the scheming coquette knew the effect she was having on her audience and I suspect enjoyed the power. In a town where white women were in such short supply, a one-eyed hag with a limp would have gathered an army of admirers. This prime piece could have ruled the colony if she chose.

The man who did rule the colony was not in his office when we reached it. His secretary, a Welshman called Williams allowed me to wait alone in his study and sent a boy to find him. It felt incongruous to step inside the governor's well-appointed quarters still dressed in the stained and tattered shirt and breeches I had now been wearing for weeks. A woman came in with a tray and I was given a cup of tea. As I sat in a comfortable armchair made in some British workshop and held the delicate porcelain cup and saucer, I realised that I was back among the things familiar to me. After all the weeks at sea in that damn boat and the foreign surroundings of the Fantee village, the jungle and Africa generally, these simple household items had a strange effect on me. I found tears welling up in my eyes and tried to dash them away before the woman noticed. The masters at Rugby would have been appalled at such a show of emotion. I thought I had succeeded in hiding it, but then I looked up and saw her walking to a sideboard. A moment later she put her hand on my shoulder and a large glass of whisky on the table in front of me.

"You look like you need something stronger," she said, smiling kindly.

I took a swig of the strong spirit feeling that familiar sensation of it warming my insides. "Thank you," I replied. "It has been a trying few weeks getting here. The sight of your crockery… I have seen that pattern in England, just reminded me of home." I tried to pull myself together and asked, "Are you the governor's housekeeper?"

Before she could reply, the door to the room banged open and a small boy stood in the threshold. He looked no more than three with blonde hair but a brown complexion and if I was a judge, his mother's nose. "I am a little more than that," she replied, and her son ran to stand beside her. "My father was another official here and my mother a local woman. My name is Hannah, Hannah Hayes and this is our son, John McCarthy."

The boy ran to his mother and then pointed at the Collier still stuck in my belt and shouted, "Gun."

"Yes, it is," I said smiling at him. "I have a daughter your age back home. No wait, that was when I last saw her, she will be around five now." I turned to Hannah, "The schooner at anchor off the coast. Will it be heading back to Britain soon or do you know of any other homeward bound craft?"

"Charles uses the schooner to move up and down the coast. The territory he governs stretches a thousand miles up to Sierra Leone. That ship won't be going back to England, but vessels from the naval squadron put in here as well as merchant ships and some of those will be heading home. Charles will know more when he gets here – he is out inspecting new farms. While you wait, I will get you a new shirt and trousers. He won't mind you using his razor if you want to shave."

Chapter 4

When I finally met Brigadier General Sir Charles McCarthy, governor of the British possessions on the Gold Coast and Sierra Leone, I was wearing his clothes and my clean-shaven chin was courtesy of his razor. Given that he had fought for the pre-revolutionary French Royal Army he must have been close to retiring from service, but there was a youthful energy to him. He was tall and while his hair was now grey, there were still streaks of the blonde that was evident in his son.

"So you are the stranger I have been hearing about," he exclaimed while shaking me by the hand. If he noticed that my duds looked familiar, he did not say. His own clothes were covered in sweat and dirt after a day out in the fields and the jungle. "Here, you will be wanting a drink and I could certainly do with one." Another whisky was pressed into my hand while he gestured for me to sit and tell him how I came to be on this shore. I told him a creditable tale of my adventures in South America and how I had ended up on the coast. Omitting any reference to Jonah, I explained how Fenwick had brought me to the settlement.

"An extraordinary tale," he said at last. "You have been most fortunate to survive and Wetherell tells me that you were previously an army man."

"Well that is a long time ago now, but I served in India, Portugal, Spain, Canada and…" I was going to mention Waterloo, but before I got the chance McCarthy slapped his knee and interrupted me.

"That's where I have heard your name!" he cried. "When you said it was Flashman I knew I had heard it before. You were in the Canadian port of Halifax briefly, weren't you?" Before I could reply he continued, "I was stationed there for seven years and left just before you arrived. My subaltern wrote to me about you. He said that you had been a spy in Paris but before that you had led cavalry charges at Talavera and had been badly wounded at Albuera but were still one of the first into the breach at Badajoz. And now you mention you were also in India. You are clearly a very capable soldier, sir."

I remembered well giving an exaggerated account of my Spanish adventures to an officer in Canada. My aim back then was to convince them that I had suffered enough and deserved a berth on the next homebound boat. Not that the tale did me much good; I was sent on to Niagara anyway, where I was stationed with the Iroquois. "That was all a long time ago," I protested. I had long since learned to play down my martial reputation, it only leads to trouble. "I am forty-two now, far too old for heroics, and I have been away from home for over two years. I just want a berth on the next ship back to Britain."

"Nonsense," laughed McCarthy. "I am sixty and I hope I am not too old for heroics. But don't worry, we will get you home, although you may have to wait a few weeks for a ship."

I sighed with relief and then remembered another nagging worry. "You are not expecting trouble from these Ashanti fellows I heard about on the way here, then?"

McCarthy gave a snort of derision. "No, they may have ambushed a patrol under my adjutant, but when another officer and a friendly Fantee chieftain led a force against them, they backed away. They are just opportunist bullies, Flashman. When people stand up to them they shrink back to their own lands. They do not want a war with us."

I had asked my question to get some reassurance I was safe, but McCarthy's answer did not entirely give me the comfort I was looking for. "But they attacked your adjutant," I persisted. "Was that in our territory or theirs?"

"Just fifteen bloody miles away," McCarthy admitted as I felt the first twinge of alarm. "But Chisholm always gets himself carried by bearers on expedition and takes no notice of local features. He probably gets lost on the way to the privy." He dismissed the incident. "There is no cause for concern, for I am presently gathering several large bands of allied warriors to give a show of strength to the Ashanti. In fact, you must join me on one of the inspections – to have a man with your martial reputation will be a boost to our soldiery. As you have probably heard, most did not come here voluntarily."

"Yes, young Wetherell told me that half of them die in the fever season and er... when is the fever season?"

"Don't worry," grinned McCarthy. "You have just missed it. The rainy season here is in the summer months. There are torrential downpours; cesspits flood and drainage ditches overflow. On top of that you have rotting vegetation and drowned animals and swarms of flies from larvae that hatch in the puddles. It is a pestilent place then. We get the first cases of fever in June and July, but in August there are also fogs, which make the air damp, and that is when the disease really takes hold."

"It sounds bloody awful," I said with feeling. "I am surprised you get anyone to come here at all. You cannot fight a fever like that if it is in the air that you breathe. Dammit, if I was offered this posting or a flogging, I think I would take the lash."

"Some do," admitted McCarthy. "But it can be a beautiful place too and the people are friendly, loyal and proud fellows for the most part. And anyway, Wetherell was exaggerating. In my time we have never lost more than a quarter of the white folk in a season." He paused, thinking before adding, "Although a lot of the survivors were old-timers, and so I suppose the deaths amongst the new arrivals were higher."

I did not know what to say to that, other than to hope that a homeward bound ship would be along soon. I pitied the poor devils that would still be here next summer and then one in particular sprang to mind. "I was surprised to see a white woman teaching in the courtyard. Surely she has not come here to escape a flogging?"

McCarthy coloured slightly at the mention of the woman and immediately began to look a little uncomfortable. "Ah, well, no. It is a little bit of a delicate situation, Flashman, I'm sure you will understand. More whisky?"

He bustled off to the decanter and was clearly hoping that I would drop the subject, but my interest and indeed ardour was aroused. If I had to spend much time on this wretched shore waiting for a ship, then the delightful Mrs Bracegirdle would be one of the few things to make such a stay palatable. "Surely you will not deny the curiosity of a brother officer," I cajoled, now playing the army card for all it was worth. "Obviously it will go no further."

"Well, I have given my word," muttered McCarthy as he put the glass down beside me. He paused, obviously hoping that I would let him off the hook, but I kept silent and stared at the amber liquid as though waiting for him to continue. "But I suppose you will be going soon and so it will not matter," he continued at last. "But I am relying on your utmost discretion, Flashman, as the lady's reputation would be ruined if this got out."

"Of course," I said, eagerly awaiting him to dish the dirt.

"Well the woman was originally a Miss Temple, a vicar's daughter from Oxfordshire. The father was due to be appointed as the canon of a cathedral when his daughter was discovered indulging her basest pleasures with two farm hands in a hayloft."

"Two at the same time," I repeated in what I trusted was a dismayed tone.

I had hoped he would give more details but instead he continued. "Yes, well, as you can imagine, there was the risk of an enormous scandal. Her father did his best to hush it up, but he had to get his daughter out of the way. In the end he married her off to an old friend of his who was home on leave from a posting here. I gather it was a condition of the marriage contract that the groom took his new bride with him when he returned." McCarthy shrugged, "I know, it does seem a rather extreme solution to the problem."

"The callous bastard, he must have known she could die here." I was referring to the father, who was evidently willing to sell his daughter down the river to protect his own career. But McCarthy misunderstood me.

"Bracegirdle is not a bad man. He is doing a great deal to help me set up the new settlements of freed slaves that are being landed here. During the fever season he asked if his wife could be berthed on the schooner, away from the contagion. I sent Hannah and young John aboard as well, to keep her company." He laughed, "Mind you, I have to say that her arrival has done wonders for attendance in church. Half the garrison seem to be there some days and I am sure it is not for Bracegirdle's sermons."

33

"Is there a conflict between these missionaries and your native allies?" I asked. "The Fantee village I arrived in did not seem too keen on Christianity." I had a sudden image of Jonah roasting on his own pyre, although I doubted he would have been killed if he had not been a certifiable lunatic. They had let me live, after all, and I was a Christian, albeit a bad one according to them.

"Fenwick brought you in, didn't he? Was it from Banutu's village? He is a strange bird," declared McCarthy in what I thought was a monumental understatement. "There is no great conflict with the locals. The missionaries concentrate their attention on the returned slaves, many of whom are already Christian. I give them parcels of land to build their communities as well as agricultural supplies and I have even built a few schools for the children. The missionaries help with those and build churches only in those settlements. I don't care who the others worship, but I will not tolerate human sacrifice, not in British settlements.

"Fenwick said that the Ashanti sacrificed three thousand for their king's funeral, most of them Fantee prisoners. Is that right?"

"It is their custom to make sacrifices when someone dies, some of the other tribes are the same. Often it is a slave girl to look after the deceased in the afterlife. There would have been a number killed for a king, but I doubt it was three thousand. The Ashanti are not that wasteful. The real number has probably been exaggerated to highlight the importance of the old ruler."

It was at this point that Hannah opened the door to the governor's office and walked in. "Mr Brandon is waiting to see you," she told her husband. "Do you want me to ask the mess orderly to prepare a room for Thomas in the officers' quarters?"

"That would be very kind," said McCarthy rising again from his chair. "Brandon is our quartermaster," he explained. "I will ask him to give some supplies to Fenwick to take back to the village. It is the least we can do after they have rescued our friend here." He held out his hand in greeting, "Welcome to Cape Coast Castle, Thomas."

Chapter 5

My life in the castle quickly settled down into a regular routine. Each morning I would arise from my comfortable billet in the officers' quarters and climb to the tallest point on the battlements to scan the horizon. I was searching for the sails of an approaching ship, but each morning I was disappointed. I would take breakfast in the mess and then spend the cooler part of the day exploring the town and surrounding area. The hotter afternoons would be spent at the castle, often observing the splendid Mrs Bracegirdle teaching her charges in the shade. Then, if the sea was not too rough, I would take a swim before dinner.

It was a fairly idyllic existence, unlike that for many of the castle's previous inhabitants. One morning I went down to the slave dungeons. By then I was used to warm weather, but the air got damp and clammy as I went down the passages, holding a lantern as there was little natural light. The huge great barrelled chambers were cooler than outside, but then they were empty, as they had been for nearly twenty years. Packed with humanity, with little if any sanitation for weeks at a time, the conditions must have been truly unbearable. It would have been stiflingly hot, dark and crowded and the desperate wretches would have known the fate that awaited them. From what I had heard, the conditions on the slave ships were even worse. Tens of thousands had passed through the place; you could almost sense the despair as though it had been absorbed by the surrounding brick and stone.

It was a relief to get back out in the sunshine. I had seen more than enough slaves in my time. There had been the slave pens in Algiers full of Europeans and Americans, then more recently Brazil, whose plantations and cities were dependent on them. It was sobering to think that there was probably a similar castle still full of them in Brazil's African colonies. At least their new emperor was trying to put a stop to it all.

When I explored the town, I found it a thriving and diverse place. The majority of its citizens were African, but judging from appearances, more than a few had traces of white bloodstock in their lineage. The castle had been started by the Swedes in the 1600s and so Europeans had been in the region for nearly two hundred years. There were also Arab traders in their turbans, with their veiled womenfolk. I noticed that even the African women were more modestly dressed here, most with strips of cloth wrapped around their bodies. The commercial area was a hive of activity with fishermen on the beachfront selling their catches, hunters nearby offering a wide variety of bushmeat and farmers trading fruit and vegetables. Beyond them were the craftsmen: carpenters, blacksmiths, an ivory carver and several who were skilfully hammering intricate patterns into metal plates and bowls.

I met Major Chisholm there, who I had talked to before in the mess. He was an old Africa hand with fourteen years' experience of the continent. I guessed that he could not afford a commission elsewhere. He had asked me about my campaigns in Europe with a note of envy, for there was little chance of advancement with his posting, yet with disease rife, there was probably a higher chance of being killed. McCarthy had been right about his sense of direction, for I'll swear he had got himself lost again. He was searching for the silversmith to repair a mounting on a pistol and must have walked right past the fellow before he found me.

As he had been beaten by them, I was interested to get his view on the Ashanti, to see whether McCarthy was being overly optimistic.

"They are hugely powerful and damned cunning," he told me. "I am sure that they bribed our guide to lead us into their ambush, not that it did him much good as he was one of the first ones killed."

"The Fantee man who brought me here told me that we pay them a tribute to recognise their dominance over us, is that true?" I asked.

"We have loaned the local people here gold to pay tributes to the Ashanti, but we have not paid them directly." He shrugged, "I am not sure that the Ashanti noted the distinction and to be honest we have behaved badly on our treaties with them."

"Why, what have we done?"

"A man called Bowdich went to the Ashanti capital of Coomassie in 1817 to agree the first treaty. But when he got back here the local director of the African Company of Merchants, a trading company that was then running the colony, decided that he did not like some of the clauses agreed. They were inconclusive about sovereignty. So he secretly changed the wording to indicate that the Ashanti had acknowledged British dominion here, before sending a copy on to London. The Ashanti also sent ambassadors here who were to be sent on to London to directly negotiate with our government. The company director refused to even receive these representatives, never mind arrange their passage on a ship to England as that would have revealed his duplicity. Two years later a British government official called Dupuis arrived in the Ashanti capital of Coomassie with a copy of the London treaty to negotiate new terms. The Ashanti soon discovered that Dupuis' copy of the existing terms differed to their own. Dupuis negotiated a new settlement, but the trading company director snubbed both him and the Ashanti after that. Dupius was scathing of the company in his final report to the government, which was one of the reasons the company was replaced. The area was then made a crown colony by the government and McCarthy, who had already been governing in Sierra Leone, was appointed governor here as well."

"Do you think that McCarthy is right, then, that the Ashanti are just bullies who will back down?"

"They don't trust us, but they don't need us either. They do most of their trade through the Dutch port of Elmina just up the coast and with the Danish settlement at Accra in the south. The governor is right that they respect strength, and that we cannot allow them to kill our soldiers without responding. But if we push them too far, the king will lose face and will be forced to retaliate. The old man has a delicate path of diplomacy to tread."

It appeared that treading paths was one thing that McCarthy was also keen to do. For a few days after this conversation, he led an expedition twenty-seven miles into the jungle. He had set off early in the morning with just a local guide for company. There were no horses at Cape Coast Castle or even mules or oxen. Such beasts of burden did not survive in the climate and so you either walked or were carried by bearers. McCarthy walked and the rest of his entourage did not catch up with him until lunchtime.

He had asked me if I wanted to come, but I saw no reason to take such a risk. Chisholm had alarmed me about the Ashanti situation and McCarthy was going almost twice as far into the jungle as Chisholm had done when he had been attacked. The governor was also only taking a small escort with him as the trip's purpose was to seal an alliance with the Fantee chieftains. Their warriors would be his security. Personally, I preferred stone walls and a few hundred redcoats.

The day after McCarthy left, I and many of the white men remaining in the garrison went to church for the Sunday service. I had been considering how best to use the information the governor had given me to get the delectable Mrs Bracegirdle into bed. The obvious approach was blackmail, but if we were caught or she had an attack of Christian conscience and told her husband, things could unravel quickly. McCarthy would learn I had abused his trust and I still needed his help to get a boat home. Anyway, from what I had heard, the girl had been ill used and deserved better. I thought a subtler approach would offer greater rewards.

As we all piled into the whitewashed chapel, the object of my desires was playing a hymn on an old wooden organ at the front of the church. It was one of those portable affairs that required a second person to work a bellows to send wind through the pipes. Two soldiers were on their knees beside her, taking turns to pump the bellows so industriously that the music was almost painfully loud. Chisholm, as the governor's deputy, took a seat in the front pew and I took the opportunity to grab a place beside him, to give me an unobstructed view of proceedings. As the major glared at the soldiers and gestured for them to slow down, the good reverend finally made an appearance, walking up to the little altar. I had seen him once before. Grey-haired and balding, he must have been nearly sixty; cadaverously thin with a yellowish tinge to his complexion that he shared with many of the old-timers in the region.

"Welcome to St Saviours," he called in his reedy voice and then proceeded to read out several parish notices. It cannot have escaped his attention that beyond a cursory glance, he had not retained the attention of his audience. Virtually every eye was fixed on his wife, who now sat demurely staring down at her keyboard, doing her best to ignore the waves of lust washing in her direction from the congregation. The next hour confirmed that people had not come for the sermon as I doubt a single one of us could have quoted from it once we were back outside. Most just sat there drinking in the vision of womanhood in front of us. She looked up only once. I tried one of my winning smiles, but her gaze went over my shoulder at the rows of faces beyond with, I thought, a touch of defiance in her expression.

All too soon the service was over and we trooped back outside and through the little churchyard. Chisholm was telling me about one of the characters buried there when a man called out in my direction.

"It is you, Yer Honour, is it not?" shouted an Irish voice from a group of soldiers standing near the church gates, waiting for their comrades to come out. As I looked up one of them came forward, a little unsteadily, clearly the worse for drink.

"Dammit, O'Hara, are you drunk already?" The look of annoyance was clear on Chisholm's features as he added, "It's barely ten o'clock on a Sunday morning. Do I have to put you in the cells again to sober up? Now leave this gentleman alone, you don't know him. I doubt that you can even see him clearly."

"Ah but I can, Yer Honour, and I know him fine well, so I do." The Irishman grabbed my hand and shook it. I studied his features but they did not seem familiar – mind you the eyes were bloodshot and the ruddy cheeks riddled with the veins of a heavy drinker. On top of that, the fumes from his breath were enough to make your eyes water.

I stared at him trying to place the face. "I am not sure…" I started.

But he cut me off with an exaggerated wink and continued, "Sergeant O'Hara, oh wait now," he said gazing sadly at the faded cloth on his sleeve, which showed where a sergeant's stripes had once been. "Corporal O'Hara at your service. But I *was* a sergeant when yer knew me before," he added. He turned to Chisholm, "This hofficer," he announced, "was with my company of the Connaught Rangers at the battle of Busaco."

Christ, now I remembered him all right. This villain had seen me trying to shirk my way out of the charge and with his mates, had picked me up and half carried me right into the thickest part of the action. We had only just survived after some desperate fighting. I had shaken his hand at the end of the day, but now I wondered if he was going to denounce me and ruin my reputation, at least in this backwater posting. The concern must have shown on my face, for he winked again before he continued.

"'E led my company right into the very heart of a French column, sor. We sent 'em running, like the hounds of hell were biting their arses," he said to Chisholm before turning to me. "D' ye think I have forgotten how ye killed that great big grenadier bastard that nearly did for me? Now sor," he beamed at me and filled my face with more of his noxious fumes. "Would you deprive an old comrade of a small drink to wet his whistle?"

"Is that true?" asked Chisholm, astonished.

"Oh, I think O'Hara exaggerates a little," I protested. If I claimed too much credit the conniving weasel could still blackmail me. I glanced across at the crowd he had been standing with to see if there were more familiar faces there who could back him up.

"Exaggerate?" protested the Irishman. "That giant fecker was as tall as a house and did you not nearly take his head off. The Captain 'ere must have cut him a score of times," continued O'Hara, "and he saved my life for sure and certain."

"Extraordinary," said Chisholm, before adding with feeling, "By God I wish I had been there." He looked like he was eager to hear more of our war stories, but I cut him off as I wanted to get O'Hara on his own to find out what the Irishman was about.

"If you will excuse me," I said to Chisholm, "I will take the corporal for a drink." As the man in question beamed his delight, I added, "One that will sober him up."

"Did ye think I would tell him how we really got you down that hill?" asked O'Hara a few minutes later as we sat alone.

"The thought crossed my mind," I admitted.

"Well ye shook me hand and shared a drink with me afterwards and you did not make trouble for us when you could have, so I would not be doing that." He paused and grinned, "Anyway, Flaherty's dog liked you, so you cannot be all bad. Good judge of character that one."

"Flaherty's dog?" I repeated.

"Yes, that big Irish wolfhound ye had back then. He had belonged to Corporal Flaherty, who sold it to some English gent. I am guessing that you bought it from him."

"The English gent was Lord Byron and he gave me the dog."

"The poet fella? I hope Flaherty got a good price, then. What happened to the dog?"

I hadn't thought of Boney in years, but the memories brought a smile to my lips; he had been a good companion. "He saved my life more than once," I told O'Hara. "He was killed at Albuera trying to protect a young ensign." We were in what passed for a coffee house in Cape Coast Castle, which is to say we were sitting on some fallen logs on the beach near an Arab who sold the strongest coffee known to man. When the African Company of Merchants had run the colony, they had tried to diversify the trade beyond slavery and had tried tea, coffee and spices as new sources of income. Tea and coffee had not proved sufficiently profitable, but as a result the colony was self-sufficient in both. Peppercorns had been their most successful cash crop and pepper was now the main export from the region. Given its abundance, the nearby coffee seller offered a drink he called 'gunpowder,' which was strong coffee with a generous dose of ground black pepper mixed in, something he assured us was a great restorative.

As I sipped my coffee and felt my eyes water, I remembered those Connaught Rangers on the Busaco ridge. They had been wild, fearless soldiers, renowned for their fighting and drinking. Coming from the west of Ireland, many of them had only spoken Gaelic when I had known them. "How the hell did you end up on this godforsaken shore?" I asked.

41

"Court-martialled for gettin' drunk and hitting an officer," O'Hara admitted before adding defiantly, "a useless prick of an English officer." He gave a heavy sigh as he considered his fate and then went on. "It was a choice of the Royal African Corps or the lash. I had been flogged before and did not fancy that again. So Seamus and I decided to come here instead. Do ye remember Seamus? He was with us at Busaco."

I nodded, I had a vague recollection of a wiry soldier who had tried to take on the giant grenadier on his own.

"Well you know the French could not kill Seamus. He fought through Portugal, Spain and France, but this place got him in his first summer. He died mewing like a cat in a puddle of his own shit. I got drunk then and I have done my best not to be sober since. We have our own still and I don't think the fever likes our *poitín*," he said, referring to his lethal homebrew.

"I am not surprised," I said grinning ruefully as I remembered the time I had tried it. "That stuff would burn the scales off a snake. God knows what it did to my insides. But did they not have a surgeon here to help with the fever?"

"Aye they did, but he was one of the first to catch it and die. If he could not save himself, what use was he to the rest of us? No, you are better off with a drop o' spirits. It either cures you or ye do not care. Mind you, the stuff we make now is not as smooth as the old days – we have to use local roots and plants." He took a sip of his coffee and grimaced. "But it is still better than this heathen muck."

"Drink it down, it will do you good. What were you doing outside the church? Had you been in to see the fragrant Mrs Bracegirdle?"

"Me in a Protestant church?" he repeated sounding genuinely appalled. "Father Maguire would have my guts for knee braces if I confessed to such a thing. No, I had been waiting to ask a favour of Major Chisholm until I saw you.

"Were you with him when he was ambushed?" I asked. "What do you make of these Ashanti warriors? They seem to go through the local tribes like a hot knife through butter, but the governor is convinced that they will not stand against us." I was keen to get an expert opinion. For despite McCarthy's high rank, as far as I could tell, he had little experience of fighting, while in front of me was an expert in the field.

"I was there," he grinned, "and if they had been the French I would not be 'ere now. They were on both sides of us and outnumbered us three or four to one. But they rushed their shots and kept their distance. I have not seen one of them with a bayonet yet." He took another swig of his spiced coffee and added, "The old boy is probably right. If you show 'em a tough defence they'll not charge home. He knows his business. He has had me and the lads with Light Company experience training the others on how to fight in loose formation. There is no room for tight ranks and volleys in that stinkin' jungle."

I was considerably reassured. If I had been asked to guess which of my former comrades had been posted to a penal regiment like the Royal African Corps, I might well have chosen the Connaughts, for they were viewed as near wild men by the rest of the army. But the one thing that they did know about, apart from drinking, was fighting. They had been in the thick of numerous battles under a variety of commanders. Even half drunk, I valued O'Hara's judgement. He could quickly assess an enemy as well as the capability of a commanding officer. Fighting in the jungle, McCarthy's plan to train his soldiers to fight in looser formations seemed very sensible. "What did you want with Major Chisholm?" I asked, conscious that I had taken the corporal away from his duties.

"Ah, I was trying to persuade him to take me on as his orderly," the soldier admitted. "I'm gettin' too old for all this running about in the heat."

"Nothing to do with the easy access to the officers' wine stores, then?" I enquired with a wry grin. "I cannot imagine why Chisholm is reluctant to appoint you."

"Have you got an orderly yet, sir? An officer of your importance needs a man watching after him, so he does." There was a cheeky glint in his half-focused eyes, but the Irish charm was not working with me.

"Why on earth would I agree to having you as an orderly?" I laughed.

"Because ye will probably leave without payin' yer mess bill, so you'll not care how much I drink," he stated perceptively. As I began to object he held up a finger to stop me, "And I can tell you where that lassie you admire so much will be just before dusk this evenin'."

Chapter 6

Corporal O'Hara was without doubt, the worst orderly I have ever had, with the possible exception of a Private McFarlane back in India. But there were compensations and as you will see from later in my tale, I would not be here now without him. The first of these was the intelligence that Mrs Bracegirdle had a penchant for an evening stroll. Nothing unusual in that, but her perambulations regularly took her along a hillside path that overlooked a stretch of beach that the men used to take a dip in the sea at the end of the day. She had been seen more than once peering over the rocks to get a view of the naked men splashing in and out of the surf. That information, together with the news offered by the governor on her background, provided an opportunity that was too good to miss.

So it was that two evenings later, I was secreted along that very path opposite the beach. I had been there every evening since O'Hara had told me, but until now my prey had not appeared.

"Wait there, Bessie," I heard her call to her local maid and then she came up alone along the path. She checked to see if anyone was coming up the track from the opposite direction, but she did not see me as I was hiding in the bushes behind her. I watched as she crouched down and moved slowly to the edge of the path, so that she could peer through the branches of a shrub. The sound of distant shouting and laughter carried in the air as the men ran through the waves, washing off the sweat of another sultry day. My beauty watched with rapt attention and while I could not see her left hand, her right began to squeeze her breast. A low groan of desire escaped her lips, which seemed to be my cue to step forward.

"Why, Mrs Bracegirdle, what a surprise to see you here." She emitted a startled scream and the poor woman half fell into the leaves she had been hiding behind.

"Mistress, are you all right?" The young maid came at a run, just in time to find me helping her red-faced employer from the foliage.

"I'm fine, Bessie, this gentleman just surprised me, that is all." She turned to me and tried to recover her dignity. "What are you about, sir, creeping up on me like that?"

Instead of replying I reached forward and pulled down a palm frond to reveal clearly to both of us the view she had been previously enjoying. Around half a dozen naked men were lying on the sand no more than thirty yards away. Two were looking around having heard the scream and I gave them a cheery wave. Beyond those, another half dozen were still running in and out of the waves. "I can see now why you did not hear me coming up the path," I said coolly.

The maid sniggered with amusement – she must have known what her mistress was doing all along. "Bessie, go and wait for me back up the path," Mrs Bracegirdle snapped, before turning those beautiful blue eyes onto me. "How dare you sir, I am a respectable married woman," she blazed. "I… I just heard shouting and wanted to check that someone was not drowning." I watched as she glanced to the bend in the path over my shoulder and tried to gauge what I might have seen. Well she was not going to get away that easily.

"Do you know, I think we have met before in England. Your face looks familiar."

"I doubt that, sir, now if you will excuse me." She turned to go as I continued.

"Yes, it was some place in Oxfordshire, where was it now? Your name was not Bracegirdle then either." She stopped then, frozen as I went on. "Ah yes, it was Temple, you were Miss Temple back then, a vicar's daughter if I recall."

She turned to face me then, a look of fear on her face as she searched my features to see if I knew her secret. "Yes, I heard the story of you and the two men," I confirmed and watched as the colour drained from her face. I gestured through the leaves, "I saw you watching those men too, so don't play the coy mistress with me. I just thought we could help each other to scratch an itch, so to speak."

"So it is blackmail," she whispered. "I sleep with you or you tell everyone what you know."

"Not at all," I replied genially. "I have not said a word to anyone here of what happened in Oxfordshire and nor shall I, whatever you decide. You have a choice. You can continue to lie with that dry old stick of a husband and creep around in the bushes clutching yourself while you watch the soldiers; at least before you are caught and humiliated by someone with fewer scruples than I. On the other hand, you can arrange an assignation with me, which I am sure we will both find very satisfying and you can rely on my continued discretion." I gave her my warmest smile. "Now good day to you. I will leave you to let me know what you choose."

With that I turned away and strolled off down the path. I could not resist a self-satisfied smile as I went, for the encounter could not have gone better. I would rather she come willingly to any meeting than under duress; she would participate more enthusiastically then. The frustration that had been in her as she had watched the soldiers was almost palpable – she was on the boil to get her muttons and I was only too happy to oblige. A day, I thought, two at the most and she would come running. Of course, if she did somehow manage to hold out, there was always the blackmail option to fall back on.

As it turned out, it took her three days to make her approach, but I knew she was interested before then. She had engineered a meeting with Chisholm to find out all about me. O'Hara had overheard some of it and the good major had waxed lyrical about my wartime exploits in Spain, inviting the Irishman to describe the action at Busaco.

"I piled on Yer Honour's glories," the corporal confided later with a conspiratorial wink. "I told them of your charge at Talavera and that you had fought in Canada and at Waterloo too. I don't know what hold ye have over that girl, but she was impressed."

"It's just my natural charm," I insisted. But the next evening as I strolled through the castle to the officers' mess, I found the maid Bessie waiting for me. She grinned and pushed a note into my hand. Without waiting for a reply, she rushed off into the shadows and away, out of the castle. I stood under a nearby lantern and read:

Dear Mr Flashman,

Given your interest in our work, I wondered if you would care to join me tomorrow on a trip down the coast to visit one of the settlements of freed slaves that we administer. A fisherman has agreed to take us in his boat. I will be bringing Bessie and for propriety you may wish to bring a companion too.

Yours sincerely,

Eliza Bracegirdle

I must have grinned in the darkness as I anticipated the pleasures to come. What I did not expect, though, as O'Hara and I strolled to the beach the next morning was to see the Reverend Bracegirdle standing on the sand with his wife. I cursed under my breath: had the damn woman tricked me after all? I wondered. The old boy was fussing over the supplies in the fishing boat, but turned when he saw us approach.

"Ah, Mr Flashman," his voice quavered. "How pleased I am to see you and grateful to you for escorting my wife."

"You are not coming with us then, Reverend?" I asked with relief.

"Goodness me no, my duties take me elsewhere today, but I know my wife will be in safe hands with you."

"You can rest assured on that score," I told him fervently and by Christ I meant it, for Eliza was looking most becoming. The crisp new blouse flapped invitingly on the sea breeze and the wide straw bonnet framed her features to perfection. I was positively champing at the bit and could not wait to get away.

In no time at all I had helped push the boat off the beach and was soon manning the tiller while the fishermen hauled on the ropes to raise the sail. The craft was the size of a small cutter. O'Hara and Bessie sat in the bows while Eliza and I were in the stern. The fishermen stayed in the middle of the boat amid a pile of nets and a cargo of supplies for the settlement we were visiting. Soon we were through the breakers and I gestured at one of the fishermen to haul on a rope to tighten the angle of the sail as I turned the boat east.

"You look comfortable sailing a boat." It was the first thing Eliza had said to me, but I had seen her watching me carefully as I had helped launch the craft.

"I should be, I was a captain in the Brazilian Navy three months ago."

"A naval officer!" she exclaimed. "But I was told that you were in the army."

"I was, but more recently I helped my friend Thomas Cochrane in South America."

"Is he the man the papers call the renegade admiral?"

"That would be him," I admitted. Then in a blatant attempt to earn favour I added, "He is currently helping the new Brazilian emperor in his efforts to abolish slavery in that country."

"So, you are a supporter of our cause, then?" She looked at me eagerly and I noticed that she rested her hand on my arm. I had not felt comfortable with the slave culture in Brazil, but I will be honest and say that at that moment, I would have sold every man jack alive in Africa into bondage, just to see this beauty stripped for action. I took a deep breath and reminded myself of the need to be patient.

"My last command was a detachment of marines who were all liberated slaves," I told her. "Now why don't you tell me where we are going."

She explained that we were heading to a settlement, ten miles down the coast. The governor had set it up for former slaves that were now being returned to Africa. Some, who were delivered back on the coast of this vast continent and left to find their own way home, came from captured slave ships. Others were former slaves from the Caribbean and the Americas. Both groups found their arrival in Africa challenging. Those recently enslaved often had no idea where they had come from and had rarely seen a map. Even where it was known from which port the ship they were captured in had embarked, it was usually not wise to return them there, for they would simply be re-captured and loaded on the next west-bound vessel. Some tried to make their way home regardless, but ignorant of local languages and customs, it was likely that only a few succeeded. Others remained in the coastal settlements, almost as lost and disorientated as when they had been at sea.

The situation was even worse for those who had lived in the Caribbean and the Americas. Many of them had been born there and were completely unfamiliar with Africa, its climate, plants, animals and people. Eliza explained that some of them were encouraged to return to Africa by well-meaning abolitionists, who felt that the blacks would never achieve equality in their countries. Others were free blacks who were sent back to Africa by slave owners, as they were worried that notions of freedom would unsettle their 'livestock'. Some fifteen thousand had been sent back so far and they were scattered in settlements from Sierra Leone all the way to the Gold Coast, which was where Cape Coast Castle was located.

"Who is organising the return of slaves?" I asked.

"Well, our navy returns most of those captured on slave ships. They often just turn the ships around and head for the nearest African shore before food and water on board run out. As for the rest, there is an organisation in America founded by George Washington's nephew which sends many back and similar groups in the Caribbean and Canada."

We arrived at noon. It was easy to spot the settlement we were going to. Unlike the African villages we had seen on the coast with their round huts, this one had rectangular buildings and ridged roofs. Its occupants had constructed in the style they knew from the Americas.

"It is a sizeable place," I pointed out. "There must be over twenty houses."

Eliza beamed with pleasure as she studied it, from its roughest shack to a large whitewashed building that I took to be the church. "I have not been here before. When Cuthbert first came to Africa, some of the settlements would disappear. The occupants would be lost in conflicts with the local tribes or sometimes sold back into slavery."

"Cuthbert?" I queried.

"My husband," she grinned. "He might be a 'dry old stick' as you put it, but he is a good man. Before, people would be landed here with little or no support. Local tribes viewed them with suspicion, especially if they encroached on hunting grounds or stole crops to

50

survive. They were seen by many as a nuisance and Cuthbert thinks that the old trading company connived in selling them back into slavery to remove them as a problem. But the new governor has already set up thriving communities in Sierra Leone. Now he is governing here too, he is supporting the missionaries and these settlements so that they survive without conflict. Once we get ashore you will see."

The fishermen skilfully steered us through the surf and onto the beach where a crowd was already waiting to greet us. They were delighted to have visitors and were even more pleased when they saw the supplies we had brought along. We were escorted up to the village and proudly shown fields where rows of young coffee trees were growing alongside vines of the pepper plant. Only one of the smaller fields looked close to producing fruit. Eliza explained that these plants had been provided by the missionaries while the rest were grown from seed provided to the farmers. There were also vegetable patches, chickens and even a few goats. The place certainly looked self-sufficient. A man called Joshua, the leader of the group, proudly showed me a warthog that he had shot that morning.

"Praise the Lord, we have a fine hog for yo' dinner. Yes indeed, after your sermon we will have a feast," he told me.

"After my what?" I asked, surprised. The man clearly thought I was a missionary too and I was just about to disabuse him of the notion when he showed me into a hut that had been prepared for our arrival.

"We hope you and your wife will be comfortable here," he beamed, showing me a room with a large homebuilt double bed. Suddenly the role of 'Reverend Flashy' was much more appealing.

"Sermon, you say... Is there any particular theme you have in mind?" I asked.

He nodded to where two pretty young women were arguing over a goat. "I fear we are having trouble with the Seventh Commandment, if you know what I mean."

I watched them squabbling over the rope that held the animal and tried desperately to recall my Commandments. "Ah you mean the one about not coveting thy neighbour's ass."

The man beamed in delight, "You are surely right there, Reverend. You tell them firm now, won't you?"

"Oh I will," I replied distractedly as I watched Eliza bend down to tickle a young child. I had been patient long enough. "My wife will be tired after such a long journey, perhaps we should rest for a while now and join you later."

"Yes sir, Reverend," Joshua replied before striding forward to shoo the children away. "You leave Mrs Bracegirdle alone now, her husband says she needs a rest and then he will preach to us before dinner." He turned to Eliza, who was staring at me, a mixture of shock and alarm fighting for dominance of her features. "Now ma'am, let me show you to your lodgings. I am sure it will not be as good as you are used to, but it is the best that we can provide."

"Why on earth did you say that you were my husband, never mind a member of the clergy?" Eliza hissed at me as soon as we were alone.

I pointed at the bed, "How else was I to explain us romping on that?"

"You fool, what if Cuthbert finds out? Besides, you can't give them Holy Communion, you are not ordained in the church."

"I have a much more personal communion in mind," I growled, pulling her towards me. Initially she was inclined to continue the argument, but once I had stopped her lips with mine and grabbed hold of one of those fine breasts, her resistance crumbled like a sand wall in the surf.

"I'll be ruined again," she wailed as she started to undo my breeches as my fingers feverishly worked on removing her blouse.

"Nonsense, girl," I declared as I finally revealed my prize. By God, they were tits to die for and I fervently declared, "Whatever we have to tell him, it will be worth it for tonight."

That bed was stronger than it looked, as were several of the hut walls as we both worked through our pent-up frustrations. It was early evening when we finally emerged from that hut and I will venture that we both had that healthy glow of a couple who have had an afternoon well spent. But there was no rest for the wicked, as immediately we stepped outside, some child started hitting a bent piece of metal on a

52

string with a spade. The resulting clanging was evidently their equivalent of the church bells. Instantly the entire community started to emerge from the other huts and head to the large one that was their church. I was reminded that my short ecclesiastical career was about to begin.

As I stood before my congregation I wished that I had paid more attention to the hundreds of church services I had been obliged to attend back in Leicestershire and elsewhere. I had fidgeted impatiently through nearly all of them. But how hard could it be, I reasoned as I looked at my flock. They sat erect on their roughly hewn pews, wearing their best clothes, all the women adorned with modest bonnets. With solemn, freshly washed faces, they were a vision of Christian respectability.

"The Reverend Bracegirdle will now give us Holy Communion and a sermon," intoned Joshua before sitting in the front row next to Eliza.

"No," said my 'wife,' "my husband is not yet fully ordained to give Communion."

"But is he not the leading missionary here?" asked Joshua, puzzled.

Eliza looked perplexed at how to answer that one and so I swiftly stepped in with the only explanation I could think of. "I believe there is some confusion," I started. "My father, the older Reverend Bracegirdle is the head missionary."

Joshua's brow cleared. "That explains it," he grinned. "I had heard that the reverend was an old man and so I was surprised when I first saw you. But surely you can bless the wine for us? We have been making it since we heard you were coming." He gestured over my shoulder to where a large bowl sat on a table that served as the altar.

Eliza looked like she was going to protest, but I got in first. "Yes, I can bless the wine," I agreed. I turned and went to stand over the bowl. I knew some priests chanted in Latin at this point and so I waved my hand over the wine and announced the only Latin that came to mind: "*Orando Laborando*," which was my old school motto. 'By prayer and work,' seemed appropriate here anyway and I lifted the bowl to take a sip. It was the local palm wine, a substance that was normally weak in alcohol. This time, however, a familiar searing heat burned my gullet and I scanned the congregation for the person responsible. O'Hara grinned happily back from the side of the room. He tapped the pocket of his tunic, where I knew that he kept a huge silver flask normally filled with his homebrewed 'tonic'.

I passed the bowl to Joshua. "This wine is enhanced with the fire of our lord," I announced as I strode to the platform that I took to be the pulpit. By the time I faced them again Joshua must have drunk, for his eyes were watering and he was gasping for air as he passed the bowl to the man sitting beside him. I waited while the wine went up and down the rows until it finally reached the back of the church. Having not given a thought to what I would say until now, I needed time to think. Perhaps it was the post-coital contentment, or the effect of O'Hara's tonic, but I was in no mood to call fire and brimstone down on them. Surely being jealous of your neighbour's livestock was not that much of a sin. How was I to know that 'ass' to Americans did not just mean a donkey, but was their word for arse as well, and particularly a woman's flesh.

"The lord says, 'Thou shalt not covet thy neighbour's ass'," I began, as the congregation settled and looked at me expectantly. I ran my tongue around my mouth and realised that I could no longer feel any sensation from my gums. I would have to keep this speech short in case I started slurring as the elixir took hold. "But the Bible was written for those in towns and cities," I told them. "In a small community like this we have to do more to help each other to get along. So I say if a neighbour covets your ass, let them have it." There were gasps of surprise at this and a frown of concern from Eliza. The two girls I had seen arguing over the goat giggled as a man next to them nudged one and whispered something. "You should share your goats too," I warned them sternly. If you give your neighbours what they need, then when you need something, they will give it to you. That is the Christian way." I finished then and stepped down. Judging from the smiling faces of the congregation, my sermon had gone down rather well.

Joshua got up and announced that the feast would shortly begin before turning to me with a puzzled expression. "Are you sure what you said is the Christian way?" he asked.

"Absolutely, old chap, now why don't you show us to this feast, I am famished."

A few minutes later and we were all sitting outside eating plates of roasted hog and a mixture of vegetables that were hard to identify in the evening light. I noticed that the bowl was still circulating and might even have been refilled as there was still plenty in it when it was handed again to me.

"What is in this stuff?" asked Eliza, taking a cautious sip.

"I strongly suspect that it has been fortified with Corporal O'Hara's home brew," I told her. "But at least it is helping people celebrate Reverend Flashman's first church service."

"I cannot believe that you countermanded one of the Ten Commandments," she scolded.

Joshua wanted one on the Seventh Commandment," I explained. "But I thought that such a small community should share its animals."

"Dear God," Eliza groaned. "The Seventh Commandment is not the one about animals, it is the one forbidding adultery. If Cuthbert ever hears about this, he will have a seizure."

"Don't worry," I reassured her. "They will wake up in the morning with sore heads and wonder if it happened at all." I spoke confidently at the time, but as the evening wore on and the bowl kept circulating, things did seem to be getting slightly out of hand. I remember one of the goat girls squealing with laughter as she was picked up by some big cove and carried off to a hut. I looked around for the other one and spotted her lying under another man among some pepper vines. As her knees were up near her ears, there was no doubt as to what they were doing. In fact, when I surveyed the clearing I could see at least four fornicating couples and several more who were clearly thinking along those lines. Even O'Hara had his arm around Bessie, Eliza's maid. Then I saw Joshua walking over. He was unsteady on his feet and clearly had been supping on the bowl more than was good for him. I thought he was coming to talk to me and so got to my feet, but at the last minute he staggered several paces to his left and came up behind Eliza.

"I am taking your ass," he announced. Then to my astonishment he bent down and grabbed Eliza across the chest, taking a firm grip on those delicious breasts, and started to haul her to her feet.

"What the devil are you doing, man?" I shouted, appalled at his impertinence. My hand dropped to my waist, but I remembered that the Collier was back in the hut. I had decided that a revolver was not something a reverend should have tucked into his waistband. I looked around for another weapon and saw a shovel resting nearby. He was a big man, but he was much drunker than me. I would break his damn legs if he did not give up my woman. But as I snatched up the spade, I saw that O'Hara had moved even faster. He was up behind Joshua and two sharp punches in the man's kidneys saw Eliza released.

"You'd better take the lady to your hut, sir," the corporal suggested. Eliza still looked shocked from the encounter and O'Hara gently took her arm and guided her towards me. "I'll stay with Bessie by the door, they won't trouble ye again."

A minute later and we were in the hut staring out of the window at the scene in the clearing. Joshua lay supine where he had fallen, but a woman was with him now and pulling on his trouser belt, clearly planning to offer some personal comfort. Two other couples could be seen in various stages of undress as they pawed at each other around the fire.

"What have you done?" asked Eliza, astonished. "This used to be an upright Christian community, but after just a few hours of your ministry it has descended into a bacchanalian orgy."

"I know," I said with a touch of pride. "With O'Hara's tonic to guide the congregation, I could start a whole new church."

"It is not funny," she chided as she leaned further out of the window to look at the couple rutting away under the pepper vines.

"I know, but it is making me as horny as hell," I muttered as I hauled up her skirt. I ran my hand around the top of her now naked thigh and felt her skin tremble with desire. "Prepare to receive the sacrament," I called as I plunged in.

Chapter 7

If the good Reverend Bracegirdle ever heard how easily I had converted one of his model settlements into the African equivalent of Sodom and Gomorrah, well he never mentioned it. But then he soon had far more important things to worry about. There had been hardly anyone around when we rose the next morning and slipped down to the boat on the beach. Given his behaviour, I doubt Joshua was minded to complain and the two fishermen, having availed themselves of the local hospitality in every sense, were also inclined to keep the matter to themselves.

The day after our return to Cape Coast Castle, Governor McCarthy marched out of the jungle from his trip up-country. He was in remarkably good spirits; there had been no trouble and Major Chisholm had even managed to keep up without getting lost. The surrounding tribes had greeted the governor as some kind of saviour for protecting them from the Ashanti. They had pledged to provide warriors to support any action that McCarthy wanted to make. With the governor's return and preparations for more expeditions, there was much more activity in the fort and town, which made it near impossible to organise another assignation with Eliza. Lustful eyes followed her wherever she went. She was terrified that someone would notice some casual familiarity between us and create a fresh scandal. I managed to get messages to her via O'Hara and her maid, so all was not lost, but then I learned that after the apparent success of our visit, Bracegirdle had decided to take her himself to one of his settlements to the west.

They were away for over a week and as I kicked my heels in frustration, I was invited on another voyage myself. McCarthy was planning to take his schooner twelve miles down the coast to Annamaboe, to another gathering of Fantee chieftains.

"Come with me, Flashman," he cajoled. "You must be fed up, you have been stuck here for over a month. I promise it will be an amazing spectacle and I will organise a runner to come to us if a ship arrives. We will leave orders that it is not to depart until you are on board."

He was right, a fresh diversion would be welcome, so I joined the governor, his secretary Williams and a Captain Rickets in the little ship and I made my way down the coast again. We passed Joshua's village en route and I studied it through the glass. It seemed that their Christian values had been restored as I saw several villagers working industriously in the fields.

It certainly was a peaceful place compared to Annamaboe; we could hear trumpets heralding our arrival when we were still a quarter of a mile offshore. At least a thousand people were on the beach to welcome us onto the sand. Tribesmen from dozens of villages had gathered, cheering and waving their weapons in the air. Large palm leaves were laid down for us to walk on as we made our way through the tumultuous crowds. Eventually we reached a dais shaded by a roof of leaves and grass where seven chieftains sat waiting, alongside them, another chair for McCarthy. One of their number, I saw, was Banutu, who nodded in greeting as I went with Rickets and Williams to stand behind the chair of the governor.

There were voluble speeches of welcome from each of the chiefs. How much of them the governor understood I could not say – even Williams looked confused as he tried to interpret parts of them. But there was no doubting their enthusiasm as they beat at their chests and held their weapons aloft. McCarthy gave a speech in return, confirming that they would work together in a new and proud alliance to bring fear to their enemies. I saw Fenwick beside Banutu for this, whispering a translation in his ear, while waving a cheery greeting to me.

One by one the chiefs made their oaths of allegiance to the new alliance. They would swear on the Bible for our benefit and then make more elaborate pledges to their own gods. This usually involved shouting at the heavens or at religious tokens that they had brought with them. They would also wave swords and spears above their heads with such a passion, that it was a miracle none of them lost an eye, or worse. After each chief's declaration his warriors would set up their own acclaim, firing weapons into the sky and charging towards the platform yelling their war cries to show how ferocious they could be.

They were pretty convincing, for at the first charge I was just about to make a run for it before Rickets caught my arm and explained that it was all a show. At the end of each charge, as the tumult died down the chieftain would look expectantly at McCarthy. Each time he would place his hand on the Bible and swear that the British would not break the alliance without first warning the tribe and ensuring that their interests were protected. After this had happened for the third time, I turned to Williams and asked why the tribes were so insistent on this. "Don't they trust us?" I asked

"They have good reason not to," he admitted. "Back in '07 the old trading company supported the tribes in a conflict against the Ashanti, but later changed sides without telling them. They handed an old chief who had sought their protection over to his enemies and he was tortured to death. Then they sold many of the local warriors into slavery."

"I am surprised that they trust us at all after that!" I exclaimed.

"I think that they recognise that the governor is a very different man to the old company administrators. They are also far more worried about the Ashanti than they are about us."

Just as I thought the ceremony was about to come to a close, word came through that a new chief was coming. The man was called Appea, and he was a powerful leader of the Adjumacon people. McCarthy was delighted at the news and announced that we would stay overnight in the local fort to greet Appea when he arrived the next day.

I saw the first of the Adjumacon when I threw back the shutters in my room the following morning. They were bearers walking towards us down the beach, each loaded with a bundle of possessions. By the time I had finished my breakfast and looked again a procession of them, now nearly a mile long, was visible coming over the sand.

"How many of them are there?" I asked McCarthy.

"There should be at least a thousand, but it is not just the numbers. Appea and his warriors have beaten Ashanti forces before and have no fear of them. That is why I am keen for them to join us. They will help give confidence to some of the tribes that the Ashanti have conquered in the past."

As we watched, the bearers were followed by the first of the warriors. There were hundreds of them, most armed with muskets but others with spears, bows and arrows and various other bladed weapons. At the head of each band was a war leader, striding under a colourful umbrella to keep off the sun, an impressive gold-hilted sword at his hip. We went to wait with the other local chiefs at the little shaded pavilion we had used before. The beach was now heaving with people as far as the eye could see as all of those from the previous day had come back to see the new arrivals. Many more from nearby villages had also come to view the spectacle. Eventually the clarion call of trumpets announced the arrival of the great king. Appea's guards cleared a way through the crowds and a new procession appeared.

First came the trumpeters, who were now blowing near continuously, but not playing any kind of tune. I was glad when they moved past as the din was awful. They were replaced by a procession of Appea's senior captains, each one lying on a palanquin borne by four soldiers and around them four more held up a canopy to keep their chief in the shade. At the sight of McCarthy each of these leaders left their conveyance and gave the governor a salute in their custom, before standing with the other local men to await the arrival of their king. A steady thumping beat could now be heard and two huge drums came into view. Each drum and its beater was borne aloft by six men. The drums were draped in a tartan plaid, which seemed an effort to hide the adornments underneath, but glimpses could still be had of the skulls and jawbones of what must have been beaten enemies. Then came warriors bearing elephant tails, emblematic of the king's power and finally ten men carrying aloft swords that appeared to have been made of solid gold. Only then did a much larger canopied palanquin make its way through the crowd, carrying a smiling monarch reclining on a satin cushion. Appea climbed out of his conveyance as it was set down before the pavilion. He grinned and held out his hands in welcome to all those present as McCarthy stepped forward to greet him personally.

"Welcome, Chief Appea, it is an honour to have you join our gathering," the governor called. I watched as the words were translated for the chief by a pretty young woman, who quickly stepped up beside him.

"The chief is honoured to be an ally of the governor," she replied on his behalf as the king stepped forward and shook McCarthy's hand in the European manner. He had another of the golden swords at his hip and I noticed several scars indicating he had fought a few wars already. He said something to the translator and she continued, "He says that we will chase the Ashanti from our lands like lions chasing cowardly dogs. None will be left alive."

"Indeed," agreed McCarthy somewhat hesitantly. He had said previously that he was simply looking for a display of strength to intimidate our aggressive neighbours, but clearly some of the tribes had other ideas. Before he could say more a huge warrior stepped forward, a good head and shoulders taller than any of the others. His massive oiled body was rippling with muscle; he looked like an ebonised Greek god.

"This is our champion," announced the translator. She looked smugly at McCarthy and then at the other chiefs sitting behind him before she announced, "The king suggests a wrestling tournament to see if you have anyone who can beat him." The huge brute could probably have beaten a grizzly bear into submission, never mind another warrior. The other chiefs evidently thought the same, for they lapsed into furious whispering between themselves as each tried to persuade one of the others to put a man up to be pulverised and have their people humiliated. As no foolhardy volunteer was forthcoming, the translator turned back to McCarthy and asked with deceptive sweetness, "Who is the governor's champion?"

McCarthy looked back to Rickets. We were still standing behind the chair he had been using. "Captain Rickets, do we have anyone among the soldiers we brought who could at least stand a few minutes against this fellow?" He must have known the answer to his question before he asked it. No single man in a fair fight would stand a chance and I would not have bet on them if they had allowed three of our men to take him on together. Rickets shook his head, at a loss at what to suggest. Then I saw McCarthy turn to me and wink before he responded. "Mr Flashman is my champion," he announced to general gasps of astonishment – not least from me.

"If you think I am wrestling that big bastard you are out of your mind," I announced firmly. I was a civilian now and could speak my mind. Governor of this part of Africa or not, there was no way that I was obeying any order to fight that giant. He was strong enough to break my back as though it were a dry twig. McCarthy just grinned at my response. Over his shoulder I could see the interpreter whispering my answer to the king, who looked at me and roared with laughter.

"He says your champion is a wise man, but not perhaps very brave," the girl translated, passing on Appea's thoughts.

"Well now, brave he is, but not foolish enough to fight your man," announced McCarthy. "Mr Flashman was formerly a soldier, a great warrior, who had many battles with the French under their great chief Napoleon. Have you heard of him?" The girl nodded that Bonaparte's fame had spread to even this remote corner of civilisation. "Mr Flashman was at the great battle of Waterloo that saw Napoleon finally vanquished once and for all."

Eventually they found three warriors willing to take on Appea's champion. The big man must have been under orders not to humiliate his king's new allies, for he toyed with each of them for a while. He even let them try to come to grips with him. I am sure one of his challengers broke his shoulder when he tried to charge the giant, as I heard a bone snap. Then, when the big man tired of their antics, he lifted them up in the air as though they were small children and then dropped them down on the sand, pinning them there with his foot.

I thought the king had forgotten about me, but when we settled down for a feast at the end of the day, I found the pretty young interpreter at my elbow. "King Appea would like you to sit with him and tell him about this battle of Waterloo," she announced.

So that evening, while McCarthy sat on the king's left, I sat on his right. Well perhaps not immediately to his right, for between us sat the interpreter, wearing a colourful blue sarong and smelling of tropical flowers. I told him the story of the battle, explaining how the French emperor had managed to get an army of over a hundred and twenty thousand men close to his enemies unseen and how he had come so close to winning. We struggled a little with numbers as their biggest number was ten thousand. So I used beans to show how many ten thousands there had been on both sides. The king asked lots of questions, but I think he struggled to understand the full horror of the barrage from the French grand battery. Or perhaps he understood well, for he suggested that Wellington would have been better off charging the gunners at the start of the battle and trying to hold the guns. Thinking back to the bodies scattered along the British ridge at the end of the day, he may have been right.

I agreed with him anyway as by then I was more than a little distracted. The translator sat so close that her shoulders brushed against both the king and me as she leaned first to one and then the other so that we could talk above the din of the feast. It was hard not to stare at the firm ripe orbs of flesh that were visible down the front of her sarong and I am sure that the garment slipped lower during the evening. Appea caught me gazing at the view once and grinned. The next thing I knew, the interpreter was turning to me and asking coyly, "The king is enquiring if you find his interpreter attractive?"

"Well... I... er... Tell him that his interpreter is as beautiful as she is skilful in languages," I tried diplomatically.

"And are my breasts that you have been admiring as pretty as those of the white women?" she pressed while holding my gaze. I was pretty sure that this was not part of Appea's question and now suspected that the cunning minx had been discreetly pulling down on her sarong to distract me with a better view.

There was a brazen tilt to her chin, but if she thought she was going to embarrass me, well she was knocking at the wrong door. "Well, why don't we arrange a private viewing after this dinner and then I can give you my expert opinion."

She turned back to the king. Heaven knows what she told him about what I had said, but he was amused and then asked more questions about how British Army regiments were trained. As the evening finished and the king got to his feet, the translator turned to me and whispered, "Your 'viewing' will have to wait as the king needs me at his side this evening. But perhaps we can meet again on the march and I can also see how white men compare with my brothers."

Chapter 8

"How is my champion this fine day?" boomed McCarthy as he strolled into my room the next morning. I was still in bed, which was not surprising as the sun was not even up.

"What in God's name are you doing waking me at this unearthly hour?" I grumbled.

"I wanted to make sure you are awake, as we are setting off in half an hour. As you will soon see, travelling through the jungle is much easier if you get ahead of the crowds."

"Through the jungle?" I queried, still half asleep. "But I thought we would be going back to Cape Coast Castle."

"Ah, that was the old plan," admitted the governor as he threw back the shutters to let a grey pre-dawn light into the room. "But as Appea has brought with him men and supplies for a month, I can hardly thank him for coming and send him straight home. We are going to make a patrol in strength up to the Pra River – it forms a natural border between the territory of some of our allies and the Ashanti."

I was awake now all right, the reek of danger filling my nostrils as McCarthy prattled on. "It will mostly be a procession, of course, just a show of strength, and the various champions will be displayed. As I have now announced you as my champion, it would be awkward if you were not there."

"But surely the Ashanti are likely to retaliate if you march a huge force up to their front door?"

"Nonsense, there is nothing to worry about. We will still be seventy miles from Coomassie, their capital, and they have no idea where we might appear. Appea's people have heard that the Ashanti army is broken up into at least twelve different divisions and scattered across the country to block any advance on Coomassie. They are on the defensive, they don't know what we are going to do next and have spread their forces out too thinly to be a threat. Even if we were to stumble into one of these divisions, we would outnumber it three or four to one. But I am sure that they do not want war with us anyway. As I told you before, they are bullies, happy to attack a weaker foe, but when someone with a bit of resolve looks them in the eye, they will back down. You need not be concerned, Flashman, the Ashanti will not bother us. This patrol will also block their trade with the Dutch outpost at Elmina, which has been selling them powder and ammunition." He grinned, "Anyway, I thought you would want to come. You seemed keen on Appea's translator and she will be coming with us. I will need someone to liaise closely with her, so we know what Appea's men are doing."

Now in the past I'll admit that such an appeal might have made me overlook the risk, but I was longer in the tooth now. I remembered all too well the times that lust and debauchery had led me into moments of stomach-churning terror. I wasn't falling for that again.

"Well obviously I wish you well with the expedition," I started, "but I doubt I would be of much help to you. I have been out of the army for years now and I have never fought in jungle terrain such as this. Anyway, as you know, I am keen to get home, my family have not seen me in years. My duty is to them now and I would be perturbed to discover that I had missed a ship home while I was up-country."

"Fear not, sir," consoled McCarthy as he gave me a manly grip on the shoulder. "My order that no homeward bound ship shall leave here without you on board still stands. You will not miss your passage back to the bosom of your kin, I will give you my word on that. A messenger will bring us news of any ship and we will quickly get you back to the coast. We are using my schooner to bring supplies up river and once we are near the Pra, you will be able to get back to the castle in a day using her if need be. But I think you will be of more use than you imagine. Word has spread amongst our own men of your exploits and now our allies are hearing of your deeds. They put great store in men of such courage. You will find that you are honoured wherever we go and your presence will add greatly to the confidence of our men."

The governor was toadying me for all he was worth, but I was not falling for such flattery, for I knew where it led. "I hear what you say, sir, but I know a champion will be expected to lead any attack and I'm afraid my fighting days are behind me. I would not want to let you down. The time of my heroic exploits is long past. I ain't as fast as I was with pistol or sword and certainly not over rough ground."

McCarthy laughed. "My dear Flashman, that fancy pistol you normally wear in your belt tells me that you still carry a martial sting, but do not worry. I give you my word that I truly believe there will be no serious engagement with the Ashanti at all, this is just a matter of show. We will merely demonstrate our strength and resolve. But if I am wrong, then the fighting will be led by our soldiers and our allied warriors. You can stand with me as we watch the attacks of our men and give me the benefit of your experience on how any battle should be conducted."

Well, I suppose he could not be fairer than that: a guarantee that I would not have to fight and a confident assurance that there would be no battle at all. On top of that, an immediate dismissal should a homeward bound ship appear. He had addressed all my objections and to continue to argue against joining him would have looked odd for a man who had previously boasted of his ordeals in uniform. And there was that translator to consider, a shapely piece who would provide an interesting diversion as we progressed through the country.

So it was that despite my initial objections, twenty minutes later I was joining the governor as he started his way up a jungle track. There were just the two of us and a couple of local guides. I could see immediately why the governor liked to set off early. The path was so narrow that at times we had to walk in single file, but we made brisk progress in the relative cool of the early morning. It was hard to imagine how several thousand warriors and bearers would follow us. They would have to hack down the foliage for several yards on either side of the track to make a road that the army could march on; it would take them days to follow in a single file.

We passed the first village an hour after dawn. It was full of women and children who stared curiously at us until the guides explained who we were. I was puzzled at the absence of men until I realised that they were all down at the beach behind us. Once McCarthy had been introduced, the families left behind by the warriors made a big show of welcome and ensured that we had a good breakfast before we moved on. We passed two more villages before noon and at each we were welcomed, again just by old men, women and children. I had thought that we were moving at a cracking pace given the terrain and the climate, but by early afternoon we began to be overhauled by some of Appea's porters who had been sent on ahead of the army to set up the next camp. I puffed and sweated through exertion and the increasing jungle heat and humidity while these hardy fellows grinned at us as they swept by on long, languid limbs. They each had huge bundles, often balanced on their heads, but did not seem remotely fatigued compared to us – my burden was merely a stick with which to beat back the undergrowth.

Before we made camp that evening, we were also overtaken by the front ranks of the army, who were cutting a wider path to help those behind. The practical difficulties of moving an army of several thousand men through a jungle were astonishing. By the time we reached the village and fields that were to be our camp, the vast majority of the army were still on the track behind us. Many must have spent the night on the trail as they were still pouring into the camp at dawn the next day. Organisation of the bivouac was chaotic, with people arguing over where they should camp and which chief should go where. Things were not helped by torrential rain, which quickly turned much of the area into liquid mud. King Appea and his comely translator must have arrived in the camp after the storm hit, for we did not see either of them that evening.

McCarthy and I, along with Rickets and Williams, who had caught us up with the small British contingent, were fortunate to be lodged in one of the village huts. As the storm lashed the grass roof we tucked into a stew of bushmeat and something called macaroni. This latter substance is, as best I could tell, a paste made with eggs and flour. It is then cut into small shapes and dried before being packed in barrels. Everything you want to keep dry must be stored in barrels or it will become damp and rot. This macaroni was a popular campaign food as it was relatively light to carry, but once added to a stew it expanded and was quite filling – if a little gritty on occasions.

For me at least, the first day's march had been relatively pleasant if a little tiring. But the second day was anything but enjoyable. Early the next morning McCarthy was keen to press on again. Rickets and Williams wanted to come with us and bring with them the few British soldiers and bearers we had. This delayed our departure until well after dawn. By then the path was already packed with porters and warriors from the other tribes. After the recent rain, the track was soon a quagmire – I slipped and fell on my arse twice in the first mile – and then we encountered a stretch that saw us wading through water up to our knees.

We staggered into the next camp late that afternoon, cut, bruised and exhausted. Rickets and I spent an unpleasant half hour using blades to scrape leeches off each other's bodies; I must have had at least a dozen on me, including one in my ear that was hard to remove. McCarthy, though, despite being nearly twenty years my senior was soon back in an ebullient mood. He was cheered by several chieftains of the Assin tribe who were waiting to meet him. They had traditionally been allies of the Ashanti, but these men were asking to join McCarthy's alliance. It was a clear sign that the local balance of power was tipping in his favour.

The following morning we set off early again for the town of Donquah. I was soon feeling thoroughly miserable, not least because I fell and twisted my ankle on the way. The 'champion' of the British forces finally arrived in Donquah carried on a canvas seat, stretched between two poles, which were borne by four natives. My spirits rose, though, when I saw the place, for compared to the villages we had seen en route it was a very pleasant settlement. The main street was some sixty feet wide with a row of trees down the centre to afford shade. On either side were substantial dwellings, some two-storey, built with wooden beams, wattle and daub walls and thick thatched roofs. Some of the houses were even whitewashed. It looked like an Elizabethan village transported into the jungle. When McCarthy talked about moving on in the morning, I put my foot gingerly down and insisted that I would go no further.

"Leave me here," I said wincing at the pain. "I will only slow you down and my ankle needs a few days of rest to recover."

"If you are sure," agreed McCarthy. "I will send a runner to Cape Coast Castle to let them know you are here if a ship arrives. They can always carry you to the coast if your leg has not healed."

"Thank you. Where will you go now?"

"Well there are a few more chiefs I want to see. Then I may go back to the castle myself to check the army is ready to advance before coming back." The man seemed to have boundless energy.

I found a room in one of the largest houses with a decent bed, a roof that did not leak and no leaches in sight. There I was content to rest. After the best night's sleep I had enjoyed in days, I got up to watch through the window as McCarthy, Rickets, Williams and the few soldiers with them marched off down the next jungle track. The governor was wearing his habitual, distinctive yellow waistcoat and he fussed up and down the column checking men and supplies like an anxious bee guarding his honey. It was a relief to see them go and leave me to enjoy some well-earned relaxation.

It wasn't exactly peaceful, however, for as I sat on the balcony that morning, hundreds if not thousands of men trudged past me on the street through the town. They still had the energy to blow into blaring trumpets, beat drums and make a heck of a din as they paused in their journey to seek out their fellows. Towards the end of the afternoon the sudden appearance of men bearing golden swords indicated the imminent arrival of Appea and, of more interest to me, of his woman of the foreign tongues. I leaned eagerly over the rail as a procession of palanquins approached. The king waved cheerily when he saw me but did not stop – his bearers carried him straight off down the next path. Behind him came his captains of war and then at last came my beauty, with that great hulk of a champion walking alongside. I waved and was rewarded with a sultry smile before she leaned forward and instructed her bearers to lower her to the ground in front of me.

"Can I offer you some refreshment?" I offered, gesturing to a pot of the local coffee.

"That would be most kind," she purred as she walked up the steps towards me. The smile was still there, but there was a calculating look too. She moved with a feline grace and I could not shake the impression that she was surveying me as a cat would a mouse. Following behind her came the champion, the boards creaking under his weight until he stood behind the chair I had set for her. "Don't mind him," my guest gestured over her shoulder. "He is as dumb as an ox and will not understand a word we are saying."

I gazed up at the champion, who regarded me through eyes narrowed slightly in suspicion, as though he could guess my intentions. I did not think he was dumb at all. I poured them both coffee, although the cup looked like a thimble in the giant man's hand. "I am glad to see you again," I continued, "although your bodyguard looks set to stop us getting as intimately acquainted as I would like."

She smiled. "There is no time for that as I will have to catch up with the king soon. We will have to travel faster than we did this morning." She looked down at her bearers, who were wearily flexing their shoulders now they were relieved of their burden. She shouted a harsh command in their language and one of them doubled off to the well with a bowl to fetch water. She turned back and surveyed me over the rim of her cup as she took a sip of the dark liquid. "Is the governor far ahead of us?" she enquired. I told her that he had left early that morning and then shared what little I knew of his itinerary. "Where do you think he will go once he has gathered his army from Cape Coast Castle?" she asked.

"I have no idea, I hope to be long gone by then." I looked at her curiously, "Has he not discussed his intentions with King Appea, then?"

"Yes of course, but not every detail has been agreed yet." She changed the subject, "I hear you are going home on the first ship heading north. I have always wanted to go to London and Paris. Have you been to those cities? What are they like?"

"They are huge and very crowded," I told her. "Much colder than here and there is no fever season, although we do occasionally have outbreaks of cholera and other diseases."

"But what of the people; how are they dressed and are there black people there?"

I laughed, "The ladies wear long dresses and the men wear much as I do now but with waistcoats and overcoats to keep them warm. Everyone wears hats outside." I thought back, "There are a few black people in both cities, more I think in London than Paris. A handful are gentlemen, writers mostly, although my friend Cochrane told me of a black chap he admired called Perkins, who made post captain in our navy. Others are servants, but some are former sailors or soldiers. There were a few in the army I fought with in Spain."

"And the buildings, do they have streets as grand as this?" she asked gesturing to the broad thoroughfare before us.

I chuckled and put a coffee bean from a pot on the table down next to her cup. "In London," I told her, "there is a building bigger than this house to the same scale as your cup is to that bean."

"That is impossible," she gasped. "Even the Ashanti do not have buildings that big, at least so I have heard. And anyway, no one would dare to go to the top of it, for it would be bound to collapse."

"St Pauls is made of stone and it has already stood for a hundred and fifty years. It has a domed top, almost as beautiful as those domes you are hiding from me. But if you lay on the floor directly under it and could walk upwards into the air, you could go a hundred paces and still not touch the top." She was silent then as she tried to imagine it. Her lips parted in wonder. I looked up at the Hercules standing beside her, but he was clearly bored with us and staring out across the street. "Why don't you lose your companion and we could go inside and talk more about domes," I suggested.

She grinned. "I don't think that would be a good idea. Appea ordered his champion to protect me and he takes his responsibility very seriously. If he caught us, it would end badly for you."

At the mention of the word 'champion,' her companion looked around. He clearly was not as dumb as she suggested, for he understood some words. He gave me a stern glare and put a proprietary hand on the girl's shoulder.

The pair of them left a few minutes later. Normally I would have felt a pang of longing at letting such a prime piece escape, but that time it was almost a relief. Perhaps I was just grateful to have escaped a mauling by a jealous Hercules, or having spent time recently with Eliza, there was no great sense of frustration. But I think it was more than that. Looking back with the hindsight of what followed, I cannot be sure, but I think even then there was something about the lady of tongues that I did not entirely trust.

Chapter 9

I spent Christmas day, 1823 in Donquah. I remember it well as two
local merchants, one black and one white, invited me to a festive
dinner at one of their homes to celebrate. It was a rather disturbing
affair, not least because they served roast monkey instead of the goose
I was used to. Skinned and gutted, the animal resembled a long-limbed
child and did nothing for my appetite. My companions were in a
melancholy mood too as they claimed that their town was in decline. It
had previously been on one of the main routes to the coast for slave
traders. They boasted that in the past they had runners in all of the
main ports, who would tell them quickly of changes in prices, which in
turn was dependent on whether they had ships to fill. Cargoes would
then be directed to the British, Dutch, Swedish or Danish slave castles
nearby to get the best return.

While they professed to be Christians, their attitude was very
different to that of the Reverend Bracegirdle. They had little empathy
for their human merchandise. They pointed out that there had been
slaves in Africa since the days of the Pharaohs and probably before
that too. Many of the local tribes had slaves of their own and there was
still a demand for them in the Americas. Even though the trade had
been banned by the British for fifteen years and by the Dutch for eight,
they were still resentful of their fall in income. The town had been
prosperous, enabling the merchants to build their large houses, but
now the little ivory and other goods from the interior gave them mean
pickings.

"What about the gold?" I asked. "This area is called the Gold Coast;
surely there should be ore to trade that would make you a profit?"

"The mines are all in Ashanti territory," explained one. "Their king
controls the trade and the mines. He must be immensely rich, but they
only spend the gold on what they need. They do not allow other
merchants to have a stake in their gold." He explained that originally
Europeans had come to this coast for the gold, not slaves, as they
arrived long before plantations were established in America and the
Caribbean. But the Ashanti and other tribes knew the value of the

metal as they had been trading for generations with Arabs to the north. They were not going to hand over ingots in exchange for a few glass beads and, moreover, they drove hard bargains for trade goods. "That is why the Ashanti are as well armed as you British," explained the merchant, "and why no European soldiers have been able to get anywhere near their mines. I doubt that many white men have even seen them."

The more I heard about the Ashanti, the less I liked the sound of them. I was content to keep a low profile and out of the way in Donquah, while McCarthy charged about the country organising his forces. I was quietly hoping that he would forget about me entirely. With Appea and the other warriors gone, the place was quiet and tranquil and my ankle soon recovered. We got word that the governor was back in Cape Coast Castle, which further convinced me to stay where I was.

After nearly two weeks my period of rest was rudely interrupted by the arrival of more soldiers. They were led by Chisholm, borne aloft in a rudimentary sedan chair, and I noticed that they did not arrive on the path that I was told led directly to the castle, so heaven knows what circuitous route they had taken. He had with him the bulk of the Royal African Corps, some six hundred men and at least another thousand local warriors. O'Hara was in the ranks and looking none too happy about it.

"He got us lost twice on the way here," he grumbled of his commander. "I am surprised he can find his cock to take a piss." He gestured to the wide path that Appea's army had cut through the jungle a fortnight before, "At least now we are here, we will have a good trail that even he can follow."

"Are you joining Appea, then?" I asked.

"Aye, that is the plan. The governor has split the army so that we can travel faster through the jungle. We will be going the furthest north on our route. As they reckon that we are the most likely to be attacked, we will have the strongest force. There should be nearly four thousand of us once we catch up with Appea."

I remembered that each one of the dozen Ashanti defensive divisions that Appea had heard about was only around a thousand men. The odds were in our soldiers' favour, but I was glad that I was not going with them.

"Ah, Flashman, I wondered where you had got to." I looked up and saw Chisholm striding towards us. He was looking pleased with himself as he added, "It is good to see the army finally on the move, eh?"

"I gather your part is the most likely to see action," I said nodding at O'Hara as my source.

"Oh the governor is still confident that they will not attack. In fact, we are hearing rumours that at least one of their army chiefs is thinking of bringing his warriors over to us. They have heard how some of their former allies have joined our ranks. No," he concluded, "I don't think we will have much to worry about. The army is travelling in four separate columns and once we join Appea, I will lead us to our rendezvous point, a town on the edge of Ashanti territory." Over his shoulder I saw O'Hara roll his eyes at the thought of more navigation from Chisholm, but I was sure Appea would have reliable guides to get them there. "Once we are all together," continued the major, "we will have over twelve thousand men, which we think is more than the entire Ashanti army. The governor says he wants a show of strength to put these rogues in their place."

"Well it is a shame I cannot join you," I lied, "but I have orders to remain here until I get new instructions from the governor." For a ghastly moment I had a sudden horror that Chisholm would produce new orders for me, but he did no such thing.

"Well then, I will see you at the rendezvous," he declared confidently, "unless your ship arrives first." I wished them well and as I watched them all march off down the path, I felt a surge of relief. For once a war was happening without me… and it felt marvellous. Major Laing was somewhere to the northeast with a force of over two thousand, and elsewhere there was yet another army of over six thousand, including some of the less reliable natives. They were all busy hacking their way through jungles, risking ambush and death, while T Flashman Esquire sat peacefully on his balcony drinking tea and waiting for news of a homebound ship.

There were no more messages from Cape Coast Castle and as the days passed, the hope that I had been forgotten by McCarthy began to grow. I would wait until we had news that he had marched without me and then I would return to the castle. With most of the garrison out of the way, it would be much easier to arrange liaisons with Eliza while I waited for a sail on the horizon. Then a week after I had seen Chisholm, a young ensign with around fifty men arrived in the town. It was Wetherell, the lad who had welcomed me to the castle when I had first arrived with Fenwick. This time his party included a dozen soldiers from the regiment, a score of native soldiers and a similar number of bearers. They were all under orders to escort me to a place called Assamacow, where I was to be reunited with McCarthy. My heart sank at the news; I had not been forgotten after all. The disappointment must have shown on my face but Wetherell, who had evidently heard the tales of my earlier exploits, misunderstood.

"Were you hoping to join Major Chisholm, sir?" he asked before continuing. "They say he is the most likely to see some fighting. Some of the chiefs do not want the governor in the field at all, they say it demeans him to fight unless the Ashanti king personally leads his army, but word is that the king is ill at Coomassie and may be dying. The governor only has a small group with him and is well surrounded by allies. I doubt we will see the enemy."

I did not take too much comfort from that for I had heard similar platitudes before, normally preceding some terror-stricken disaster. Instead I searched for an excuse that I could use to return to the coast, but none came to mind. McCarthy would lose face with his allies if his 'champion' was not on hand and I did not want to lose the governor's goodwill. If he did not help me get home, then I could still be here during the next fever season – the thought filled me with horror. No, I would have to go and rely on McCarthy's promise that I would not be expected to fight – something that Wetherell's news about the Ashanti king being ill made more likely.

We set off early the next day. It is difficult to describe how disorientating travel through the jungle is. At times it was hard to see the sun through the tree canopy and we crossed several paths along the way. Within an hour, I doubt I could have found my way back to Donquah through the maze of tracks we had passed. Wetherell and his guide, though, were confident that they knew where we were going and so, proceeding in single file, we did not have to cut through too much of a trail. At one point we came to a particularly wide stretch of track that had been recently cleared, with lots of broken branches lying about. I thought it was pleasant to have some space around us again, at least until Wetherell told us that we had to hurry along it.

"It has been made by one of the water horses or possibly elephants," he explained. "They are creatures of habit and often use the same paths repeatedly. We don't want to come across the owner of this one while we are using it, or they will charge and trample us." I had already discovered that those water horses were surprisingly fast over short distances and felt a sense of relief when we emerged on a narrower trail.

At length we arrived at Assamacow, which was another prosperous town, similar to the one I had departed from. I found McCarthy in one of the merchant's houses. He had been waiting there for three days, not for me but for the rest of his supplies, and he was fuming with impatience.

"Most men want to carry weapons and fight rather than act as porters. Those that will carry things are demanding a ridiculous amount. Instead of solving the problem, Brandon has come on ahead to complain to me. The man is useless," he grumbled of his quartermaster. He lashed the table top with a fly whisk in frustration, sending several of the insects into the air. I got the impression that if McCarthy had been the head of a school, the unfortunate Brandon would be heading for a caning. "Now Captain Rickets has to manage the rear-guard," he continued, "and press women, boys and old men into service as porters, many of whom have abandoned their loads at the first opportunity."

Assamacow was a sizeable place to wait for them to catch up and I was not unduly perturbed until McCarthy spoke again. "Two local tribes claim that they have Ashanti warriors in their territory, but I do not believe that they could be that close. I have sent Williams to investigate. He has negotiated with all the local kingdoms, including the Ashanti in the past. He should be able to give them some backbone. They are timid and nervous people and will run from their own shadow if we are not careful."

From what I had heard of the Ashanti, the caution of the local tribes was entirely reasonable and I began to feel a familiar twinge of alarm. "How many men do you have here?" I asked.

"When they all arrive, there will be around five hundred, but half of those will be Fantee tribesmen. The rest are soldiers and militia."

"If those local tribes are right and even just one of the Ashanti divisions is in the vicinity," I cautioned, "then we could be outnumbered two to one. That is if the Fantee men stand and if the local tribes are falling back, there is no guarantee of that." Even as I spoke I felt a growing sense of trepidation. Each Ashanti army was said to be a thousand men. In thick jungle they could advance virtually unseen until they burst among their unsuspecting enemy. "As a precaution, sir, should we not order Major Chisholm to close with us? He has six hundred redcoats with him not to mention another three thousand warriors."

"Are you sure that is really necessary, Flashman?" McCarthy gestured vaguely out of the window towards the nearby jungle, "Williams should be able to give the local tribes a stern talking to. Then, once our men arrive, we should have plenty to teach one of their columns a lesson – if such a force exists, which I doubt."

"I have fought in numerous countries around the world, sir," I said reminding him that I had more military experience. "And if you do not know precisely where your enemy is and in what strength, then I would strongly advise caution and summoning Major Chisholm's forces."

I could not have put it more firmly than that and McCarthy sat back in his chair for a moment as he considered what I had said. To unite his forces would slow them down as they travelled through the jungle, but he must have been conscious that he had not been in a battle for twenty years and had never commanded a force in the field. "Well you are my military adviser as well as my champion here, Flashman, so I suppose that I should heed your judgement. Get Wetherell to send a runner to Chisholm, would you? He is only three days' march away and it will take nearly that long to gather up our supplies."

I went away feeling well satisfied, confident that for once disaster had been averted. The young ensign sent one of his best men to Chisholm with orders to join us a few miles further forward on the banks of the Pra River, which was to be our next stop. Then I went to check on the supply situation, which was suitably shambolic, guaranteeing that we would not be moving any time soon. A steady stream of bearers had started to arrive in the town and now surrounded Brandon, squabbling over how much they should get paid. They were all shouting and following him around, like a pack of dogs at feeding time. How he worked out how much to pay was anyone's guess as some were coming in with a single load while others arrived in pairs sharing a burden – perhaps having abandoned one on the way. Once paid, around half went back down the track to collect some more, but the rest slipped away down other trails into the jungle. I sat and watched as a pile of supplies steadily built up. There were barrels of cartridges and the macaroni, which had to be kept dry; large sacks of meal, cooking pots and the poles and canvas for tents, but not yet nearly enough for five hundred men on a march.

Williams, the secretary, arrived back in Assamacow the next day. He told us that the nearby chiefs were sure that Ashanti were in the area, but did not know how many or precisely where. While the local warriors were said to be retreating before this force, Williams had spoken to their leaders, who had assured him that they would stand and fight with us. Despite these reports, McCarthy was still not convinced on the existence of the Ashanti. He thought frightened villagers might have invented them to save face as they moved back. But nodding at me he told Williams, "Mr Flashman has persuaded me to recall Major Chisholm's force, which will rendezvous with us at the

Pra River. That should give the tribes some comfort. Go back to their chiefs and tell them that I expect their warriors to meet us at the river too."

Two days passed after that meeting as we sat in relative comfort at Assamacow. Slowly the pile of supplies in the centre of the village grew and more soldiers gathered in the town. It was a paltry force to go to war with, but by then Chisholm's force was marching towards the river too. I thought I would feel more comfortable when I was surrounded by sturdy backs draped in red cloth.

We finally had enough supplies to leave Assamacow, with a twenty-mile march to reach the river where I hoped Chisholm would be waiting. As we stood in the central square preparing to depart, it was clear that we had nowhere near enough bearers to carry the barrels and bundles that the army needed on the march. There were wails of complaint as Brandon's men started to round up virtually every villager they could find to serve as porters. Old men, women and children were all protesting that they did not want to go near the Ashanti. Meanwhile McCarthy and the quartermaster insisted to all who would listen, that the rumours were false and the Ashanti would be nowhere near the line of march. The chief of Assamacow supported the governor. He was a thin, crippled old man who needed porters himself, as he was carried down the track suspended from a pole in a large basket.

I was soon envious of the old chief and his mode of transport, for it was a miserable journey. There was torrential rain that made the paths almost impassable. The heavily laden bearers soon fell behind and even unburdened; it was a struggle to make progress. At the bottom of one valley we must have spent hours crossing a mile of malodourous ooze. Each step saw you sinking knee deep in the foul-smelling mud, so that every pace was an energy-sapping effort. I ceased to care about the leeches or even snakes that I saw worming away from our path. The exhaustion even dulled my fear of the Ashanti.

We had hoped to make the meeting point by nightfall but as the sun came down we were still several miles short. I found some high ground and slumped down, content to let a fresh rain shower rinse some of the mud from my clothes. It was at least warm. I must have fallen asleep in the rain, as I awoke the next morning with my clothes still damp and muscles as stiff as boards.

Many a time I have topped the crest of a hill to see an army, friendly or hostile, spread out before me. But when I came over the last rise before the meeting point, I saw nothing but jungle. This was despite shinning up the slimy bark of a nearby tree for a better vantage point.

There were supposed to be thousands of men beneath the forest in front of me but there was no sign of them: no recently hewn clearing, no campfires, no glimpses of men moving through the trees. I knew that there had to be several hundred of our force down there as they had gone past me on the path, but the jungle was so thick there was no trace of them either. All I could see was a solid wall of green separated by a meandering strip of brown water, the Pra River. On the positive side, there was no sign of the enemy either, for the far shore of the river looked just as peaceful as the bank I was on. Perhaps McCarthy was right, I thought as I pressed on, searching eagerly for any sight of Chisholm and his men.

It was mid-afternoon when I finally tracked down McCarthy. For once his ebullient energy had deserted him. He was covered in mud and looked exhausted, having surveyed the jungle for several miles around the camp.

"Any news on Chisholm?" I asked, having already established that none of his men had arrived.

"No," sighed McCarthy wearily. "But he must be close, I have sent out half a dozen messengers in various directions to guide him here as quickly as possible."

The urgency of the governor's orders gave me a frisson of alarm. "Do you think that the enemy is close, then?"

"The local tribes are convinced they are and some of their warriors have already tried to desert. I had to summon their chiefs, who have again insisted that their men will stand with us and fight." He looked up at me then and I must have looked nearly as tired as him for he smiled and gestured to a metal pot hanging over a small fire. "There is tea in that, help yourself." He stretched his tired limbs and looked around to check we could not be overheard before continuing. "I doubt the chiefs can control all of their men, especially at night. We will put the local tribesmen in the centre of the camp and I have asked Captain Rickets to have some men stand guard to stop them escaping."

I sipped my tea with a growing sense of anxiety. "If there is one of those Ashanti armies out there, then they already outnumber us two to one. More if some of those natives manage to run while it is dark. You don't think the Ashanti will attack during the night, do you?"

"That is one thing that you do not have to worry about," McCarthy grinned. "Williams tells me that the Ashanti will only attack in daylight. They have probably learned that battles at night are too chaotic with warriors blundering about in a pitch-black jungle. Anyway, I am still not convinced that they are there at all and if they are, they still have to cross the river, and that bloody thing is full of crocodiles."

"Well I for one will be damned glad to see Chisholm and his men," I said fervently. "That will change the balance of things. We will outnumber the enemy and our allies will be less prone to run away. Are you certain he will arrive tomorrow?"

"I am sure he will," breezed the governor, although I noticed he did not look me in the eye as he said it. Instead he stared into the flames of the small campfire. I suspected that, like me, he was praying that the stupid bastard had not got himself lost again.

Chapter 10

Dawn on the Pra River at the place now known as Nsamankow on the twenty-first of January 1824, gave no hint of the horror that was to follow that day. The night had passed relatively peacefully, apart from one bloodcurdling scream when a sleeping warrior had been snatched by a crocodile. I had slept close to McCarthy's fire with the loaded Collier in my hand, in case one of the great scaly beasts came our way. Supplies were still only slowly trickling into the camp from the long train of exhausted porters that we had left on the path behind us, but some meat and macaroni were boiling in the pot for breakfast.

I went to find Rickets to take him a bowlful and discovered that he had managed to stop most of the local warriors from escaping during the night. Some eighty of them *had* slipped away, though, and judging from the resentful glances of those that remained, I would not have bet a farthing on the ones left staying long if we were attacked.

"I would send some of them out to look for Chisholm if I thought that they would actually search rather than run away," grumbled Rickets, who clearly shared the same opinion of their resolve. I walked cautiously down to the water. While there were some reptilian marks in the mud, the crocodiles had moved away in daylight. The river was sixty feet wide and its muddy waters the colour of milky tea and about as transparent. Heaven knew how deep it was and what manner of deadly creatures could be lurking unseen beneath its surface. I was reassured that it was a considerable obstacle to stop any attack. I studied the far shore and listened for any sign of distant voices or of men cutting their way through the forest, but apart from the usual screeches of jungle creatures, there was nothing. It looked as benign as the other landscape we had passed through, and yet the hair on the back of my neck was prickling with alarm.

By noon there was still no sign of either Chisholm or the enemy. But spirits had been lifted by the arrival of two hundred fresh warriors from Appea, which the king had sent to reinforce the governor's party. If these men had found us having covered a longer distance than Chisholm, then surely, we tried to convince ourselves, the major could not be that far away. We had a small marching band with us amongst the redcoats and McCarthy now ordered the bugler to sound the 'recall' every hour, in the hope of guiding our reinforcements towards us. As the strident notes echoed through the trees at midday we all strained our ears for an answering call, but there was nothing. I remember cursing the silent jungle, but, as it happened, you should be careful of what you wish for. When the bugler put his instrument to his lips an hour later there *was* a response, a distant strident blare of a horn… but from the other side of the river.

I was standing with Wetherell, Rickets and McCarthy and for a moment we all stared at each other in silent astonishment. "Could Chisholm somehow have crossed the river?" I asked.

"That was not a bugle," replied Rickets. "It sounded like a native instrument." We looked around; virtually the whole camp had fallen silent at the sound and of those we could see between the trees around us, all were staring expectantly in our direction. Rickets turned to McCarthy, "We do not have much ammunition yet, sir. The men only came with twenty rounds each and only one of the barrels of spare ammunition has arrived so far."

McCarthy nodded thoughtfully. "We still do not know who they are or what they want, but it pays to be prudent." He turned and found the person he was looking for standing by a pile of supplies. "Mr Brandon, a word please." The quartermaster came over, his eyes widening in alarm as the horn sounded again from over the water. "Brandon," said the governor quietly so that only those near him could hear. "Is it true that you only have one spare barrel of ammunition?"

"Yes sir," replied the quartermaster. "The rest are scattered back down the trail. A lot of the porters have abandoned their loads and left them in the mud, but some are still getting through."

"Take half a dozen strong men," instructed McCarthy, "go back down the trail and bring back some of the barrels of ammunition as quickly as you can." He nodded across the river, "I pray we don't, but we might need it later this afternoon."

"Right away, sir," said Brandon moving off, the colour draining from his face as the implications sank in. He was not the only one going pale; I could feel a familiar tightening of fear in my stomach and Rickets had begun licking his lips nervously. Then we heard a second horn sounding through the trees, this time two rising notes instead of one. I saw the young ensign immediately stare at Rickets, who nodded as though this new sound had special significance.

"What is it?" I asked, not sure I really wanted to know the answer.

"The tribes use the horns to keep their regiments together in the jungle," explained the captain. "They each have their own horn call. It is possible that there are two Ashanti columns out there instead of one."

"Oh Christ," I muttered for this meant that there could be at least two thousand against our five hundred, many of whom were likely to run at the first opportunity. I glanced across to where the native warriors were gathered and noted that the significance of the second horn had not been lost on them either. Some were in a fine old taking, ranting and pointing into the jungle on the verge of panic. I knew exactly how they felt, as when I thought about our plight, I nearly brought back up my breakfast macaroni. Why were the Ashanti closing in on our pitifully small force when there were much larger armies nearer to their lands to attack? The answer came after just a moment's thought: the Ashanti knew far more about our disposition than we knew about theirs. They must have spies in our forces who told them where McCarthy was and they were evidently determined to capture or kill the governor.

The man himself seemed blithely unconcerned. "That is only a theory," insisted McCarthy. "For all we know the man blew two notes because he had inhaled a fly."

Well he might have been trying to convince himself, but he was failing with me. I looked fiercely about, like the fearless hero I pretended to be, while inwardly I desperately thought about how to escape. My first inclination was to run back down the path we had used and keep running until I got to the coast. In fact, I may even have taken a couple of hesitant paces in that direction before a new horn call brought me to my senses. It was from the other side of the river and two short notes this time, signifying yet another column was closing in.

The Ashanti, I realised, had played us for fools. They had tricked us with tales of their dispersed regiments, when in reality, much if not all of their whole army, was together and coming up fast. If they were half as clever as I suspected, they would not just try to cross the river in front of us, but instead send forces – unopposed – over the river on either side of us to come up from behind. If I fled, I was likely to run slap into one of these encircling armies. I would certainly not survive for long in the jungle on my own, especially with thousands of Ashanti combing it for fugitives. "Our only hope is Chisholm," I said at last, for his force would at least even up the numbers. Then I had an awful thought. "You don't think that they have destroyed his column already, do you?"

"Surely he would have sent word if he is under attack?" suggested Rickets uncertainly.

"Gentlemen, we are getting ahead of ourselves," announced McCarthy. "We should prepare for an attack, but we have no idea of the enemy's intentions. Remember that there were reports that some were looking to join our forces. Alternatively, it may just be a show of strength to get us to stop our advance. I am still of the opinion that they are not going to want a war with us."

Rickets and I tentatively agreed with him, but I don't think either of us was remotely convinced and that conviction decreased further over the coming hour. As Rickets lined the force we did have along the river bank and distributed what spare ammunition we possessed, a steady cacophony of horns came from the other side of the river. I counted at least ten different calls, all growing steadily louder. Surely they had not managed to get ten thousand men through the jungle, past Chisholm and without anyone warning us? More in hope than expectation I sought out Williams, as he knew more about the local tribes than anyone.

"It is possible, I suppose," he said, in response to my suggestion that they might be blowing different horn calls to deceive us as to their number. Williams was a thin man with the yellowish tinge to his skin of those who had survived the fever at least once. He cocked his ear to listen across the river; we could hear distant shouting now and the noise of branches being broken as they cut tracks through the jungle. "But I fear," he continued, "that it is more likely that they have ten thousand warriors out there."

I felt numb for a moment as the last of my hope evaporated. If they had that number, then even the miraculous arrival of Chisholm's larger force would not save us. I felt a sudden pang of self-pity as I thought back to my wife and family in Leicestershire, who, it now seemed, I would never see again. I was a white man in Africa, unfamiliar with the jungle, and even if I survived the coming battle, I could not see how I would escape. The Ashanti were bound to hunt down survivors and threaten the local tribes to hand them over. My colour gave away my nationality. "Do the Ashanti er... take prisoners?" I asked hesitantly. "I mean, well the governor does not think that they will want a war with Britain."

"Sometimes they take prisoners," said Williams. "Especially fit young men who they can put to work in their mines." He glanced across to where McCarthy was supervising men near the river bank. "The Ashanti know a little of Europe and they realise that they would lose a war there. But here in the jungle, they know they will win and so they do not worry about a war with us. I warned the governor that they would not welcome us stirring up other tribes against them and now I fear that it will be us who is taught a lesson."

So that was it, then, I thought. The best I could hope for was to end my days slaving away in an African mine. Before I could say more there was a sudden volley of musket fire from our men and looking across, I could see the first Ashanti soldiers appear on the far bank. They did not return the fire, but instead slipped back into the foliage.

"Don't shoot," ordered McCarthy. "They are not firing back. They may be coming in peace, perhaps to join our forces." He turned to Rickets, "Have the band stand in that clearing and get them to play the national anthem, if they are looking to join us, then they will know who we are."

"Are you sure, sir?" asked Rickets, who evidently thought that the Ashanti were already in no doubt as to who we were, but McCarthy insisted. A couple of minutes later the dozen members of the band were – very reluctantly – gathered in full view of the other side of the river. They were arranged in a semi-circle and no doubt only stayed put because the governor himself was standing in their centre. He seemed determined to act as their director.

"Steady now, men," he called. "We will play them some proper stirring music and show them some British spirit." With that he started to wave his arms and count them in.

The first strains of *God Save the King* rang out through the jungle and across the river. Understandably, most of the bandsmen were anxious to get through the tune as quickly as possible and were soon playing in different time. Despite McCarthy bellowing at several musicians to slow down, after the first few bars the noise was barely recognisable. The situation was not helped when the Ashanti began to express their musical appreciation with a fusillade of shots. McCarthy stood firm as the balls whistled about him, but when a trumpet was shot from the lips of its player, the band finally broke and ran for cover. The governor, though, was made of sterner stuff and he turned to glare at the Ashanti, who were now visible again on the far bank. He actually wagged his finger at them in admonishment.

To my dismay, he then turned and walked towards me, bringing a barrage of fire with him.

"They are starting to get a little unruly," he commented as I discreetly edged back behind a tree trunk for protection.

"Unruly?" I repeated in disbelief. "I think that they are way beyond that. They are not errant children; the bastards are trying to kill us."

"And you think we should teach 'em a lesson, eh?" replied McCarthy, grinning and completely misunderstanding my point. He stuck his thumbs in his yellow waistcoat pockets and continued, "They are testing us, like boys do a weak master. They want to see if they can smell fear. Well we will teach them some British resolve," he said triumphantly as a musket ball slammed into my tree trunk just an inch above his head. He patted me on the shoulder and went off to inspect more of his defences. If the Ashanti were trying to smell fear, I must have reeked of the stuff.

"Well I think we can rule out them wanting to join us," I muttered as I watched the governor calmly stroll away. He was brave, I will say that for him, but as Ashanti musket balls began to lash all along our side of the river, I felt a growing anger. He had evidently ignored the warnings from Williams and pressed on with his own foolhardy scheme to suppress the Ashanti. It was clear now that he had totally misjudged not only the Ashanti resolve to resist him, but also their military capability. There was a scream from a few feet away. When I looked around I saw one of the local tribesmen staggering back, whimpering and holding the side of his face, which had been smashed by a musket ball. Two more men immediately dropped their weapons and started running, but I saw now that Rickets had placed a score of redcoats in a line behind the river to stop just such a thing a happening. A gun fired and one of the deserters fell, clutching his leg. The other held up his hands and started to edge back to the river.

I breathed a sigh of relief; the captain clearly knew his business. If the first two had been able to run it would only have been moments before many others joined them. Not all the natives were ready to flee, though; I saw one of the chieftains berate the deserter as he returned to his post and while I could not understand him, he was obviously haranguing the others about standing firm as well.

There was a steady crackle of fire from our side of the bank now too, but looking across the river, few Ashanti were to be seen: most of our people were firing blind into the undergrowth.

"Hold your fire unless you can see one of the bastards," I yelled. We would be through what little ammunition we had in only a few minutes at this rate. My Collier was useless at such a long range and I edged back to where I had seen the wounded warrior. The man, the first victim of McCarthy's stupidity, was leaning against a tree, and judging from the blood pouring from his wound he would not be alive for much longer. I found his musket in the bushes and near it a pouch with a dozen cartridges. If I was going to die, I was damned if I would not take some of the swine with me. I settled down beside a tree trunk for cover, but, squinting through the foliage, I could not see a single one of the enemy. There was now just the occasional puff of musket smoke as one fired in our direction, but no sign of an imminent attack.

Rickets and McCarthy were yelling for our men to hold their fire too and it seemed that the battle might be over before it had really begun. With the river in the way, neither side could reach the other, and I remembered O'Hara talking about the reluctance of the Ashanti to press home an attack. But just as I wondered if there could be a glimmer of hope after all, an ominous sound of axes biting into tree trunks came from the far bank, indicating that this deadlock might not prevail for long.

I edged back to where Rickets and the governor were holding an impromptu council of war. "Even with the spare cartridges distributed, they still only have about thirty rounds a man," the captain was saying. "If Brandon does not get here soon with some more barrels, it might be too late."

"Ask King Dinkera," said the governor, gesturing to the chief I had seen railing at his warriors, "to send two of his more reliable men after Brandon to hurry him along. Send some more out after Chisholm too. If the Ashanti know we have reinforcements coming, they may hold back."

"Should we not try to retreat back along the path we used to get here?" I asked.

"No," said McCarthy. "I will not be seen running away from them. And anyway, if they were to attack us strung out on the trail, they would cut us to pieces. We are in a much stronger position behind the river here and besides, Chisholm must surely arrive soon."

I was harbouring doubts that the major would ever arrive or that it would make much difference to the outcome if he did, but I kept those thoughts to myself. For the next half hour very little happened. King Dinkera sent off his various messengers and the rest of us sat behind trees and repeatedly counted the few paper-wrapped tubes of ball and gunpowder we had left. A good soldier could easily fire three shots a minute and so most only had enough ammunition for ten minutes. But then I remembered Williams' confident assertion that the Ashanti did

91

not fight at night. It was only two or three hours before it would be getting dark. Perhaps, I thought, there was still a slim hope after all. I could slip away after dusk and get as far as I could before dawn. Then I would hide up during the day to escape whatever search parties the Ashanti sent out. I was just trying to convince myself that I stood the ghost of a chance of reaching the coast in this manner, when I heard splintering wood.

The first tree trunk bridge crashed down into the jungle to my right. There was an immediate flurry of shots from our side of the water, but no one tried to come across. We could still hear the sound of chopping from the jungle opposite as the Ashanti hacked at more trees to bridge the river that would divide our fire when they attacked. A few minutes later another tree crashed down to my left and at almost the same time two more fell across the river to my right. There were now four thick trunk bridges in place and our men gathered around the branches ready to defend them. The Ashanti were certainly organised, however, for nothing happened until one of their wretched horns blew. Then there was a fusillade of fire from their banks, which flailed through the branches at our ends of the bridges. There were screams as men waiting among them were hit but fortunately, the thick wood provided secure cover for many more. I had stayed in my place between two of the bridges and while our men blazed back, obscuring their view with musket smoke, I could see clearly a score of Ashanti who now tried to make their way across. None of them made it. I think I accounted for one myself as the man I aimed at clutched his guts and pitched into the water after I fired.

A furious volley of fire came from the Ashanti side of the river to clear those who were stalling their advance, and as the smoke gave away their positions, our fellows shot back with equal enthusiasm. I only fired when I had a clear target to aim at, but I was soon down to just five of the paper tubes for my musket and could hear others calling out for ammunition. Rickets yelled at his men to save their cartridges, while McCarthy shouted for his bugler to sound the recall, whether to direct Chisholm or Brandon it was hard to say.

Sensing a lull in our fire the Ashanti made another effort to cross the bridges, with a dozen men charging across each of the trunks. I watched the bridge to my left and shot into the crowd of men. There were enough of us loaded to take out at least half of the enemy, but a handful made it to our side of the river where they started a frantic melee with our defenders. Spurred on by this success, the Ashanti sent more men across. I now only had four charges left but by the time I had reloaded with one of them, the trunk was full of men pushing others to make their way across. I could not miss as I fired again. I saw another man go down, grabbing at one of his comrades as he fell and taking a second man into the water. The river was littered with bodies now, some dead or dying and others making for one of the banks. Amongst all the splashing, I thought I saw the flicker of a reptilian tail, but I only caught a glimpse as I realised that the Ashanti had nearly broken through on the bridge to my right. I fired two more shots into the men crossing that tree and was down to just one cartridge as I watched King Dinkera lead a band of his warriors to kill those who had broken through. It was desperate hand to hand stuff and I knew that we could not last much longer.

I glanced up at the sky; it would still be at least an hour before it started to get dark, but I had waited long enough. The sound of shooting from our side had virtually died away as few had any cartridges left. The next charge would see the Ashanti over the bridges and then the defenders would be done for. *It's time for you to leave, Flashy old son*, I told myself as I moved back into some undergrowth. I had planned to move discreetly through the camp without attracting attention, but as I reached the first clearing I heard the blare of more trumpets behind me signalling the start of another attack. My nerve broke then; I did not want to die in that infernal jungle and as panic gripped me I ran as fast as I could go.

"Flashman, where are you going?" I heard McCarthy call behind me. Then as I ignored him and pushed one of the local warriors out of my way, he must have realised what I was doing. "Come back, you damn coward!" he roared.

Chapter 11

I had spent a career protecting my precious reputation, but I did not care any more. We were all likely to die anyway so what did it matter? I pushed through another bush and then literally cannoned myself into salvation. The next moment my limbs were tangled in the mud with those of two sweating natives, while a barrel lay just a few feet away. I heard my name again and this time looked up into the face of the quartermaster and saw that natives were carrying two more barrels behind him. Ammunition had arrived in the nick of time.

"It's Brandon!" I shouted getting to my feet and as I pushed back through the bush I saw McCarthy staring at me in astonishment. "He has more cartridges," I yelled at the men near the river. Suddenly dozens were running towards us like hungry orphans for the poorhouse gruel pot.

"It is good to see you Flashman," gasped the quartermaster, who appeared to have run the last mile. "Break open that barrel, will you?

I raised my musket butt and brought it down heavily on the circular top of the barrel. The wood splintered easily and then there lay before me a sight for sore eyes: hundreds of fresh, dry cartridges. I grabbed a handful and stuffed them in my pockets before I was jostled out of the way by several soldiers, who raced to fill hats and anything else they were carrying with the precious ammunition before running back to the river.

I breathed a sigh of relief – we would have enough cartridges now to see us at least until nightfall.

"I'm so sorry, Flashman, I did not realise..." McCarthy was now at my shoulder and looking distraught as he gripped my shoulder, "... that you had seen Brandon."

I nearly laughed at him. With our lives hanging by a thread, he was more worried by calling me out for the coward that I was. "It's nothing," I grunted as I raised the butt of my musket again to bring it down on the top of the second barrel. Then I stared, frozen in horror.

I have looked aghast on a fair few grim sights in my time: the final advance of the Imperial Guard at Waterloo; Procter's army dissolving before the charge at Moraviantown or the last desperate defence at the Alamo, but none was as horribly unexpected as what I saw that day. For as McCarthy and I stared down into the barrel, we saw not the desperately needed cartridges, but instead… macaroni. I remember plunging my hand into it, willing my sense of touch to correct what my eyes were telling me. The governor stepped back as though he had been struck, his jaw sagging in disbelief. Then shaking himself like a bear from a stream, he snatched up my musket and smashed it through the lid of the third and final barrel. I did not need to see the contents, for I could tell from his reaction.

"You bloody fool," he roared at the hapless Brandon. "See what you have done!"

The quartermaster was similarly stunned as he gazed into the barrels and saw what he had been struggling through the jungle with for the past few hours. "I… I didn't know," he gasped, which only served to make McCarthy angrier.

"You incompetent imbecile," he shouted. "You will be court martialled for this, I promise you that." He turned and called out to Rickets, "Captain, the quartermaster is to be placed under arrest."

The poor captain, who was desperately overseeing the defence at one of the tree bridges, glanced over his shoulder in astonishment. Men were running towards him with the first hat-fuls of cartridges to be distributed amongst his men. He was too far away to hear the exclamations of dismay as others looked into the two barrels of macaroni. "Please sir," he shouted, "first we should get cartridges to the defenders." The single barrel of ammunition was already half empty as a steady stream of soldiers and warriors came up to replenish their comrades still fighting.

I could see more Ashanti pouring over the log bridges and Rickets shouting at men to stop them. Brandon, still in a state of shock, was staggering towards the river while McCarthy started to stride through the camp, muttering something about having his quartermaster hanged. Everyone had forgotten about me and as I looked about, I saw two of the men who had carried the barrels, start to back away into the jungle. They were obviously quick-witted lads who had seen that the situation was lost. There did not seem a second to lose as I followed their example.

As I pushed my way onto the trail behind them, they looked over their shoulder, perhaps expecting me to stop them. "Run, you fools!" I bellowed, gesturing them on and despite their earlier efforts to carry the barrels, they went like the wind. I followed, puffing, in their wake, but they were soon twenty yards ahead and then forty, barely visible amongst the thick foliage as they went down twisting forest paths. I caught a glimpse of one as he crested a shallow rise and was just in time to see him throw up his hands and fall. With the noise of the battle behind echoing through the trees around me, it took me a second or two to realise what had happened. Indeed, if a new warrior with a smoking musket had not appeared to stand over the corpse, I might have even run on. Instead, I threw myself behind the thick trunk of a tree and stared around in a fresh burst of panic. The newcomer was not another porter. Before I could even begin to gather my wits, I heard other men moving in the jungle around me. Was it Chisholm's men here at last? Or was it one of the columns I had anticipated the Ashanti would send across to attack our flanks?

My deliberations were answered succinctly by a yell to my right. I looked up and saw some evil, black villain running towards me, a large cleaver raised in his hand. The Collier barked in my fist, without me even thinking about it. Before his corpse had hit the ground I was off and running, back the way I had come, with what sounded like a dozen shrieking fiends hot on my heels.

I don't think I have ever run so fast in my life, certainly not over rough ground. I would have won the cross-country cup at Rugby with ease if I had been pursued by murderous Ashanti. I did not dare look over my shoulder, for to stumble would have been fatal. I remember crashing through a bush and finding myself back in the clearing with the three barrels and a few startled soldiers. I did not stop, but I heard the Ashanti behind me begin to engage with those in the clearing. It was a scene of utter confusion. More Ashanti had made it over the log bridges and now men were fighting and running everywhere I looked. My overarching memory is one of terror and it is hard to say what happened when. As I write this, I have before me the account of the battle from young Rickets and between our two memories, I will try to recount what happened.

The British and their allied warriors were trying to fall back from the river, but there was no order to the withdrawal. I remember Brandon staggering back towards me with his shirt covered in blood, then a dozen redcoats in a tight circle trying to fight their way clear as Ashanti soldiers poured fire into them. One of the attackers virtually ran into me and I pulled the trigger again to send him sprawling in the mud. Then I saw King Dinkera's feathered hat, visible above the heads of his men as they fought their way back into the trees. Rickets shouted out a warning to a soldier as another Ashanti ran towards the captain's exposed back. Instinctively I thumbed back the flint of the Collier and twisted the chamber round to shoot the man down, earning a nod of appreciation from Rickets as I cursed my impulsiveness. The Collier only had five chambers and now there were just two left.

"Where is the governor?" I shouted at the captain. If the Ashanti were to spare anyone, it would be McCarthy. Now my instinct was to be with him when he was captured, in the hope of being spared too. Rickets gestured over his shoulder and I ran on in that direction, weaving between various running battles. I distinctly remember dodging two wild-eyed jungle deer stampeding through the clearing. They must have been driven towards the battle by one of the flanking forces and were now desperate to escape to safety. I knew how they felt. As I moved among the trees I caught a glimpse of my quarry. McCarthy was a hundred yards away, one hand clutching at a dark stain in his yellow waistcoat, the other holding a pistol. He was shouting angrily over the heads of around a dozen soldiers who were desperately trying to keep the Ashanti away from him, while young Wetherell stood protectively at his side, sword in hand. The governor showed no fear even then; I am still not sure he understood the situation. Perhaps he yet believed that a stern reprimand would make the Ashanti back down. I lost sight of him then as a score more Ashanti ran through the trees in front of me to attack his party. It was more than enough to overwhelm the small group around him and in a moment, weapons were rising and falling. It was clear that no one at all would be spared.

I stared frozen in horror but did not have time to think, for at that moment an Ashanti burst out of a gap between two big bushes. He was right in front of me and swung his musket round in my direction as I moved the Collier to cover him. It was just a second of raw survival – I had less distance to move and fired first. He went down, but then I heard another man running towards my back. I twisted and dropped to one knee as I thumbed desperately back on the Collier's flint to re-prime the gun and move round the last loaded chamber. He was just a yard away as I fired into his chest, the ball knocking him back off his feet. All around me now was hand to hand fighting as soldiers and allied natives desperately tried to fend off a rising tide of Ashanti.

My gun was empty: I needed to hide within the next few seconds or I would be a dead man. I stared wildly around but saw no one else coming for me. The only cover nearby were the two bushes that the first warrior had come through. I half rolled in that direction and as I squeezed through the branches I saw that there were three large shrubs growing together. An Ashanti, one of their chiefs with a leopard skin over his shoulder, ran past. I was sure he had seen me crouching in the gap, but he did not stop. He just ran on towards the group around McCarthy. It would only be a moment before someone else saw me and then it would be all over. I had to find a better hiding place. I pushed myself into the largest bush, half climbing into the middle of it, careless that the foliage must have been moving wildly as I did so. Then, half-lying over two forks of branches, I froze. I expected rough hands to grab me and pull me out at any second, but none did. I cautiously moved my head to check that my whole body was enclosed in the thick leaf cover. It was, but I then discovered that I was sharing my hiding place with a green snake, who hissed angrily at the intrusion. I bit back a sob of terror, for I hate snakes and for a moment I was torn between fear of the serpent in the bush and the Ashanti outside it. The Ashanti won and I stayed where I was, watching as the snake slithered higher into the branches.

I don't remember much about the next few minutes other than I could hear my heart beating in my ears at an alarmingly fast rate and I gradually started to tremble, whether through fear or shock I could not say. Probably both. I twisted my head occasionally to check on my scaly companion, but other than that I stayed as still as a rock.

Around me the noise of battle gradually moved away. Peering through the gaps in the leaves I could see the ground covered by the dead and the dying and beyond them, several hundred Ashanti who were celebrating their victory. A large crowd had gathered around where McCarthy had made his last stand and there was lots of shouting from that direction, but no English voices that I could hear. I wondered if I was the only survivor, and then, if I would survive much longer. It would soon be getting dark, but the Ashanti did not look like they were moving any time soon. I doubted I could spend a whole night and a day suspended in the middle of a bush without being discovered. If the snake did not bite me in the night, then I would probably be crippled by cramp and give myself away.

As my shaking started to diminish, I watched the Ashanti warriors move across the clearing to loot the dead. Occasionally they would finish off a badly wounded man. Although most had muskets slung across their shoulders, they would use a knife for this purpose, usually slashing across the throat. I offered a silent prayer that I had not attempted to hide amongst the dead, a sentiment that became even more fervent a few moments later.

Ten yards from my bush lay the body of one of the allied warriors. The fellow had a cloth over his shoulder that marked him out as one of their chiefs. I watched as one of the Ashanti walked up to the prone figure and kicked him. The wounded man groaned and it clearly pleased the Ashanti that he was still alive as he called some of his mates over. The Ashanti talked with the wounded man, which only served to make the warriors about him even more excited as they whooped and taunted the poor devil. Then, to my undying horror, one of them bent down to cut away the wounded man's loin cloth. Taking a firm grip of the fellow's wedding tackle, with a swift cut of his knife he emasculated his victim. The wounded man screamed then all right, as blood gushed all over the leaves between his legs. He tried to sit up as they waved his genitals in the air, but, perhaps mercifully, he was pushed back and despatched with a gurgling cut across his throat.

I watched the scene feeling whatever is far beyond appalled. Even the snake above me was indignant, for it hissed angrily, but that could either have been due to all the shouting or because it smelt that I had just pissed myself. Unconsciously I reached one arm back to cup myself to reassure that all was present and correct. Then realising that I had been holding my breath as I watched the awful stroke of the knife, I slowly breathed out. It was at that precise moment that I felt a hand close around my ankle.

After what I had just witnessed I could not begin to describe my terror. The hand at my foot tried to pull me out of the bush while instinctively I grabbed at the branches to stay inside it. The bush was swaying now as we tussled and I remember the snake hissing angrily again just above my head as it was shaken about. My assailant was shouting and now more hands reached in to grab me. I saw the snake strike one with its fangs before it fell through the bush to the ground. My shirt was torn open and I was punched and pulled in two different directions. The men around me were laughing in triumph.

Then one of the branches I was holding on to for my life snapped and I found myself tumbling out at their feet. I was surrounded by a circle of grinning faces, one of whom I recognised as the chief with the leopard skin who had seen me earlier. The bastard must have come back to get me. Several of them were holding knives and I nearly spewed at the thought that they would serve me as they had the native chief. A new panic gripped me and I struggled desperately to get away from them, anywhere, even though I knew it was impossible. My feline-coated friend shouted an order and arms grabbed at me again. Before I knew it I was being born aloft, my limbs held tightly as I twisted and turned in their grip.

"Please don't kill me!" I wailed, and I wept as they carried me forward, still frantically trying to escape. I managed to get an arm and leg free at one point and half fell to the ground, but all I got for my trouble was a musket butt around the side of my head and then I was carried face down. That was even worse, as I was hauled, half-stunned, over various dead bodies with terrible fresh wounds to remind me of my imminent fate. I managed to look up and realised that I was being carried towards the group of men standing where McCarthy had made his last stand. There was a crowd of well over a hundred of them and they started cheering and waving their weapons in the air as they saw me approach. I was still howling when they threw me down in the centre of the circle. Then I properly retched to bring up my breakfast at the sights I saw.

The little clearing was puddled with blood and there, on one side, was young Wetherell's body. At first I just registered the familiar uniform of an ensign, but then to my horror I saw that it was missing its head. I whirled around to see, half leaning against a fallen log, another headless corpse, this one wearing what was left of a yellow waistcoat, although there was little of the yellow left to be seen. For as well as removing McCarthy's head, they had also cut his chest wide open, leaving lungs and entrails gaping from the wound. Another chief pointed at me. He must have been wounded in the mouth as there was blood all down his chin and I noticed it around his gums as he shouted for me to be laid over a log. I struggled again but they forced me down on my back, the log under my neck. A man behind me gripped my head to keep it still; I could no longer see my own body, but I felt others holding me down. Then above me, in my line of vision, came a new Ashanti. He was grinning and in his hand he hefted a massive bloodstained axe. That was when I knew I was about to die.

Chapter 12

Heaven was surprisingly warm and humid, I thought, as I drifted back into consciousness. But then I heard the crackle of flames and realised that I was in the other place. Not surprising, really, given the life I had led. Slowly I opened my eyes to see what hell looked like and found it was remarkably similar to the jungle clearing I had died in. Perhaps hell was what you feared most, and as I had just proved, I was more afraid of Ashanti than snakes. There were several of them talking and laughing by a big campfire in the centre of the space. From the light of the flames, I could still see headless corpses lying on the ground.

I went to move but found that my legs were tied together by a strip of creeper. That seemed odd – after all you cannot run away from hell. Gingerly I raised my hand up to my neck and found it intact.

"You're awake, then," gasped a voice beside me. I turned to find Williams resting his back against the same log as I. He clearly had not been as fortunate, for he had a bandage around his neck and from the blood, it looked like someone had tried to cut his head off. There was another wound to his thigh.

"Am I still alive, then?" I asked in wonder.

"For now," he grunted ominously.

"But how?" I gasped. "I mean, I remember their executioner swinging his axe."

"I think you fainted. Then one of the chiefs saw that mark on your chest and stopped the killing." He winced in pain and added, "That is a masonic mark, isn't it?"

I looked down at the tattoo on my chest in wonder. "But surely the Ashanti are not masons?"

"You would know more about that than me. From what little I know of masons, they do favours for each other and help their brothers to trade. The Ashanti are the biggest traders in the region. While precious little of that goes through Cape Coast Castle, they would want to avail themselves of every advantage."

"I am not a mason either," I admitted quietly. "I let a Fantee chief called Banutu give me this mark as I thought it would stop him killing me."

Williams was quiet for a moment as he considered this and then he began to chuckle. He laughed until the tears were streaming down his face and then slowly the tears were accompanied by sobs. I said nothing, waiting for the outburst to pass.

"How were you saved?" I asked as he lapsed into silence. At first I thought he would not answer, but then he whispered, "Two years ago during a visit to their capital, I helped one of their chiefs negotiate for a wife. He saved me, but not before someone had started sawing at my neck with a knife."

I thought back to the man who had ordered my own execution. "Was it the chief who had been punched in the mouth?"

"What?" asked Williams, puzzled.

"The man who was going to have me killed had been punched in the face. There was blood in his mouth and all down his chin," I explained.

"Are you feeling strong, Mr Flashman?" asked Williams quietly. Now it was my turn to look confused and on seeing my expression the secretary continued. "That chief is one of their leaders. He had not been punched. He had the governor's heart cut out of his body; he ate it." I thought back to McCarthy's mutilated body and knew it must be true. I swore softly but Williams held up his hand to stop me. "I know it is hard for us to understand, but to them it is a sign of honour. They were impressed by his courage."

"I saw them cut the cock and balls off another wounded man," I challenged. "Were they impressed with him as a lover, then? The bastards, they are bloody savages."

"No, Flashman, they are just different to us and I suspect that you are more likely to see that than I."

"Why? What do you think they will do to us? Will they send us down the mines?"

"No, they have their spies at the castle. I imagine that if they do not know already, they will soon learn who you are. You have seen that

103

they value men of courage and as a distinguished soldier, they will probably view you as a valuable hostage. When their king hears what has happened here, he will want you as a bargaining chip in future negotiations with our people."

"Surely they will want you as a hostage too? Won't your friend save you?"

"Normally yes, but I rather fear that this wound in my leg will see me off. The ball is in deep and it will soon become gangrenous."

I looked at the hole in his thigh. He had the limb slightly raised and so I knew the bone was not broken, but there was a ragged, raw hole that was still bleeding. I looked at my own body and apart from a few scratches from when I was torn from the tree, I was miraculously unhurt. My shirt, though, had been torn to shreds when I was captured, with one sleeve held on by just a thread. "Here," I said tearing the sleeve off entirely. I leaned forward and tied it around his wound as tightly as he could bear. We sat quietly through much of that night talking about the battle and whether there were any other survivors at all. Williams had seen King Dinkera and his men moving off into the jungle, pursued by a large party of Ashanti. He mentioned that he had seen the new surgeon shot early in the battle and two more of the militia officers killed during the retreat. I told him that I had run past Brandon, who looked mortally wounded.

There was sporadic shooting from the jungle during the night. It is hard to imagine now, but I think we must have slept a little. In the morning new horrors awaited us. We both sat quietly, trying to avoid drawing attention to ourselves as the camp slowly came to life. Various Ashanti came over to look at us as though we were specimens in a zoo and I half feared that they would decide that our survival had been a mistake. That trepidation only increased mid-morning when drums began to beat and they started preparing for some sort of ceremony. Had they saved us as a sacrifice? Perhaps the pleas from our separate saviours had been overruled and we were to be put to death after all. My fears seemed confirmed when we were dragged to our feet and, after my bindings were cut, driven forward. Williams put his arm around my shoulders to take the weight of his injured leg and we hobbled along until we were told to sit again beside a large drum. In front of us was a log and my old executioner friend of the night before. By then continuous fear had exhausted me. I remember thinking that if I had to die, at least it would be quick. To our surprise, several badly wounded Ashanti warriors were carried forward and one by one, their necks were placed over the log. There was cheering and chanting at each execution. Williams, who had a little of the language, turned to the man beside him to try to find out what was going on.

"They are killing those with five wounds," he told me. "They believe that these men must be sacrificed to their gods." Well they can kill as many of their own as they like, I thought before swiftly counting the scratches I had incurred. Judging from those brought to the log, the wounds had to be serious to count and most were near death anyway. That was certainly the case with the last body carried forward and we were aghast to see it was a white man.

His face was covered in blood and I could not make him out, but he was still alive, for he groaned loudly when he was laid over the log. "Who is it?" I asked Williams. "Can you see?"

"It is Mr Jones," he told me. "He is one of the traders in the castle, but he also serves as a captain in the militia." I did not know the name, but I was glad it was not Rickets. After the axe had swung, the body of Jones was laid with the other Ashanti sacrifices and they were all treated with more ceremony before the gathering broke up. Soldiers started collecting their possessions and moving on, some over the log bridges and others down the track we had taken from Assamacow. For a while we were ignored. So we staggered over to where I had last seen Rickets, to see if his body was there. It wasn't, but that of another militia officer, a man called Robertson was, not to mention a score of other soldiers, all now long dead. There was still the occasional and now distant crackle of musketry from the jungle, indicating that the pursuit of fugitives was continuing. By the time they had finished, I doubted that there would be any other survivors.

"What a bloody waste," I said vehemently. "McCarthy said he was going to give the Ashanti a rap across the knuckles. Huh, all he has succeeded in doing is killing hundreds of fine men."

"Don't forget that the governor did a lot of good along the coast, more than any of the company men," said Williams with surprising softness. "He just did not understand the Ashanti. He thought that a nation that had defeated the likes of Napoleon would instil fear and respect. But we are not the British lion here. In Africa we are more a goat, surrounded by hungry predators."

I gave a snort of derision and turned to find an Ashanti officer walking towards us with a squad of soldiers. He gave a long command that I did not understand. Realising he was wasting his time, he then just said, "Assamacow," and pointed in that direction. I gathered we were on the move. With Williams holding on to my shoulders and our escort surrounding us, we hobbled off down the path, back the way we had come.

Chapter 13

It took us three days to reach Assamacow, double the time it had taken to go the other way. At the end of the first afternoon, we were joined by a third prisoner, driven on by his own escort. His white skin was covered in scratches and bruises, but other than that he was unwounded, at least in his body. The shock of the battle and his capture, however, had clearly taken his wits. He was naked when we saw him and he never uttered a word. Williams told me he was another merchant and that his name was Raydon. I vaguely recalled him laughing on the march and wearing the uniform of a militia captain. Well, he was not laughing now and just stared vacantly around him, showing no interest in us or anything else. We were given some water and food, – ironically, macaroni from a barrel abandoned on the trail – but he refused both. We tried to talk to him and jostle him along, but he had given up and seemed to just want to die. On the second day as he grew weaker and slower, the Ashanti obliged. After some discussion between the soldiers and our escort commander, two soldiers took him off the path into the jungle. There was the sound of a shot and only the soldiers came back.

With little food and only three working legs between the pair of us, Williams and I felt near death ourselves when we finally reached our destination. It was strange to see the Tudor-style architecture of Assamacow again. Where British officers had stood and marshalled supplies just a few days before, now the Ashanti were in charge. This time we were not in one of the grand merchant houses, but instead in what must have been a shed for animals, for it had straw strewn about and a wooden trough for feed. We threw ourselves down, exhausted. Williams' leg was now swollen and looked bad. We had fashioned crutches from some long sticks and I had helped him hobble along – I could not have abandoned him, for we had seen the fate of those who refused to move. Not only that, he was the only one with a sense of the language. When you are lost in a foreign land and are prisoner to a very strange enemy, it is a great comfort to have one of your own people with you, especially one who can tell you what is going on.

We had been there some hours when the door was thrown open and three Ashanti officers stood staring at us. One had a cruel face and he said something that made the others laugh. A moment later a soldier with a sack entered and turned the wooden trough upside down to form a narrow platform. On it he started to place items from his sack. When he stood back we viewed the grisly spectacle he had created. McCarthy's head glared at us indignantly, while that of Ensign Wetherell was frozen in the grimace he must have held when the axe fell, with his eyes tight shut. To our surprise there was a third head in the display, that of Mr Buckle, who had been the colony's engineer. If they were expecting a reaction of horror they were to be disappointed, for we were too exhausted to feel much at all. After a career fighting on land and sea, I had seen far worse sights. Anyway, it was always the wounded that were more distressing than the dead, for whom help was too late.

I was more concerned about Williams, whose thigh had started to smell ominously as though rot was setting in. It looked like my companion would not be around for much longer and I did not fancy my chances alone. I pointed to the injury and mimed him being shot and pulling the ball out, but the man in charge showed little concern. He just grunted and shut the door, leaving us under the surveillance of the row of severed heads. There was enough light coming through the big gaps at the top and bottom of the door to show the governor's features. The heads were remarkably well preserved and perhaps it was the movement of shadows through the afternoon, but McCarthy looked increasingly disappointed in us. It was as though we had let him down. In the end I got up and turned all the heads to face the wall.

Williams managed to get some sleep, and that evening we were finally given some food. A spoonful each of a mushy mess that my companion told me was snail porridge. I was past caring now and would probably have given a leach a taste of its own medicine if I could find one. I wolfed it down and then asked Williams what he thought would happen next.

"I imagine that they want to take us to Coomassie as hostages, he whispered. "But that is near an eighty-mile walk, I would never make it. They will leave me to die here or speed me along like poor Raydon. You will have to go on your own. But don't underestimate them, Flashman. You might think of them as savages, but they are clever and sophisticated fellows in their own way."

There was no doubt of that, I thought, as I stared at the heads in front of me. The Ashanti had run rings around McCarthy. "What about your friend who saved you?" I asked. Will he not help you again?"

"He probably thinks his debt is settled," grunted Williams. "Anyway, my leg is so swollen, I think even one of our surgeons would struggle to get the ball out now." We lapsed into silence then, both aware that the only trained surgeon we knew of in the colony was presently lying dead by a river a few miles away. It turned out we were wrong in that assumption, although given the pain inflicted, Williams might to this day disagree.

The next morning two elderly Ashanti men did come and look at his wound. They sniffed it and prodded it, to grunts of pain from their patient, and then went away again. They came back with two lengths of rope, which they proceeded to tie around his leg on either side of the hole, over the swelling. By now the secretary had guessed what they were intending and was struggling and begging them to leave him alone. More guards came to hold him down and two more stood at my side to stop me intervening. Then the two Ashanti sawbones put sticks in the rope loops and started to twist them like a tourniquet. Williams started to writhe and scream in agony and it took four warriors to hold him down. I watched in fascinated horror as pus started to ooze from the wound, but there was still no sign of the ball. After what seemed an age, with Williams now weeping from the pain and begging them to kill him, they covered the wound with some paste and then some leaves, before wrapping the leg in a clean cloth bandage.

I watched my companion sleep for a while after they left. He was trembling a little now and appeared to be coming down with the fever. While the Ashanti may have had the best intentions, their ministrations looked certain to kill him. Their efforts to force the corruption from his body, must also have pressed it into his blood. That evening more snail porridge arrived. I was ravenous and, mindful of the adage that you must 'starve a fever,' I decided to eat Williams' share as well. He awoke in the middle of the night and asked about food, but I told him none had been delivered.

"Ah, they are leaving us to die," he whispered. "Flashman, I have some money. If you ever get back to the castle, you will find the details in my quarters. I would be grateful if you would see that it gets to my sister."

Of course, I promised that I would and he settled back to doze. In the morning he was still alive but in such a deep sleep that I could not wake him. When the door to the hut opened, I thought it would be their doctors again, but this time they came for me. I was pulled roughly to my feet and out of the door. As I left, I glanced back over my shoulder. Williams was still lying with his eyes shut on the straw and I did not imagine I would see him again. I thought he would probably die in his sleep and as I was dragged off to a very uncertain fate, I did not know whether to pity or envy him.

I will spare you the details of the next two weeks, for they were spent on the road to the Ashanti capital of Coomassie. I was taken with one of their regiments, perhaps a thousand men. Half a dozen were assigned to guard me. I had a rope around my neck like a dog and at every moment of those two weeks there was always someone holding on to the other end of my leash. While I could not understand them, I could tell that the soldiers were in good spirits; they had enjoyed a prestigious victory and humiliated an enemy. A number of them were wearing clothes that they had taken from the dead, including several redcoat uniforms removed from our soldiers. Some used the clothing to taunt me in my rags, but I was too tired to give them much of a reaction. Another showed me a watch he had taken, yet there did not seem a huge haul of loot as our numbers had been pitifully few compared to theirs. Doubtless they expected more spoils of their triumph from the royal treasury when they got home. But about a week into the journey they received news that spread consternation through the ranks. I did not understand it then, but I later learned that the Ashanti king had died. Many of the officers rushed on ahead, leaving the soldiers and I to follow on behind.

We must have passed through half a dozen villages on the way, which did not look any different to the ones I had seen outside of Ashanti territory. The roads got steadily better, though, not paved or anything like that, but wider and clearly well travelled. We no longer had these tracks to ourselves and strangers stopped to stare at me as they went past. Farmers were moving food to the capital on small carts they drew themselves – there were still no horses. I doubted that such animals would survive any longer there than on the coast. Others carried bundles on their heads. Intermingling with the locals were various Arab traders, some heading to the capital and others walking towards the coast.

The road felt endless and I began to think that we would never arrive, but then one morning we rounded a corner and there, laid out before us, was the outskirts of Coomassie. I stopped in astonishment and was nearly pulled off my feet by the man holding my tether.

There was a rising sea of rooftops and buildings in front of me, with the meanest hovels on the outskirts, but the walls of much grander buildings beyond. It was huge, far larger than anything else I had seen in Africa. It was not as big as London, but perhaps the size of a small city like Coventry. There were no city walls, but then they probably did not think they needed them as they were the dominant force in the region. The soldiers gave a cheer at the sight of it but as they marched on towards their capital, my guardians tugged at my rope and drew me away a hundred yards from the road to wait in the shade of a tree. Grateful for the rest I dozed for a while until I felt another pull on my leash. I opened my eyes to see a handful of Ashanti officers watching me. One looked familiar and I realised that it was the one who had seen me hiding and later pulled me from my bush. He grinned broadly when he saw the recognition cross my features. Then he pointed to what looked like a large wooden coffin and gestured that I should get inside.

For a moment I was alarmed – were they going to bury me alive? But then I thought that if they wanted me dead they could have killed me at any point since I had been captured. There was no hostility in my captor's face, he just pointed to his eyes and then at the city and back at the box. I realised that they wanted to bring me into the city without anyone seeing. Heaven knew why, but as I was in no position to argue, I got up and lay down between the rough-hewn planks. A lid was placed on my 'coffin' and then I felt myself being hoisted into the air and carried down the street. It was a strange way to travel, although I probably will not care so much the next time I am carried in that manner. I twisted around to squint through a gap in the wood at my surroundings as we passed by. As we got closer to the city centre I noticed more of the half-timbered houses that I had seen the merchants build nearer the coast. Many of them were painted in colourful patterns with swirls and blocks of colour. Unlike the villages, where there was just a cluster of large houses, here there were long streets of them on either side of wide thoroughfares that thronged with people. Many of the houses had large open porches at the front that their owners sat in to watch the goings on in the city.

I saw that many of the grander houses had bundles of small gold bells hanging from the upper floors, presumably to show off their wealth as well as to make music in the light breeze. But when I looked about, I saw a profusion of gold amongst the citizens of the city. Rich men wore gold necklaces down to their navels; others had bands of the metal around their head or limbs. As well as jewellery, the wealthy citizens were adorned in the finest fabrics. Often they were worn thrown over one shoulder like Roman togas. Some looked to have been made locally, but others were clearly of European manufacture and at least one was of silk. Arab traders in their robes were also much in evidence, particularly in what I judged to be the commercial district, with its rows of stalls selling all manner of goods. There were stacks of weaponry, piles of pots and pans, bolts of cloth and baskets of meat, fish and vegetables. But alongside this great wealth there were also slaves. As I had seen in Rio, they were one of the main beasts of burden in the city.

After my bearers had carried me for half a mile through the streets, we turned down a narrow alley. At last I was set down and as I heard a gate close my lid was removed. I found myself in a small courtyard surrounded by a substantial property. I gathered that this was the home of the leopard skin-adorned chief as a young child came running out to greet him. The general threw him laughing up into the air as a father would a son.

For a man who had previously tried to kill me, he now seemed most concerned with my comfort. While his son watched me curiously, I was shown into a store room, which had already been prepared for me. There was a bed with a straw mattress, a bucket for a toilet, a small table and a stool to sit on. It was far more comfortable than I had been expecting. As I sank gratefully down on the bed, the chief stood in the doorway, telling his son all about me. While I could not understand the words, he acted out pulling me from a bush and my flailing reaction, which had the lad howling with laughter. Then before he left, a servant came in with a bowl of meat stew and a wooden spoon. I was famished and fell on it with relish. It seemed that I was a guest of this man, but I also noted that after he'd turned to leave, the door was bolted behind him.

I did not even think of escaping. I was now a hundred miles from the coast in an enemy capital and with my white skin, I doubted I would get a hundred yards before being apprehended. I was just grateful I was not losing my head or being taken down a mine. In fact, for reasons I did not understand, I appeared to have fallen on my feet. It at least gave me the opportunity to regain some of my strength. The previous days of near starvation and the long marches over rough country had taken their toll. My cheeks were sunken and my ribs showed to such a degree they made a Whitechapel orphan look like an army cook. I ate greedily whatever was provided in the Dutch blue and white china bowl my food came in. Whether it was the strange vegetables I was not used to or the cloudy water, I cannot say, but on the third day my stomach was hit with the gripes. I spent two days filling my bucket and I had to take to my bed. I had dysentery and in my weakened state it, nearly did for me.

I was ill for several weeks and even though I was a prisoner, I could not fault my care. My memory is vague as I drifted in and out of consciousness. I must have also had a fever. I remember a kindly woman of the house who came often to my bedside to dribble water into my mouth. I may be wrong, but I think at one point some of their doctors put a burning brazier in the room and wrapped me with leaves and then tightly in a cloth so that I could not move. I have other memories, too, that must be due to the delirium, for example I clearly recall the severed heads of McCarthy and Wetherell having a heated conversation about their favourite cheese.

As the illness abated the old lady still came to sit by my bed and brought me small pieces of freshly roasted meat from the kitchen. She would stay there, feeding me like a child, while talking to me quietly in a language I did not understand. I have no idea who she was, but without her I fear I would never have left Coomassie. Eventually I had the strength to get up and walk unsteadily around the courtyard, with my constant companion holding my arm. Others must have been watching my recovery, for three days after I started walking again I had another visitor.

I was at my table, soaking up some meat juices with a flatbread my companion had brought me, when the door to my room opened. I looked up to see the leopard-skinned general walk in and behind him a stranger. The woman immediately jumped to her feet and, bowing, tried to make for the door, but the general stopped her. He spoke to her kindly and gestured at me. I guessed he was complementing her on my recovery, but she was still frightened and slipped away as soon as she could. Then the general said something to me, but of course I could not understand him. It was then that his companion spoke.

"Would you please tell us your name?" asked the newcomer in perfect English.

I goggled at him in astonishment. It was the first time I had heard words I understood in over a month. "It is Flashman, Thomas Flashman," I admitted. The stranger looked down at a document he had taken from his pocket and started to refer to a list of names before pointing at one and whispering something to the general. The reaction from my captor was extraordinary; he gave a yelp of delight and punched the air as he discovered who I was. I felt a twinge of unease: what did all this mean for me?

The stranger looked up and must have seen the concern etched on my face. "Please do not be alarmed. Your owner thought you were an important prisoner as you had an extraordinary pistol. Now we know that you were McCarthy's champion and a renowned British soldier."

It was the first time I had ever heard anyone referred to as my 'owner' and it did not make me feel any more comfortable. It only served to show how powerless I now was. "What, er, what does he intend to do with me?" I asked hesitantly, not sure what to hope for.

The stranger smiled and came over to sit on the bed beside me. "Did you know that the old Ashanti king has died?" he asked.

I shook my head and then a memory came back that filled me with horror. I recalled Fenwick telling me that at the funeral of a previous king they had sacrificed thousands of prisoners. Was that why they were so pleased, I wondered? Was my death to be the finishing touch to an old man's burial?

"He died on the same day as your battle," the stranger continued. I sagged slightly in relief. That must have been nearly two months ago; surely they had planted the old bastard in the ground by now? But before I could relax the stranger continued, "The new king is building his court and the general wishes to win favour with him. He is going to present you to the king as a gift."

"Oh," was all I said as I wondered what this new development would mean for me. My mind was distracted with an image of me standing, freshly scrubbed, before a throne with a big ribbon around my neck as one might present a kitten. I looked down at the bowl of meat on the table and now understood a little more. My host had not been arranging such extraordinary care for me out of any sense of kindness; I was his slave and he merely wanted me fit and healthy so that I would be more valuable as a bribe. A few extra pounds around my ribs might make the difference between him getting a promotion or not. I doubted that my new owner would be so considerate. "What will the king do to me?" I asked.

Instead of answering my question, the stranger asked one of his own. "What will the British king do when he learns of the defeat of his army?"

I had been wondering about this myself on the march to Coomassie and had concluded that the government would do very little. It would be the fever more than the Ashanti that would deter them. They could land enough soldiers and guns to capture the capital, but it would take a large army, for it would be bloody work. I suspected that the Ashanti would retreat into the jungle and, avoiding the main force, attack the lines of supply. It is what I would have done in their place. The British might well burn Coomassie, but I would be long gone if they did. Then like Napoleon in Moscow, the redcoats would lose more men on the retreat. This time with fever instead of frostbite adding the *coup de grâce*. If they were still there during the fever season then they might, with battle casualties, lose three-quarters of the total force. You can fight men, but there is nothing you can do about disease. Tens of thousands of casualties to conquer a place few Britons had heard of. This was the kind of shambles that could bring down a government and I was sure our politicians knew it. So they would play down the defeat and perhaps suggest McCarthy had been reckless. Then after a respectable delay, a new emissary would be sent to rebuild bridges with the Ashanti. They would not want to lose the prospects for trade. It turned out that I was right about much of that too, but at the time, I did not see how it would help me to say so.

"Our king will be angry," I told them. "What he does next will depend on what he is told of the Ashanti and whether they are honourable men." I nearly added something about treating prisoners fairly, but I thought that it would be too obviously self-interested, which would diminish my earlier statement.

"The British king is not honourable. His people have broken treaties with the Ashanti. It is well known that they are not to be trusted," the visitor responded.

"That was the African Company of Merchants, not the king. Only McCarthy was appointed by the king and while you might not have liked what he said and did, he was straight with you." The stranger nodded to acknowledge the point. He appeared well informed on state affairs and Ashanti politics and so I asked, "Who are you?"

"My name is Quashie, I am one of the king's official interpreters. I suspect your owner did not bring me sooner in case you died and I told the king about your death. We interpreters speak to all the king's foreign guests and tell him if we think that they are telling the truth." He was in effect, then, a councillor to the king and, I guessed, a pretty shrewd one.

"What do you think the king will do with me?" I asked. "Will he send me back with a message for the British?" I continued hopefully.

Quashie smiled and gently lowered my expectations. "I rather think he is more likely to hold you hostage to deter your people from doing anything rash. But at least you will be kept safe, unless of course the British launch another attack." He paused then to hold a brief conversation with the general, presumably to bring him up to date on our exchange, and then he turned back to me. "The general will present you tomorrow. The king is new and is still finding his way. He must appear strong to his court to deter rivals from challenging him." He looked me sternly in the eye then and waved his finger at me. "It is important that you remember this – your life may depend on it. You are a slave now and not a British master. You must not look the king in the eye or challenge him in any way or he will be compelled to treat you harshly."

If he was worried that I was some proud officer who would not bend the knee to save his own life, then he was utterly mistaken. If my skin was at stake I would kiss the king's royal black arse if that was what it took. Stay alive and wriggle out at the first opportunity was my motto, not like those fools who put their honour above everything. I well remembered how my old nemesis, Colquhoun Grant, had dragged me all the way to Paris during the war to avoid breaking a promise – nearly getting us killed on several occasions. I assured them both that I would not cause offence and while they did not seem entirely convinced, they nodded and took their leave. I was left alone again with my lunch, but now my appetite had gone.

Chapter 14

I awoke the next morning with a feeling of trepidation. I had been lulled into a sense of false security in my little store room. My world had thus far only extended into the courtyard outside and as I recovered from my sickness, with regular meals and even the occasional cup of palm wine, things had been very comfortable. Now I was to face an enemy king and by all accounts, a deuced sensitive one, who could get the vapours if I so much as looked at him. One false move and it could be my last.

I was reminded of my changing status when I came to get dressed. The old lady had taken away my locally made gown and on the table I found folded neatly the clothes I had been captured in. It was an unwelcome reminder of my earlier plight. At least there was a healthy breakfast of meat, eggs and flatbread although I wondered what the food would be like in a royal prison. As I munched disconsolately on this final repast, I watched as soldiers gathered in the courtyard outside. The general appeared, resplendent in two leopard skins and with a thick gold band like a crown around his head. He climbed into a chair with a bearer at each corner and then looked around to my store. One of his soldiers entered and as I got up, a rope leash was once more slipped over my neck. It was clear I was to be presented as a captive of the victorious commander. I was led to a place behind the general's chair in the middle of the little procession and then the gates were thrown open.

Trumpets blared to announce we were on our way and with musicians to the fore, we set off down the street to the palace. I was led along by my halter, like a prize bullock at a county fair for others to gawp at. I could only hope that my fate would be better than those creatures. I knew that other white men had visited Coomassie, but they had been honoured guests, not prisoners. My appearance was a novelty. Even though I was an enemy, there was no great hostility from the crowd, probably because they had won the war so easily. Indeed, several were pointing and laughing, no doubt commenting on what a miserable specimen I was. My one-sleeved shirt was tattered and torn while my trousers were barely decent. I had not been able to shave in captivity and so I now also sported a shaggy beard.

The cacophony of instruments from the front of our procession was attracting more and more people and so by the time we got to the end of the first street, the crowds were several deep. There were wealthy local citizens, slaves, Arabs with their veiled women and some other strange black tribesmen who did not look like Ashanti at all. All were cheering the general while I received less favourable attention. Several children ran alongside me now, darting between the soldiers guarding me and, when they had the chance, throwing mud in my direction. Perhaps I am prouder than I think, for when one of their balls of dirt hit me on the side of the neck, I dearly wanted to give the little brat a damn good thrashing. Instead I was yanked on by my tether.

We went down two wide avenues in this manner, with me feeling increasingly vulnerable as the mob jeered. I was sweating in the heat and covered in dust and mud by the time we reached a large square. Opposite us I saw a huge complex of buildings. The outer walls facing me were plain and windowless single-storey structures, but beyond them two- and even three-storey edifices could be seen. Many of the taller buildings were covered in ornate decorations and glittered from gold ornamentation. It had to be the royal palace; I felt a tightening of my stomach. I looked around at a sea of unfriendly faces surrounding me and wondered if I would ever see the outside of this complex of buildings again. Leicestershire had never felt so far away.

As it turned out, it is probably easier to get *out* of Newgate Gaol than it is to get *into* Coomassie Palace. The general and his men had to negotiate with the guards at the palace gates for a full five minutes before they would let us enter. We then found ourselves in one of the outer courtyards, surrounded by store rooms and barracks, before progressing on again. A new gate and a new debate on whether we should be admitted led us into a second square, much like the first. The third square with its two-storey residences looked to be where some of the courtiers lived. Many of those who stopped to give me a curious stare I saw were wearing gold jewellery. We had turned at least twice when we reached the fourth square. I was already losing my bearings in this maze of buildings as I saw a gate glittering with gold decoration on the far side. This time negotiating our entry took nearly half an hour and even the general had to get down from his chair to speak to whoever was on the other side of the little window in the gate.

Eventually, however, the portal was pulled open and we entered the space beyond. Unlike the previous squares, this one was nearly empty. Down the left side was a most ornate building, covered in carvings that were painted or covered with thin sheets of gold. I thought it must be the king's residence, yet it was a dark and secretive building, with intricately carved screens over the windows to hide those inside. Silhouettes of the occupants could be seen moving within the palace, though. Several were watching us cross the ground in front of them. There were guards at the entrance to the building; the only other way out of this square was through a gate on the far side and that was where we headed. My companions had fallen into a hushed silence now and I guessed we were close to the inner sanctum. The band, the general's bearers and most of the soldiers stood back – only the general and the man holding my tether went forward to the far gate, with me forced to follow reluctantly behind them. There were yet more discussions at the gate and beyond it I could hear the murmur of voices. Then finally we were admitted into the royal presence.

I have been in a fair few foreign courts in my time, but none like that one. As the gate opened we found ourselves at one end of a long open-air corridor. On either side sat rows of richly dressed courtiers, many clothed at least partly in silk and glittering from jewellery of every description. Above their heads were huge colourful umbrellas to keep them in the shade. As they turned to stare curiously at us, I in turn looked at the figures at the far end of the space. Fifty yards away, under a canopy of gold cloth a large man sat with what must have been a score of courtiers all gathered behind him. He was glaring at us and seemed annoyed at our intrusion, before reaching forward to rummage in a large bowl of fruit held by a slave at his side. Even the general hesitated in his presence, but a fat, gold ring-adorned finger gestured to us to come forward. The man holding my rope snarled something at me that I did not understand, but I remembered that I should not look the king in the eye and so I advanced with my eyes fixed on the heels of the general.

We came to a halt around ten feet short of the throne, which I now saw was a stool that appeared to be made from solid gold. I felt a downward yank on my rope and had little choice but to fall to my knees. I watched the general's feet as he stepped forward a couple of paces to speak to the king. I could not understand a word but could imagine the gist.

General: My king, I present to you as a gift this miserable specimen of a British soldier. I found him cowering in a bush after the battle.

King: He is a squab-kneed little wretch, isn't he. I hope you are not expecting a big favour in return. I would have much preferred another of these bowls of fruit.

General: I agree he is not worth a bunch of grapes, but he does seem to be one of their officers.

King: Then why on earth did you not cut his head off with the rest? His skull could have been fashioned into something useful, like the drinking cup I had made from McCarthy's.

General: Because he had this, Your Highness and I thought he might show you how to use it. If we had more of them, our army would be even more powerful.

The general stepped forward to present the king with something and instinctively I looked up to see what it was. There in the king's pudgy fingers was my Collier pistol; I had wondered what had happened to it. He gave a grunt of surprise and as I watched he clicked round the next chamber in the gun to see how it worked. Several of the courtiers standing behind the king leaned over his shoulder to study the weapon as well. They were all wearing robes, and several bore symbols of gold to indicate their office. One had a gold bird hanging around his neck, another had crossed swords while a third had what appeared to be a golden turd against his chest. Whether he was keeper of the royal closet or in charge of yams it was hard to say. Then I saw Quashie. He had a tall gold-topped cane, which was evidently the symbol for the interpreters. As I caught his eye, he glared at me and nodded downwards towards the king. As I looked down I found the king staring at me with small piggy eyes and hastily dropped my gaze back to the ground.

There was a whispered discussion amongst the courtiers as the king played with his new toy. Then his voice rumbled an enquiry to those about him and I heard Quashie respond. He must have been telling them what he had learned from his interrogation of me the previous day, for I heard the word 'Flashman' amongst the other unintelligible chatter. I kept my head down as the Coomassie debating society prosed on. Then I heard another word I thought I recognised: 'Waterloo'. I glanced up and saw an old man, also with the staff of an interpreter, pointing at me and talking urgently in the king's ear. He paused as someone behind him tugged on his sleeve and whispered something and then continued talking to the king and this time I heard the word 'McCarthy'. The king said something back and waved dismissively at the old man, who now spoke to me directly.

"We hear that you were McCarthy's champion," the old voice quavered, "and that you are a famous general among the British. Is it true that you beat the French king called Noleon at the battle of Watterloo?"

Where on earth had they got that idea? I wondered, but before I could even begin to reply another heated debate broke out amongst the courtiers. An old man with gold swords around his neck was most indignant. He appeared to be implying that Napoleon would have to have been a prize plum to be beaten by me when the Ashanti had defeated us so easily. Then I heard another voice mention someone called 'Wellyton' and 'Watterloo'. The king held up his hand for silence and the old translator started again. "Did you beat the French king?" he repeated.

I looked up, unsure what to say and what they knew of events in Europe. Then I saw Quashie and almost imperceptibly, he nodded at me. "Well, I was at Waterloo," I told them. "General Wellington and I beat Napoleon together." That was not an outright lie, I had played my part. I had poisoned the French emperor just before the battle and had been with the British at the end, although I doubt Arthur Wellesley would have agreed with my assessment.

Confirming my earlier suspicions, the old interpreter now asked, "So is the Ashanti army much stronger than the French?" The interpreter repeated the question in their language for the benefit of the king and his courtiers. Most of them smirked happily, confident of my answer. I dearly wanted to tell them that on an open plain, the Imperial Guard would have knocked their vaunted army into a cocked hat in five minutes, but I doubted that would be diplomatic. Again, I saw Quashie nodding at me. So, I swallowed my pride and said, "The Ashanti army is indeed formidable."

That was the cue for smug looks all round and then the king gestured for me to come forward. "Show the king how to load your gun," ordered the interpreter. My former owner, the leopard-skinned general, also stepped forward and I saw he had a flask of powder and some balls that looked the right size. He had evidently anticipated this request and he stayed close to see how it was done.

I crouched down beside the king and took the weapon from his hand. There were huge rings on all of his fingers and several necklaces of coloured shells as well as a shell circlet on his head. Most striking, though, was a red cord over his shoulders, from which were suspended three large sapphires mounted in gold. I swiftly removed the ramrod and started to load charges in each of the chambers. Then I showed them how the priming mechanism worked, which prompted a grunt of surprise from the general, who had obviously been trying to work it out for himself. Finally, with the weapon ready to fire, I handed it back to the king.

The king shouted something, clearly intending to test the pistol himself. The courtiers sitting on either side of the corridor I had walked up earlier, now began to move hurriedly back. They must have seen the king shoot before and it was obvious that they had little confidence in his accuracy. As the coloured umbrellas and stools began to topple over in their hurry to get out of the way, I saw soldiers move into the throng and grab slaves, who had been serving food to guests. As five of them were pushed into a rough line just ten yards in front of the king, I realised that these poor devils were the targets for their monarch's practice. They stared wildly about, struggling to take in their unexpected change in roles. The first man was still holding a large pottery jug that moments before he had been using to refill cups. He glanced over my shoulder and when I looked behind me, I saw that a thickset man had stepped up to join the courtiers. I did not need the large golden axe blade emblem hanging around his neck to tell me he was the royal executioner. He hefted a huge hatchet in hands adorned with large gold rings and there was a bloodstained stool by his feet, which must have left the slaves in no doubt as to their fate if they moved.

The king cocked the flint, pointed a wavering hand at the first slave and fired. The jug exploded into fragments and the slave went down squealing in agony. The king was already laughing with delight as he clicked around the next chamber and cocked again. The second slave was hit in the shoulder and fell writhing in pain. I am pretty sure that the king missed the third slave, but the smart lad clutched his chest and also fell groaning to the ground. The final two were not so lucky. They stood there shaking in terror as their monarch casually pointed the gun in their direction, showing no more concern than if he had been shooting bottles. One was shot in the hip and the last in the throat, which sent a spray of blood all over the courtyard.

There was a burst of sycophantic cheering from the courtiers, who now surged forward to regain their places. The king beamed in delight and passed the still-smoking gun to one of those standing behind him. No one gave a fig for the poor wretches lying in the dirt. With a chill, I realised that I was now a slave just like they were. I was perhaps fortunate not to be prostrate amongst them. More slaves were whistled up to carry their fallen comrades away, while others spread fresh dirt over the bloodstains to stop them attracting flies. I noticed that one of the 'fallen bodies' leapt to his feet and ran away as soon as he was through the gate, confirming my suspicions that the king had missed one of his targets.

For a while I was forgotten. I edged back and crouched behind the slave holding the king's massive fruit bowl and wondered what I should do. The general I had arrived with had joined the courtiers and the fat occupant of the golden stool was shouting to one of the nobles under the umbrellas in front of him. Was I a prisoner or a slave? And how had they heard about my being at Waterloo? They must have had spies amongst Appea's people and possibly our own too – it was the only explanation. Then suddenly everything became a little clearer, for as I looked up among the crowd of courtiers behind the throne, I saw another familiar face. Holding another gold-tipped staff and standing at the back was a woman I had last seen when we shared a coffee in Donquah. It was King Appea's comely translator. Now, just a couple of months after I had seen her serving that king, she was looking very comfortable in the court of his most mortal enemy. She must have felt my gaze and looked across at me and at what must have been an expression of shock on my features. Various details now started to make much more sense. She tilted her chin up with a sideways glance, perhaps of triumph, or was it contempt for her enemies, and turned to talk to one of her companions. Before I could even begin to marshal my thoughts for something to say, I felt a tug on my leash and found myself being led away.

Chapter 15

I have been in far worse confinement than that I experienced at Coomassie. My cell was as well appointed as the store room in the general's yard. Even the rations were very acceptable; there was no snail porridge here. I got the distinct impression that I was living better than any royal slave. My only complaint was that it was rather dark as there was a thick grill at the only window, which faced onto a yard. We were even allowed out to exercise every day for an hour or two. There was no great security – the covering across my window was made of wood and I could probably have kicked it out, but where would I have gone? I was still in the heart of the palace, less than a hundred yards from where I had met the king. If I broke out I would have to negotiate a myriad of courtyards and gateways. Back then escape seemed impossible.

There were half a dozen other prisoners in the row of cells. Five of them always got together as soon as we were let out while the other wandered alone, spending most of his time throwing pebbles in the dirt. They all ignored me, but I did not mind that, for I would not have been able to talk to them anyway.

I spent the first day and much of the night in a growing rage as I considered how thoroughly we had been humbugged by that wretched woman. As McCarthy had told Appea about our plans, he had been obliged to communicate through her. I did not doubt that every word was passed on to the Ashanti. But it was worse than that. McCarthy had only divided his forces because Appea had convinced him that the Ashanti army was divided into a dozen smaller forces. But it was the translator who had told us that. I would bet a guinea to a farthing that she gave the same news to Appea and told him it came from us. The damned bitch had dangled her tits under my nose and I had answered all her questions without a hint of suspicion. She had played me for a fool and it had worked. How she must have laughed when we set off into the jungle, full of plans for our own attack and completely unaware that a massive army was being guided to literally cut off the head of our command.

On the second day as I strolled in an impotent rage in the sunshine, I looked up to find I had a visitor.

"I trust you are comfortable, General Flashman?" It was the translator called Quashie.

"As I suspect you know, I am not a general," I admitted grumpily. "I was a colonel in the French Army and a major in the British, oh and a captain in the Brazilian Navy, but I have never been a general."

Quashie raised his eyebrows at the variety of my appointments and then grinned. "Yes, I know you were just a civilian when you were in the castle. Malala is not the only one to have spies amongst the British. But it enhances her reputation, and that of my friend the general, to have you as a more exalted prisoner. It is better for you too, as you are more comfortable here in the palace than in the mines."

"Malala, is that the name of the treacherous snake who acted as Appea's translator and betrayed us?"

"Yes, she is a very ambitious woman. The first to become a court translator, but I suspect that she has set her sights even higher." I swore softly and he laughed. "King Appea shares your view and is determined to see her killed, but she is well protected here." He grimaced slightly before adding, "She is becoming very powerful, a favourite of the king, and few would dare challenge her now, especially after she helped to deliver such a decisive victory."

I got the distinct impression that Quashie did not like Malala. She must have ruffled quite a few feathers when she pushed her way into the inner court circle. I gestured around at the yard we were standing in and asked, "What is this place, is it the royal prison?"

"Only for the most important prisoners," replied Quashie. "Those men over there," he said pointing to the five prisoners who always exercised together, "are some of the king's brothers and cousins who were rivals for the throne. He did not want to kill them, but he cannot trust them not to plot against him and so he keeps them here."

"What about that one?" I pointed to the old man still throwing his stones in the corner of the yard.

"That is King Azi. The Ashanti conquered his lands, but they keep the king alive so that his people do not rebel."

"And what is that place?" I asked pointing to another side of the highly decorated building with the shuttered windows we had seen on the way to visit the king. It formed one wall to our yard and I had already discovered that the guards did not allow me to go too close to look inside.

"That is the women's house, the part of the palace where the king keeps his wives. Apart from his eunuchs, no other man is supposed to see them.

"How many wives does he have?"

"There are all sorts of tales, most to show the prowess of the king. Some say a thousand or even two thousand, but as no one can see them we are not sure. I suspect it is much fewer, a few hundred at most." As I wondered if I would ever see my own wife again, Quashie continued, "Most of the women in that building were the wives of the old king. Our new ruler is currently deciding which ones to keep, the others will be given to his courtiers."

"Do you think I will ever get out of here?" I asked, feeling depressed.

"It is possible," said Quashie patting me on the back. "But only with the king's permission and that will only come when we are at peace with the British. Perhaps they will exchange you for a thousand of those clever pistols." He sighed, "But it will not be for a while as it looks like war with the British will continue. The king is planning to send a new force to drive the British from Cape Coast Castle and our shores entirely."

With that cheery news Quashie left, promising to come back soon. Even if I had still been in the army, I doubted that the British would have traded a hundred Colliers for me, never mind a thousand. But it did not matter for no one in Britain knew I was here. Those in Africa who did were either already dead or, from the sound of things, soon would be. I felt my despair growing. In fact, over the coming days I must have looked so miserable that King Azi tried to teach me his game of stones to cheer me up. It was essentially a game of bowls with pebbles.

Two weeks later I had another visitor and initially this one did not improve my mood at all. I was lying one evening on my bed and feeling sorry for myself when the door suddenly swung open and a female voice called out, "Would you like a book?" I looked up and there was Malala, holding of all things a copy of *Gulliver's Travels*. She came in and put the volume on my table and as I swung my feet onto the floor she asked, "Are you being well looked after?"

"What is it to you?" I snapped. "Have you come to gloat over your victory?"

To my surprise her chest heaved a big sigh and she looked tearful. "I knew you would not understand," she wailed. "I did not want to spy but they made me. They threatened to kill my father if I refused." As I stood up she threw her arms about my neck, and with those splendid bouncers pressed against my chest, seemed to be sobbing as she pleaded in my ear, "I really did think that the Ashanti army was divided. I had no idea that they were planning to ambush McCarthy. I swear I would have done nothing to put you into danger."

It was a good job that her chin was on my shoulder and that she could not see my face, for I'll wager it was a picture. Astonishment, disbelief and then anger chased their way across my features. What kind of fool did she take me for? Had I not seen her standing smugly behind the king as I knelt in the dirt? I was on the verge of pushing her away when I stopped myself. Rather than get angry, I preferred to get even, and this was a delicious opportunity to play her at her own game.

"You mean you really are loyal after all?" I gasped. It was not hard to sound astounded. "I just cannot believe it."

"I swear it is true," she whispered, glancing nervously at the door as if worried we would be overheard. "I would not be here if it wasn't. You must know I am fond of you, that is why I told them that you were a general, so that you would be well treated. Oh please, tell me that you know I am true," and before I had the chance to say anything she reached up and pressed her lips passionately on mine.

I kissed her back automatically, my mind still reeling from this sudden change in circumstances. Whatever it is you want, my girl, I thought, you are going to pay handsomely for it. Then, taking advantage of the situation, my hand reached up and popped one of those ripe breasts out of the top of her dress. She stiffened momentarily and then, as though it were an effort, I felt her body melt into mine. I had been led by my loins into enough danger in the past, but this time I was playing a part, one that I hoped would have some compensations. "Could you stay the night?" I gasped as I broke off the kiss. "We never did get to know each other properly, you know."

"Darling, I wish I could, but they will notice I am missing and come looking for me." Seeing the genuine disappointment on my face she added, "Perhaps another night I can slip down here after dark, when they think I am asleep."

"That would be wonderful," I said with feeling, although I knew she had no intention of a midnight tryst. She backed away from me then for a moment and stared into my eyes, as though struggling to believe that I had been fooled so easily. But I have spent a long lecherous lifetime pursuing all kinds of women and it was not hard to give her a leery grin, running my eye down her body, taking in all of her obvious attributes.

"You know, old girl," I said, smacking my lips in appreciation, "I think I always knew you would not play me false."

Apparently reassured that I was just a randy simpleton, she sat down on the bed and patted the space beside her for me to sit down too. "I want to help you escape, but it may not be safe. The king is planning another attack on the coast. What do you think the British will do? Will they stay and fight or will they abandon the port if they know the Ashanti are invading?"

Aha, I thought, now we are coming to the real reason for your visit. Trick the gullible fool into giving you more information and then leave him to rot in his cell. Well two can play at that game. I wrinkled my brow in concentration as though giving the matter some thought. "I can't tell you until I know what has occurred since I was captured," I told her. "What happened to Chisholm and our other armies? Were they attacked too?"

"No, Chisholm is now acting governor with most of the British soldiers back at Cape Coast Castle. But many of the other tribes have abandoned them and gone back to their own lands. Only King Dinkera and Appea's people look likely to fight again."

"Have any ships arrived there?" I asked.

"Yes, two ships arrived just after the battle."

"I see." My heart lurched in frustration at how close I had been to sailing home and avoiding this catastrophe entirely. But I pulled myself together. "Well that means that news of the defeat will soon be reaching London if it has not already. If the British government sends reinforcements, then any Ashanti near the fort will be destroyed."

"But you said the Ashanti army was formidable when you spoke to the king." She sounded petulant and disappointed and I guessed that she had been pressing for a second attack.

I laughed, "Well of course I did, with the king's executioner standing nearby." I looked around to check we were not being overheard before whispering, "But just between us, the British have new weapons that will beat the Ashanti."

"What do you mean?" she whispered, her eyes glittering with interest.

"Well you have seen my Collier pistol, they are making muskets with the same mechanism and rifles that are accurate at two hundred yards. You would need to have five times our number to stand a chance or your soldiers would be cut down before they reached our lines."

She considered this for a moment and I suppressed a smile of triumph. Collier had indeed made such weapons, but reloading them took too long for consideration by the army. Yet with my pistol as evidence, she could not easily dismiss the threat. "How many men can your big ships carry?" she asked. "If we have an army of fifteen thousand soldiers, we could have over five times as many men as yours."

"The British Army was seventy thousand at Waterloo," I told her, neglecting to mention that less than half of it was actually British. She still seemed doubtful and so I gave my imagination free reign to come up with yet more weapons. "They are using a much larger version of the Collier device on cannon too," I explained. "The empty chambers are reloaded by gunners as the cannon fires, so that an endless stream of shot can be fired into our enemies. They can also fire shrapnel shells that explode, spraying balls over a wide area. The British will also come with hundreds of rockets that they can fire into the trees to explode, sending splinters everywhere." I paused and reached out to hold her hand. "I am only telling you this because I would not want you near any attack, it would be too dangerous. But please do not tell anyone else."

"Of course I won't," she assured me. She prattled on for a while about court gossip – the king was getting rid of most of the old king's wives – but she was fidgeting and impatient to leave. Eventually she gave me a light kiss on the cheek and whispered, "I will try to come back again soon."

After she had gone I leaned back against the wall and smiled to myself. I had done what I could to stop an attack on the coast, but more than that, I had hopefully damaged Malala's credibility as an informant. By the time the next ships from Britain arrived, I was sure that the Ashanti would have spies at Cape Coast Castle. They would report that the mythical weapons did not exist. Quashie had indicated that Malala had enemies in the court and I hoped that they would then begin to move against her. It was a revenge of sorts and there was something satisfying at the thought of her eventually realising that I had played her this time.

She came twice more over the next few weeks, each time she brought a small gift and kissed me. Then, presumably to protect herself from further molestation, she would suggest we walk around the exercise yard. She promised that she had tried to get away to visit me at night, but that it was impossible. She also insisted that she was still working to help me escape. After around five minutes, she would work the conversation around to what she really wanted. The first time it was the calibre of the mythical Collier artillery and the second time it was the accuracy of our rockets. While she swore that she had not spoken to anyone about what I had told her, she claimed that she had found out from papers in the palace a little about shells and rockets and wanted to know more. I thought that the existence of a Coomassie reference library with a section on modern weaponry was as likely as Collier artillery, but I played along. I told her about the fins on the rockets and implied that they were unerringly accurate, when in reality they were a damned menace on the battlefield and could explode anywhere.

They were small victories of deception that gave me some heart, but it was a depressing existence. There was no hope of escape and the highlight of my day was playing pebbles with King Azi. I was feeling truculent when Malala came the fourth time and pretended I was hurt by her long absence and did not want to speak to her. She had brought a sweetened cake, but I insisted that if she wanted to talk we had to go outside the prison as I was fed up of seeing the same walls. "You are a counsellor to the king, you must have the power to take me out of here just for a walk," I challenged.

She studied me and must have recognised the genuine anger and frustration in my spirit, for after a moment she agreed. A few minutes later and we were strolling around the large courtyard where the general and his retinue had waited before being admitted into the king's presence. The guards had leapt to open the gate as Malala, holding her gold-topped cane of office, approached. She was clearly well known as a powerful woman about the palace. We were not entirely alone, two guards had fallen in behind us when we left the prison, but they stayed a respectable distance behind to allow us to talk in private. There were also a few maids carrying supplies into the ornate women's house that formed one side of the square. Some were dressed in African robes, while others were the veiled servants of the king's Arab wives.

"Are you enjoying being out?" Malala asked smiling. "It is a nice sunny day."

"It is good," I admitted. It might seem strange as I was only a hundred yards or so from my cell, but seeing something different after well over a month of captivity in that prison did lighten my heart.

"I wanted to ask you about the weather," continued Malala. I cocked an eyebrow in surprise and she went on, "When it rains, do your new guns and rockets still fire?"

"The rockets are difficult to light in torrential rain," I admitted, "and of course priming and cartridges can get damp, but gunners often cover them with canvas to try to keep them dry."

"But as they uncover the guns to fire, surely the weapons and powder soon become wet?"

"They do," I conceded. "I have heard that no one around here fights during the rainy season for precisely that reason."

"This is true," she admitted. "But the Ashanti generals have learned of the new weapons from their spies. I have heard them talk of attacking the British during the rainy season, when they believe these new guns will not work. Our muskets will not fire either, but we will have the advantage of much greater numbers.

I did not say anything for a while as we paced along, but my mind was whirling. Had all my talk of mythical weapons changed the Ashanti's plans? And if they had, were the British better off or worse? Little did I know it then, but my intervention was to give us the most unlikely victory – but that was hard to imagine back in that yard. For it seemed to me then that the British garrison was doomed either way. If fifteen thousand well-armed Ashanti marched down the road to Cape Coast Castle, there would be little that the few hundred British soldiers and their native allies could do about it. They might be able to hole up in the fort for a few weeks until they were starved out, but there was no chance of a relief force to drive the Ashanti back. The best that they could hope for was being allowed to evacuate the garrison onto a passing ship. If the Ashanti attacked during the rainy season, the situation would be far worse, for half of the garrison was likely to be incapacitated with fever.

"I know you say that you want to help me escape," I said at last, "but it does not look like there will be anywhere to escape to soon."

I half expected her to look triumphant and to finally drop the pretence of being on my side. She had, with my unwitting assistance, helped the Ashanti to develop a plan of attack that would strike the British at their weakest time. But instead she looked as sad as I did. It was strange as, despite her protestations, I was sure that her loyalty was not to me or my countrymen. "I doubt I will be able to help you at all for much longer," she sighed. The king wants to marry me."

"You mean you will be a queen?" I asked, surprised. For such an ambitious woman, she did not seem pleased at achieving the ultimate position.

"I will be one of his principle wives," she corrected. "But if we have a son he might one day be king." Her chin tilted up a little at that, showing her old pride, but as I looked across at the women's house on the other side of the square, the reality of her fate dawned on me. She would be just as much a prisoner there as I was in my cell. Unable to leave or even be seen by male members of the court. While she might exert some influence through her pillow talk, she would lose access to sources of information such as me, that had helped her gain status. Her rival counsellors would hold sway with the king and she would have to share even that greaseball with all the other wives. The chances were he would soon find other favourites and she would disappear into obscurity. I *almost* felt sorry for her.

She saw where I was looking and must have guessed my train of thought. "The king has shown me around the women's house, it is brighter inside than it looks out here. There is a central courtyard with no bars on the windows."

"I have stayed in worse prisons," I conceded. "There was a bottle-shaped one in India that was pretty grim."

"You have been to India as well as France and Spain," she exclaimed. "What is India like?"

"Well there are some stone carvings on the temples there that show every conceivable position for lovemaking, and quite a few that I found impossible. It is hot like here but very different, with huge palaces, different religions and an energy and bustle to the place that I found nowhere else."

She laughed and added wistfully, "You will have to sit under my window in the women's house and tell me all about your travels. Have you been anywhere else?"

"I have been to Canada. You would not like it there in winter. The water freezes into ice and the rain comes down as snow so that the ground has a deep white covering. It looks magical, but it is bloody cold."

"And I suppose that there are dragons and flying horses there too," she laughed. "Do you take me for a fool to believe such things?"

It took me quite some time to convince her that snow and ice did exist or that the weather ever got cold enough to necessitate a sensible degree of clothing. To prove that water became a solid, I had to explain how it became steam too. When I mentioned that I had once travelled in a ship powered by a steam engine, she was overawed by all the sights she had not seen. By then we were back near my prison cell. As she turned to leave, I wondered if I would ever see her again.

Chapter 16

When the mathematician Archimedes had his moment of revelation, legend tells us that he leapt out of his bath yelling 'Eureka!' My moment was a little less dramatic, although I flatter myself that it was just as ingenious.

It had all started two days before at my regular game of pebbles with King Azi. At first it just looked like a regular reflection of the sun from the many gold decorations on the walls of the women's house. Then I noticed that the beam of light was unsteadily circling the white stone that served as a jack. Even though we had no common language, I saw that Azi had noticed it too. He gave a slight grunt of surprise and then slowly turned to survey our guards. They were both sitting in the shade of the cells and one looked to be asleep. There was no cause for them to be concerned as the scene was the same as it was every day, with Azi and I playing our game and the other prisoners sitting in another patch of shade and talking among themselves. The light moved once more around the jack and then darted off in the direction of the women's house. As it did so I noticed the glint of light on metal from one of the ground floor windows.

We finished throwing our pebbles. As usual Azi was extraordinarily accurate; it was though he had been throwing those stones for years and perhaps he had. But when he picked up the white one, with a glance at me, he threw it on in the direction that the light had taken. It took two more games to get close to the window in the wall – it was here that the guards would normally yell at us to move away. Azi looked up and saw the one conscious guard watching us. He waved an acknowledgement at the man, even though he had not yet shouted, and then made a big show of throwing the jack this time away from the women's house. The guard sat back and looked at his other prisoners, content we were not causing trouble. He did not see us take a couple of steps back, closer to the window.

"Engleeshman," a voice whispered. "That black cow Malala is fooling you. She is not your friend, she tells the king everything you say."

"I know," I called back softly. "Who are you?"

"My name is Jasmina. I am one of the king's wives, at least for now. The new king does not like Arab women and I am to be sold to a merchant in town."

"You speak good English," I told her.

"I was born in Cape Coast Castle, but my father traded with the Ashanti. He was forced to give me as a wife to the old king before he was exiled back to the coast."

"When you get out of here, will you be able to get a message to the British for me?" I asked suddenly realising what an opportunity this chance meeting was.

"Of course, my maids and I will leave in the next few days. My new husband is a trader, he will not let me go home, but I can send a message to the coast."

"Thank God," I breathed. "Tell the British that Thomas Flashman is a prisoner of the Ashanti and that they plan to attack during the rainy season."

She promised that she would and as I threw my last stone I felt a surge of elation. Now at last someone would know that I was here, and I had further thwarted Malala's plans. It was a start. The British may have to abandon the coast, but they would be back. When they knew I was here, I prayed that they would include my release in any new trade negotiations. It was only as I went to bed that night that something began to gnaw at my brain. I was missing something, but I could not work out what it was. All of the next day I wracked my addled wits to find what I could not see, but it was not until the next night that the last piece finally dropped into place. If I recall, I whispered, "Bloody hell," instead of 'Eureka' and then I lay there trying to work out if it was really achievable.

It was a mad scheme and there were dozens of things that could go wrong, but it was the only plan I had, or could see ever getting. The alternative was spending the rest of my life in that prison with perhaps a letter every few years to remind me of the life I was missing. With that perspective, everything was possible and I spent the rest of the night pacing restlessly around my cell. Suddenly freedom seemed at hand and so close I could almost taste it.

The next morning, I was in a fever to begin. As soon as I heard them moving I hollered for a guard. "Malala," I shouted at him. "I must see Malala." Of course he could not understand me, but he knew the name and that she had visited me before. So it was not hard to guess what I wanted. He nodded and ambled off while I rehearsed in my head for the hundredth time what I was going to say. It would be no easy task, for my whole plan relied on the loyalty of a woman who had made her name with treachery and deceit.

"What do you want?" asked Malala curtly when she finally arrived. She had taken three hours to respond to my request and I was on the verge of giving up hope.

"Could we go and walk again in that square…?" I started.

"What? I do not have time for this, I have matters of state to attend to. You cannot just summon me every time you want a fresh view." She was angry and turning to go.

"Please," I pleaded. "What I want to talk about will greatly benefit you as well as me." Her eyes narrowed in suspicion, she clearly thought I was lying just to get out of the cell, but she could not be sure. After a moment's hesitation, she nodded to a guard and the door was thrown open.

"So what is it that will be of great benefit to me?" she asked a few minutes later as we walked into the other square.

I took a deep breath, this was my moment of truth and all of a sudden my plan felt entirely absurd. "You have often told me of how you would like to help me escape," I blurted out. "What if I could help us *both* escape?"

"Escape!" she almost shouted the word at me. "Why would I want to escape? I am about to marry the king and I already have more power and influence than any woman in Coomassie."

I gestured at the women's house, "If you are telling me that you are happy to spend the rest of your life behind those four walls – and we both know that your influence will wane once you are trapped there – then take me back to the prison now." I paused as she looked across at the decorated carvings and the partially shuttered windows. "But if you want to see stone buildings the size of small mountains, travel in ships powered by steam, walk the streets of London and Paris, perhaps travel to India and explore its exotic temples or go to Canada to see ice and snow, then I can help you." She stared at me then, her mouth half open in wonder as she started to imagine it. "You would drink cold champagne in the finest hotels, visit royal European palaces, perhaps even see people flying high above your head in hot-air balloons."

"What are hot-air balloons?" she asked.

"They are huge silken bags, as big as this square that are filled with hot air and rise high into the sky. Underneath is a basket which can carry two or three people and the balloonist who guides the craft."

"There is truly such a thing?" There was no doubting her interest now.

"There is, I swear it, and if you help me I will show you, although we may have to go to Paris to see them. I have even seen a woman jump from the basket when it was high in the air. She used a huge umbrella to drift safely back to the ground."

We walked a few paces in silence as she considered the wonder of what I had told her, but then her natural cunning reared its head again. "Wait, how can I trust you? You whisper of these fantastic things to get my help, but how do I know you will show them to me? If I get you to Cape Coast Castle, you might leave me behind when the ship comes or denounce me to the British as an Ashanti spy."

I was ready and waiting for that one. "The very fact that you have helped me escape from the heart of the royal palace and guided me to safety will be proof to anyone that you are not an Ashanti spy. If anyone remembers you from before, I will vouch that you had no choice and believed that the Ashanti army was divided. It is the least I can do if you get me out of here. As for the rest, you will have to trust me, just as I must trust you not to betray me."

She thought about that for a few more paces and then stopped and studied me carefully. "You are very different today," she said at last. Then a more knowing look crossed her features and she asked quietly,

"Do the British soldiers really have Collier rifles and artillery and accurate rockets?"

I smiled. "No," I admitted. "And did you ever visit me unless you wanted information?"

She smiled back, "No," she conceded. "So, we are both liars and yet now you say we must trust each other."

"If we don't, we will both spend the rest of our days in our respective prisons. I imagine that you cannot turn down a marriage proposal from the king."

"Not if I want to keep my head. But you are asking me to give you what you want first; how can I be sure that you will keep your end of the deal?"

"Look, I'm not going to travel the world with you, I have a wife and family that I want to get back to. But I can show you around London when we get there, Paris too once I have spent some time at home. If you want to go to India or Canada, I have contacts in those countries that I can introduce you to. I also know people who would pay handsomely to hear all the details of the mysterious Ashanti army that has just vanquished the British governor. But let us suppose I let you down; if you have gold, you will still be able to find your own way in London or Paris. I imagine that you can get your hands on some gold. That bracelet you are wearing now would pay for a small town-house with a maid for a year. But I will not let you down. If you bring her husband safely home, my wife would not allow it." I grinned at her and I think she was convinced. Mind you, back then I wasn't lying. I did not trust her an inch, but if she got me away from this nightmare existence then I would happily do all I promised and still feel I had got a bargain from the deal.

"Wait though," she said frowning. "This is all very well, but I still cannot get you out. The guards open the gates for me here as we are still in the heart of the palace. They may let me take you into the next courtyard too, but no further. You are the only white man in Coomassie and everyone knows that you are a prisoner of the king. The guards would never let you walk out of here, even if I ordered them too. They know that their heads are at stake if you escape."

"Don't worry, I have a plan."

"You cannot walk out of here and don't think you can go out hidden in a cart either, for they are all searched. Unless you have one of those hot-air balloons hidden in your cell, I cannot see how you can escape."

"I have a plan," I insisted. "It will give us both what we want and if you swear to help me, I will tell you what it is." I held out my hand to shake on the deal and after a final moment's hesitation she took it.

Chapter 17

If Malala had been doubtful of the plan when I had revealed it, her reservations were nothing to those of Jasmina. I whispered my idea to her through the bars of the women's house during the next day's game of pebbles. She was sure that Malala would betray us and wanted nothing to do with the scheme at first. We had to play the game past her window twice for me to assure her that while she had the least to lose, like the rest of us, she would get what she wanted if it worked. Reluctantly she agreed.

There was not a moment to waste if the plan was to work and that night I paced impatiently up and down my cell, listening for any noise to indicate that the scheme was afoot. All I heard was the gentle snoring of the guards at the end of the passage. Then at last I heard the familiar creak that indicated that the door to the little prison was opening. I held my breath as a shadowy figure appeared at my cell door and there was a scrape as the locking bar was lifted out of the sockets.

"Quickly," Malala whispered as she pulled the door open. I did not need asking twice as I went past her into the corridor. Three more dark figures stood silently at the end of the passage, right next to the sleeping guards. "Don't worry," Malala continued as she saw me stop at the sight. "The guards have been drugged – they will not wake up for hours." She closed my cell door again and put the bar back in place.

"Why are you doing that?" I asked.

"It might buy us more time before they realise you have gone," she explained. Nodding at the guards she continued, "They will wake with sore heads, so it will be a while before they bother to check on their charges. Now come on, we must get you ready."

Malala had led three veiled Arab women into the part of the palace that contained the prison, but there were four with her when she came out. The maid walking behind Jasmina was unusually tall. Close inspection would reveal that her left breast was larger and lower than her right and where her robe stopped an inch above her ankles, some large manly boots were visible. Her mistress looked rightly terrified at the risk of being caught and for good reason, it was as well that the escape was taking place at night.

While we were still in the prison, the maids had helped me on with my gown and then pinned the dark scarf around my face so that only my eyes were showing. With all the time I had spent in Brazil and Africa, I was sufficiently dark to pass for an Arab. One of the maids, a large black girl, had insisted I stroll up and down the prison passage for their inspection. I had been walking nearly all my life and grumbled that I did not really think practice was necessary. But they insisted and when I turned around after a brief strut down the corridor I found them in a state of horrified consternation.

The small thin maid threw up her hands in resignation and issued a stream of voluble oaths that appeared to suggest that they would save time by handing themselves to the executioner right then and there. I had no idea what she was complaining about and she must have seen the bewilderment on my face. Cursing again, she then did an imitation of my gait, which I had to concede was not exactly feminine. The robe came off again then while they adorned me with breasts made from cloth bundles tied in place with a strip of linen. The small maid then had to teach me to walk like a girl, involving a step more like that of a tightrope walker, which she gestured would make my backside swing in a more authentic manner. It is not often I have been invited to study a woman's behind as she walked, and I know mine was not nearly as comely as hers.

With my gown and veil back on, a generous dose of a pungent perfume, and a large bundle of clothes to carry like the other maids, they said I was finally ready to step outside. Despite my near total covering, I still felt exposed and vulnerable. There was one more thing I wanted: a weapon. As I cast a final look around the prison that had been my home for the last two months, I noticed a sheathed knife tucked under the belt of one of the snoring guards. I gently pulled it from him and buried it deep in my bundle of clothing.

"Say nothing, whatever happens," Malala warned us as she led the way. The first gate was something of an anti-climax. The guards had already let Malala pass once and were pulling the timber door open again as soon as they saw us heading in their direction. I kept my head down to keep my features in shadow from the flickering torchlight, but they did not seem to be paying us any attention.

"We are through," sighed Jasmina as the gate shut behind us.

"There are three more gates," warned Malala. "That was the easiest. Now, no more talking in English." We were walking past the front of the women's house now and I saw her glance across at its brooding black mass. If we were caught, at least for Malala and I, we were likely to lose our heads. I was frightened but elated at the same time. Before my situation had looked entirely bleak; I may have been alive, but it was hardly a life worth living. Now I had hope and that is a marvellous thing. I had a chance of going home, seeing my family, feeling the bite of a frosty morning in Leicestershire and never going near Africa again.

I was still lost in these happy thoughts when Malala rapped her gold-topped cane on the next gate. A tired soldier wearily emerged from the gatehouse but leapt smartly to attention when he saw who had summoned him. I knew that Malala would be explaining to him that Jasmina was being sent to her new husband in the city and that this was being done at night to save any embarrassment to her and to the king. The palace was a tight-knit community and the guards would have known that the king was adjusting his harem to his own tastes. Some of the wives had left already. The story evidently was plausible to the guard, for with very little ceremony he threw the gate open, seeming anxious only to get us through it so that he could return to his bed.

The next square was completely dark apart from a flickering torch by the gate on its far side. Shadows danced across the ground and I started a couple of times as I thought sinister figures were moving in to ambush us. The big black maid behind said something in Arabic and patted me on the shoulder with a quiet chuckle to calm me down.

Once more the gold-topped cane rapped on the door and again a man emerged from the nearby guardhouse. This one, though, did not rush to open the gate. Instead he took the flaming torch from its bracket and walked towards us, asking a question of Malala. I imagined that he wanted to know what the deuce we were doing wandering around the palace in the dead of night. She answered his questions and followed him as he held up the burning log to illuminate our little party. As he ran his watchful eyes over Jasmina just in front of me, I shifted the bundle of clothes I was holding to cover my uneven breasts. I had a bad feeling about this encounter and slowly slid my hand inside the bundle until my fingers closed around the hilt of the knife inside. Then as I kept my head bowed I sensed him coming alongside me. I was slightly taller than the guard and out of the corner of my eye I saw him glaring at me with suspicion. He gave a sniff, probably catching the pungent perfume I had been doused with earlier and then grunted. I could feel my heart racing; in the next few seconds everything could fall apart. Malala must have seen my hand inside the bundle and quickly distracted the guard by asking him a question. He turned to her and replied then she passed on the information in Arabic to Jasmina, but at the end of the words I could not understand, she said something in English that was really intended for me. "There are two more guards watching us through the gatehouse door, so do not do anything stupid with that knife."

Now the guard was turning his attention back to me. The hand holding the knife was on the far side from him and I dared not move it. He started to run his eyes down my body and I cursed myself for not changing out of my boots. Barefoot or sandals would have been far less conspicuous. Then I heard a squeal from behind. The big black maid had dropped her bundle at my feet and turned to berate the younger maid behind. The two of them started a furious row in Arabic, with one pushing at the other. The guard laughed and stepped forward with Malala to keep them apart. As peace in our little party was restored, the guard strode off and to my relief headed towards the gate. One more courtyard between us and freedom and I desperately hoped that the next guard would be as pliant as the first two.

I was to be disappointed, though, for as the doors to our square opened, we could immediately see the far portal that led to our liberty. It was illuminated by four torches, two on either side, and around the gate were the same number of guards. Getting past one man had been hard enough, but four in a well-lit space felt impossible. I heard Jasmina give a little wail of despair, but Malala was swiftly alongside and whispering something in Arabic. Then she turned to me and said quietly, "This is the last gate so for God's sake, when you approach it remember to walk like a woman."

We went forward once more, this time with a sense of foreboding. The fair maiden Flashy swung her hips for all she was worth and while it may not have been aimed at me, one of the guards gave a low whistle of approval. This time they did not seem the least bit intimidated by Malala's cane of office and it was soon obvious why. They reeked of palm wine and I saw a jug on the ground near the gate. As Malala tried to negotiate with the man in charge, the other three crowded around us. As a former wife of their king, they steered clear of Jasmina, but clearly thought that her maids were fair game for their amorous attention.

One leered up at me with unfocused eyes and whispered what I think were some words of admiration. I glared back silently in response, but then the impertinent swine took a mauling clutch at my left buttock. Well I have clutched a rump or two myself in my time and I knew all too well what the response was to an unwelcome approach. It was refreshing to be the giver rather than the receiver for a change. I emitted a suitably feminine high-pitched squeal of indignation and swung my open palm round to give him a resounding slap across the cheek as hard as I could. He staggered back a pace or two and rubbed his face. But rather than being cowed by this robust defence of my womanly virtue, he was only encouraged and cackled with delight.

The black maid was clearly a resourceful woman who had come prepared for just this type of encounter. She tried to distract my assailant by unpinning her veil and beaming broadly at the guards around her. She had uncovered a black gown that had been cut to reveal a generous glimpse of a very ample cleavage. The guards hooted in delight and I thought I might escape any more amorous attention, but my admirer was not going to give up that easily.

147

The man turned back to me and cooed more Ashanti words of endearment, while gesturing for me to remove my own veil for him. I doubted three months' beard growth would do much for his ardour and stepped back, but now I was up against the wall. I kept my cloth bundle tight against my chest in case he tried to grab me there and looked around desperately for help. The black maid was keeping two of the guards fully entertained by virtually pushing their heads into her breasts while Malala was still arguing with the man in charge. Jasmina stepped forward and tried to order my admirer away, but he was having none of it. He was still cackling as he rubbed his cheek again and then squeezed his own bicep before pointing at me. He seemed to be saying that he liked his women nearly six-foot-tall and with the slap of an angry costermonger. Then, before I realised what was happening, the lecherous villain lurched forward and grabbed me between the legs.

For a split-second time stood still. I remember gaping in astonishment and seeing that expression mirrored in the drunken face in front of me, as the man realised he had got a handful of far more than he expected. The younger maid gave a little squeal as she realised that the game was up, while her companion grimaced in horror. Then, almost unable to believe what had just happened, I dropped my bundle and roared in indignation. I remember my right fist swinging. The man stepped back but had no time to defend himself. I struck him plum on the jaw. His knees were already buckling as my left fist hit him hard in the solar plexus. I sprang forward past my victim who was now falling to the ground and gasping for breath. I expected the other guards to rush me and raised my fists again to defend myself. My veil had slipped round as I had thrown my first punch and so I could only see from one eye. But when I looked up instead of charging, I saw that the guards were backing away, holding up their hands in submission.

Malala stepped forward and spoke sharply to me in Arabic, wagging a finger as she scolded me, and pointed to the man lying at our feet who was still wheezing and struggling to breathe. Then she turned to the man in charge, who to my astonishment was now gesturing for the other guards to open the gate. Jasmina stepped up beside me and whispered, "She is telling them that you are a bashful virgin, determined to protect your honour." She chuckled before adding, "I think it will be a while before they assault an Arab girl again."

Already the gate was swinging open and I stared across the open ground at the dark silhouette of the streets of Coomassie. "Well we had better leave quickly," I said in the highest voice I could manage, "before that fellow can tell the others what he just got a handful of."

We grabbed our bundles and hurried out of the gate, walking quickly. I glanced over my shoulder, expecting at any moment the start of a pursuit, but instead I saw the gate close behind us. We broke into a run then, all the way to the first street and then Jasmina led the way up an alley between two rows of houses. "This way, we will go by the Arab quarter. Veiled women will not stand out there and I know a place we can hide if they raise the alarm."

I fell in behind the maids and heard Malala come up beside me. She gave me a sideways glance and grinned, "Perhaps you should walk a little less like a woman after all if you are going to attract *that* kind of attention," she suggested.

Chapter 18

We waited for half an hour in the Arab quarter, where we would not be so conspicuous, expecting at any moment to hear shouts of alarm coming from the palace and the sound of soldiers running through the streets. Instead the place was as quiet as a grave. We heard nothing; no one was moving. We had to be out of the city by dawn, when my escape was bound to be discovered, and so now Malala led the way. She went at a fast pace and we all stumbled once or twice moving over rough ground in the dark, but as the sun began to lighten the eastern horizon, we found ourselves in the green hills that surrounded the city.

"Hang on," I said as I got my bearings. "The sun is behind us and so we are heading west, but the coast is south."

"Yes," said Malala. "What do you think will happen when they find your cell empty? They will think that you have gone south to the British. So the king will send hundreds if not thousands of soldiers south after you. They will sweep through the jungle for several miles on either side of the road and search every village. He will be determined to get you back. So we will head west. First to a village where a guide is waiting for us and then after a couple of days we will turn south, but wide of their search parties."

I had to concede that her plan was sensible and an hour later we arrived at a small village. We hid behind a large fallen tree while Malala went in search of our guide. He turned out to be a taciturn grey-bearded fellow, who just nodded at us and led the way into the jungle until we came to a cleared field of crops with a covered yam store on one side. As he led us to it I saw that the yams had been piled up on four sides to leave a clear hidden space in the middle.

"We stay here until nightfall," announced Malala. "This close to the city, the villagers may hear of our escape and so we do not want them seeing strange Arab women during the day."

I was glad of the rest and as soon as the old man had gone, I pulled off my veil. I doubted my amorous friend would have found me quite so attractive now. I was hot and sweaty. Apart from the beard, I was also a little lopsided as my left tit had fallen out of my gown on the way out of town. The other veils came off too and for the young maid and Jasmina it was the first time I had seen their faces.

"Why do you think the guard who grabbed you did not raise the alarm when he could speak?" asked Jasmina.

I had been wondering that too. "Perhaps he was not sure what he had felt, although he got a bloody good grip."

The black maid chuckled, but then put forward another theory. "A few years ago, a man was found smuggled into the women's house. He was killed, but so were all the guards who should have stopped him. Perhaps they were worried for their heads."

"They will lose them anyway when the king finds out that they let us escape," said Malala abruptly. It was a harsh reminder of the brutal world we had just escaped from. Mind you we had a long way to go until we were safe. In fact, knowing that the huge Ashanti army was soon to be on its way to Cape Coast Castle, I knew that I would not feel safe until I was on a homeward bound ship with the white cliffs of Dover on the horizon.

We sat and ate some boiled yam that our guide had provided and listened as a rain shower began to beat down on the grass roof above us. It was the start of the long rainy season and the shower soon became a deluge. Streams of water were running off the thatch above us and into the field, which was being lashed by the rain. It was now hard to talk, but at least there were few leaks from the covering over our heads. We were all tired from the tension of our escape and a long night-time walk, so we set about trying to make ourselves comfortable to sleep. For a while my mind would not let me rest and I remember looking across at Jasmina, who was dozing curled up in the corner. She was very pretty and looked remarkably like a girl I had known in London over twenty years before. Their names were almost identical. That earlier girl had died horribly in my arms... Even then the memory made me shudder a little.

When we awoke that afternoon, the rain had stopped and everything looked green and fresh. Our guide brought more food and then as evening drew in, he led us off again into the jungle. He used a machete to cut away the foliage that had encroached on the old path we were using, while the rest of us followed in single file. Apart from Malala, we were back in our gowns and veils as other villagers could be in the jungle or out hunting, even at night. While I saw the sense in it, I hated having the damn cloth over my face. It was hot and stuffy and you could not see clearly where you were going, particularly down by your feet. I was forever tripping over roots and once I heard a rustle in the leaves at my side and just caught a glimpse of a snake disappearing into the trees.

"Don't worry," laughed Jasmina on hearing my shout of alarm. "It is not poisonous and most of them are more afraid of you, than you are of them."

I was not so sure about that, particularly after the black maid spoke up behind me. "Apart from the mamba," she added helpfully. "They don't give a damn as they know they can kill you. You die within hours if one of those bastards bite you."

"What do mambas look like?" I asked nervously.

"They are green – but they live up in trees and bushes, you rarely see them on the ground." This was hardly comforting as we were surrounded by trees and bushes, many of them growing over our heads. I had a sudden memory of the green snake I had shared a bush with at Nsamankow and wondered if I had been much closer to death then than I thought. It was now dusk and I opened my mouth to ask if mambas hunted at night, but then decided that I did not want to know the answer.

We fell into a routine over the next three weeks. Once further away from Coomassie, we travelled by day, although always veiled. After a couple of days heading west we turned south and mercifully, did not see a single Ashanti search party. While the Arab women chattered amongst themselves, the interpreter said very little. Malala would generally stride on behind the guide, her gold-tipped staff in her hand and a heavy leather bag over her shoulder. I heard a metallic clink from it occasionally and guessed that she had followed my advice about bringing gold. It was obvious that she did not like Jasmina – a feeling that seemed entirely mutual – and on the second night she tried to persuade the Arab girl to stay at a nearby village.

"It will be a long and dangerous journey," she said. "Stay with your women in the village and we will get word to your father so he can send men to fetch you safely. Perhaps with a boat to save you walking all of the way."

It seemed practical advice but Jasmina would not hear of it. "I do not trust you," she said bluntly. "You say you are loyal, but I have heard you boasting of your victories to the king. How do I know that you will not leave me in the jungle to rot? I have been abandoned before; it is not going to happen again."

I had discovered that she was only fifteen when the old king had demanded her as a wife from her father. He had displeased the king over some trade and to refuse would have meant death for her whole family. Even then, once she had been delivered to the palace, the rest of the family were banished from the kingdom. The king had never slept with her, he had a dozen or so favourites for that, and so like many other women, she was kept as a prisoner to his whim. Several times when we were alone she would warn me about Malala, who she was sure would betray us sooner or later. But as the days passed I was more convinced that she was wrong.

Malala appeared genuine in wanting to see the outside world and if she was going to have us ambushed, it would surely have been on the streets of Coomassie rather than deep in the jungle. Malala had more to worry about in me keeping my end of the bargain, but if I could get myself on a ship before the Ashanti attacked, I did not care who came with me. Malala was welcome and I would keep my promise to show her the sights. It would be more than worth her help in the escape. Mind you, I suspected that Malala was rather more worried about what Jasmina might say to her father about the translator's loyalty and if this would be passed back to the British authorities. I doubted that Chisholm would believe Malala's claims of allegiance any more than I did, but rescuing my unworthy carcass would stand in her favour. She would just need to leave the coast before King Appea learned of her return, as I doubted he would be as forgiving.

Our luck changed one evening and our spirits rose when the guide announced that we had less than a week to travel before we reached the coast. None of us, I think, had realised the progress we had made. It was tough going travelling through the jungle; it rained heavily on average every third day and then the ground was often boggy. There were streams and rivers to cross, two of which we had been forced to wade through with the constant fear of crocodiles. Now it felt we were so close that I could almost smell the salt tang of the ocean in the air. We all went to bed that night with smiles on our faces.

The next morning, however, one of us was not smiling. It was the young maid. She had been stung on the sole of her foot, I thought, by one of the big scorpions I had seen in the jungle. The things are the size of small lobsters, but while the stings are painful, they soon ease off. In fact, there were loads of vicious creatures in that jungle, which was why I was now very grateful I had kept my boots during our escape. When I looked, there was a small red mark about the size of a farthing on the ball of the maid's right foot. It did not look too bad and with padding around it we set off as usual. But she was limping and we had to slow our pace so that she did not fall behind.

By midday the other maid was giving her a piggy back while I carried two of our bundles of supplies. When we stopped and unbandaged her foot, I was surprised to see that the red mark, instead of diminishing, had spread to cover the whole front part of her foot with a livid purple bruise. It looked nasty and the poor girl was in agony. It was obvious that she could not now walk, but we were miles away from any villages where we might get help. The guide cut down a long pole and we used some of the cloth we were carrying to fashion some slings to it so that the girl could be suspended in a form of hammock. Thank heavens it was the lighter maid, as she did not really slow us down at all. We all took turns carrying one end of the pole, but the girl was getting worse. She was feverish now and drifting in and out of consciousness. We were still in the forest at dusk when we put her down. By then the redness had spread to her knee.

"I have never seen a scorpion sting like this." Jasmina looked distraught as she raised the girl's gown to see how far it had spread.

"I think the poison is in her blood," Malala said dispassionately and turned to look at me. "I had a brother who had a sting like this. He died, there was nothing anyone could do."

"Died?" repeated Jasmina, appalled. "No, she is not going to die. We will build a big fire and try to sweat the fever out of her." So that was what we tried to do, but privately I thought that Malala was right. There was only one way the girl could be saved and that was to remove her leg, but you would need a skilled surgeon for that. We wrapped her up in every scrap of cloth from the bundles we had been carrying and placed her near the fire. Jasmina and the other maid stayed with her through the night, mopping her brow and trying to encourage her to pull through. Malala and I sat nearby, listening to the maid's laboured breathing. The rasping gasps for breath got louder through the night until, just before dawn, they stopped. We all sat there in silence for a moment, listening for her lungs to work again, but there was nothing. I felt a sense of relief as it had been obvious for the last few hours that she would not recover. It was no more than twenty-four hours since the poor girl had been stung and now she was dead.

We sat around feeling shock at the quickness of her death, all too aware that whatever had caused it could have struck at us just as easily. As the sun's rays started to shine down through the leaves, the guide reminded us that the village we had been aiming for to get help was still a few miles away. We wearily wrapped the corpse back into her slings and carried her on her final journey.

It was a miserable place when we got there, just a few huts and a handful of families that barely survived on what they could grow and harvest from the jungle. But they welcomed us and if they noticed that one of the veiled women was suspiciously tall and spoke with a deep voice, they kept those thoughts to themselves. They helped the guide to dig a grave for the maid and we stood by it as Jasmina and the other maid said some words from their faith, before a local man muttered some incantations of his own. Then we found that they had cleared one of their huts for us to spend the night in. The five of us ate a meat and yam stew that night, sitting in a small circle outside our hut.

"I told you that this journey would be dangerous." Malala spoke in English so that only we could understand. She looked at the Arab women and continued, "Please, it would be much safer if you and your maid stayed here. We can get a message to your father when we reach the coast and he can send a strong party out to collect you. The people here will look after you." She patted her leather satchel before adding, "I will even give them some gold so that they treat you well."

It was a generous offer, almost too generous, and I saw Jasmina's eyes narrow slightly in suspicion. "No," she said at last. "I do not trust you. We have travelled for three weeks now and we only have a week to go. It makes no sense to stop now. I want to see my father when he learns I have escaped."

"If you do not trust me," persisted Malala, "then tell Thomas where your father can be found. He will tell him where you are."

I nodded in agreement but Jasmina was having none of it. "No!" she shouted, causing the guide to look up in surprise. "You are not leaving me behind," she said with finality and turned to go into the hut.

Not a lot was said next morning as we set off once more. The path out of the village was wider than the normal track and Malala walked on ahead with the guide while Jasmina fell in beside me. "I don't trust her," she whispered, gesturing towards the pair walking in front of us. "Jana," she said referring to her surviving maid, "said she saw that witch sneaking around the fire the night that Salma was stung."

"Oh come on!" I exclaimed. "You are surely not suggesting that Malala found one of those giant scorpions or a snake and got it to sting Salma. That is ridiculous. She would be at far more risk of being stung herself." I thought the idea was absurd at the time, but the next morning I was not so sure.

Chapter 19

As the camp stirred itself into life, I was surprised to see Jana the maid still asleep. She was normally the first up, cooking breakfast and when we had it, making coffee. The villagers had given us a fresh supply of roasted beans and I had been looking forward to waking up to the aroma of fresh coffee. I went across to shake her shoulder to get her up, but as I bent down over her I froze. Her eyes were wide open, fixed on the sky above and from her slack jaw a trail of dribble ran down her chin. Slowly I reached out and touched her shoulder; her skin was cool and the joint felt stiff. She had been dead for a while. I looked up. The guide was busy tying up his blanket ready for the day's walk and Jasmina was in the trees conducting her toilette. Only Malala, still sitting on her bedding, was watching me. There was no concern or alarm on her face, just curiosity as she waited for me to react.

"Did you do this?" I asked quietly.

"Perhaps now she will wait in the village," she whispered not answering my question.

"And will you kill her too if she doesn't?" I persisted.

"Do you want her to tell your commanders how the great British hero was found hiding in a bush in the middle of a battle, or how you begged for your life and showed the Ashanti king how to use your latest weapons? You have as much reason as me to stop her reaching Cape Coast Castle before we leave." As she spoke, she uncoiled herself from the floor and stood up. I was not sure if I had shared that bush at Nsamankow with a green mamba, but Malala looked just as deadly. There was an impassive calm to her, with not a shred of remorse over the death of the maid. There were probably countless other victims lining her rise to power and I did not have a shred of doubt that she would despatch me too if I became inconvenient. I was only alive because she wanted something: heaven help me if I stood in her way.

"Leave her alone today," I whispered. "I will try to persuade her to stay in the next village."

"It is up to you," shrugged Malala. "You can try your way first, then we do it my way." She went off into the jungle then to conduct her own toilette and so was not there when Jasmina returned. Malala might not have been present, but she would have heard the screams of anguish when Jasmina found the body. They were swiftly followed by shouted Arabic oaths and curses as she made it very clear who she thought was responsible. We looked over the maid's body but there were no signs of any wounds at all, although a tiny insect bite would have been harder to spot on her darker skin.

"We don't know what killed her," I said gently, trying to placate Jasmina. "It could have been anything."

"It was her," spat Jasmina gesturing into the jungle. Malala was nowhere to be seen but I was sure that she was nearby and eavesdropping on the conversation. "She used poison or snake venom and she is going to pay for what she has done."

"Look, supposing you are right, and I'm not saying you are. That means that she has killed two people already and she will come after you next. We still have five days to go and neither of us can stay awake all night every night. Stop at the next village and I will get your father to send some people to collect you."

Jasmina thought about what I said for a moment. "What if she kills you?"

"She won't kill me because she wants me to take her to London. I will get to the castle and then I will speak to your father." Of course, if Malala was standing over me with one of her scorpions, I would delay speaking to her father until a ship was in sight, but Jasmina was not to know that.

She seemed to see the sense in what I was saying, "Tell her I will stop at the next village if you want." I breathed a sigh of relief before she added, "But as soon as you are out of sight I will pay the villagers to take me to the coast. What do the British do with traitors, do they hang them?"

That's it, my girl, I thought, certain that Malala was nearby, you have just signed your own death warrant.

158

It was impossible to carry the dead maid any distance and we did not have the tools to bury her. Instead we had to make do with covering her body with cut down branches. The guide chopped most of it with his machete, but I hacked at some large leaf fronds with the knife I normally kept in my bundle of clothing. This time, though, when I had finished, I pushed the blade up the arm of my gown, tucking the hilt into the remaining cuff of my shirt that I wore underneath. Malala reappeared while we worked, but made no effort to help. She could not have failed to notice the hostile atmosphere in the little clearing as Jasmina pointedly ignored her.

"Jasmina has decided to stay in the next village," I said cheerily in an effort to lighten the mood. My reward was a stony glare from both women. Once more the mistress said a few words in her religion over the grave of a maid and then we set off. As usual Malala strode on ahead with the guide while Jasmina and I followed on behind. My companion was muttering darkly about what revenge she would wreak on the translator, but I was not listening. Instead I was lost in my own thoughts.

I liked Jasmina; she was pretty, brave and passionate in her feelings. She had been dealt a raw hand with her forced marriage, but she had leapt at the chance to get away. Her only reservation had been Malala's involvement and she had been proved right there. I realised that I had feelings for the girl, but for once they were not driven by lust. She greatly reminded me of her namesake who I had known years ago in London. There had been lust then all right and more besides. But despite those feelings, the poor girl had come to an awful end. Now I felt that history was about to repeat itself. Jasmina might be brave, but she was up against a ruthless predator who would not hesitate to kill anyone she viewed as a threat. I was only safe as long as I could give Malala something she really wanted, although as we walked, I started to wonder if I would outlive my usefulness once we were in London. Perhaps she would worry that I would reveal her part in guiding McCarthy into an Ashanti trap and decide to tidy up a loose end.

Malala thought I was tied to her for fear of my reputation being damaged, but she could not have been more wrong. I had enough ill-deserved credit in the bank not to worry about a rumour from darkest Africa. Anyway, as possibly the only survivor from the entire British force, few would blame me for trying to hide when everything was clearly lost. I wanted to protect Jasmina, but I was damned if I could see how with five days still to travel. I could feel the weight of the knife in my sleeve, but it was obvious that Malala had hidden weapons of her own. She would be on her guard even now. Even if I got close enough to use the blade, I feared that I would be struck with some lethally poisoned point in return. If I sided openly with Jasmina then neither of us were likely to survive the next night.

The precarious nature of my plight was brought home to me an hour later when we reached a wide stretch of brown water. The guide babbled something to us and then announced "Pra," as though this was something that even I should comprehend. It took a moment, but then I realised that this must be the Pra River, the one that we fought alongside at Nsamankow. Suddenly Cape Coast Castle was a lot closer. We followed a path along the river bank until we came to a huge fallen tree. It must have been blown down in a storm as it had been taller than the other trees nearby. It had certainly not been felled by a man as the splintered break in the massive trunk was some twenty feet in the air. It spanned the river at the same height, its canopy having brought down several trees on the far side. Thick creepers grew up the side of the trunk to help us climb up the still standing part, but we would still need both hands for the climb. We put down our bundles of clothes and food and surveyed this new obstacle.

"We cross here," announced Malala as she put down her satchel and leaned her gold-tipped staff against the trunk. Then she turned to me, "Thomas, we will climb first to see how easy it is to get across. Then we will come back and help the others." Jasmina looked as if she was about to object at being left behind, but then changed her mind. She probably did not relish the thought of standing on a precarious tree trunk with Malala over a crocodile-infested river. I knew exactly how she felt. I was none too keen on the prospect myself, but could not think of a good enough excuse to refuse without increasing the animosity between us.

Malala sprang up the tree trunk with the agility of a cat, while I followed more steadily behind her. She waited for me at the top and then, with a little smile, gestured that I should go first along the trunk over the river. "I think I would rather have you in front of me," she said.

"What, don't you trust me any more?" I asked as I gingerly stepped out onto the log. This end was quite wide, but it got decidedly narrow near the far bank.

"Should I trust you?" she asked, following me. "You seem to be getting very friendly with that girl."

"Of course you can trust me," I insisted. I felt a trickle of sweat run down my back that I was sure was not due to the heat. I did not like having her behind me, especially as it was impossible to look round at her while I had to watch my footing on the log. "I am a British gentleman, a man of his word. I said I would take you to Britain and if you get me safely on a ship, so I shall."

"And what of the girl?" she asked. We were halfway across the log now and my foot slipped for a moment on a strand of loose creeper. As I steadied myself I noticed the flick of a scaly tail in the brown water beneath me.

"What of her?" I repeated.

"How will we deal with her?" Malala persisted with a note of anger in her voice.

"Well, she says that she will stay at the next village," I replied. I tried to sound as casual as I could but the hair on the back of my neck was starting to prickle in alarm.

"And do you believe her?" Malala spoke softly but there was undeniable menace in her voice now.

I took two more careful paces forward before I answered. The tree trunk was now little more than eighteen inches wide and sprang slightly as I moved. It was all I could do to keep upright on it – I would have felt much safer sitting astride. I was still over the water and whatever beasts it contained, twenty feet below. I could not run, I did not even want to turn, but I sensed that a lot was riding on my next answer. "No," I whispered back.

"Look at me," Malala spoke sharply. I put out my hands to help keep my balance and slowly started to turn around. I had almost made it when a branch snapped in the foliage behind me and the trunk lurched slightly to the left. With a wail of despair, I felt myself start to fall to one side and threw myself forwards, wrapping my arms and legs around the trunk like some desperate lover. I had half expected to hear a cry of alarm from Malala too, but when I was able to look up, she was still standing, regarding me impassively, with what looked like a conductor's baton in her hand. Seeing I was safe, she held it up and continued, "If you had lied to me just then, the venom in this dart would have killed you. Not instantly, but it paralyses muscles and the crocodiles would have done the rest."

"I didn't lie to you," I gasped as I adjusted my grip amongst the network of creepers growing over the log.

"But you thought about it," she said quietly taking a couple more paces towards me. "If you even think of lying to me again, you will die," she said. As if to emphasise her point, she raised the little wand to her lips and with a slight 'pfft' noise, a small dart with a yellow feathery head appeared embedded in the log a foot in front of me. She sneered at the look of horror on my face and continued, "I do not think that you are the brave soldier you pretend to be. If you were, you would not have hidden in the bush during the battle and by now you would have tried to attack me with that knife you have hidden. Or have you given it to the girl?" She gave a little humourless laugh and went on, "It does not matter. When we make camp tonight you will go for a walk by yourself in the jungle. By the time you come back, the girl will be dead. Do you understand?"

I nodded, unsure what else to say. I did not care that she implied I was a coward – it was true and if anything, I was proud of the fact. What was the point of being one of all the brave men who had died at Nsamankow? No, she could insult me all she liked. Staying alive was my first priority; getting even was the second. The tricky thing was, I was now sure that when we got to London, I would become an inconvenient witness to her past and suffer the same fate as she had planned for the unfortunate Jasmina. But sprawled on the log in front of her gave me a new perspective on the situation, and an opportunity to achieve both my priorities.

Malala gave a slight grunt of contempt at my apparent abject submission and then said quietly, "Let's go back and get the others." She started to turn on the log. Where she was standing it was closer to two feet wide and she moved with casual ease. What she could not see that I could, however, was that one of the vines that had been between her feet was in fact loose in my hand and not entangled with any others until some distance beyond her. I saw at once the opportunity and knew that with Malala there would be precious few others to grasp at. I eased my knees forward as though preparing to stand again. As Malala stepped around so that both her feet were briefly on the same side of the loose creeper, I struck. I yanked the vine high into the air as she tried to step over it. Then as she was unbalanced on one leg, I swung the creeper as far as I could to the left to push her off the log.

She moved fast, I will say that for her. Even as her foot was sliding off into the void she somehow managed to throw herself in the opposite direction. She landed with her chest over the top of the log but with her waist and legs dangling over the muddy brown water below. Her hands scrabbled out to clutch at the vines to stop herself sliding off the trunk.

"Help me," she shouted as she grasped a new creeper with one hand and held the other out to me as I edged on my hands and knees towards her.

She had been facing away from me when I moved the creeper. I wondered if she realised that I had yanked on it or if she was just too desperate to survive to think. "I am coming," I shouted and shuffled forward another three feet until I could reach out and grab her hand.

She clutched at me with a vice-like grip and then gave a small grimace of triumph as she tugged again with her other arm to move further onto the log. "Pull me up," she demanded, "If I fall I am taking you with me."

163

"I would not be so sure about that," I replied gesturing to the back of her hand that gripped mine. She followed my gaze and I saw her eyes widen in horror as she noticed the yellow tuft at the end of the poisoned dart.

"Pull it out, please," she gasped. "I will let the girl live, I will do whatever you want but please get it out of me."

Already I could feel the grip on my hand loosen, but I held on tight to hers to let the poison do its work. It felt good to give the evil bitch a taste of her own medicine. I thought back to all those men who had died not far away on the shore of this same river, not to mention the two maids and countless others I did not know about. I have felt pity for many of the people I have killed, but as Malala wailed and begged for her life, I did not feel a shred of remorse. For I knew one thing: if she lived after this, I would be a dead man. Eventually as her arm began to shake I released it. The trembling was now spreading to the rest of her body. The venom had done its work and we both knew it. Her left hand, though, still remained clenched around the first vine that she had grasped and showed no sign of slackening. I sat up and pulled the knife from my sleeve. Her mouth opened and shut and a rasping croak came from her lips, but she said no more as the steel began to cut through the plant stem. It was time to bring this to a close. The last strands parted and with a gurgling cry Malala disappeared from view. I expected to hear a splash as she hit the water but there was nothing. Instead I heard creaking from the vine further along the trunk and realised that Malala had somehow managed to hang on with her good hand. I did not dare lean out to look, but now I also heard shouting from Jasmina, who had seen her enemy dangling over the water.

The dart must have lost some of its venom when it was fired into the log. I was surprised that she had been able to maintain her grip and began to wonder if the poison would wear off. The thought of a murderous Malala climbing back up the vine filled me with horror. I began to edge further along, back to the thicker end of the log, where the other end of the vine she was clinging to twitched and moved with the strain of her weight. I could not see Malala, which perhaps made things easier as I started to cut the strands again with my knife.

"I don't want to keep you hanging around," I muttered as I kept a wary eye out for a clawing hand climbing back up. Then, with a twang, the creeper parted. This time there was a splash. Taking a grip on other firmly anchored vines, I risked leaning out a little to look into the river below. Malala was flailing around in the brown flowing water, but she was not alone. A scaly snout surfaced, its jaws opening like a giant trap but before it could get a good grip, something unseen pulled her violently below the surface. A second later the only sign of Malala's existence was a slowly widening circle of ripples.

Chapter 20

My limbs were shaking almost as much as Malala's had been as I climbed back down the tree stump to where Jasmina was waiting. It was probably delayed shock from yet another close shave with death.

"I am getting too old for this," I said as I dropped the last two feet onto the soft earth.

"You were wonderful fighting her like that," gushed Jasmina as she threw her arms about me. "I knew you would not let her kill me."

"Did you now, well that is youthful optimism over experience if ever I heard it. I say, where is the guide?"

"He ran off when he saw her hanging from the creeper. Did you see her fall? There were two crocodiles fighting over the body; they will have torn her to pieces."

Even though she would probably have killed me in the end given the chance, I could not quite share Jasmina's delight at Malala's death – if it had not been for the interpreter I would still be in prison – but then it was not my maids who had been poisoned. Perhaps I was also mindful that we still had to cross the log bridge, over those same hungry reptiles. I looked around but could see no sign of the guide fleeing through the trees. I wondered if he had taken Malala's bag with him, but then saw it was still resting near the bottom of the tree. I peered inside and gave a low whistle. It was full of gold ornaments, bracelets, a cup and, wrapped in a leather pouch, was a large gold-mounted sapphire, almost as big as the ones worn by the king. It was a handsome haul. Leaning against the trunk was the translator's staff of office with its ornate gold top. I picked it up wondering if I could pull off the metal. After a couple of tugs, I found that it twisted off easily. I was on the verge of dropping the staff when I saw that it was hollow and there was something inside.

"Look at this," I said tipping the contents onto the muddy bank. There were two glass phials, one empty and the other half full of a cloudy liquid. Glinting in the mud was also a silver needle. I picked it up carefully and saw that it was hollow with a widened top like a funnel. "This is how she poisoned your maids," I said. I broke the phials with the staff and pushed the pieces and the needle deep into the mud. "We had better get going. Without the guide, we will head south and find out where we are when we reach the coast."

With the heavy satchel around my neck, I felt even more vulnerable as I edged out over the log bridge again. I only walked for the first few paces and then dropped to my hands and knees before finishing the crossing shuffling forward astride the log. Jasmina followed on behind with a bundle of provisions around her neck. I helped her down and we swiftly found a trail on the other side of the river, which headed off in roughly the right direction. The guide had taken the machete and it would have taken too long to hack a new path through the thick jungle with the small knife I now had stuck in my belt. We had no choice but to follow the existing trails and hope that they did not lead us into an Ashanti patrol, for as we drew closer to the coast and the castle, we also ran a greater risk of coming across our enemies.

For two days we trudged through an endless jungle. For much of that time we endured torrential rain. I could not help but notice that when soaked through, Jasmina's robes stuck to her in all the right places. She had not been bedded by the king and I wondered idly if she had ever been with a man. Perhaps because I was still feeling protective of her, I did not try to remedy that situation. It might also have been because we were close to exhaustion. We were now having to ration out the last of the boiled yam and the constant showers turned the paths to thick, sucking mud that made every step an effort. We had previously tried to light a fire at night during our journey, not for the heat, but for the light and to keep animals at bay. I spent half an hour that first evening we were alone with a steel and flint trying to start a fire from some shavings I had scored from the middle of an old log. Despite trying to shield the kindling, raindrops soaked my effort. I gave up and we slept huddled together in the dark.

Towards the end of the second day the trail started to widen and then in the distance we heard the unmistakable sound of voices. I had taken to keeping my robe and veil stuffed into the satchel, but now I hauled them out and put them on. Earlier in our journey, one of the maids had sewn a strip to the bottom of mine so that at least now my boots were hidden. We had come so far and were now so close to our goal, that it was unthinkable that we would be stopped. Cautiously we moved slowly forward until our path emerged onto a much wider track, almost a road, and from the muddy footprints in both directions, it was a well-travelled one. It ran almost exactly north to south and so we turned south, towards the sea. We had only been walking an hour when we caught up with the voices we had heard earlier. It was a trading caravan, a mixture of Arab and African traders, along with a dozen slaves carrying bundles of goods for sale. We held back, walking a quarter of a mile behind them and they took no notice of us. At dusk they pulled up at the side of the road to make a camp and we had to decide whether to stop too or press on. We were both light-headed from hunger and had already eaten the last of the yam so when I saw that they had managed to light a fire, my mind was made up.

I sat at the edge of the road and opened the satchel. Inside was a small gold chain. I cut it in half with the knife – it would not do to show the traders too much wealth. Then with some thread from one of the gowns I fashioned a necklace and put it around Jasmina's neck.

"Go to one of the Arabs and see if you can barter this necklace for some food," I told her. "Try to drive a hard bargain so that they do not suspect we have more. They would probably kill us both for what is in this satchel."

She laughed. "An Englishman does not need to teach an Arab to haggle, we are gifted with this skill from birth." She headed off a little unsteadily down the track. I watched anxiously, wondering what we would do if they refused or worse, held her captive. I needn't have worried, though, for five minutes later she was back with some fruit she had got for nothing.

"We are on the road from Coomassie to the Dutch port of Elmina," she told me. "We are invited to their camp and for two links of the gold they will give us bowls of meat stew, but it will not be ready for an hour."

I grinned with relief. Elmina was just seven miles up the coast from Cape Coast Castle. The Dutch, though, did a lot of trade with the Ashanti and I doubted they would help us, but I knew there had to be a way to get to the castle from there. "I can't go into their camp," I said. "They would soon realise I'm not an Arab woman if I do."

"I have told them that you are deaf, said Jasmina brightly. "So ignore their questions and just sit quietly, you will be fine."

So it was that just over an hour later I was in the traders' camp. There were several fires; most of the men sat around one and all of the women around another. To my horror I saw that the Arab women removed their veils to eat. Jasmina had already removed hers and one of our hosts gestured for me to remove mine. I shook my head and shot a mute look of appeal to my companion for assistance. She said something to the others, but whether she claimed I was horribly disfigured or just shy I could not say. Whatever, they were satisfied with the explanation although one or two looked at me curiously as I shovelled food behind the veil and into my mouth. It was good to feel full again.

We stayed with that caravan for the next two days and as it happened it was a good job we did. But it was a struggle not to show that I could hear. Twice when I looked up as people called out, I caught a woman with a red headscarf looking at me curiously, but she did not say anything. When we were back on the road we passed several groups of travellers heading inland. Then early on the afternoon of the second day we saw a group of men blocking our path. There must have been at least fifty of them, all well-armed; they looked to me like Ashanti soldiers. I started to hang back but the woman in the red scarf shouted at me. When I looked up she smiled, by then she must have known full well that I was not deaf and she clearly suspected that we were on the run. She gestured for us to come forward and pushed us into the middle of the group of women. We stood nervously, hiding in the centre of the crowd as two of the leaders went forward to talk with the Ashanti. Knowing the way of things, I saw that they had taken gifts to smooth our passage. After a couple of minutes, the soldiers stood aside and the caravan moved on. Once more I breathed a sigh of relief and wondered how many more obstacles there might be left between us and our goal.

I'll swear I smelt it, before we saw it. There was a definite tang in the air just before dusk. Then as we rounded a bend a cheer rang out from the men in front. I ran forward to where they were standing. In front of us was a town with another large castle but beyond that was the sea. It was a joyous sight, like liquid gold in the setting sun. I reached around and hugged Jasmina and there may even have been a tear in my eye as I gazed along the shore.

"Elmina," said the woman with the red scarf behind me. "Dutch," she added pointing at the town. Then giving me a shrewd look, she pointed east and added, "British." The jungle obscured any view of the British settlement, but I knew it was little more than a couple of hours' walk along the beach. The woman had started talking Arabic to Jasmina, who explained that we would have to wait a little bit longer.

"The Ashanti are on the shore between here and Cape Coast Castle," she warned. "They have the British surrounded. There are also many of them in Elmina and if they discover we are there, the Dutch may hand us over. But this lady says we can hire a fisherman in Elmina to take us around them."

I wondered if I was about to jump from the frying pan into the fire. It sounded like Cape Coast Castle was already under siege and I did not fancy our chances of fighting off thousands of Ashanti. But what was the alternative? I could hardly stay dressed as a maid in Elmina. At least one woman had already seen through my disguise. Staying in the town, it would only be a matter of time before I was discovered. I could not bear the thought of being taken back to Coomassie and whatever fate awaited me there. At least at Cape Coast Castle I could get rid of the wretched gown and veil and if there was a God in heaven, there might also be a ship in the bay to carry me home.

Chapter 21

To get into the town of Elmina, you had to cross a bridge over a river by its castle. It stands on a little promontory out to sea. As we walked over the rough-hewn planks, I eagerly looked to my left, down the coast. My veil hid a beaming smile as I saw anchored just off Cape Coast Castle, not one but several ships. My heart soared; salvation was at hand. We spent that night in one of the traders' warehouses, but I barely slept. I was burning with impatience to complete the final stage of our journey. Then at first light the lady in the red scarf took us down to the river mouth and found us a boatman who could be trusted. She hugged us both and we climbed down into the canoe, which was soon being skilfully paddled out through the waves.

"The woman said you should keep your veil on until we are sure you are safe," shouted Jasmina over the sound of the surf. "The Ashanti will have spies and agents in the town and possibly in Cape Coast Castle itself."

"One more hour won't be a hardship," I yelled back. "Then I might burn the bloody thing."

"I doubt my father would approve of me doing the same," Jasmina laughed and then she reached forward in the canoe to grip my hand. "Thank you, Thomas," she said. I could see that her eyes above the veil were brimming with tears. "I would never have made it without you."

"Come now, I could not have made it without you either. I would have looked damned odd in this rig by myself and that caravan would probably have set the dogs on me rather than helped."

"But you risked your life to kill Malala and save me. I owe you a great debt."

Veils can be damn useful after all, for they hid a smile of surprise at that remark. Yes, I had been feeling protective of the girl, but there was more than a shred of self-interest involved when I tried to pitch Malala off that log. It was only a matter of time before the translator would have tried to kill me too. Jasmina knew nothing of the dart that the translator had threatened me with and I thought it better that she remain in ignorance. In fact, I spent a moment wondering just how indebted she might feel she was.

The fisherman soon had a sail up and the canoe fairly skidded over the water until we were coming up fast on the beach by the British settlement. He was not landing in the town but on the beach just outside, I did not care as there were no Ashanti in sight. Soon came the welcome hiss of the wooden bottom of the boat on sand. We jumped out onto the shore and just hugged each other as our captain used a paddle to get the boat turned back into the waves. Against all the odds we had made it, we had only flaming well escaped! We had done what had seemed utterly impossible during those weeks I was held in a cell in Coomassie. Breaking out of what was probably the tightest palace in Africa, evading the whole Ashanti army and killing a ruthless agent to boot. As Jasmina dropped to her knees to offer a silent prayer of thanks to her god and perhaps for the souls of her maids, I did not know whether to laugh or cry with relief and came close to both. I looked up and saw the mud brick wall that marked the edge of town just twenty yards away. I remembered too well walking up to the identical wall on the opposite side of the settlement all those months ago. As we held hands and strolled towards the gate now I recalled how Ensign Wetherell had welcomed me on my previous visit. Then, unbidden, came the memory of his severed head on the upturned trough.

Instead of soldiers, two sailors appeared in the gateway as we approached. They ran their eyes over us and then one turned to the other and said, "I don't fancy yours much. That tall one is a right ugly munter. I'll take my chances with the pretty young one."

Jasmina burst out laughing but I was less impressed.

"'Ere, that girl understands English," said the other sailor.

"So does the ugly munter, damn your eyes," I growled. I took off my veil and had the satisfaction of watching their jaws drop in astonishment as my bearded features were revealed. "Major Thomas Flashman," I announced, resuming my former military rank. "Now I would be obliged if you would let us through so that I can report to whoever is in charge."

172

With a final embrace, we parted once we were through the gate. Jasmina running to the town surrounding the fort to look for her father, while I headed to the gate of the castle. A bearded white man wearing a woman's gown brought me more than a few enquiring stares, but I did not give a fig about that, for I was finally safe. I must have been striding with an air of authority – the goggling sentries did not attempt to stop me – and soon I was in the main courtyard. I glanced across to where I had seen Eliza giving her lessons, it must have been at least six months before, but there was no sign of her. I had just climbed some steps to the officers' quarters when I was finally intercepted.

"You, sir, what is your business here?" A captain was standing in a doorway. He was so cadaverously thin, that it took me a second to recognise him, but when I did I beamed with delight.

"Rickets, what kind of welcome is that to an old comrade? The last time I saw you, I was plugging someone running at your back with my Collier and now you treat me like the town tramp."

"Flashman?" he gasped and he took an unsteady step back as though I had punched him in the gut. "But we thought you were dead."

"I damn nearly was on several occasions," I told him, enjoying the look of astonishment on his face. "You must forgive my attire, I have recently been disguised as a veiled Arab woman as we passed through Ashanti patrols hidden as part of a trading caravan." If I had told him I had passed through the jungle as the back end of a pantomime horse I doubt he would have looked more astonished, for he just goggled at me speechless.

"But… but where have you been?" he stammered. "The battle was four months ago."

"I was taken prisoner along with Mr Williams, although he was wounded in the leg and when I last saw him it did not look like he would survive their medical ministrations."

This explanation only left Rickets more dumbfounded. "But Williams is here. He was returned to the Dutch at Elmina a couple of months ago, naked and bound. He has written a report of his captivity, but he did not mention you."

Now it was my time to be surprised. "Damn the man, is he here? Can I see him?" Rickets led the way along a veranda. As we went I stripped off my Arab gown to reveal the tattered garments I wore underneath.

I was shown into a room with an old bearded man lying on a bed, that I only just recognised as the secretary. He had evidently endured a tougher ordeal in captivity than I, not that I felt too sorry for him at that moment. "Williams, why did you not tell them that I was a prisoner with you?" I pointed to my bare arm, "Do you not remember me tying this sleeve around your wounded leg or helping you walk all the way to Assamacow?"

By way of response, poor Williams gave a start of surprise and then fainted clean away. When he came around again, he explained that he had been delirious for much of his captivity and could not remember what was real and what was not.

"I thought you were some kind of guardian angel," he admitted sheepishly. "You weren't there when I recovered. I was half out of my mind back then, I used to have long conversations with those severed heads and in my imagination, they answered me and talked amongst themselves."

Well it was the first time I had been confused with an angel. "They did not argue about their favourite cheese, did they?" I asked idly, but seeing a mystified expression on his face, I went on. "They took me away while they were trying to get that ball out of your leg." I turned to Rickets, "They tied ropes to either side of the wound and tried to squeeze that and the pus out."

The captain went green at the thought, but Williams spoke up. "I don't know how, but they did get the ball out and the wound is now healing well."

"Did you hear anything about a new Ashanti king?" asked Rickets. "We have had rumours that the old king has died and a brother of his has taken the throne."

"I have done more than hear about him. I have met him and was his prisoner in Coomassie for two months before I escaped."

"You have been to their capital and escaped all the way back here?" repeated Rickets, fresh astonishment crossing his features. "But how?"

I laughed, "Who is the governor here now? Perhaps we should go and find him so that I only have to tell this tale once."

I discovered that the acting governor was still Major Chisholm and I was soon shown up to the study where I had first met McCarthy. On the way Rickets explained that he had escaped the battle running after King Dinkera, but he could not keep up in the jungle. He and a warrior had hidden up as the Ashanti search parties roamed about after them and during this time he had come down with a bad dose of fever. Chisholm's part of the army had found him days later being cared for in a village and close to death.

The major himself was in no great shakes when I finally met him. He was reclining on a day bed and occasionally shivering despite being wrapped in a blanket.

"No, don't get up," I said as I saw him struggle to rise. Is everyone in this fort ill, then?" I asked.

After expressing surprise at my miraculous return from the dead, Chisholm explained that of the three hundred and sixteen men then in the garrison, no less than a hundred and four were listed as sick.

"Things would not normally be this bad," added Rickets, "but for damned Sutherland."

"Captain," reprimanded Chisholm, "there is no need for that in front of *Mr* Flashman."

Rickets stuck his chin stubbornly out. "Major Flashman is ex-army and he deserves to know what is going on. He saved my life at Nsamankow and this affects him too."

I was already feeling more than a qualm of disquiet and this only grew as I was then told of the involvement of Lieutenant Colonel William Sutherland. He was a ruthlessly ambitious officer who had been sent to West Africa to take charge of military affairs after the death of McCarthy. He had arrived at Cape Coast Castle with a new surgeon, a quartermaster and forty men. He had assumed command of the army and on hearing that an Ashanti force had been spotted some ten miles away, he ordered an attack by the entire garrison. Then to the disgust of his new officers, he ordered Chisholm off his sickbed to lead the assault. Sutherland was taking no chances of suffering the fate of his predecessor: he sailed back to the safety of Sierra Leone the very next day.

"I warned him that this would leave the castle undefended and that we had no idea of the size of this enemy force, but he would not listen," complained Chisholm. "We hacked through jungle paths for a week before we encountered the Ashanti. We had five hundred Fantee warriors with us too, but they ran on hearing the first shots, taking a number of our militia with them. We fought a running battle for five hours. I have no idea how strong the enemy was as we only had fleeting glimpses of men running between the trees, but eventually they retreated, taking their dead and wounded with them. We only lost four men killed and twenty-one wounded in the battle, but by the time we got back to the castle around a third of the command were unfit for duty."

"That is not the worst of it," added Rickets. "We have seen a copy of a despatch that Sutherland sent to Lord Bathurst in London. In it, he claims that under his command, we beat a force of ten thousand Ashanti." He gave a snort of disgust. "We know all too well the outcome if an army of that size meets a small British force. He is just trying to prove he is better than McCarthy. We hear that he is pressing his friends in London to find him another appointment before he is proved wrong."

"More worryingly," added Chisholm, "if London think we can beat ten thousand Ashanti with just a few hundred men, then we will get precious few reinforcements above what we have now." He gave a heavy sigh, "We have no idea what size force they might attack us with."

It was a depressing picture and while at last I thought I had some information to add to the discussion, I did not think it would lighten the mood. I shared it nonetheless. "One of the king's most trusted advisors, a woman called Malala, told me that the Ashanti would send around fifteen thousand against us."

There was a silence in the room as the other two officers considered the almost inevitable outcome of such an imbalance of forces. Then Rickets' brow furrowed. "Malala," he repeated. "Wasn't she the translator that King Appea used? He is convinced that she had betrayed us all to the Ashanti and he now blames himself for McCarthy's death."

"The poor devil insisted on accompanying me when Sutherland ordered us into the jungle," added Chisholm gloomily. "Now he is down with the fever too. His men and those of Dinkera, are the only reliable native troops we have. Heaven help us if he dies and they go home."

"Well in that case he will be pleased to learn that she was torn apart by crocodiles in a river a week's walk from here. I saw her die myself." I remembered something then, and suddenly I saw grounds for hope. "But I don't think they will attack yet. When I was here before, people told me that the fever comes with the rains. The worst of the fever season is in August: that is when they will attack."

"Why will they wait?" asked Chisholm.

"Because they saw my Collier pistol and I convinced them that all British soldiers are being equipped with Collier-style muskets and rifles. I also told them that we have similar devices on our artillery that will send down an endless stream of shells into their forces. So, you have longer to prepare or," I added hopefully, "abandon the territory."

"But why will all these imaginary weapons make them attack in August?" repeated Chisholm. "Are they hoping that we will all be down with fever?"

"Partly that," I admitted. "But all these weapons rely on dry gunpowder and they are planning to come when the rain is at its worst as then our powder will be wet."

Chisholm and Rickets exchanged a glance and I had a nasty ominous feeling. "August is the worst month for fever because of the damp mists," said Chisholm at last. The worst month for rainfall is normally June."

I had lost track of the seasons during my captivity and time on the road, "What... er... is today's date?" I asked hesitantly.

"Sunday the sixth of June," said Rickets quietly as, with perfect timing, there was a crash of thunder and some raindrops splashed onto the windowsill.

Chapter 22

In the circumstances, the two officers took my unwitting part in their imminent destruction quite well. There was no sobbing, wailing or biting at the rug, which might have been the result if the situation had been reversed. They just sat there calmly as though fifteen thousand angry Ashanti about to attack, behead and possibly eviscerate them was not the worst news they had heard that day.

The only thing that kept *me* from chewing on the carpet was the thought of those vessels in the bay. "What is happening with those ships at anchor off-shore?" I asked. "Surely the sensible course of action is to try to evacuate the garrison?"

Perhaps mindful of McCarthy's previous promises to find me a berth on the first available ship, Chisholm was quick to dash any hopes of escape. "Sutherland has ordered them all to stay here until the danger is passed. Most of the crews are already ashore to help with the defence as are many of their guns."

I felt nauseous for a moment as the implications of those words settled in. There was a grim inevitability to it, really. When in my entire career of dangers and disasters had I ever been given the opportunity to duck quietly out of the way at the critical moment? Despite everything I had been through, it seemed that I would have to face another Ashanti attack, with the odds of success pretty much the same as McCarthy's last stand. The only comfort was that the ships were there at all. There would be an unavoidable fall back to the beach and the boats once the fortress was stormed and some would get away. I was going to make damn sure I was one of them, for my destiny if I fell back into the hands of the Ashanti king did not bear thinking about. I looked up and saw Chisholm and Rickets watching me closely as realisation of my fate sank in. I knew that the gallant hero I was supposed to be would be ready with some offhand response. "Well that is just as well, really," I managed to say. "I always get seasick at the start of a sea voyage."

"That is the spirit," said Rickets patting me on the back. "I will be proud to fight again alongside you, sir."

Before I could say more the door to the room banged open and a small boy entered. I recognised him as McCarthy's son. "Hullo, young shaver," I greeted him with forced cheeriness. "What are you doing here?"

Despite the beard he must have recognised me as he pointed at my waist and shouted, "Gun."

"I can't show you my gun today," I told him. "The Ashanti king has taken it." I turned to Chisholm, "What is going to happen to McCarthy's wife and son?"

The major glanced at the boy, who had now run off to play with a wooden carved animal on the floor in the corner of the room. "His mother is ill with the fever. I am letting them stay here so there is no need to disturb them." He rolled his eyes towards the still open door and added, "This morning my orderly is supposed to be looking after the boy." I had a sudden memory of the severed head of the boy's father and wondered what the son's fate would be if he was not able to escape in the coming battle.

"Jaysus, Mary and the fecking Holy Ghost, I thought ye were dead." I turned and there was O'Hara, standing a little unsteadily in the doorway with another wooden toy in his hand. He shook his head as though he could not quite believe what he was seeing and then stared at me again. "How the blazes are ye here?" he demanded before taking in the others in the room and belatedly bringing himself to attention and adding, "Sor."

"It's good to see you too, O'Hara," I grinned at him and noticed that somehow, he had managed to recover his sergeant's stripes. "The Ashanti king got bored of my company and so I decided to leave." I nodded at the boy and added, "I see you are as good at being a nursery maid as you are an orderly. Your charge has escaped."

Before he could reply the boy ran to him and hugged his leg shouting, "Paddy Ginty, Paddy Ginty!"

O'Hara gave a rueful grin back and explained, "I have been singing *Paddy McGinty's Goat* for him, the clean version," he added hastily glancing at Chisholm. He turned back to me, "Am I to be *your* orderly again, sir," he asked with a note of hope in his voice.

"I think you will have to serve us both," answered Chisholm. The major turned to me, "There is still a chest of McCarthy's clothes here that you can borrow from and there is a spare razor you can use. I am sure that Mrs McCarthy would not mind."

An hour later and I was looking quite respectable. O'Hara had offered to shave me, but having seen how his hands shook, I did it myself. He cut my hair, though, and found me some decent clothes from McCarthy's chest. The boy had been passed to a kitchen maid to look after and had bawled at being parted from the Irishman.

"He seems fond of you," I said.

"Ah he is no bother. When the maids cannot watch him, I put four drops of tonic into his glass of goat's milk and he sleeps like a log through the night. Would ye like a wee nip?" He held out the huge silver flask.

"God no, I am surprised you have not killed the child, giving him that."

"It's safer than water," insisted O'Hara sounding offended. You go and look in the rainwater tanks on the roof," he said. "They are full of green slime and all sorts of wriggling little creatures. I can't be drinking that, and neither should you. Not unless you put some tonic in it to kill the bugs."

"Where were you when we were attacked?" I asked.

"I was with Chisholm. We did not know anything about them bastards attacking you until the day after your battle. McCarthy's first messenger had got lost and arrived with the second one that day. The major was in a fever to get to you, but we had to cross two rivers with only one canoe. Most of us swam across, but we had to keep the muskets dry and some could not swim. It took forever with that bloody boat going backwards and forwards. Then we got word that Cap'n Rickets was lying ill in a nearby village. That was when we discovered that we were too late. The major thought that the Ashanti would attack the castle straight away and so we rushed back. Hardly anyone returned from McCarthy's column; only King Dinkera came back with a group of survivors."

"What about this Colonel Sutherland?" I asked, knowing that O'Hara would not be as diplomatic as Chisholm.

"He is more dangerous than the bloody Ashanti!" exclaimed the Irishman. "He has no clue what he is doin' but he does not let that stop him giving orders. He is also determined not to get his own hands dirty with any actual fighting. He damn nearly killed all of us, sending us out like that when we had no idea what we would be facing. He left the castle defenceless."

We were interrupted by a knock at the door. A bemused sentry appeared to ask if I could go down to the main gate where a big Arab gentleman was insisting on seeing me. I pulled on one of McCarthy's waistcoats and followed the sentry through the castle. As I approached the gatehouse I saw Jasmina standing beside a man I presumed was her father. As she pointed me out he started wailing and throwing his arms about and actually prostrated himself on the ground in front of me.

"He is pleased to have you back, then?" I asked Jasmina with a wry grin.

She winced with embarrassment as her pater pounded the dirt at my feet and continued to shout and wail. "He says that you have done him the greatest service a man could do and he will forever be in your debt," she shouted over his din.

I reached down and started to pull the old man back to his feet, he was causing a scene. He must have brought half the town with him on his way up to the castle and they were all standing around and watching curiously. "Tell him that I am in your debt too and that we helped each other," I told her. She smiled at me and I realised that now she was home again she was no longer wearing the veil with her Arab scarf. She passed on my reply, yet this only resulted in more wailing until she reached forward and kissed me firmly on the lips. "My father is not the only one indebted to you," she whispered. There was a scandalised murmur from the watching crowd, but she did not care. She took the arm of her father, who had at least been shocked into silence, and turned him back towards the village. I watched her lithe body move under her gown and realised that I had perhaps misjudged my feelings for her after all.

Chapter 23

I spent the next two weeks helping the garrison prepare for the expected onslaught. Despite reinforcements from the crews of the ships offshore, it was backbreaking work and no one could be spared. We all knew that the Ashanti could arrive at any time and that every ounce of effort now could be critical in delaying them. Many of the soldiers and sailors were confident that we could stop their army, but then they had not been with McCarthy. I knew that the Ashanti weren't just well armed and would arrive in huge numbers; they were also likely to be well organised. They had used diversionary attacks to distract us at Nsamankow from their larger flanking forces and I did not doubt that they would assault us on several fronts at the castle. My main fear was that they would send an army along the beach to cut us off from the ships.

Each morning would begin with a funeral service for those who had died the day before. Around half of those who caught the fever died from it and the rest resumed light duties, looking pitifully thin and weak.

Of those that were fit and able, none were excused. O'Hara and I soon found ourselves put to work preparing the defences. On the highest hill nearby was a large mudbrick tower that served as an observation post. But the sailors soon made it much taller by building a wooden tripod on the top, secured with stay ropes and with a rope ladder to a platform at the summit like a fighting top on a mast. They armed it with swivel guns and swore that on a clear day they could see for over twenty miles. Most of that was thick jungle, however, so unless the Ashanti started to chop down trees to make roads for the handful of cannon I had seen at Coomassie, they might still approach unobserved. But if they built any cooking fires then the rising smoke would soon give away their position.

Two new mudbrick forts were being built on the outskirts of town. I spent most of my time with the one on our right, on a hill top named for McCarthy. There was no time to properly dry the bricks, but I knew from experience that wet mud was far better at absorbing shot than brittle, dry clay. When I was not helping to make mud bricks, I was wielding an axe and chopping down trees and brush to give the fort a clear field of fire. The timber was then used to provide supports that the mud bricks were built against or to make temporary roofs to stop our work being washed away in the torrential rain. There was a downpour at least every other day and sometimes for several days in a row. A huge trench had been dug around the fort to excavate the mud, but this quickly turned into a moat. More pits were dug nearby but each time they filled with water as the ground was now almost entirely waterlogged.

At the end of each day an army of brown men, caked in mud from head to foot, would stagger wearily down to the beach. We would leave our tools on the sand and wade into the sea to wash the stinking ooze off our bodies and clothes, emerging as different people once more: white, black, soldiers, sailors and civilians, but all of us exhausted from our labour.

O'Hara was right about the water. From my time on board various ships I was used to the greenish tinge, but when I poured some into a glass I saw that it was alive with tiny wriggling creatures. The Irishman had supplied me with a small jug of his tonic. When I poured a splash into the glass I watched the little critters in it slowly die. After half an hour they had all sunk to the bottom. Despite its dilution, the tonic still had a considerable kick to it. It reminded me of its effect during my preaching down the coast. One evening I asked O'Hara if he had any news of Eliza. I had been looking out for her as we walked through the village to and from our work and in the castle where she had taught, but there was no sign of her. I had feared that she had died of the fever, but instead it turned out it was the reverend who was ill.

"She is nursing her husband," O'Hara said. "I have seen Bessie a few times and she tells me it is bad. He has been ill for weeks; it is over a month since you Protestants gathered in your church." I felt a pang of sadness for Eliza. Often those that nursed the sick got ill themselves and from the sound of things old Bracegirdle was fighting the fever hard. It was probably not his first dose. Those that had suffered it before recovered more often that those catching it for the first time. I wondered if she knew I was back, but I realised that she could hardly abandon her saintly husband's sickbed and rush to see me without creating scandal in the tightknit community around the fort.

On the first Wednesday after I returned, I received a note from Chisholm asking me to call on Appea. The major had relayed to the king details of Malala's death, but the African had wanted to hear the story first hand from someone who was there. So that morning instead of heading out to the quagmire, I tooled along to the king's room. He was there with several of his courtiers and it was immediately apparent to me that he was not long for this world. The room stank of vomit and worse, and several of his servants had cloths tied around their faces. I made a point of going no closer than the foot of the bed. On seeing me the king summoned a smile and whispered the word, "Champion," while pointing weakly in my direction. Then he gestured in the corner of the room and repeated the word. Looking around I saw Hercules, his own giant champion, regarding me impassively from a face not protected by a kerchief.

"The king wishes to hear about the death of Malala," a wizened old man requested in English. So I slowly told him the tale, much as I have described it here. How I tricked the spy with tales of fictional weapons, then persuaded her to help me escape with promises of foreign travel. The king beamed with delight at the news of his nemesis being bested, but when I glanced over my shoulder his champion looked singularly unimpressed. I was sure he thought I was telling stretchers. But when I explained how she had poisoned the maids, Hercules did react. He babbled excitedly in his language to the king and was most agitated. Eventually the translator explained that one of the guards detailed to protect Malala had died in a similar manner. They now suspected that this guard had discovered her treachery and been killed for it. I told them about the tools that we had found hidden in her staff. While she did not have a staff when she served Appea, there was little doubt that she had her instruments of death on her person somewhere.

"But tell the king how she died," persisted the translator. "The king wishes to know if she suffered."

So I told him about the blowpipe on the log and how I unbalanced her and stabbed her with her own dart. They chuckled darkly at that and then again as I described cutting the creeper. I had seen little of her fall into the water, but I knew what my audience wanted and so I relayed – with some embellishments – what Jasmina had seen.

"She fell into the jaws of two crocodiles. There were horrible screams as they bit into her and tussled between them for the prize. The river turned red with her blood and she went under the water twice, still gripped by their teeth. The larger crocodile tore her free, leaving a leg in the mouth of the other. Then they both disappeared beneath the water and were not seen again."

The king beamed with delight at this graphic description. I had clearly given him the news that he wanted. "The king says he would give the last days of his life to have been there to witness her death. He will die knowing that this treachery has been avenged and that the British know him to be a loyal friend," the translator told me.

That evening when I returned to my quarters from another afternoon of shovelling mud, I found, lying on my bed, a sword covered in gold. It was a generous gift and must have come from Appea as it was identical to those I had seen carried by his captains months before. I realised as I held it, that it was in fact made of steel, but with a thin sheet of gold along the blade almost up to the edge. The handle, which was engraved with swirling patterns, was also covered in gold. It was a well-balanced weapon, with a leather scabbard that hung over the shoulder.

We finished Fort McCarthy the next day. The men had been working on it long before I arrived, but it was not a thing of beauty. A squat round tower only two storeys high, built on the top of a hill. Three cannon had been hoisted onto the top by sailors using spars and ropes. A thin roof of large leaves and grasses was being placed on a high wooden frame covering the platform. This was not to provide shade for the gunners, but to stop the rains from weakening the mud walls. There was even a thick hawser tied around the top of the tower to stop it falling apart. Despite its appearance, however, I thought that it would be a formidable obstacle. On three sides it was surrounded by a wide moat of liquid mud that had been dug out in its construction. The hill it stood on had been cleared of all vegetation and cover. We could all vouch that the wet mud made it extremely slippery. The Ashanti would not cover the ground quickly and would have no protection from the cannon at the top firing grape shot at them. With the ships in the bay, there was now no shortage of powder and ammunition. The ground floor of the tower had been filled as a magazine. It was a safe place as there was no door to the tower on the ground floor, just a hatch from the roof. To get in you had to climb a wooden ladder up the side and then drop down.

As I stood back to admire our handiwork, Chisholm came up to stand alongside. Like me he was covered in mud. He and Rickets were both weak from their recent sickness, but they always made a point of helping out with the construction. I doubt they did much actual labour – I had seen Chisholm climb the hill to the tower and the poor fellow looked exhausted by the time he had made it to the top.

"Do you have some water, Flashman? I am very dry," he croaked. I passed across my flask and he took a swig. "Ugh," he gasped after swallowing. "That has O'Hara's tonic in it. Foul stuff, but I have to concede that he is right, it does kill the bugs. I just wonder what it does to my insides." He looked up at the tower and added, "Tell me, you have more experience of battles and sieges than I do, what do you make of our defences?"

I stared around. There were three fortifications inland from Cape Coast Castle roughly in a line parallel with the coast. With my back to the sea, Fort McCarthy was on the right; there was a similar construction on the left and in the middle, opposite the castle was the tall observation tower. It was a five hundred-yard run from Fort McCarthy back to Cape Coast Castle, downhill most of the way. "How are you planning to allocate the men?" I asked.

"I was hoping that you would take command here," Chisholm said quietly and I felt my guts tighten in alarm. "I will ask Rickets to command the fort on our left. King Appea speaks highly of you and so I will place his warriors here too, while King Dinkera's men will be with Rickets." I felt a small sense of relief at that, for Appea's men were well organised and more importantly there were around two thousand of them, dwarfing the size of our regular troops. Chisholm continued, "The navy will provide the gun crews and I will keep our regulars in reserve to support whichever side is attacked."

"What if they come through the middle?" I asked. The tall observation tower was our weakest defence.

"Then they will be fired on by both fortresses in the flank and face the full force of the castle guns in the front."

"That seems sensible," I agreed. Then I lowered my voice so that we could not be overheard. "But we should make sure that we have plenty of guns loaded with grape to cover the beach and all the boats should be brought up close to the castle. We can try to hold them here, but if we need to fall back to the castle, we must be sure that they cannot cut us off from the sea." I tried to sound positive but if the Ashanti came in force, I could not see how we would be able to offer anything more than a fighting retreat. When we got down to the sand it would be every man for himself. If I could not get near the boats, at least I was a good swimmer. "I suppose that they will definitely attack?" I wondered aloud. Our position seemed hopeless and I was clutching at straws that might herald our survival. "I mean, McCarthy was sure that the Ashanti did not really want a war with the British."

"I think the fact that they killed him rather disproves his argument," Chisholm countered wryly. "Where I was born they had an expression: If you are going to be hung for stealing a goose, you might as well steal a cow. They have killed the British governor and so they might as well try to drive us out of the country entirely. Anyway," he added looking at me curiously, "you should know their intentions better than me. You have met him; do you think that their king wants war?"

I thought back to my audience at the palace. "They are certainly not frightened of us," I admitted. "They truly believe that their army is stronger than Napoleon's Imperial Guard."

No work was done on the defences on Sundays. Not just for religious reasons, it was more to do with the fact that the men were exhausted after six days' toiling in the mud and needed a day of rest. I had only arrived the previous Sunday, but after a week of hard labour, my muscles ached and almost every part of my body was stiff. I was hoping for a dry day that I could spend resting in a shady spot on the beach and getting thoroughly clean in the sea.

O'Hara was off to work on his still. "I'll soon be having a new batch of the tonic ready, but this won't be as smooth as the last," he warned ominously. I groaned but by then I was getting used to the taste of the vile brew. Its lethal bug-killing properties made it essential in any water that I drank.

After a leisurely breakfast I found a towel and strolled out of the castle. There was still no sight of any Ashanti from the watchtower, although I could not help but wonder if my next Sunday would be quite as relaxed. As I passed the gateway I heard a voice call out my name from the crowd of traders that normally gathered there to sell wares to the soldiers. I turned around and there was Bessie, Eliza's maid. She held out a letter for me. At first, I assumed that it was a note from her mistress, but the spidery writing was from the good Reverend Bracegirdle. It was a very formal invitation to call on them at my convenience. My immediate response was reluctance; I wondered if he had heard of my impersonation of him at the village down the coast. Furthermore, I certainly did not want to spend time with someone suffering from the fever. I was minded to send a message to say I was busy until I read some more words in a feminine hand added at the bottom of the note: *Please do come, Cuthbert is not infectious, E.*

Memories of my time as the Reverend Flashman brought a smile to my face, particularly the hours spent in the guest quarters. If I had to endure a scolding from the priest, it would be a small price to pay to spend time with Eliza again and so I bid the maid to lead the way.

The Bracegirdles occupied a small cottage next door to the whitewashed church. The maid held the door open for me and I stepped into a small hallway with rooms off either side. As soon as the front door was shut behind me, Eliza came out of one of the side rooms and threw her arms around my neck.

"I thought you had been killed," she whispered in my ear as she squeezed me tight. "I have been so worried and we hear that there will be more fighting…"

I stopped listening and just relished the smell of her and the feel of her body against mine as I returned her embrace and then bent down to kiss her.

"Why does your husband want to see me?" I asked.

"He wanted someone to talk to and I suggested you. You must have some tales after your adventures. People say that you met the Ashanti king at Coomassie." At this we heard the old man's voice croak out from one of the side rooms and Eliza took me through.

Bracegirdle had never been stout, but now he looked thinner than ever. I learned that he did not have the fever at all. He was suffering from a growth in his stomach and the new surgeon had told Eliza to prepare for the worst. "The doctor has given me some opium to help me sleep, but he does not have much to spare," wheezed the reverend. "Your orderly has given Bessie some of his tonic for me and if it does not exactly ease the pain, it makes me less mindful of it."

"It is certainly powerful stuff," I agreed, remembering that the first time I had taken a swig of O'Hara's undiluted homemade spirit, it had literally taken my breath away. In Bracegirdle's slender frame, one sip of it would probably leave him drunk and insensible.

"I hear that you have been to their capital and met the Ashanti king," Bracegirdle continued. "I wanted to ask you what we can expect if they come here. Will they attack the Christian settlements that the governor and I have worked to establish? Do they respect gods other than their own?"

"Well I saw plenty of Muslims in Coomassie who were able to practice their faith, but they were there for trade and I think that purpose protected them." I looked down and saw desperate hope in his features. He was a dying man who wanted to believe that his life's work would not be destroyed around him within days of his death.

You could not help but feel some compassion – even if you had not been sleeping with his wife behind his back. I was just working out what lie to tell when Bracegirdle held out his hand for me to hold. It was like grabbing a bundle of leather-covered sticks. "Tell me the truth, lad," he whispered.

I took a deep breath, "Well you would probably know about this better than me, sir, but I hear that when the Ashanti conquered the Fantee lands they rounded up all they could find and took them into slavery. I imagine that they will do the same for the people they find here. Some may be kept as prisoners or hostages against retaliation from the British government, but I doubt London will want to commit the forces needed to defeat the Ashanti and force their return."

Bracegirdle thought about this for a moment. He was probably imagining all the communities of freed slaves he had established along the coast being rounded up and taken away for a second life of bondage. "Their king," he asked at last, "is he a cruel man?" I told them about the target practice with the slaves and Eliza gave a gasp of horror. "That is what I feared," said Bracegirdle and then he turned to his wife. "You must ask Major Chisholm to put you aboard one of the ships now, we cannot risk you falling into their hands."

"No," said Eliza fiercely. "If we must leave, we will go together. I vowed that I would stay until death parted us and I am not going to leave you when you need me the most." She turned to me and I saw that there was a tear in her eye, "Anyway, I hear that the Ashanti army has not even been spotted by our lookouts. It is possible that they may not come at all, isn't it, Thomas?" I agreed that such a thing was possible and then steered the conversation around to the safer topic of my adventures in South America. There at least was the prospect of more slaves being freed.

When I took my leave, Eliza escorted me out to the hall. "I will not leave him," she whispered. She blushed slightly as she looked at me, "I have already broken one marriage vow, but I will not let him die alone. He is a good man and he does not deserve that."

As I left their cottage there was a rumble of thunder and the first drops of another heavy shower began. I ducked into the porch of the little church and found that O'Hara had been wrong. The Protestants had not been deprived of their church, just their minister. The door was unlocked. Judging from the muddy arse-prints on some of the benches, more than a few had been in there to pray for deliverance from the coming onslaught. I found myself wandering down to the front pew

191

and sitting where I had once ogled Eliza playing the organ. I had prayed in the past, usually when I was utterly desperate for help, but as I looked up at the carved wooden cross in that church, I wondered if there was really any point. After all, if the Almighty saw reason to take saintly characters like Bracegirdle and the well-meaning if naïve McCarthy, what chance did I stand of Him listening to a sinner like me? But as the rain thundered down on the wooden roof, I found myself praying anyway. I made all sorts of promises of what I would do if I was spared... and I kept them all too.

Chapter 24

Any doubts we had over the intentions of the Ashanti king were resolved two days later with the arrival of a young white boy. He was not white because he was European, but instead because he had been painted. It had been done as part of a ritual for the Ashanti gods to sanctify him as he was a messenger of the king. He was found by one of our advance guards and brought back to an interpreter to recite a message he had been taught for Chisholm's ears. "You should build the walls of your new castles higher," the boy said, "and land every gun from the ships. You should even arm the fish in the sea, but nothing will stop the king of the Ashanti from throwing every trace of the British into the waves."

He said it in the form of a song, presumably to help him remember the words. It was not a cheery ditty and I would have happily painted some obscenities on his lily-white skin and sent him back where he came from, but Chisholm let him go.

"They clearly have spies among us if they know about our new fortifications," said the major.

I pointed out to sea where a dozen fishing boats could be seen out with nets on the waves around the bay. "A fishing boat from Elmina could easily sail seven miles down the coast and mix with the local fleet. The towers can all be seen from the sea." I was thoughtful for a moment before adding, "But their king's foolish boasting might give us a small advantage. We now know what he knows and so we can anticipate what he will do about it."

"What do you mean?" asked Chisholm.

"Come, I will show you," I replied as I began to put myself in the enemy's shoes.

We spent the next week considering how the enemy would attack and building further defences to thwart them. If the Ashanti tried a frontal attack past the observation tower and straight up to the walls of Cape Coast Castle, they would be attacked on three sides: from the guns of the castle and the new forts on either side of their advance. By now with all the rain, the ground in front of the castle was extremely boggy and it would slow their men down. They would be stuck in the mud and flailed with grape shot. I thought we stood a reasonable chance of stopping any attack like that, but I had already learned that the Ashanti generals were wily devils and I doubted they would be so obliging. It was far more likely that they would assault one or both of the new forts first and whittle away at our defences. So we set to building new gun batteries on either side of the towers. Each had three guns and a roof to keep off the rain, but they were also covered with tree branches and bushes to hide them from the enemy and any passing fisherman until we wanted to reveal them. Then anticipating that the Ashanti might try to go around the forts and attack them from the rear, we built more new batteries nearer the town to cover that approach. Chisholm also put more guns on the beach by the walls that led down to the sea. We had at least taken the Ashanti advice; virtually all of the guns from the ships in the bay were now on shore.

As well as building batteries, I also spent time with Hercules and King Appea's translator to discuss tactics. Appea's men were used to jungle fighting, but not battles over open ground with cannon. I had to explain to him that his men could not charge forward as usual or they would block the fire from our guns. Instead I persuaded him to let the enemy struggle up the muddy hill towards us. They would be tired and slow when they neared the top and easier to kill. We had already cleared a wide expanse of jungle in front of the guns and as an experiment Hercules had a dozen of his fittest warriors race from the jungle edge to the batteries. The gunners estimated that they could get at least three rounds off before the men reached them.

We did not have the time or any translators to train the men to fire ordered volleys. Instead I had to suffice with drawing lines in the mud on either side of the new batteries. Appea's soldiers were ordered not to advance beyond the line until ordered, but to fire at the enemy as soon as they came within range. If this all sounds as though I was being quite diligent and industrious, well I was. I generally am when my own precious hide is at stake. That is not to say that I was foolish enough to think we would win the coming battle. We might slow them down and inflict heavy casualties but, in the end, I suspected that the sheer weight of numbers would win the day for the Ashanti. That was why I made a few additional personal precautions.

Depending on the tide, the area of beach in front of the castle was narrow and rocky. I pictured it full of panic-stricken soldiers, sailors and civilians desperately trying to escape as Ashanti warriors poured into the fort behind them or along the beach. I realised that this would be no place for me. Boats would be overloaded, smashed against the rocks or, if the sea was rough, broached in the surf. Instead, there was a path that led directly to the nearest beach from my tower. I could be there in barely over a minute. All I needed was a boat ready and waiting. That was when I went to see the two fishermen who had taken Eliza and me down the coast to Joshua's village. I had already discovered that they spoke some English and with the aid of a map drawn in the sand, they understood what I wanted. When the Ashanti attacked they would take their boat and anchor it a hundred yards offshore from the path to my tower. I did not want the boat filled with refugees before I reached it and I was fairly sure I could swim that far. In return I would give them the solid gold top from Malala's cane. I showed it to them and their eyes lit up at the sight of such wealth, but I insisted they would not get it until I was safely alongside one of the ships in the bay.

The following Sunday I even had a practice swim out to the boat, which the fishermen had anchored in the place I had instructed. I made the distance easily and was just sitting on one of the thwarts drying out in the sun when the bang of a cannon rang out. Looking around I saw a plume of gun smoke by the observation tower. It was the signal that the enemy had been spotted. I listened for a while for the sound of crackling musketry which would indicate that the Ashanti had somehow got close without us spotting them. If they had, I was probably safer where I was. Instead all I heard was the usual bustle from the shore, the breaking of waves and the shouts of distant fisherman. I could see my fort and while a few of the men around it were staring curiously at the observation tower, there was no indication of alarm. I told the fishermen to row me to the castle jetty and once there I made my way to Chisholm's office. I arrived at the same time as a sweating young naval midshipman who had run down from the observation tower.

"We can see a plume of smoke in the distance, sir. A big thick one, much bigger than a campfire." We all looked out of the window but our view was blocked by the hills and we could see no sign of smoke.

"How far away is it?" asked Chisholm.

"About four leagues nor' nor' west, sir," said the midshipman breathlessly.

Chisholm's brow furrowed in puzzlement and so I enlightened him. "About twelve miles away," I announced, looking down at the map on the table, "and it seems to be coming from near D'Jouquah. Do you think that they are burning the town?"

"It's possible," admitted the major. "Perhaps they want to signal to us that they are on their way." The news that the Ashanti were coming spread quickly through the town. By late afternoon a straggling column of Africans could be seen approaching us from the jungle inland of the castle. Villages there were being abandoned before the enemy army rolled through them, killing and taking prisoners. Others were heading away from the town. Some along the coast west to Elmina where they would seek the protection of the Dutch, who had been friendly with the Ashanti. More were heading east, along the coast into Fantee territory and beyond to get out of the way of the coming attack.

I wandered back up to the tower I was destined to defend. There was a handful of sailors in one of the gun batteries – the rest were still enjoying some rest in town. I saw them whispering and nodding at me as I came up the hill. By now they all knew that I was the officer who had been captured at Nsamankow and one of the few survivors of that awful day.

"Don't you worry, sir," called out one of the gunners. He patted the breach of his gun and added, "When they come, our guns will mow them down like hay." They did not seem to have the slightest concern about the coming conflict, but then they had not faced the Ashanti before.

I did not want to dishearten them and so I forced a smile and replied, "Just make sure you have plenty of powder and ammunition to hand when they do come, for it will be a prodigious harvest." They chuckled at that and then I noticed a score of men moving at the edge of the forest in front of our guns. "Hey, who are they?" I shouted, pointing. I felt the first twitch of alarm: surely the enemy were not here already?

"They are our lads," called back one of the gunners. "That big fella took a couple of 'undred of them into the jungle when 'e 'eard that the 'Shanti were on the way. Look," he pointed at the other side of the tower and I noticed now a pile of long straight sticks. "I reckon they are makin' bleedin' spears, although Christ knows why they want those when they 'ave all got bloody muskets."

"Perhaps they are going to throw them when the Ashanti get close," I wondered. I did not recall the Ashanti using spears at Nsamankow. There had been a few archers, I remembered, but most had muskets, swords or axes. They did not have shields, yet I did not imagine that throwing sticks at them would do much damage. I started to walk down the hill to find Hercules and see what he was about, but I had underestimated just how boggy the ground was. I slipped on my arse twice climbing down the slope below the moat and then when I got down to the valley bottom I found my feet sinking ankle deep into the muddy ooze. "To hell with this," I muttered to myself and turned to go back the way I had come. I would find out what Hercules was about in the morning.

Things were little clearer the next day, not least because it was pouring with rain again when I climbed the hill to the fort. There must have been a hundred of Appea's men industriously working in the downpour, but at what I was not entirely sure. Most of them were cutting the sticks that they had gathered the previous day into two-foot lengths. At first I thought they were making arrows, but then I saw that they were sharpening both ends. The pointed sticks were tied into bundles and one end of them then dipped into a large pail that seemed to contain black tar.

"What on earth is going on?" I asked Hercules when I saw him. Even though the translator was not on hand, he must have guessed what I was asking by the confused look on my face.

"Come," he said and he led the way down the side of the hill. He took a different route to the one I had taken the previous day and as we got to the bottom of the slope I saw that a thin trail of logs and tree trunks had been laid over the mud. Some of them were slippery or partly submerged, but it was still much easier to walk across them than the boggy ground I had slipped on. We headed out across the valley floor. Squinting through the rain I could see more men working at the forest edge. As I got closer I saw they were digging, which seemed a pointless exercise as the ground was sodden and the holes must have filled with water as soon as they were dug. We stepped off the wooden trail and Hercules led me splashing through the mud to the nearest group of workers. Only then did I realise what they were doing.

The holes they were digging were filling with water as I had suspected, but they did not mind a bit. The excavations were only a foot deep and about the same distance square. Into each hole a warrior pushed five of the sticks with the blackened ends pointing upwards. They were pushed down hard into the mud at the bottom of the hole so that the points were submerged. The hole looked no different to the thousands of puddles that now littered the plain but if one of the Ashanti stepped in it, he would be out of the fight. I guessed that the black liquid the stakes had been dipped in was some kind of poison. Appea's warriors had kept several paths marked with taller canes through their field of traps. Men were using them to scatter large leaves and other foliage over the ground to make the traps even harder to spot.

As I stared about I could see that holes were being dug across our entire front; virtually all of Appea's two thousand soldiers were working industriously on the task. I had to admit it was a stroke of genius. Even if they did not kill many of the Ashanti, the traps would force our enemy to advance slowly across the mud, for they would have no idea where the ground would be safe. Our guns would scythe through them as they edged forward. I beamed with delight and reached up to clap Hercules on the shoulder so that he knew I was pleased with what they were doing.

I was soaked to the skin when I got back to the top of the hill. I saw the gunner who had thought that they were making spears the previous evening. With his mates he was standing under the roof of thatch over his guns and staring with barely disguised contempt at the warriors as they cut and shaped their sticks and dipped them in the tar. I went over to them and pointed out to the valley. The rain was still coming down in sheets and it was impossible to see the forest edge from the hill top. "Do you want to know what they are doing with those sticks?" I asked. When I told them, the sailors were delighted.

"They are crafty bleedin' buggers, aren't they, sir," said the gunner, grinning. "That will slow the 'Shanti right down, we will have a field day with them."

"That is if we can bloody see them in this rain," said one of his mates gloomily.

"Well," I said. "As they are helping you and you are all bone dry while I am soaking wet, I think you can come out from under your roof and give them a hand." A couple of the sailors looked resentful at the order, but the rest jumped out handily enough. "But don't touch whatever is in that bucket," I warned. "It smells foul and will not do you any good."

The rain only began to ease off later that afternoon. It reduced to a light shower and from the top of the tower I could now see the full extent of the work of Hercules and his men. They had dug holes in a strip of land fifty yards wide from the jungle near the central observation tower all the way round to our right flank. Judging from the men beetling backwards and forwards down the safe paths into the forest for more wood, they were not stopping yet. A score of gunners sitting in the mud behind me with other warriors were busily turning sticks into sharpened stakes, while we had got through at least half a dozen buckets of the black tar. As I stood on the tower watching, heavy footfalls up the steps behind me heralded the arrival of Hercules and his interpreter.

I asked him how many stakes they were planning to put in and got a reply that the job was half done. A hundred yards of the pit traps would be a daunting obstacle, although if we had a few days of dry weather they might be easier to spot. "Do the traps work well in the rainy season?" I asked.

The translator did not bother to check with his master to answer. "We never normally fight in the rainy season," he said. "The Ashanti have never attacked during the rains before. Nobody fights then."

It was an unwelcome reminder that the timing of their attack was down to my invention of modern weapons, while we were now relying on traps that had probably been used since the beginning of time.

"Do you know why they are attacking during the rains?" asked the translator, who had been watching me closely.

"No idea at all," I said hastily and then changed the subject by asking about their stores of ammunition.

Hercules came up to stand beside me. He stared proudly around at the growing arc of traps. Then he looked to our left, across the valley that was now waterlogged with big puddles of standing water, to the far tower. Rickets had done a good job of building in more batteries there too and King Dinkera's men looked a fearsome bunch. Many of them had been in the group that had fought their way clear at Nsamankow and they were now burning for revenge. With a score of cannon in the main castle aimed out across the valley, we had built a formidable defence. Hercules rumbled some words from that huge chest as he surveyed the scene and the translator said, "He thinks we will stop them here."

At that moment I wondered if he could be right. I turned and stared back out to sea, looking at the spot where the fishing boat should be waiting for me when the battle started. Then out of the corner of my eye I spotted a new sail coming down the coast. Little did I realise the danger it contained.

Chapter 25

Lieutenant Colonel William Sutherland was possibly the biggest fool I have ever fought with. He was a lieutenant at the start of the Peninsular War and his regiment fought in many of the fiercest actions. Simply by staying alive, any half-decent officer should have seen at least one and possibly two promotions by stepping into dead men's shoes. Hell, even a regimental mascot could probably manage at least one promotion in that bloodbath. Sutherland remained a lieutenant for the whole campaign – clearly no one thought he could be trusted with the command of a single company of British infantry.

He must have purchased his promotions after the war and bought the cheapest he could find. His colonelcy was in the West India Regiment. They had bought slaves to fill their ranks until the practice was abolished and now they sought volunteers, not from West India as their name suggests, but from the West Indies. Like the well-meaning Christians in America, who thought that any black man would thrive in Africa, the British Army often sent the West Indies men to the Gold Coast, but they suffered from the fever just like everyone else. That was bad enough, but to put a cloth-headed dunce like Sutherland in charge of them was just brazen cruelty.

Even though he had previously only spent one day at Cape Coast Castle, during which he had ordered a near disastrous attack, given his rank, Colonel Sutherland was the senior officer for our defence. His ship appeared on the twenty-second of June, two days after the Ashanti had been spotted. I got the distinct impression that he thought he had rather mis-timed his arrival – not that I could blame him for that. Given half a chance, I would have much preferred to be safely in his regimental barracks up the coast in Sierra Leone too.

"The enemy were spotted here on the twentieth," explained Chisholm, pointing at D'Jouquah on the map. "They advanced to within five miles of us yesterday and now King Dinkera's scouts report that they are just three miles away. It is impossible to ascertain numbers clearly as they are spread out through thick jungle, but

Dinkera's men captured a prisoner who claimed that the Ashanti have brought at least fifteen regiments with them."

We were standing in Chisholm's office around a map on his table. As well as Chisholm and me, there was Rickets, the midshipman from the observation tower, a couple of the garrison officers and two of the naval captains. "Can this *Dinkera* be trusted?" asked Sutherland imperiously. He pronounced the king's name as though it was some kind of disease and wrinkled his nose in distaste. It was clear that he would rather put his trust in a Cheapside pickpocket. "Perhaps we should interrogate the prisoner ourselves," he suggested.

"I rather think that the prisoner did not survive King Dinkera's questioning," said Rickets, suppressing a grin. "They are not in the habit of keeping prisoners alive for long." Sutherland shuddered with distaste as the captain continued, "But King Dinkera is entirely loyal. His men stood with Governor McCarthy until it was clear that all was lost. I would trust his men with my life. Indeed, I did after Nsamankow, as they were the ones who got me clear when the Ashanti were in pursuit."

"Mmm," Sutherland made the noise with a frown to indicate he was still far from convinced. "But Major Chisholm, you reported that most of our native allies ran away at the first shot during the attack that I ordered when I was last here."

"They were from the Fantee kingdom," Chisholm reminded his commander. "Their lands have been ravaged by the Ashanti in the last few years and this has instilled considerable fear in their people."

"And how do we know that these others will not lose their nerve as well?" Sutherland grumbled as though Rickets had not spoken at all. He paused staring at the map, his brow furrowed in concentration while one hand drew on the sides of his chin. He was the picture of a man lost in calculating thought, but I doubt that many of us around that table were deceived. Nobody was expecting inspiration from that quarter, for he had already proved himself to be a dangerous bloody menace with his previous visit. Most of the garrison officers had complained bitterly of his arrival as soon as they realised who was in the approaching vessel. Many had been in Chisholm's abortive attack and knew how close they had come to disaster.

"I would have preferred to see the Ashanti arrive than that rascal," one of the militia officers had grumbled.

Sutherland had already complained that the guard of honour who greeted his arrival looked dirty and disreputable and that parts of the castle were flooded from the heavy rain. Then he had been offended by my presence in his military council. "What the deuce is a civilian doing here?" he demanded, jabbing a finger in my direction.

"While he does not hold rank here, Mr Flashman has had a most distinguished career. Most recently as a captain in the Brazilian Navy." Chisholm started to explain my presence although mention of my South American experience only caused the Colonel's frown to increase. "But prior to that he served as a British diplomat; he was with Wellington at Waterloo and was a major in the army serving in Canada and the peninsula. You may recall him from your service there," added Chisholm hopefully.

"Flashman," grunted the colonel, "Yes that name does ring a bell." Would he remember my charge with General Cuesta at Talavera, advancing with the Connaughts at Busaco, being one of the first through the breach at Badajoz, I wondered? Of course not. I knew all too well what story was likely to come to mind – it had haunted me ever since a damned Catholic priest had vowed to blacken my name with the exploit. "Ah yes," muttered Sutherland as the memory came to him. "You were with some girl in Seville, weren't you? Disgraceful behaviour. You had better not indulge in any of that damned nonsense here."

I ground my teeth in frustration as the other officers stared with open curiosity. It does not matter what acts of unintended valour you perform, fornicate with a girl in Seville Cathedral and the tale will follow you around like a bad smell. "There were some scurrilous rumours about me that circulated in the peninsula," I admitted. "But I assure you, sir, that they were grossly exaggerated. The Bishop of Seville himself condemned them as tavern gossip." That was true as far as it went, but then the cleric had been half asleep during my misdemeanour and had even blessed me while I was in the act.

"Major Flashman has proved himself to be a very able officer since he was shipwrecked on our shore, sir," Chisholm added hastily, while he shot me another inquisitive glare. "He was one of the few to survive the action at Nsamankow and was captured by the Ashanti. After interrogation by the Ashanti king, he managed to escape from his prison and make his way back here. I have put him in charge of the defences around the east tower on our right flank."

"Mmm," grunted Sutherland again as he stared at the map. At last he came to a decision. "It won't do, gentlemen," he announced. "I do not trust our native allies and if they do give way, half of the garrison could be trapped outside of the castle walls. Let this Dinkera and Appea and their men defend the towers if you must, but we should keep the garrison within the castle walls." He paused, ignoring the stunned look amongst his audience and then added, "And while I think of it, there are a couple of houses in the village that are too close to our walls. They should be knocked down, or they will provide cover for the enemy to fire on us when they reach the town."

As he finished speaking everyone else started at once, voicing their protests over each other so that no one could be heard. Sutherland held up his hand for silence and only one of the naval captains ignored him. "But what about my sailors, sir? I have gunners at both of the towers manning cannon taken from my ships."

"Who authorised cannon to be taken from the ships?" Sutherland demanded. "They will fall into enemy hands and be turned against us. No, no that will not do at all. They must be brought back to their vessels at once." He turned to a bewildered Chisholm, "I am surprised at you, Major, for allowing such a thing."

Rickets was red-faced with repressed fury and opened his mouth to retort, but an anxious Chisholm waved him to silence. "With respect, sir," the major started, "we have carefully calculated a double line of defence, to which the cannon are a critical part. We hope to hold the enemy well away from the castle and the town. We currently have around three hundred men in the garrison fit to fight, but over four and a half thousand men from our native allies. They are better equipped to fight in the open, and in any case, there would be no room for them all to fight from the castle."

"If we retreat to the castle," I added, "we cannot expect any great relief force to rescue us. The Ashanti will probably hide in the rocks on the beach and kill anyone trying to move between the castle and the ships offshore."

"We might as well abandon the territory now," said Rickets hotly.

Sutherland turned on him angrily, "Thanks to you building batteries around the towers," he snapped, "we could see our ships being driven away by our own guns."

I glared at Rickets to shut him up and held up a hand for calm. Perhaps being a coward myself, I can sense it in others and I knew Sutherland was afraid. He had found himself reluctantly in command of an impossible situation that he did not really understand. He was seeking whatever security he could find. The stout walls of the castle gave him more reassurance than an exposed muddy hillside. He felt he had to show the authority of his rank, but he must have been all too aware that old Africa hands like Chisholm and Rickets knew far more about the territory than he did. Butting heads with him would not work. I had to play on his insecurities.

"I am sure that you remember from our days together on the peninsula, Colonel," I began, "that Wellington never liked his forces holed up in a fortress. He preferred to have the freedom to manoeuvre." I was playing the 'old comrade' card first, reminding him of a campaign in which he had more experience than most of those around the table.

"Indeed," agreed Sutherland, watching me warily.

"The Ashanti are used to fighting jungle ambushes," I continued, "but as you will have seen, we have cleared a wide expanse across our front to force them to meet us more on our terms. We have built a range of batteries with crossing fields of fire and tried to anticipate what moves they will make when their initial attacks falter." As I spoke, I pointed them out on the map. "You are our commanding general here, sir." I flattered the fool with a promotion and then with a comparison that I knew he would appreciate. "Like our mentor, the duke, you will see that your forces are also making full use of the surrounding hills. We must have stood together on the same hillsides in Spain and I am sure you will recall that it invariably resulted in victory."

"Hmmm." A grunt from our gallant commander was the only result from this blatant flattery, although I noticed that the edges of Chisholm's mouth were twitching upwards as he tried to suppress a smile. Sutherland must have seen a fair degree of toadying in his career, enough to recognise my efforts, anyway. He was still unconvinced, but I had not finished yet.

"I am certain, sir, that our outer lines of defence give us the best chance of stopping the enemy," I continued. "But if we fail, I would suggest that we conduct a fighting retreat to the boats. We should not try to hold them at the castle." For once I was speaking with an honest conviction, for while I fully intended to be one of the first to climb aboard a boat, I could not see how the rest of them could hope to hold the castle for long.

"Flashman," admonished Chisholm. "The castle is to be our second line of defence."

"I know, but if you think about it, I don't see how it will work." I pointed at the map, "If that prisoner is right, they have more than three times our number. Even if we killed half of them with our first line, they would have more than enough to lock us up tight here. We would never be able to break out again and drive them back. The best we could hope for is a fighting withdrawal to the boats. So it makes sense not to retreat into the castle at all."

"But the walls are thick and we have plenty of stores," protested Rickets. "We could wait them out."

"We have enough stores for the garrison," I shot back. "But not for all the sailors and say half of our native allies that might make it back to the castle, never mind the families they brought with them and the rest of the town that will seek shelter behind our walls. I doubt we could survive a week and we would be so densely packed that the fever would spread like wildfire." There was silence as they all considered this. A minute earlier Sutherland had been advocating just the course of action I was now criticising. He glared at me with suspicion; he clearly did not like his commands being questioned. He probably thought that some of the other officers such as Chisholm and Rickets would support him, but I doubted he could see a flaw in my assessment. One of the naval officers spoke in my favour.

"It will be bad enough to lose my guns, but to lose most of the gunners too would be intolerable. I will certainly want my men lifted off the beach. We can come in close and provide some covering fire from the few guns we have left, but it will be a bloody business if you leave it too long."

"Hmmm," said Sutherland as he rubbed his chin again. He stared vacantly at the map, like a drunk seeking inspiration from his tankard. He just needed one more push to help him make the right decision and I had my ace card to play.

"I know you will always put duty above your own personal safety, sir," I said quietly, "but were you to die here, it would do immeasurable damage to our reputation in this region."

"What do you mean?" demanded Sutherland.

"You heard how Governor McCarthy died?" I probed.

"He was beheaded," replied Sutherland briskly. "A most unpleasant business. I hear that they still have his skull and that the Ashanti king has boasted of using it as a drinking cup." He paused as he tried to follow my line of thought. "Are you saying," he added more quietly, "that they might… er… do the same with me?"

"I am afraid he did not die from the beheading," I answered. "That came later. They thought that McCarthy was a brave and honourable adversary, as I am sure they would you if you were to lead our defence. Consequently, when he fell, one of their chiefs cut open the governor's chest and pulled out his still beating heart. Mr Williams witnessed it and I was on the scene moments later. The chief ate the heart raw, I saw him just afterwards with the blood still dripping from his chin. Then the body was beheaded, but the rest of his corpse was not spared. It was divided up as keepsakes of the battle. Ashanti warriors wear pieces of his bones around their necks or in their ammunition pouches and believe that they imbue some of McCarthy's courage. Right now, I suspect that most of Governor McCarthy's body is no more than three miles away, but probably in at least a hundred pieces."

In truth I did not know if McCarthy was dead or headless when his heart was removed, but it did not matter. Sutherland's face had turned ashen as I told him of his predecessor's fate. Malala had told me how various parts of the governor's body had been divided up among their soldiers. I had even seen what looked like a small square of leather, but which was said to have been a piece of his dried skin.

"That is unspeakably barbaric," gasped Sutherland at last and there were murmurs of shocked agreement from others around the table.

"Quite so, sir," I agreed. "But having McCarthy's remains seems to have given the Ashanti more audacity to attack us. I understand that they have not been this close to the castle in many years." Chisholm nodded his agreement. "If they were to kill another brave senior British officer then this would only embolden them further. Who knows where that might lead?"

I stopped talking then for I was not sure that Sutherland was still listening. His mind seemed frozen around the possibility that his living heart could be wrenched from his chest and that his mortal remains might end up as a collection of native beads. He stepped back a couple of paces, unsteady on his feet. For a moment I thought he might faint but then he recovered himself and at last spoke with some resolve. "On reflection I think Mr Flashman is right. We will maintain the first line of defence and if that fails, we will fall back on the boats."

Chapter 26

"You are a cunning devil, Flashman," said Chisholm with a smile. "You played our *commanding general* like a trout yesterday. Giving him some line and letting him think he was winning, before reeling him in."

"I wasn't wrong about holding this castle, though," I replied. We were standing on the battlements and while I think Chisholm had been annoyed with me at the military council meeting, now there was little doubt that my advice had been good.

That morning the observation tower had signalled that the Ashanti were right up to us; we had even heard a crackle of musketry from around the tower itself. Others swore that they had seen enemy troops moving at the edge of the forest and thick plumes of smoke marked where two of the nearest villages were being put to the torch. The effect on the populace living around the castle had been dramatic, and every man, woman and child not already in service had pressed to get within its walls.

Sutherland had refused to open the main gate, in case it was rushed by Ashanti spies, he said. Instead only the small wicket gate was used, allowing just one person at a time to enter. The colonel had insisted that two sentries be posted to inspect the entrants – as though Ashanti spies wore some kind of uniform. I had already seen Jasmina, her father and some of her other relatives come through, but there was still a large crowd of several hundred outside. Many of them were wailing and screaming as though enemy hordes were already charging along the beach. I did not doubt that some of the elderly and children would be wounded in the crush at the gates, but the situation was little better inside.

Chisholm had visited the Bracegirdles and insisted that they come to the castle. The reverend had claimed he was too ill to be moved and certainly he would not have been able to queue with the others. But the major had got some of the sailors to rig a boom over the walls and he was hauled up, still lying in his bed. Eliza was pulled up after him in a bosun's chair.

There was little more than standing room in the main courtyards and the old slave dungeons had been reluctantly pressed back into service to give people more room. Despite this, we would be chock full when the last of those outside were through the gate.

"Yes," agreed Chisholm, "you were right. I hope that many of this lot brought food with them," he said gesturing to the sea of humanity in the yard below. "Yet I doubt that we can hold out for much more than a week. Sutherland was up here earlier and I admitted to him that I thought your advice was sound. I think even he could see the sense in it when he saw the crowd outside the gate."

"Then it is probably the first bit of sense he has seen in a while," I grumbled. "The bloody fool will get us all killed if we are not careful."

He laughed and added, "Thanks to you I think we could soon be left to manage things ourselves. What you told him yesterday about McCarthy seems to be playing on our general's mind. He told me that he would leave me in command of our defence as I had more experience of this coast and its people."

"More likely he does not think we can win and wants someone else to take the blame. That and the fact that he does not want bits of him hanging around the Ashanti king's neck."

"Well now you mention it, having seen how crowded we are here, he does believe that it would be better for him to observe proceedings from the deck of his brig. He claims that he will be better placed to manage the evacuation if necessary. Ah, speak of the devil, where is he now?"

We had heard Sutherland's voice shouting over the babble in the courtyard but staring around there was no sign of him.

"Major Chisholm, down here!" The voice was coming from outside the castle. Taking a step to the battlements, I looked down and saw the colonel standing next to one of the huts in the village. "Chisholm, I told you to have some men demolish these two huts, they are too close to the castle walls."

"But… well I thought that as we were no longer defending the castle, it would not be necessary. Chisholm shot me a glance, clearly confused now as to whether the colonel had changed his mind again.

"When I give an order, Major, I expect it to be obeyed. Now get these huts demolished."

"It will take some time, sir. The men have been hard at work all morning preparing for an attack and those walls are over a foot thick of dried hard mud.

"Nonsense, man, it is a matter of a few minutes." With that, Sutherland started to pull at the thatch of the nearest hut until he was holding a large handful.

"Is he planning to pull the bloody thing down by himself?" I whispered as the colonel strode inside the dwelling.

"Perhaps the strain is getting to him," suggested Chisholm. I just hope he does not change his mind about letting us command the defence."

"If he does, I will come up with some tales to frighten the living daylights out of him," I promised. "Hello, what is that? Smoke?"

We watched as the first tendrils wafted out of the hut door, followed by Sutherland, now carrying a burning torch made from his bundle of roof thatch. "There, how hard was that?" he shot up at us before marching resolutely on to the second hut.

Chisholm opened his mouth to shout a warning, but I stopped him. "Don't bother, you will only anger him again and it is too late now." Already we could hear the crackle of flames from the nearest hut and see more wisps of smoke emerging from the thatch. Sutherland had been standing in the lee of the castle walls, where there was no wind. But from the battlements we could feel a strong breeze at our backs. The top layers of thatch were damp from the recent rains but underneath they were bone dry and the fire took easily. Sutherland came out of the second dwelling and stood back to admire his handiwork. The first flicker of flame was already showing through the roof of the first hut now and thick clouds of smoke were billowing from the door. I could hear shouts of alarm from the townspeople in the courtyard behind me as they saw the thick column of smoke appear over the battlements. The colonel turned towards the beach, apparently satisfied with a job well done, and did not see the first smouldering pieces of thatch getting caught in the wind and blown over the rest of the town.

I will say one positive thing about Colonel Sutherland: when he wrote later to Lord Bathurst in the government to describe all the happenings at Cape Coast Castle, he at least admitted that he was responsible for burning down the town. He claimed that just the thatch burned and many of the contents of the huts survived, which may have been true of the mud-walled buildings. Other structures, though, such as the church and the Bracegirdle's cottage beside it, were burnt to the ground. The fire caused considerable panic, not only in the castle as the inhabitants of the town realised it was being put to the flame, but also in the surrounding hill encampments. Many thought that the Ashanti had somehow got behind them and were responsible. Warriors, sailors and soldiers rushed back down the hill to either counter attack or make for the boats. If the enemy had chosen that moment to attack, they would have beaten us easily. Instead, they must have been staring curiously at the coast and wondering what on earth had possessed us to burn down our own town.

Once we had the men back in their places we watched anxiously for any sign of an assault, but there was nothing. All we saw were a few fleeting figures at the forest edge. That evening I returned to the castle. Everyone was adamant that the Ashanti would not attack at night and so only a light guard was left. Sitting around the mess table, Rickets announced that the latest of the prisoners captured by Dinkera had revealed that the Ashanti king was joining his army to see our destruction for himself. The enemy had formed a huge camp half a mile into the forest, where they waited for their monarch to join them. They sent out large patrols though and some of Dinkera's men only narrowly escaped capture.

It rained heavily again that night. I at least was comfortable in my room, but it was hard to sleep with the wailing of the refugees outside. When I got up the next morning and left my quarters, I had to step over dozens of bodies trying to sleep on the damp stone. Every available flat piece of space was taken, and some had even managed to get up on the battlements. I remember passing a whole family hunched, wet and miserable on the steps down to the courtyard. The place stank too; the few latrines we had were hopelessly overwhelmed and people did not want to leave whatever space they had found, even if that meant fouling it. I was glad to get out of the castle gates and up the muddy hill to my tower.

That day passed and then another with nothing happening. After two days of living in the hellish interior of the castle, a few had decided to take their chances in the town and some were even trying to rebuild or at least re-roof their homes. Others tried to head east along the coast, but most of those came back a few hours later as the Ashanti had now encircled us and were capturing those trying to get away. It was too late to escape by land, but the enemy showed no sign of wanting to bring our ordeal to an end. I guessed that their king had not yet arrived but if he did not come soon, I feared Mother Nature might do his grim work for him.

Fever deaths were increasing; instead of individual graves a large trench was dug, which was extended each day by a few more yards, the spoil covering some fresh bodies. The stench in the fort was appalling and O'Hara warned me not to drink any of the castle water, even if purified with his tonic.

"There is shit all over the place," he complained, "and when it rains the muck gets washed into the water tanks. We can boil it, but it still tastes bad."

"What the hell are we supposed to drink, then?" I asked.

"I've left an open barrel out where I keep the still, with a piece of canvas nailed to it to collect rainwater. I'll get our water from there, mixed with tonic, of course."

God knows whether some vengeful local pissed in his barrel, or if I caught it some other way, but over the next day or so I came down with the fever myself. It had been the thing I most feared ever since I had heard of the dreaded fever season, but at least for me it did not turn out to be fatal. It was similar to what I had suffered in the general's yard in Coomassie. This time, though, instead of a silent maid, I had a noisy Irishman looking after me. O'Hara was convinced that I had fallen ill because I had not drunk enough of his vile potion and so he did his utmost to remedy this at every hour of the day. His latest batch was the most incendiary yet. As it seared its way through my insides I was by no means certain whether it was killing or curing me. On one occasion I used a silver spoon to stir in some fruit juice to disguise its taste and I noticed that it took all the tarnish off the spoon!

I was bed-ridden for days and roaring drunk for much of it. Apart from O'Hara, no one came to visit, and I could not blame them for that. When I was sober enough to think, I imagined that they would be fighting off the Ashanti without me. I made the Irishman promise that if our defences failed he was to get me on a ship at all costs. Thinking back now, I doubt a captain would have risked letting me board and infect his ship. I would have been left to perish.

Chisholm finally came to see me as I started to recover. I had already made it out to the balcony overlooking the nearest courtyard. It contained no more than half the number of people there that I remembered from before, but if anything, the latrine stench was even worse.

"It is good to see you getting back on your feet," the major grinned. "O'Hara has been giving me regular progress reports and claims that your recovery is entirely due to his homebrew."

"Well I am glad he is telling you things as he has refused to tell me what is going on outside. He says I'm not to worry until I am better. But as you are here, I take it that we have beaten the Ashanti?"

"Heavens no, we are still waiting for them to attack."

"But I don't understand. They were on the verge of attacking when I got ill. I must have been on my back for a week... What day is it now?"

"It's Friday the ninth of July, you were on your back as you say, for *nearly two weeks*. Are you well enough for a walk up to the battlements? Here, take my arm." He led the way slowly up the stone steps. As we went he explained that a lot had changed while I had been out of action. We had received some reinforcements by ship from Accra down the coast as well as some Fantee warriors. Chisholm thought that the latter had come to protect themselves from Ashanti raids rather than to help us. He had put them on our left, furthest away from their lands to reduce the chances of them running as soon as any battle started. When we got to the top of the walls I saw that there was another ship in the bay, a large frigate. "That is *HMS Thetis*," Chisholm explained. "Her guns will be invaluable in covering any withdrawal and she has added her marines to our defence, I have put them to help with your tower on the right." He sighed and gripped my shoulder before adding, "The lieutenant in charge of them has no experience of organising a battle, in fact none of us do apart from you."

"That's nonsense," I protested. "You and Rickets have faced off to the Ashanti far more times than I have."

"We have fought them in the jungle and in ambushes like Nsamankow. But this will be a battle on open ground with artillery and the closest we get to ranks of infantry. Your knowledge of where to place the guns so that their fields of fire overlap and anticipating what they will do next has been invaluable. I don't think we can win without you, which is why I am damn glad to see you back on your feet again."

I could not think what to say to that. Perhaps I was too ill or empty to feel that all too familiar churning of fear. I just felt numb as I was thrust forward into the gaping jaws of danger again. I gave a grunt of acknowledgment. Almost of its own volition, my hand reached into my jacket for the bottle of O'Hara's raw tonic that he now insisted I carry with me. I took a swig and gasped as it burned through my insides, but at least I felt a little better. I looked around. A few people were moving around the charred walls of the town and I could see that some had chosen to rig temporary shelters rather than stay in the castle. Near the beach a handful of soldiers were working industriously around a fire. "What is going on there?" I asked.

"Many of our new recruits from Accra and the Fantee did not come with arms or ammunition. We have given out what we have, but we are low on ball. We are melting all the lead water pipes in the castle to make more."

I gave a wry grin, "Sutherland won't like that – he was complaining about the flooding before."

215

"Thankfully he has stayed out of our hair. He has only been ashore twice while you have been ill. And anyway, it has not rained for over a week."

I continued to survey the land around me and stopped suddenly when I saw the funeral trench. It was now well over a hundred yards long. "Good God," I exclaimed, how many have we lost?"

"Around twenty soldiers and far more from the town. With the overcrowding they were dropping like flies. Corporal Evans has gone, did you know him? Mr Jarvis and John Henderson have both perished, oh, and Hannah McCarthy finally succumbed too.

"So that poor lad is an orphan now."

"McCarthy told me that he has a sister," responded Chisholm. "Perhaps she would look after the boy if we can find her. He said that she married a French officer and is now a countess. She is already guardian to one of his sons born here."

I stared gloomily at the trench which was still open at its far end awaiting yet more occupants. With a chill I realised that I could so easily have ended my days inside it too. No stone monument in an English churchyard, just a foot or two of space in an overcrowded ditch that would probably soon get dug over by wild dogs. "What about Reverend Bracegirdle?"

"No, he is still hanging on, but he cannot survive much longer."

I transferred my gaze up the valley between the hills towards the enemy. Smoke from cooking fires was visible, drifting above the treetops, but beyond that, no sign that a huge force was hidden there. "Do we know why they have not attacked yet?"

"No, their king arrived well over a week ago but apart from raiding the countryside around us, they have made no serious move on our lines. Just a few firefights with our skirmish parties. The only thing I can think of is that it has not rained. Perhaps they really are worried about those repeating weapons you regaled them about."

Not for the first time, I wondered whether all my stories about Collier-style artillery and rifles had been a blessing or a curse. When I had first started to recover from the fever I assumed that we must have beaten the Ashanti while I was unconscious. I had felt considerable relief that for once I had missed a battle in circumstances that were beyond reproach. To say that I was disappointed to learn that the maelstrom of their attack was still to come, is something of an understatement.

I was even more distraught the following day when, with O'Hara's help, I slowly made my way up to my tower on McCarthy Hill. When I had last been there I had taken considerable comfort from the hundred-yard-wide swathe of traps that lay between me and the enemy. Back then they had all been hidden under puddles on waterlogged ground and under a carpet of leaves and foliage. Nearly two weeks of unrelenting sunshine had undone all the hard work of Hercules and his men. The ground had dried up, the covering leaves had shrivelled in the heat and now virtually every single trap was clearly visible. You would have to be blind to fall in one. But just in case, I saw that the Ashanti had been busy during the dark evenings, for there was now a large gap in the line where I guessed that the stakes had been removed and all the holes had been filled in with fresh earth.

"Christ, will you look at that," I said to O'Hara as I leaned on his arm. "That gap is on our side of the valley. If fifteen thousand of the bastards pour through there, we do not stand a hope in hell of stopping them." All we had to oppose such an attack were twelve, six-pounder guns thinly spread between four batteries, two thousand of Appea's soldiers, forty marines from *HMS Thetis*, and, if they made it up the hill before we were overrun, around two hundred men from the garrison. "They will tear us apart," I added as I turned to look back down the hill to the sea. It had taken me half an hour to climb up the slope. In my weakened state it would probably take half that time to go back down again. Even if my fishermen were waiting offshore, I would almost certainly be overhauled by the enemy on the way to them. If I did somehow manage to reach the sand, I doubted that I would be in any condition to swim.

All of my preparations and planning were likely to come to nought. I had a nasty feeling I would soon envy those unfortunate souls buried in the ditch. If I survived the battle, I doubted that the king of the Ashanti would be the forgiving sort.

217

I spent most of the day up on the hillside – it was good to be away from the fetid stink of the castle. I introduced myself to the commanding officer of the marines, a Lieutenant Drew, who happily admitted that he had not been to Africa before. "Will many of them have firearms, sir?" he asked. "Or will they have spears and bows and arrows?"

"They will all have bloody muskets," I warned him. "Few bayonets, though, and they shoot wildly, but with fifteen thousand of the buggers coming at us, some of the devils are bound to hit something."

I took a sadistic pleasure in watching the colour drain from his cheeks. "Fifteen thousand," he repeated softly and then he looked around at our paltry defences. Then I remembered all the times some evil swine had said something that had sent my bowels chattering in terror and began to feel sorry for him.

"Well lad, if we get through this, you will have a story to tell all those army veterans that boast of being at Waterloo. Mind you," I added quietly, "it would be a good idea to give your men some practice in firing volleys while moving backwards. There is a reasonable chance we will have to conduct a fighting retreat back to the beach." It seemed only fair to warn him and as my skin would rely on the effectiveness of that withdrawal, I wanted it as robust as possible.

"Don't worry, sir," he grinned at me, seeming to recover some confidence. "We have been practicing manoeuvres with those soldiers of the African king." He pointed to where Appea's men had built some long open-sided shelters on the slope facing the sea from some of the wood they had cleared from the battlefield. "They are getting quite good, but of course we have not been able to fire ammunition as supplies of ball are short."

I wished him well with his endeavours but did not hold out much hope. In the heat of battle, fingers always fumble loading a gun. The only way was to drill men so that they went through the motions automatically like machines, and to do that you needed to fire the guns for real.

As the day progressed I felt a little better and was strong enough to eat a hearty lunch of some bushmeat stew. Back on the beach I even went for a short swim – it was good to wash the dirt of sickness from my skin and feel clean again. As I dried myself on the sand, lying in the rays of the late afternoon sun, I reflected that at least the good weather meant that we might be safe a while longer. But surely it would rain sooner or later, or the Ashanti king would grow impatient.

I should have known that with my luck things would change, for as I lit the candle in my room that evening, I heard the first distant rumble of thunder.

Chapter 27

I lay in bed that night hardly able to sleep. The rain thundered down on the roof, sounding like a waterfall just the other side of my chamber. The removal of the lead piping meant that a torrent of water was smashing into the stone flags outside and soon it was coming under the door too. I must have slept for a while, but when I awoke at dawn it was still pouring. I undid the door and could barely see through the rain to the huddle of poor wet miserable villagers that were crouching under a roof on the far side of the courtyard.

I took my time getting ready – I half hoped that the Ashanti would launch their attack as the sun rose, then I could go straight to the boats and forget about my hill. But I dare say that they could not see what they were doing either.

O'Hara brought me some breakfast and some of his 'fortified' coffee. It did not taste too bad and he proudly told me that it was made from fresh rainwater, "before the bugs and shit had a chance to mix in it."

It soon grew lighter and I knew that I would have to reluctantly climb to the tower and face whatever came. I hung my new gold sword over my shoulder and put my refilled flask in one of the pockets. We set off; I was soaked to the skin in the first minute. The rain was so heavy, I thought if I turned my face upwards I would probably drown. We passed the end of the funeral ditch where half a dozen men were standing by three corpses lying on the ground. They were staring disconsolately into the hole at the end of the channel, which was now flooded with several feet of water. I thought they would have to abandon the burial, but as we moved away I heard a splash as one of the bodies was thrown in. O'Hara chuckled as he looked over his shoulder, "The bloody fools are learning the hard way that ye have to weigh a body down to bury it in this weather."

As we moved to the side of the hill, I looked down the valley towards the distant forest, but all I could make out through the rain was the dark smudge of foliage. It was impossible to tell if the Ashanti were in the trees or indeed if they had started their advance. We were already splashing through ankle-deep mud but moving over the flat land was nothing compared to ascending the hill. For every three paces we climbed, we generally slipped back one. At some points we were forced to use our hands as well as our feet to keep a grip, for much of the grass and other plants growing on the hill had been cleared by the building work and there was little on which to anchor ourselves. Now little rivulets of water poured down the slope like small streams.

I sprawled flat on my face once and was aware of someone stepping to my side to help me up. As a huge hand reached around my arm, I looked up into the face of a grinning Hercules. He led us to one of the shelters where his men were standing. The grass roof kept them dry and more importantly, their muskets were stacked out of the rain too. The soldiers about us looked curiously at the mud-stained, sunken-cheeked Englishman that was destined to lead them in the coming battle. Compared to the strapping and healthy Hercules, I must have seemed a poor specimen. Four young boys eased their way to the front of the crowd, not bothering to hide their disappointment at my appearance, but the sight of them gave me an idea. I turned to the interpreter, "Tell those four boys to follow me to the tower. You had better come with me too."

The man gave the order, but Hercules stepped in their way to block them and addressed the interpreter, his smile giving way to an expression of anger. "He wants to know if you are going to use the boys as a sacrifice for our victory," the translator said.

I laughed. "No, their eyes and ears will be younger and better than ours. I want them to stand at the tower and to watch and listen for the enemy's approach."

Hercules beamed in delight. I later learned that one of the boys was his son, which explained his concern. He came with us as we climbed the rest of the way up the hill. The gun positions were half flooded, but they also had roofs of straw to keep the powder charges dry. The naval gun trucks rested on wooden planks and while the wood was submerged, it would be much easier to move the guns on them than through liquid mud. I placed the boys on either side of the tower and told them through the interpreter what I wanted them to do. They beamed with delight at the responsibility. We had once used the sharp eyes of a boy in Brazil to spot the enemy and I hoped that the trick might work here too, but I could only see clearly for a few hundred yards and I doubted that their eyes could see that much further.

We stood there all morning. At one point, Chisholm sent a runner to report that our skirmishers had sighted some enemy soldiers moving at the far end of the valley, but we saw nothing. Then at last, around noon, the rain began to ease. Slowly but surely, we began to see further across the valley until we could clearly make out the canopy of the trees. The boys saw them first, shouting out in their excitement. Lieutenant Drew of the marines heard them and ran up the ladder to see what had been revealed.

"They can see men moving under the trees," called the interpreter. "Near the gap in the line of traps." We all stared in that direction and soon we could see them too, like an ominous dark tide of humanity washing around the trunks of the trees.

"Should I get the men to stand to, sir?" asked Drew anxiously.

I laughed. Suddenly I found the whole situation absurdly funny. My reaction may have had something to do with the fact that I had nearly finished the flask of O'Hara's tonic as we had waited during the morning. "No, leave them be." I told him. "They and their weapons would be better keeping dry until the enemy are climbing the slope towards us. Anyway," I slapped the young lieutenant on the back and grinned, "they might be over there intimidated by the numbers we have. There is no need to terrify them just yet by showing them your forty marines."

I chuckled again as Drew ran off down the ladder and drained the last of the liquid in my flask. "You know," I said to O'Hara, "this last batch is all right. Very smooth."

He sighed and then replied, "By the saints, ye must be as drunk as Father Maguire. It is the very same batch that a few days ago you swore felt like a wire brush tearing up your insides. Now, sir, do ye want to sit down afore you fall down?"

"I'm fine." I waved him away and then stared curiously to our front. "Look," I pointed, "the rain has flooded all the traps and half of them are hidden again." Hercules had noticed the same and was shouting the information to his men in the shelters behind us. The centre of the valley was completely water-logged and even their cleared path was under water. Only away to our right were the traps still visible.

"Yeah but they know they are there now sure enough and where their path is, even if they do have to get their feet wet," grumbled O'Hara. As he finished speaking I heard the first of the Ashanti horns; they were summoning their regiments to the attack, just as they had done at Nsamankow.

I turned to the three gun crews on top of the tower. "Right, gentlemen, we will have some customers for you presently, so load with roundshot and aim for just beyond where their path is. It will be full of their soldiers in a minute and I don't want any of them getting here to ask for their money back." I did not feel drunk, but I must have been as, for once in my life before a battle, I did not feel afraid. I leaned over the parapet and gave the same instruction to the battery on the left of the tower, who now started to remove the cut down bushes that had hitherto covered their guns. Hercules was about to climb down the ladder to his men, but I held him back and turned to the interpreter. "Remind him not to release his men to charge until the Ashanti are at the top of the hill. I don't want them blocking the guns. Let the cannon and the mud do their work before we fight them."

The big champion nodded in understanding as the interpreter spoke to him and then he was away. That's it, I thought. The die is cast and we will have to see now how the cards fall. The last of the rain was dying away now and between the horns I could hear the cheering of distant men and see hundreds of them milling around the jungle edge. "Right," I called pointing in that direction and looking at the nearest gunner. "Let's show them that we are open for business. Send your balls into those bastards."

The guns fired and a moment later those in the battery to my left opened fire too. Nearly all the balls fell short as the barrels were cold. I watched the shots splash into the water in front of the enemy – the ground was far too wet for them to bounce. The gunners quickly reloaded and then threw themselves at the traces to pull their gun carriages back into position. I had hoped that I might have provoked the Ashanti into a disorganised attack, but they were too professional for that. Their only response was more horn blowing as their men were rallied into their regiments. Our second salvo was much more successful. It was hard to see damage and injuries from that distance, but I saw one of the trees shudder as it was hit and knew that at least one cannonball had sent wooden splinters scything into the men around them. Then, as the gunners reloaded for their third shot, the Ashanti finally attacked.

God knows how many of the fiends there were. We found out later that it was not the full fifteen thousand, but I will swear that there were at least ten thousand, if not more. They poured through the gap in our traps like water breaking through a dam, spreading out as soon as they thought it was safe. I watched with grim satisfaction as a few turned off the path too early and others were pushed into traps by the sheer volume of men. In no time at all there must have been a hundred men down, clutching at injured feet. The cannons started to roar again and at least one ball carved a bloody trail through the enemy coming towards us. They were endless in number, the first of them charging straight up the valley towards the castle. Others turned to their right and yet more to their left, seemingly intent on going around our right flank, while a good number headed straight towards us. All of them came at the run, anxious to get away from where our cannon fire was concentrated, although they soon slowed down as their feet sank into the heavy ground and they floundered in the mud. As well as muskets, I saw a few with what looked to be heavy boxes on their backs, while others were carrying scaling ladders. There was a roar from behind me as the cannon in the castle now opened fire on those in the valley and the guns on Rickets' hill banged out too. King Dinkera's men were visible now, standing around Rickets' tower while the soldiers on my hill were still obeying orders and staying out of sight. Perhaps that had been a mistake on my part, for I now saw that more of the attackers were heading in our direction.

Our cannon must have fired at least half a dozen balls at the breach in the line of traps but still the Ashanti were coming through; the far side of the valley was alive with their soldiers. From my higher vantage point they looked like a disturbed ant's nest, although I was all too aware that they had a more powerful sting. There were a number wearing European clothes and I spotted at least a dozen sporting the red coat of British soldiers, presumably these were trophies. I guessed that their former owners had fought with me at Nsamankow. I watched them quite dispassionately. I was aware that I should be feeling fear or even terror, but instead I had a calm detachment as I went about the business of managing my command. I watched as those who ran to our right found firmer ground and hence made swifter progress than those struggling through the valley. I ordered the battery to the right of the tower to be uncovered and then to open fire. I also sent a message to our remaining battery on our far-right flank to stay hidden until the Ashanti were much closer. I remember calmly speculating on whether the shock of their appearance, which would mean that the Ashanti were being fired on from two directions, would cause their faster attack to falter.

Was this how Wellington had felt at Waterloo? I wondered. He was notorious for his coolness under fire. I had always thought he had repressed any feelings of fear, but perhaps he did not have them at all.

"Are you all right, sir?" O'Hara was at my elbow and looking at me with concern etched in his features.

"Yes of course, why on earth should I not be?"

"Because you are singing some ditty about a lock-keeper's daughter, so ye are, as you stroll around grinning at people." He lowered his voice and nodded at the nearby gunners, "You're gettin' the men worried."

"Nonsense man," I beamed at him and then turned to the gunners. "I am not making you nervous, am I?" A couple of them grinned awkwardly back at me as I continued, "You just keep firing that pepper at them and we will do fine. Few will make it to the top of our hill and the rest will be beaten and back in their camp by tea time." It did the trick, as the petty officer in charge of the gunners evidently thought that such a rousing speech should be answered with a huzzah. The gunners stopped reloading for a moment to give me a cheer and then their cannon fired once more.

"You see?" I turned back to O'Hara. "There is nothing to worry about. We will soon have them on the run. Now hand over that big flask of yours, I am parched."

For the next half an hour or so it seemed I was right, as the battle was a very one-sided affair. The Ashanti made slow progress towards us and once they stopped pouring through the gap in the traps, the cannon concentrated on where any large groups of them gathered on the clear ground between the jungle and our hill. The enemy had brought no guns of their own and so we were taking no fire at all. Yet slowly and surely they closed in around us. If they thought that they were nearing victory, though, they were soon mistaken. As they reached the bottom of the hill most were already exhausted from struggling through half a mile of thick mud, but they now discovered that had been the easy part of the journey. The sides of the hill, as I remembered all too well, were slick and slimy with mud. Men slipped and fell and tumbled into each other, knocking others down. All that would have been bad enough but our cannon at the top of the hill had now switched to grape shot. They could not depress their barrels enough to fire directly down the hill and so our guns fired obliquely into the men climbing to their left or right. Masses of them were knocked away as though blown off by a deadly wind. The numbers were so great that the gunners could not miss, but if any managed to escape this storm of shot, either side of the hill was now lined with muskets firing down at them. Lieutenant Drew and Hercules had done a fine job in drilling their men; not one tried to move in front of the cannon. King Appea's soldiers even managed some rudimentary volley fire. They were arrayed in three loose ranks and when the front rank fired they would retire to the rear to reload while the other two lines stepped forward. It was rough, but it worked. We were keeping the Ashanti at much more than arm's length and across the valley they were making no progress getting closer to the castle or Rickets' hill either.

I was feeling ebullient, my defensive plan was working perfectly, albeit massively helped by the recent weather. If they had come the day before, I suspected that the Ashanti would have bounded across the dry land towards us and up the slope like a herd of vengeful antelope. But they hadn't, they had come today and they were getting stuck in the mud and mown down by the hundred. I was probably still humming the tune about the lock-keeper's daughter when I looked over my shoulder and down at the sea. There, as arranged, was the small fishing boat, a hundred yards offshore and beyond it, the larger ships. Well I won't be needing those today, I thought as I patted the gold top of Malala's cane, which I had placed in my pocket back at the castle.

"Sor, look out!" I whirled round at O'Hara's shout and caught a glimpse of him raising his musket, and then my eyes locked on to the extraordinary sight of an Ashanti soldier climbing over the low battlement wall at the front of the tower. He was shrugging the musket from its sling over his shoulder when there was a bang from beside me and he flew backwards over the edge.

"How the devil did he get across the moat...?" I started but blow me if another head was not appearing at the same spot. O'Hara was furiously reloading, but he would never be ready to fire in time. In any event the Ashanti had seen what had happened to his fellow and he was bringing his musket forward before stepping up onto the parapet. Now I'll admit that I was not thinking clearly. My wits must have been addled by O'Hara's tonic and I could not understand how they had come so close without being killed. Yet it was not puzzlement, but fury that I remember being my overriding emotion at that moment. I had been conducting what I had thought was the perfect defence and now these blighters had bloody well gone and ruined it.

"Oh no you don't," I roared as he started to take aim at one of the gunners. I was running towards him with my arms outstretched. I had no idea what I would do when I reached the villain, I was just filled with an anger that they had thwarted my plan. The rogue saw me and tried to swing his weapon around, but it was too late. The barrel knocked against my side as my hands closed around his throat.

It was only then that I belatedly remembered that I was on top of a tower and realised that he must be standing on the top rungs of a scaling ladder. I had a brief glimpse of the ground below: a plank had been laid across the moat and other men climbing ladders were on either side of me. They looked up, startled, as I grabbed their comrade and then I was falling through the air. Whether I had over-balanced or my victim kicked off against the wall I cannot say. One moment I was standing on the tower parapet and the next the muddy brown water of the moat was looming towards me.

I realised then what had happened. While the batteries and soldiers on either side of the tower covered the ground in front of them, the gunners in the tower itself were aiming further ahead and could only see what was immediately in front of them if they leaned over the edge. We had relied on the moat for protection, but some cunning Ashanti commander had seen this dead space in our defences and sent his men to exploit it.

I did not let go of the man's neck and likewise, he clung tightly to the ladder. When you are falling through the air you naturally hang on to anything you can get hold of, even if it is the throat of your enemy. We splashed down hard into the liquid mud that filled the moat. We both went under, the rungs of the ladder cracking me across the shins. I felt the ooze close over my head, filling my ears and blocking my nose. It was like drowning in thick soup. With my eyes tight shut I pushed down hard against the man underneath me and felt him start to struggle to reach the surface. After a moment my head emerged and I opened my eyes. There were a score of Ashanti moving around the mud bank in front of me, some carrying ladders and preparing to cross the moat. Others were shouting at those further down the hill to hurry up and one or two were starting to fire muskets up at the tower.

To my surprise no one was paying any attention to me, but then they probably could not identify which head was poking up out of the mud. I could have been a white man, a black man or a basking water horse from what little they could make out. Floating in the mud, the whole situation was confused. My mind was still trying to fathom how I had ended up in this stinking ooze. The dead body of the man O'Hara had shot was sprawled in the mud beside me. It all felt unreal, as though I was now an invisible spectator on the scene. Suddenly, a hand reached up from below to claw my face. It was an unwelcome reminder of the precarious position I was in and brought me a little to my senses. At least I knew enough that I could not afford to let him reach the surface. I took a deep breath and pushed him back down into the mud, squeezing on his neck for all I was worth. I went under again myself as I wrestled to stay on top of the man beneath me, who writhed and thrashed his limbs with the desperation of a drowning man. I came up again just in time to see another of the ladders crash back down into the moat from the side of the tower, its occupant screaming in terror.

"Are yer down there, sor?" I heard O'Hara's voice shout down, but I dared not answer. There must have been thirty Ashanti on the bank in front of me and they were starting to open fire on the top of the tower to keep the defenders' heads down. It would only take one to notice me and I would be dead, I was barely ten feet away. Several more men came running up with ladders that they started to push across the moat. Still no one took any notice of the mud-covered head observing them. It was like watching a battle in a dream; I found time to study the tower and wondered why we had built a parapet wall at all. It protected the gunners, yet it also stopped them from lowering their barrels to sweep the enemy away.

Evidently some of our soldiers must have joined O'Hara in the tower, for there was a growing crackle of fire from that direction and one ball struck the corpse just beside me. I remember idly watching the resulting stream of red blood mix with the brown of the mud. The body beneath me had finally stopped struggling. I released my grip on his neck; it is so much easier to kill a man when you cannot see him. Then I slowly eased myself around until only my face was above the surface. With my ears submerged I could hear very little, which only added to the strange sensation of being a disembodied witness to proceedings. My head rested against another corpse, which must have given me some cover. I could no longer see the Ashanti on the bank, but by squinting down my nose, I could just make out the soldiers on the top of the tower.

There was a battle royal raging above me now. I could hear the Ashanti firing from the other side of the moat and at least a dozen soldiers, including O'Hara, firing back at them. It did not take long to realise that our side was losing. Twice soldiers on the tower leaned over the parapet to shoot at those standing at the bottom of the walls and both times they were hit with a hail of fire from the far bank. One toppled into the moat while the other managed to fall back, wounded. As soon as even a head showed itself over the top of the wall it was met with a crackle of musketry, as the Ashanti kept the defenders at bay. I watched as twice my Irish orderly appeared and managed to fire his gun. The second time, I saw him drop his musket and clutch his arm as he was hit. Half a dozen Ashanti warriors had managed to cross the ladder that served as a bridge and had taken two fresh ladders with them. It looked like another effort to scale the tower walls was imminent, but our gunners were not beaten yet.

As a new ladder was raised, two hands darted over the wall and dropped a pair of cannon balls on the men below. One splashed harmlessly into the water and the other stuck in the mud, but I had just enough time to notice a burning fuse poking out of one side. They were explosive shells. The implications of what my eyes were seeing burned through to my brain only slightly faster than the burning fuse to the gunpowder. Taking a deep breath, I quickly ducked under the water again. I felt the impact through the mud rather than heard it and when I gingerly surfaced again, all that was left of the men at the bottom of the ladders were pieces of offal and a range of fresh body parts floating in the water.

There were shouts of fury from the Ashanti and then I felt the corpse beside me move. I had been sure that the man was dead. Without thinking I jumped in alarm, sending out ripples over the mud, and turned to look at the body. Two Ashanti were on their knees by the edge of the moat, pulling the corpse out of the water. When I looked beyond them the rest were preparing to pull back. Perhaps, I thought, they were taking their dead with them – at least the ones that were relatively whole. They both looked up and saw me staring at them. I took a deep breath preparing to go under the mud again, for surely they would shoot me, but instead of reacting angrily or reaching for their guns, they smiled at me.

It was all very confusing. Why weren't they killing me? For a moment I wondered if they were Appea's men who had somehow retaken the hill top, but no, several were still taking pot-shots at the tower as they pulled away. One of them said something and gestured for me to come out of the water. He pointed at the tower and continued talking, grinning again. God knows what he was saying, but if I did not get out of the mud he would be suspicious. I moved to the side and started to climb, but the bank was as slippery as a wall of wet tripe. His mate had staggered off with the corpse thrown over his shoulder, following the rest of the Ashanti down the slope, but my new 'friend' held out his hand to help me out. He clearly thought I was one of his comrades and there was no reason to disabuse him. I stuck up my mud-covered paw and took a firm grip.

"Heave ho!" I recall shouting and a moment later we were both sprawled on the bank. He laughed again, he was a cheery fellow, and then he gestured to my sword and asked me a question. I wondered if only officers had those in the Ashanti army, as in ours. I staggered up to my feet and drew the weapon from its scabbard. I remember being surprised at how clean and shiny it was despite its immersion in the muddy water. I glanced down the hill; apart from my companion, the nearest Ashanti was now thirty yards away with a corpse still on his back but there must have been at least a hundred of them well within musket range.

"Go on lad, shove off," I said to the Ashanti, who only now was getting to his feet. He looked little more than twenty. He turned to me frowning, probably as he could not understand my words. I still had no comprehension of the danger and I gestured with the sword for him to go down the hill. As I did, I saw his eyes widen in surprise. I realised afterwards that when he had released my hand, he had taken much of the mud with him and he must have seen the white skin of my fingers holding the hilt. He shouted in alarm at his mates nearby, but they were still jogging down the slippery slope of the hill and would not easily be able to come back to help him.

"Run away, you bloody fool," I shouted at him. He had helped me out of the moat and I had no wish to kill him. If he had made to escape I would have happily let him go, but instead, he made a lunge towards his own musket.

I remember thinking as the gold blade glistened in the sun, that the sword handled well. It was not as sharp as my old sabre at home, but it bit deep into the man's arm causing him to stumble and roll away from his weapon.

"Clear off," I roared at him, pointing again down the hill and making no effort to follow up the attack. He squealed, clutching at his limb. Then seeing that I was not coming for him again, he got hastily to his feet and staggered unsteadily down the hill, whining in pain as he went. "And don't come back," I yelled after him.

"Is that you, sor?" asked an Irish voice from the top of the tower.

Two Ashanti muskets fired from further down the hill before I could reply. A handful of them were stopped fifty yards away, now waiting for their wounded comrade. A well-aimed shot could be accurate at that distance, but, perhaps influenced by the spirits I had on board, I was confident that I would not be hit.

"You can bugger off too," I yelled at them. "Go on, get off my hill." And with that I brandished my sword again and took several steps in their direction. I grinned as they started to back away. Christ knows what they thought a drunk Englishman armed with just a sword was going to do to them. Then I turned my attention to O'Hara, who I now saw standing at the tower battlements with a white bandage around his sleeve. "Of course, it's bloody me. Now start knocking the bricks in the parapet down in front of those cannon so that they can aim them down the hill."

"Knock 'em down?" I heard one of the gunners protest. "They were the only things keepin' us alive back then."

"Do what I tell you," I roared, feeling master of my own domain again. I watched as one of them used a gun rammer to push some mud bricks off the top of the wall between the guns. Shaking my head in exasperation I added, "Just in front of the muzzles, you blockhead. Don't knock the whole sodding wall down."

Chapter 28

I strolled around in front of the tower as though I owned the place, stopping only to toss the ladder that the Ashanti had used as a bridge far into the middle of the moat. There were still at least two corpses and various body parts floating on top of the ooze. The nearest Ashanti were now over a hundred yards off and still retreating, although there were maybe a thousand still milling around on the flat land between the tower and the jungle. I stared to my left into the valley in front of the castle; the attack had stalled there too. The Ashanti had pulled back out of effective grape shot range. Now the castle guns just boomed occasionally to send a solid shot towards large groups. They would be lucky to kill many, though, for our cannon balls just buried themselves in the mud rather than bounced through their targets. More gunfire to my right signalled that the battery covering our right flank was also in action. I stared in that direction and saw hundreds of the enemy milling about in confusion as they were caught in the crossfire from two different sets of guns.

As I watched a big figure loomed into view, jogging around the edge of the moat. It was Hercules and he beamed in delight when he saw me standing alone amongst the remnants of the last attack. "Kala ba!" he exclaimed, gesturing to my bloodstained blade, then he swept me up in a great embrace, squeezing my innards with a force that a python would envy. "Kala ba," he repeated, although I had no idea what it meant.

"Put me down, you great oaf," I gasped with what little breath I had left and when he did, I looked up to see Lieutenant Drew and O'Hara hurrying around the edge of the moat, followed by a mixture of marines and Appea's warriors.

"The gunners said you were dead for certain," declared Drew looking about him and then staring uncertainly into my mud-covered features. "How ever did you survive, sir?"

I paused before replying as a grinning O'Hara appeared alongside him and wordlessly held out his huge silver flask. I took it gratefully and gulped some of the spirit down – it was definitely getting smoother. "Well, young fellow," I said to Drew while passing the flask back. "As you can see, I managed to disguise myself as one of those water horses. That notion struck me as most amusing. I stood there giggling to myself as I watched the Ashanti try to re-organise their men in the valley in front of us."

"Are ye sure you are feeling well, sor?" asked O'Hara quietly. "Perhaps you should not have any more," he added putting the flask back inside his coat.

"Don't make a fuss, I am fine. In fact, I have never felt better in a battle," I declared. Strangely, I think I meant it then too. "How is your arm?" I asked, gesturing to the bandage.

"The ball went straight through, barely more than a scratch. Jaysus I was lucky. I take it back about them not being able to shoot straight. Their shots were coming at us thicker than flies on a turd." He grinned at me and added, "Speaking of turds, you don't want to know what has been going into that moat for the last few weeks. We had better get some rainwater and clean you up a bit."

Until that moment, all I had smelt on me was mud, but now I detected a more unpleasant odour. Two pails of rainwater were summoned and I started washing the worst of it off. Soon my hair and head were clean again and most of the mud had been washed out of my clothes. I stood dripping like a wet dog and surveyed the scene as Lieutenant Drew pointed out where the enemy were now regathering at the bottom of the hill. "Attacking here has been the closest they have come to victory, sir. Do you think they will try to test us again?"

"I am sure of it. Look over there near the jungle. There is a crowd of them carrying straight logs and sticks from the forest, they are probably making more ladders and platforms that will serve as bridges."

For the next hour we stood on that hill top and watched the enemy prepare for another attack. They must have chopped enough branches and sticks, lashing them all together, to build at least a score of ladders. Others were building ramps out of bundles of sticks to throw across the moat to make a bridge. Our gunners did their best to disturb this industry by firing solid shot and some exploding shells in their direction, but the Ashanti were too well dispersed for them to do much damage. I stood and watched proceedings with a growing sense of unease. The attack on our right flank had already died away and many of the survivors of that venture were gathering with those preparing to renew the attack in our direction. Horns were blowing and we could hear the distant shouting of their officers as they began to gather and organise troops for the coming assault. Soon there must have been at least four thousand of them. I felt a growing need for some more liquid courage.

"Sorry, sor, it has all gone," said O'Hara shaking his flask to show it was empty. "Anyway, it is best to have your wits about you, with that lot," he gestured down the slope, "comin' up in a while."

The problem was that they did not 'come up in a while'. We stood and paced on that hillside for another hour as the enemy preparations dragged on. Some disappeared into the trees again and yet more fresh troops arrived, but they did not form up in any kind of order. For all the blowing of horns, instead of columns or lines they were just in a loosely formed mass, and if anything their numbers had grown. Chisholm joined us with some of the reserve from the castle as no new attack was aimed in their direction. That gave us some two hundred regulars and the forty marines as well as the gunners. But by far the bulk of our defence was still the two thousand warriors of Appea's army. We divided our forces evenly on either side of the tower, so that the guns had a clear field of fire down the slope to the enemy.

We would still be outnumbered by at least three to one, but our men would be fresh while theirs would be tired out by a long slippery climb and being peppered with shell and shot. Several times I found myself looking wistfully back to the fishing boat still anchored off the beach and wondering if I would be swimming out to her after all. To my surprise, even O'Hara had lost his usual belligerence. I found him staring forlornly at his flask. "I should never have tipped it away," he admitted. "I could do with a wet now."

"I thought you Irish love a good fight," I chided. "You did when I first met you."

"We like a drink *and* a fight," he corrected. "One generally leads to the other. That day we carried you down the hill at Busaco, most of us had half emptied our canteens before the battle began, and they were not filled with tea." He laughed. "I think what ye drink changes who you are. If I had drunk fine French brandy, then I could have been a gentleman. If I had drunk a good claret, I could have been a priest like Father Maguire. But in our cottage, all we could afford was a soldier's liquor." He gazed glumly at his flask again before adding, "And now for the first time since I landed on this cursed shore, I think I might be getting sober." He glared down the slope at the enemy and shuddered with distaste, "And I don't like it one bit."

"You will be all right," I assured him. It felt strange to now be comforting O'Hara when in the past the man's fearless attack on the French had terrified me. But then perhaps the effects of his tonic wore off quicker for those who were more used to it.

"Have you seen how many of the murderous heathen are waiting down there to butcher us?" countered the sergeant.

"Can you swim?" I asked quietly. When he said he could, I led him behind the tower and pointed out the fishing boat in the bay. "That boat is crewed by the two lads that took us down the coast with Eliza and Bessie. If things go badly here, we make for that. But make sure you bring me with you as I have the payment for them," I added patting my pocket. "They will take us to the ships – it will be a lot safer than trying to get a passage by the castle.

O'Hara grinned at me. "I always knew you were a cunning bastard."

"I would not have got away from Coomassie if I wasn't," I told him. "Now go back to wherever you have hidden your supplies and refill that flask. We will both feel better for a nip of it and I suspect that the Ashanti will be a while yet."

He was gone for half an hour, but I was right, all the Ashanti did was blow their horns and march about. They were clearly waiting for something. I paced about impatiently until the sergeant returned. A few minutes later, after a couple of gulps of the tonic, I was much more sanguine about proceedings. O'Hara too was back to his belligerent self, sharpening his bayonet while humming some jaunty tune. "Would ye look at that," he said, gesturing down the hill. "Some fat fella has turned up on a chair. Ye don't think that they are going to burn him as a sacrifice like that other fella you told me about, do you?"

I stared to where a procession was emerging from the trees. I did not need to see his features to recognise the man being born aloft on the shoulders of his subjects. The glint of gold on the marks of office of his entourage confirmed who he was. "That 'fat fella' is the Ashanti king," I announced. "They must have been waiting for him to arrive before starting the attack."

I was not the only one to recognise our visitor. A growl of recognition spread among Appea's soldiers; it was clear that they relished the chance of getting to grips with him. They were soon chanting something in their own tongue. I could not understand it, but judging from their grins and waving of weapons, the king would do well to stay out of their clutches. Their din almost drowned out a clarion call of trumpets from the valley below. On a gesture from their corpulent monarch, the Ashanti had finally started to move towards us.

Chapter 29

It took over half an hour for the first of the Ashanti to make it to the top of the hill. Given the barrage they endured on the way, I was surprised that any of them made it up at all. I had organised our force of defenders, now numbering around two and a half thousand men, so that most of them stood behind our little fort and did not get in the way of our cannon. As well as the guns from the top of the tower, the ordinance in the castle and in Rickets' bastion on the other side of the valley also opened up on the attackers they could see. The Ashanti tried to spread out to make themselves less of a target, but this only brought them in range of the two batteries on either side of the tower, who now also lobbed shell and shot in their direction. I went to the top of the tower to monitor progress, but it was hard to see through the gun smoke. You could hear them coming, though, especially when the gunners switched to grape shot. Each belch of iron into the oncoming mass of humanity was met with a chorus of screams and wails from those who had been hit. I remembered all too well being on the receiving end of such a barrage at Waterloo and could not help but shudder in sympathy.

The dead and the dying must have provided a further obstacle to those struggling up the wet slippery mud of the hillside, which was still littered with debris from their earlier assault. They were taking a terrible punishment and hundreds of them must have been hit. I thought that sooner or later they would be bound to turn tail and run.

"My arse, they would beat the Imperial Guard," I scoffed as I squinted at them through the smoke for the first sign of retreat. They were still coming on, but at least I could wait safely for them to break, and if they did not, we had a surprise or two waiting. I strolled around the top of the tower, singing once more about the lock-keeper's daughter and trying to keep out of the way of the gunners. My serenade was rudely interrupted by the clang of a musket ball hitting a cannon muzzle.

"They are getting quite close, sir," called out one of the artillerymen.

I peered over the parapet and was shocked to see that some of them were no more than sixty yards off. I only got the briefest of glimpses through the smoke before a musket ball thudded into a mud brick right next to my head. "Keep firing over the heads of the defenders for as long as you can," I shouted to the petty officer in charge. Then I leaned again briefly over the parapet, and yelled, "Now, Chisholm, now is your time."

I could not help but smile at the memory, for Wellington had used the exact same words to Maitland at Waterloo. Then as now, a double rank of redcoats rose up from the ground on which they had been lying to avoid enemy fire. Back then they had risen to face a column of Napoleon's Imperial Guard, whereas now they were standing to meet pretenders to that acclaim. As I moved back across the tower, I heard the first ordered volley crash out and knew that it was the start of a steady hail of lead into the leading Ashanti ranks.

Hercules was waiting eagerly below the tower for the word. "Go!" I bellowed and while he might not have understood the word he knew its meaning. He shouted a command and with a throaty roar his men surged forward down the paths around the moat on either side of the tower. I went back to view the effects of my handiwork.

Moments before, the front ranks of the Ashanti must have believed that despite their gruelling climb, they were close to their objective. Now they found themselves assailed from four different directions. Chisholm's infantry was sending regular crashing volleys into their front, while over their heads our cannon continued to blast grape shot into the main body of their attack. Now, from each side of the tower came a thousand of Appea's soldiers, firing and charging into the flanks of the Ashanti force.

No assault could withstand that and squinting through the smoke, I finally saw the Ashanti giving way. "Fix bayonets," called out Chisholm as Appea's men started to encroach on their line of fire. Then I saw the familiar sight of a line of redcoats advancing on their enemy. Feeling well satisfied with myself, I climbed down the ladder to the ground where I found a grinning O'Hara waiting for me. He was standing beside one of the batteries where he had a good view of what was happening.

"Ye timed that sweeter than a harlot's kiss," he declared.

"It did go rather well," I agreed smugly. "Shall we go and examine our fleeing enemy?"

We made our way around the tower. By now the cannon at the top of it had stopped firing. At a distance, with our men hot on the enemy's heels, it was hard to make out friend from foe. The ground from fifty yards in front of the moat was littered with the bodies of the dead and injured, and I was pleased to see that there was only one redcoat among them. The rest of the redcoats were in a solid line some hundred yards ahead of us, their bayonets jabbing at any who dared to resist.

Chisholm looked over his shoulder and waved when he saw us approach, "Well done, Flashman, we have them licked," he called.

O'Hara tugged at my sleeve, "Look over there." He pointed at the flat ground at the bottom of the hill and I grinned in delight. A fat man was being carried aloft back into the forest with an anxious group of courtiers following on behind and shooting nervous glances at the men coming after them.

"It looks like the king is not staying around to witness his defeat," I crowed. Without the gaze of their king and his executioner, I thought, the Ashanti would have much less incentive to make more of a fight of it. I was feeling cocksure and safe, which was a mistake, for that is invariably when danger strikes. We might have been winning the battle, but there were still several thousand more of the enemy than us and it only takes a few of them to ruin a good plan. While Appea's men were fighting in a crowd that was probably half a dozen men deep, the line of redcoats was still only two ranks, a fragile screen compared to the mass of soldiers it was driving on. There was a yell of alarm from the middle and then several of the British soldiers began to fall back as some of the Ashanti burst through. Chisholm shouted for the rear rank to close up the gap and advanced on it himself, but it was too late. Half a dozen Ashanti were already through, some falling on the men around them to widen the gap and others looking for new targets. One advanced on Chisholm, only to fall from his pistol shot, but then I saw a familiar figure emerge from the melee.

It was the officer who had captured me before and who had held me in Coomassie. I recognised him and his leopard skin at the same moment he spotted me standing no more than ten yards behind the line. The mere sight of him brought back memories of the terrible moments of my capture at Nsamankow. I felt my guts tighten; he must have seen the fear cross my face. If they broke through our line, our defence could collapse, but more importantly I would be in mortal peril. I remembered those headless corpses after the last battle and had a sudden premonition that I would see the executioner again. The Ashanti officer grinned and ran towards me, two of his soldiers following on close behind. I was frozen, I could not move as my mind tried to rid itself of the image of the bloody axe and focus on the danger ahead.

"He's mine, sor," called out O'Hara as he stepped in front of me. With an unhurried gesture that he must have used a score of times in countless battles, he raised his musket and deftly demonstrated why a soldier with a seventeen-inch bayonet on the end of their Brown Bess musket will always defeat a man with a sword. The Ashanti's sword point did not get anywhere near the Irishman before the officer was impaled on one of Sheffield's finest steel tips. The sergeant was wrenching his gun free, but the next man was already on me. It was sword versus musket again, but crucially the Ashanti did not have a bayonet and it seemed he had already fired his weapon. Reversing it, he swung the stock at my head and without thinking I got my gold blade up to block the blow. For a second the sharp edge got stuck in the wood and I struggled to wrench it free. Out of the corner of my eye I saw the other Ashanti close in on O'Hara, but he was already turning to meet the threat. I did not consciously think about what I was doing – training from my first voyage with Cochrane many years before took over. As I tugged on the sword, I brought my right boot up to kick my opponent hard in the balls. As he doubled up in agony my sword came free and I hacked down on his exposed neck. O'Hara's man was also down, judging from his bloodied and broken face: a brass bound musket stock had just been smashed into it. The Irishman finished him off with another stab from his bayonet.

I was already dashing forward. More Ashanti were trying to push through the gap in our lines and the red ranks were desperately trying to hold them back. There is a moment in many battles when there is a brief tipping point which will decide victory. This was one of them and both the Ashanti, and the redcoats fighting desperately to hold them back, realised it. One of our redcoats was half wrestling with an Ashanti. He must have seen me coming up, for he twisted round to expose his foe's back to my blade. I duly obliged and thrust the gold weapon up under the man's ribs. I barely had time to twist the steel free when another warrior was on me. But before I could get my blade up, O'Hara's bayonet was in the man's throat. It was a brutal, bloody fight, just the kind of action that I am normally desperate to avoid, but now it was kill or be killed.

I hacked at one man and then another. As one fell, I saw another man level a musket at me. I was hemmed in. I did not have space to move or time to reach my foe before he pulled the trigger. I tried to shrink back, but at that moment I was bodily thrown forward into the throng as new men surged into us from behind. I could not turn to see who they were and for an awful second I wondered if the Ashanti had sprung a surprise of their own. Then a huge arm with a cleaver reached forward over O'Hara's head and split the skull of the man who had been trying to kill me. It was clear that the new arrivals were friendly after all! The next few moments were like a particularly bad scrimmage at my old school, as men pushed and shoved at each other, but only those at the edges had room to use their weapons. I found myself pushed up against the back of an Ashanti, my sword trapped uselessly between our bodies, and then I heard the cannon from the tower fire again.

I found out later that Hercules had seen the precarious position of the line of redcoats and had led a hundred of his warriors round as reinforcements. They had arrived just in time to save the day, but while they had stopped the redcoats from falling back, they were not enough to get the Ashanti to retreat. Then, as we were all packed tightly together, the gunners on the tower took a chance to win the battle. If they had miscalculated, their cannon balls would have hit us and the day would have been lost, but their aim was good. Their barrels were still hot and they had been aiming shot for most of the day. There was a ripping sound as cannon balls whizzed low over our heads. Then screams from in front, as they ploughed deep furrows through the packed humanity before us.

I doubt the dead and wounded had room to fall and at first there was no relief from the pushing and shoving. But when the three guns fired a second salvo, I think the enemy finally realised that the game was up. They could not move forward now and were hemmed in on three sides while the cannon assailed them from above. Beyond the screams of the dead and dying, we now heard more shouting as men fell back and yelled for others to do the same. Within a moment the whole mass was moving back down the hill, like water released from a dam. Many of Appea's men continued the pursuit. I saw Hercules grinning at me as he went past. "Kala ba," he shouted again as he waved a blood-stained cleaver above his head. I pitied the next Ashanti he came across. The redcoats, though, largely stayed where they stood, some still looking shaken from the crush and our lucky escape.

Lieutenant Drew sat on the ground nearby cradling what looked like a broken arm, while many of his marines and the redcoats pillaged the dead and wounded. One soldier gave a cry of delight as he pounced on a treasure hanging around the neck of an Ashanti corpse. Judging from his feathered headdress, the dead man had been an officer and the soldier held up his trophy. "Look at this, sir, a gold-plated bone!" It looked like a finger bone, with a thick strip of gold hammered around it. With an expert twist of his bayonet, the soldier soon detached the soft metal and casually tossed the bone away. It landed in the mud near me and as I looked down on it, I wondered if the relic had once been part of McCarthy.

Without saying a word, O'Hara came over and offered me his silver flask. I accepted and took a swig. The battle had been far too much of a sobering affair; now the danger was past, intoxication seemed a welcome prospect. "That was a damn close thing," the sergeant muttered as he took his tonic back.

"You are bloody right there," I agreed. I could feel my hands trembling slightly, which I thought was more due to my close brush with death than the drink. "Remind me to thank those gunners. That was some fine shooting to break the attack. Look, there must be hundreds, if not a thousand of them scattered down this hillside." The bodies were lying so thick that I was sure I could have gone from where I stood all the way to the bottom of the hill without stepping on the ground once. The Ashanti had taken many of their wounded with them, but there was still a pitiable wailing coming from the few that remained. More than once I saw a bayonet stab down to finish one off. From the state of some of the wounds it was an act of mercy.

"Well done, Flashman," a voice called. I looked up to see Chisholm walking towards me, wrapping a kerchief over a cut on his hand. "I knew your battle experience would pay off. Rarely have I seen a more complete victory and to use the cannon to break them like that was a masterstroke. Well done indeed."

I was about to explain to him that the gunners had acted on their own initiative, but instead O'Hara held up his flask and offered the major a drink.

Chisholm must have assumed that it was the diluted mixture I had been drinking before my illness rather than the neat raw spirit, for he took a large gulp. He gave a wheezing gasp and then his mouth started to open and close like a startled trout as his eyes bulged and watered. "Christ in his heaven," he croaked at last. "I would rather face the Ashanti once more than drink that again."

O'Hara looked quite hurt at this critique of his fermenting skills. "It is an acquired taste," I admitted, "but you do get used to it."

"Used to it?" repeated Chisholm, appalled. "If we had rolled a barrel of this into the Ashanti camp, we would not have had to fight them at all."

Chapter 30

For the next two days I was showered with praise for my strategic cunning in organising our defence. Even things that had happened by accident, such as me leaving a blind spot right in front of the tower, were acclaimed as a stroke of genius to draw them in to a trap. In the end I gave up trying to correct people and basked in a rare moment of military glory. After all, if you have read this and my previous accounts, you will know that there were precious few of those. I had suffered from hardship almost continuously from the moment I had set foot on the shores of Africa. It was pleasant to have some good fortune for a change.

One person who did not see fit to compliment me, however, was Sutherland. He had watched the battle from the safety of his brig and only deigned to come ashore several hours after the fighting finished. Having been repeatedly assured that the Ashanti had now retreated into the forest, he finally came up to the tower to view the scene of the fiercest fighting. Whenever Chisholm mentioned my part in planning the defence, our gallant commanding officer cast me a wary and suspicious eye. Based on the rumours he had heard in Spain, he still seemed to think of me as some blasphemous degenerate. Certainly, when he finally wrote his report for the government, he gave Chisholm most of the credit. The evening after the battle he weighed anchor and sailed back to Sierra Leone. Perhaps fearing another attack, he was anxious to get away from the Ashanti as soon as he decently could. I could hardly blame him for that, as it was a sentiment I heartily shared.

The Ashanti did not reappear, although we heard that many were still in their camp just a mile or so into the forest. The day after the battle we buried our dead. Considering we had been attacked by thousands of the enemy, the butcher's bill was surprisingly light. One hundred and two men were killed and four hundred and forty wounded. Most of the casualties were among Appea's soldiers as they made up the bulk of our force, but several redcoats and one of the garrison officers were also among the dead. In comparison, the enemy must have lost several thousand dead and wounded, although as they carried many of their wounded away, it was hard to be precise. I was just glad to see the back of them. Others, however, felt differently as I found out when called to a fresh council of war in Chisholm's office.

"Appea's men and particularly King Dinkera are keen that we do not let the Ashanti stand," Chisholm told a gathering of officers. "They want to cut a path through the jungle to the Ashanti camp and take the attack to them."

I had spent the last forty-eight hours congratulating myself on surviving this nightmare, but now it appeared that some were intent on an act of almost criminal stupidity. "For heaven's sake," I exploded. "Have they forgotten how many men the Ashanti have compared to our own? Have they taken leave of their senses?"

"Steady on, Flashman," the major soothed, trying to calm me down, but I was having none of it.

"We won the last battle because we fought them on our terms. To go marching off into the forest will give the enemy a fight on exactly the terms they are used to." I shot a glance at Rickets before adding, "We all know how *that* is likely to end. And as for marching our force up to theirs, well, it is like marching a child into the lair of a tiger: they won't stand a chance. You can go if you like," I concluded, "but I want no part of it." I turned to Chisholm, "I would be obliged if you will release me from this command so that I can finally get a boat home. I hear one of the merchant ships is due to weigh anchor in the next few days."

There were several murmurs of agreement around the table. What I said made a lot of sense and there was no suspicion that I was simply frightened of making another attack. My reputation and recent exploits made that idea seem absurd – they were not to know that I had been roaring drunk throughout. Chisholm, though, was not agreeing, the sombre look on his face resembled that of an undertaker trying to present his account to a grieving widow. "I greatly regret, Thomas, that I cannot release you just yet from my command."

"What the deuce, why the hell not?" I demanded.

"Your friend Hercules and King Dinkera both have the highest regard for your military expertise. They are insisting that you accompany them in their endeavour and advise on strategy."

"Pah," I snorted in derision. "Since when has His Majesty's government been at the beck and call of native princelings? Look, I am grateful to them for standing beside us, but if they want to put their heads in the lion's mouth, they can hardly expect us to come with them. You will just have to tell them to go to the Devil without me."

"I can't do that," said Chisholm quietly. He looked me firmly in the eye and continued, "Right now we *are* at the 'beck and call of native princelings,' as you put it. They came to us in our hour of need and now they expect us to do the same. They are the only reliable allies we have. If they were to abandon us, then our position here would be untenable. I'm sorry, Flashman, but you will have to go with them." He looked around the table, "We will *all* go with them to show our support."

I knew I was beaten then. Others around the table were clearly not keen on the idea, but they all piped up that if king and country was at stake then of course they would do their duty. To refuse would mean disgrace, but more importantly I would lose their support for an early berth on an outgoing ship and the worst of the fever season was only a week or two away.

"Is it wise to abandon the fort?" asked one of the other officers.

"Dinkera's scouts will warn us if the Ashanti approach the coast. Right now, the nearest are in their camp a mile away." He paused to show us the place on the map.

"But we will be hugely outnumbered," I persisted. "Surely we can try to get Dinkera to see reason?"

"On the contrary," countered Chisholm, "I think he may well have a point. You don't know these people, Flashman, but for any native ruler there is a lot of pressure from rivals. The Ashanti king is new on his throne and he has brothers and cousins who would take the crown from him given the chance."

"That is true," I admitted. "I spent time with some of them in his palace jail, but how does that help us?"

"His army has taken a crushing defeat, and his generals and soldiers will probably blame him for it. They may be losing confidence in his leadership."

"But surely that means that he will be more anxious to fight us to save face?" I interjected.

"Possibly," admitted Chisholm. "But Dinkera, who is a fellow king after all, thinks he cannot risk another defeat and is more likely to head back to Coomassie to shore up his support there. If he is not in his capital when news of what happened here reaches the city, then he may not be king for much longer. The momentum is now with us. We will look weak if we do not exploit it and push the Ashanti back to their own lands."

I still felt sceptical. It seemed to me that we were giving the Ashanti king a chance of an easy victory to restore his credibility, but as I had never been a king, my views did not seem to count. That night I found myself praying that the Ashanti would make some move to put us back on the defensive, as that would force us to abandon this mad scheme. Instead, all we heard next morning were rumours of enemy forces moving around in the forest and raiding local villages for supplies. When I met Hercules and his interpreter, they both appeared entirely confident of our success. "We will chase their armies all the way to Coomassie," the translator told me of the champion's booming declaration. "Their forces are in disarray, we must not give them time to regroup."

To my surprise, even O'Hara thought the attack was a good idea. "We cannot just sit on our arses and wait for them to come at us again," he explained. "Sooner or later they will come on a dry day and then we will be properly buggered. Far better to try to chase them off while we have the chance."

It was a strangely perceptive and pithy view from a man who was normally unceasingly intoxicated. I had to concede that he had a point. I was waiting for a passage home and so was only taking a short-term view, yet for the long-term future of the colony I understood that we had to drive the Ashanti back away from the coast. O'Hara now sported a new bandage around his arm, but it was only a flesh wound and he had still been declared fit for duty. There was no room for him to linger in the sickbay, which was full of those with far more grievous injuries. We were standing on McCarthy Hill watching the first of Dinkera's warriors begin widening a path through the jungle by the gap in our line of traps. As the Ashanti had cut a trail coming the other way, which our allies were using as a starting point, they were making good progress.

"I suppose we should go down and join them," I said gloomily as I watched the rest of the garrison forming up in the valley and preparing to move forward.

"Aye," agreed O'Hara pulling his flask from his coat for a final swig. He caught my eye and grinned, holding up his flask. "Are you still foresworn off the neat stuff, then?"

"Yes," I smiled. "That gut-rot nearly got me killed last time. I am sticking to the watered-down mixture in my bottle." The night after the battle I had sat horrified as various people recounted my heroics during the day. I had forgotten much of it, but as the tales were told the details came back to me with horrifying clarity. What in God's name was I thinking when I pushed the man on that ladder or when I stood alone by the moat, shouting at the enemy to clear off. It was little short of a miracle that I had survived. I was not going to take chances like that again, so I had vowed never to drink the tonic unless it was diluted. Now I only used it to kill any bugs in the rainwater but even so, it still had a worrying kick.

We made our way down the slope, past several hastily dug mass graves. They had already been disturbed by wild creatures, and I saw a half-eaten arm poking out of one of them. We joined Chisholm as he led a column of the garrison down the widened trail. From my perspective, we made worryingly quick progress as there were at least a thousand of Appea's warriors in front of us. Dinkera's men were there as well, although some were running down parallel paths to our own. I strained my ears for the sound of shooting or the shouts of battle but there were none, just the crack of machete on wood and the casual chatter of the men around us. We pressed on a while and then suddenly we heard yells from the jungle ahead. A rousing cheer went up and the warriors in front of us pressed forward hastily to see the cause for celebration.

You could smell the Ashanti camp long before you could see it. There was a terrible stench of sickness and decay, but little could prepare me for the sight of the clearing when we rounded the last bend. Bodies covered the ground as far as the eye could see. Some were dead and bloated in the heat, although there were moans from many still alive. A stream meandered through the campsite. A score of men had expired, leaning half over the bank to drink, while a similar number of bodies now formed a small damn, which half flooded one end of the clearing. The corpses were wedged tightly between the narrow banks and a waterfall splashed over the top of them. The native soldiers as well as the British were quick to spread out to loot the dead. O'Hara and I moved through the bodies too, quickly tying kerchiefs around our faces to fend off the stench and the crowd of flies that rose into the air as soon as a body was touched.

"There are piles of shit everywhere," moaned O'Hara. "They must have had fever and dysentery. I'm not surprised if they were drinking from that," he said, gesturing at the stream. "The rain must have washed the filth into the water."

There were shouts from the centre of the camp. Hercules and others were helping some men, presumably prisoners, who they had found in chains. As I looked back on the ground I saw a large axe and was about to take it over to help break the bonds when I hesitated.

"If ye don't mind, sor, I will check those bodies over there. No one has been there yet and there might be something worth taking."

"No, wait," I called O'Hara back. There was something familiar about that axe. Then I saw a small stool lying on its side in the mud and I remembered where I had seen it before. I searched among the nearby bodies and then I saw him. In death his shoulders were still broad and powerful, but now he looked a pathetic figure. He was wrapped in a cloak and had died lying face down and clutching his guts. "Help me turn this one over," I gestured to the man. "If I am right, we will find rich pickings to share."

I grabbed the man's shoulder and with his good arm, O'Hara helped heave him over. The released stink and flies made me wretch, but above my gagging I heard the sergeant exclaim in wonder, "Jaysus, there is enough gold there to choke an elephant."

Through now-watering eyes I looked down. Four fingers on each hand were still adorned with heavy gold rings while around the dead man's neck was the gold axe head I remembered. It had several links of thick gold chain connecting it to a cord that went around his neck. "We'll share the rings half each and you can have the links in the chain, but I want that gold axe head," I stated. "He was the royal executioner. I thought the bastard was going to do for me when I was back in Coomassie."

We swiftly split our haul and hid it away before anyone else noticed what we had found. The axe head was too big for my pockets and so O'Hara hid it for me in his coat lining. "If I ever get out of this accursed shithole of a country, a haul like that will make me a rich man in Galway. I'll be able to drink brandy like a gentleman."

I laughed. "Trust you to think about drinking your wealth. If you get out of here, you can afford to get sober occasionally and buy a farm."

He grinned, "Or I could buy a distillery and brew the finest *poitín* in Ireland. Then I could get drunk and rich at the same time."

"Not if it is anything like what you brew here. Now pass me that big axe and let's go and see who those people in chains are."

One of them turned out to be a brother of the king of the Fantee people, who had been a prisoner of the Ashanti for over fifteen years. He sobbed with delight as Hercules brought the axe down to break his bonds. He had been an umbrella-bearer to the king and had come with him on his slow progress from Coomassie. He told us that his master had ordered his army to wait for his arrival and then the right weather before starting their attack, as he wanted to witness his victory over the British. While they kicked their heels in frustration, the soldiers soon found that their rations were running low and then fever or dysentery broke out. It had spread like wildfire in the crowded and dirty camp. When the attack was thwarted the king tried to blame his soldiers, but many had endured enough. Whole regiments deserted and marched off. The king then left in a hurry, presumably worried he would be overthrown if his army arrived home before him. Hostages like the Fantee king's brother were just forgotten in the rush to get away.

I found Chisholm and King Dinkera with Hercules and his interpreter discussing what to do next. Dinkera was preparing to take his men on to pursue the Ashanti and force them to leave the lands of his people. I was more than a little relieved to hear that Chisholm thought our work was done. "If the Ashanti are heading back to their own territory then that is good enough for me. We have taught them a lesson and had our revenge for McCarthy's defeat, but it makes no sense to humiliate them further. We are here for trade, after all; we do not want a long and bloody war."

I agreed wholeheartedly with him there. Then Hercules started to speak, gesturing at the dead around him. We waited for the interpreter. "He says he does not understand why the Ashanti attacked during the fever season. In all the wars we have ever had, he does not remember any other time when an army has chosen to attack during the rains. It makes no sense, for an army will always get sick when so many are living closely together in the open. He thinks that the gods have chosen to punish the Ashanti for their arrogance."

Chisholm agreed that divine assistance was entirely possible, but I could not help but smile. After the battle at the tower I had been showered with praise for my planning, when in reality, many of the events had happened by chance. Now this final defeat of the Ashanti was being attributed to heavenly help, but I wondered if there might have been an earthlier explanation. Had my tales of Collier artillery and other inventions driven the timing of the enemy attack? Of course, they had probably not anticipated a lengthy wait for their king to arrive and that was what had allowed the disease to take hold so vigorously. But if they had attacked outside of the rainy season, with their huge numerical superiority, they would probably have rolled over us with ease.

Things even out; I had received plaudits for a battle that I had stumbled through while drunk and now no words of praise or admiration for persuading the Ashanti to attack at the worst possible time. But suddenly I did not care, all I wanted now was to go home.

Chapter 31

It was the middle of July 1824 when I stood on the beach with Chisholm for the last time. We had been in the Ashanti camp just two days before and now, at last, I was destined to leave that accursed shore. It was not a moment too soon, for August, with its heavy mists that would carry the fever into every nook and cranny, was a bare two weeks away. The sickness looked like it was already creeping up on the major – he looked terrible.

"Are you all right?" I asked. "You look like death only slightly warmed up."

"Well the last week or two has been a little tiring, but I am sure that I will recover in time."

"If there is any justice, you should get a promotion and a new posting for what you have achieved here," I told him. I meant it too, for apart from his appalling sense of direction, he had done a sterling job. He had been everywhere during the defence, leading the garrison and helping, encouraging and liaising with the disparate groups of our allies. I thought that Sutherland was bound to claim all the glory for himself, but I was wrong about that. Chisholm was promoted to lieutenant colonel, although he died of fever that October before the news reached him.

"I am grateful to you for taking the boy," Chisholm said gesturing at the little group gathered by the ship's boat waiting to take me away. There, holding the hand of a woman in an Arab robe and veil was McCarthy's young son. He was cajoling O'Hara into a sword fight with two sticks. "If you can get him to the governor's sister then I am sure she will take him in. It will be a weight off my mind to have the lad taken care of."

I patted my pocket where I kept the paper with the name and address of the Countess de Mervé. Don't worry, I will take care of it and I'm grateful to you in turn for releasing O'Hara from his enlistment.

Chisholm laughed, "Well you'll need an orderly and between ourselves, with that Irishman and his foul concoctions out of the way, I suspect that incidents of drunkenness in the garrison will drop dramatically. He has served more than half of his sentence and I know he saved your life at the tower. I am happy for you to take him. But," he gestured to my fellow travellers, "I hope I am not going to have to deal with Jasmina's angry father when he learns that you have taken her as well."

"Fear not," I replied. "I can assure you that Jasmina's father is entirely happy with that arrangement." I held out my hand, "Good luck to you and thank you for your help in arranging our passage."

Our party climbed into the cutter as they saw me walking towards them across the sand. I was feeling jubilant and anxious to get on our way. I helped the two sailors push the boat the final few feet over the sand until it was afloat and then swung myself on board. The others made room for me on the thwarts and I stared down at the pile of luggage between us. Among it was Malala's leather satchel, which was now impressively heavy with the big gold axe blade emblem inside as well as the recently captured rings. I had left England nearly three years before hoping to gain a fortune in silver from South America. Instead, I was coming home with a fortune in gold and gems from Africa. I just hoped that I had not gone bankrupt while I had been away, although if anyone could keep me solvent it was my wife. She knew the farmers and lands on my estate better than anyone.

"Is France further away than Sara Lone?" asked the boy.

"Sierra Leone," I corrected. I guessed that young John must have been there with his father in the governor's brig. "Yes, it is much further away than that and we will have to sort you out some more clothes on the way, for it is much colder than here too." I looked up at the merchant ship we would be travelling in, a sturdy three-masted barque. Already I could feel my pulse quickening at the thought that I would soon be on home soil.

I waited on deck while they raised the anchor and the first sheets of canvas pulled the bow around to the open sea. I watched that fetid green shore fall astern and wished with every fibre of my being that I would never lay eyes on the wretched place again. My thoughts were interrupted by someone who shared them. "I wanted to thank you for gettin' me off, sor." O'Hara stood beside me and added softly, "I've left some good mates buried back there."

"What are you going to do when you get back home?" I asked.

"Well I have been thinking about what you said. I might get my own distillery after all. I have enough gold to get a business started. I sold enough of my brew out here and even you got a taste for it."

"Mmm. That was largely because you were the only producer. I don't want to be rude, O'Hara, but do you seriously think that people will drink your tonic if there is *anything* else available?" He looked a little hurt at that and so I suggested we went below and joined the others. As we swung open the door to the cabin, the woman half jumped up in alarm. "It is all right," I told her. "We are underway, you can remove the veil now."

She reached up and unpinned it. Instead of the dark hair of Jasmina, the blonde locks of Eliza were revealed. "Do you think anyone guessed?" she asked.

"Chisholm certainly didn't, he was worried about Jasmina's father." I replied. "They will all think you are still at your husband's side."

"Perhaps I should be," Eliza replied and I saw her eyes fill again with tears. Reverend Bracegirdle had heard of my imminent departure the previous day and had insisted that I take Eliza with me. He knew he had only days to live and was worried that she would succumb to fever in the August mists. He made her swear on the Bible that she would go, but she could not bear the thought of being seen to abandon her husband on his deathbed. That was when we came up with the idea of using my old Arab gown as a disguise. I have to say that she looked a lot better in the robes than me.

"Bessie will look after him," said O'Hara kindly, "and he has enough tonic to make sure that he is not in any pain. He will go more peaceably knowing that you are safe."

"I know," said Eliza, dabbing her eyes.

"Where is the boy?" I asked looking around.

"One of the crew has taken him off to the galley," she said. "I have been thinking," she continued. "If you wish, I will take him on to his aunt for you when we dock in France."

"Are you sure?" I asked. I had been wondering if I could persuade O'Hara to do the job for me.

"Yes. My father would not welcome me home. All that waits for me there is scandal. I would like to see France. Perhaps I will stay in Paris for a while."

"You will need money, then." I pulled the leather satchel towards me and took out one of Malala's thick gold bracelets. "Take this, you can sell it to a gold dealer in Nantes. There will be more than enough to pay for your journey and some time in Paris. There is an army officer I know well who lives in the city. I can write you a letter of introduction and he will help you settle in." The last I had heard from de Briqueville was that his wife had died. I wondered if my old comrade would offer Eliza rather more than a roof over her head...

I got up and walked to a sideboard, feeling the ship moving on the swell under my feet. There were some ship decanters in a rack and having removed a stopper and smelt the contents, I poured three glasses. Taking them back to the table I put them in front of my companions.

"What is this?" asked O'Hara suspiciously.

"From the smell of it, fine French brandy." I winked at him, "It's the drink of gentlemen, remember, the stuff that you hope your tonic can compete with."

He sipped it warily and then his eyes widened in surprise. "It's as smooth as a babe's arse," he declared with relish before having another taste.

"Perhaps you should go to France too," I suggested. "You could find out how they make it. The best is made in a region called Cognac. It is not that far from the town of Mervé."

"I might just do that," he agreed, glancing at Eliza to see if she would mind him coming with her at least part of the way.

She smiled back at him and then raised her glass. "Gentlemen, let us have a toast: to the future."

"I'll drink to that," said the Irishman, as our glasses clinked together.

258

Historical Notes

As usual, I am indebted to a variety of sources for confirming the information in Flashman's account. Principal amongst these were Captain Rickets, who wrote a detailed account of the first Ashanti War and the situation in West Africa at that time. In addition, Mr Williams reported his experiences, which were recorded by others, including Rickets. Sutherland's despatches to the British government are also in the archives. While none of these individuals visited the Ashanti capital, Thomas Bowdich, employed by the African Company of Merchants and Mr Dupuis from the British government did and they both left detailed accounts of life there, including illustrations in Bowdich's case, which can be viewed in the copy available from the British Library website. This also confirms the existence of Quashie as one of the Ashanti interpreters.

Flashman uses the same place names and spellings as Rickets, possibly as he had the captain's account with him when he was writing his own memoir. However, over the intervening years, the spelling of many place names has changed. Coomassie is now Kumasi, D'Jouquah is now Jukwa and Donquah now Dunkwa. Annamaboe where McCarthy went to meet King Appea is now Anomabu. There are some vestiges of Flashman's time still standing and these include Cape Coast Castle and the Dutch fort of Elmina seven miles up the coast, of which there are plenty of photographs online as these are now major tourist attractions. Rickets' journal includes drawings showing the towers around Cape Coast Castle built for its defence and at the right level of magnification you can still see McCarthy Hill (the site of Fort McCarthy) marked on Google Maps.

Other elements of Flashman's tale have also been confirmed by online resources. While the masonic organisation is notoriously secretive, there are references to Masonic Lodge No. 621, Torridzonian Lodge at Cape Coast Castle, which was inaugurated in 1810.

Sir Charles McCarthy

Charles McCarthy was born in Ireland to French parents. He joined the Irish Brigade in the French Army and changed his surname to McCarthy at around that time. He enlisted in the British Army in 1799, spending much of his time in Canada before being appointed to the Royal African Corps in 1811. In 1814 he was appointed governor of Sierra Leone and took an active role in managing the colony. He founded various settlements for freed slaves and supported missionaries in their attempts to establish schools. He was knighted in 1820.

The African Company of Merchants was abolished in 1821 for its failure to suppress the slave trade and the Gold Coast became a crown colony. McCarthy became the territory's governor while also retaining the governorship of Sierra Leone. He was soon introducing the same improvements for freed slaves in the Gold Coast that he had already established in his first colony. The dispute with the Ashanti arose originally as a result of the murder of a sergeant in the Royal African Corps. Opinion is divided as to whether McCarthy was just taking a firm hand with the Ashanti or whether he wanted to provoke them into war. Regardless, it is certain that he catastrophically underestimated their ability to prosecute that war once it began.

He did have a sister who married the Comte de Mervé. One of McCarthy's sons, also called Charles, was adopted by them and succeeded to the title on his uncle's death. The fate of his son John by Hannah Hayes/McCarthy is not recorded.

Battle of Nsamankow

The accounts of Mr Williams and Captain Rickets largely confirm Flashman's description of this extraordinary action. McCarthy and his allies were convinced that the Ashanti army were divided into around a dozen divisions. When in Assamacow, McCarthy was highly suspicious of local reports that Ashanti forces were approaching his army. Rickets confirms that McCarthy did indeed organise the band of the Royal African Corps to play *God Save the King* as they heard the Ashanti on the other side of the river. It seems that McCarthy was still entertaining the hope that some of the enemy were planning to defect. Having finally accepted that the enemy was not divided but opposing him in overwhelming force, McCarthy set to with the organisation of a defence across the Pra River.

The Royal African Corps and the native allies who had not run away at the start of the attack, managed to repel several assaults across the river over makeshift bridges made from cut down trees. However, ammunition was soon in short supply and so the arrival of Brandon with fresh supplies was initially very welcome. Contemporary sources confirm the astonishment of the defenders when it was discovered that most of the barrels contained not desperately needed cartridges, but macaroni. Rickets describes McCarthy as being so angry he would have had his quartermaster hung.

The Ashanti soon noticed a slackening of fire from the defenders and launched fresh attacks across the tree trunks as well as from both flanks. The final moments of McCarthy were not entirely as described by Flashman, although he was understandably distracted. According to some Ashanti accounts, it seems that McCarthy died by taking his own life with his pistol when it was clear that he was certain to be captured. His heart and head were removed, but this happened *post mortem*. There were reports that the Ashanti king did use his skull as a drinking vessel and that other parts of his body were taken as tokens by soldiers. The British government spent several years negotiating, unsuccessfully, for the return of McCarthy's skull.

Defence of Cape Coast Castle
There is no detailed account of the defence of Cape Coast Castle against the vast Ashanti attack, which began on 11 July 1824. This is probably due to the fact that the two people from whom we have records – Rickets and Sutherland – were some distance from the main action. Sutherland confirms that the attack was concentrated on the British right, around McCarthy Hill and that the engagement lasted from two in the afternoon until dusk at around six-thirty. He also includes the casualty numbers in his report. With just 103 killed and

448 wounded from a four-hour battle against overwhelming odds, this would indicate that the defenders used their cannon to keep the enemy at bay for much of the time. Sutherland records that the total allied force defending the castle was just over 5,000 with 4,650 of those being from their allied local kings and chiefs.

Further Ashanti conflicts with the British
The Ashanti were one of the most powerful kingdoms in West Africa and as this account shows, were able to deal robustly with European powers. They fought a further war with the British fifty years later in 1874, when a road was built to the Ashanti capital and some parts of the city were destroyed. But as Flashman had predicted, the Ashanti had evacuated Coomassie in advance of the British and there was no appetite to place a garrison there.

The British invaded again in 1896 and this time exiled the Ashanti king to the Seychelles. A British resident was left in the capital with a small garrison. In 1901 he caused great offence by demanding to sit on the Ashanti golden stool. This object is sacred to the Ashanti and appears on their flag to this day. A revolt ensued, the resident was rescued but the British never did get their hands on the golden stool. The Ashanti king was returned from exile in 1924.

Slavery in West Africa
The common perception is that white slavers would turn up on the coast, round up some Africans and load them into a ship to take them off into bondage. However, as the facts in this book make clear, that was not usually the case. Any white slaver rounding up people within the Ashanti dominion, for example, was likely to lose their head long before they could get back to their ship. The situation would be the same for many other powerful kingdoms.

Slavery existed in the region long before the plantations in the Caribbean and Americas. Slaves were also often treated cruelly. It was commonplace for a slave to be killed after their master died to serve their wealthy owner in the afterlife. Indeed, it was not always just slaves who were sacrificed. Bowdich reports that after the death of a member of the Ashanti royal family, most of the nobility made themselves scarce for the funeral as it was the custom to kill one of the mourners to give the deceased a more honoured companion in the next life.

White settlements on the coast were originally established for trade in items such as gold and ivory. However, as demand for slaves increased on the other side of the Atlantic the European traders were not slow to spot the opportunity. Initially buying from established slave markets, they were soon sending out agents to work with dealers and local chiefs to bring more slaves to the coast. As prices rose, the more powerful African rulers started to view their weaker neighbours as sources of revenue – while warily watching over their shoulder to ensure that some even stronger kingdom was not considering them in the same manner.

The African Company of Merchants were certainly not paragons of virtue in this period, operating from 1752 to 1821 in the Cape Coast Castle region. They were heavily involved in slave trading and, it would seem, not beyond re-writing treaties after they had been signed and selling out their native allies. There is evidence that they also turned a blind eye to continued slave trading in the region even after its abolition by the British government. This ultimately led to the company being disbanded and the region becoming a crown colony.

Various well-meaning – and some not so well-meaning – groups did try to return freed slaves back to Africa from the Caribbean, the United States and Canada. One of the leading organisations was the American Colonization Society, co-founded by Bushrod Washington, a nephew of George Washington. These returned settlers suffered high degrees of mortality from fever and struggled to thrive in an unfamiliar country without local support. There was often conflict with existing tribes and in some cases these new settlements disappeared – possibly having been sold back into slavery.

Settlements established in Sierra Leone and on the Gold Coast during McCarthy's governorship fared rather better. He was a passionate anti-slavery campaigner and ensured that freed slaves had land grants; he helped them to develop trades and encouraged missionaries to set up schools. Unfortunately, many of these initiatives ceased after his death. In the decade after McCarthy died, the territory had fourteen different governors or acting governors, with many incumbents dying of fever in post. Consequently, there was no consistent policy to develop the territory or support its inhabitants.

Thank you for reading this book and I hoped you enjoyed it. If so I would be grateful for any positive reviews on websites that you use to choose books. As there is no major publisher promoting this book, any recommendations to friends and family that you think would enjoy it would also be appreciated.

There is now a Thomas Flashman Books Facebook page and the www.robertbrightwell.com website to keep you updated on future books in the series. They also include portraits, pictures and further information on characters and events featured in the books.

Also by this author

Flashman and the Seawolf

This first book in the Thomas
Flashman series covers his
adventures with Thomas Cochrane,
one of the most extraordinary naval
commanders of all time.

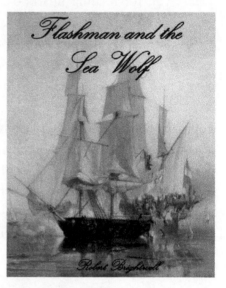

From the brothels and gambling
dens of London, through political
intrigues and espionage, the action
moves to the Mediterranean and
the real life character of Thomas
Cochrane. This book covers the start of Cochrane's career including
the most astounding single ship action of the Napoleonic war.

Thomas Flashman provides a unique insight as danger stalks him like
a persistent bailiff through a series of adventures that prove history
really is stranger than fiction.

Flashman and the Cobra

This book takes Thomas to territory familiar to readers of his nephew's adventures, India, during the second Mahratta war. It also includes an illuminating visit to Paris during the Peace of Amiens in 1802.

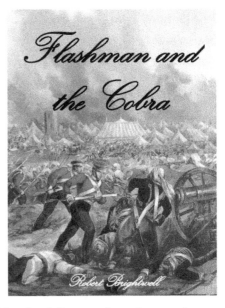

As you might expect Flashman is embroiled in treachery and scandal from the outset and, despite his very best endeavours, is often in the thick of the action. He intrigues with generals, warlords, fearless warriors, nomadic bandit tribes, highland soldiers and not least a four-foot-tall former nautch dancer, who led the only Mahratta troops to leave the battlefield of Assaye in good order.

Flashman gives an illuminating account with a unique perspective. It details feats of incredible courage (not his, obviously) reckless folly and sheer good luck that were to change the future of India and the career of a general who would later win a war in Europe.

Flashman in the Peninsula

While many people have written books and novels on the Peninsular War, Flashman's memoirs offer a unique perspective. They include new accounts of famous battles, but also incredible incidents and characters almost forgotten by history.

Flashman is revealed as the catalyst to one of the greatest royal scandals of the nineteenth century which disgraced a prince and ultimately produced one of  our greatest novelists. In Spain and Portugal he witnesses catastrophic incompetence and incredible courage in equal measure. He is present at an extraordinary action where a small group of men stopped the army of a French marshal in its tracks. His flatulent horse may well have routed a Spanish regiment, while his cowardice and poltroonery certainly saved the British army from a French trap.

Accompanied by Lord Byron's dog, Flashman faces death from Polish lancers and a vengeful Spanish midget, not to mention finding time to perform a blasphemous act with the famous Maid of Zaragoza. This is an account made more astonishing as the key facts are confirmed by various historical sources.

Flashman's Escape

This book covers the second half of Thomas Flashman's experiences in the Peninsular War and follows on from *Flashman in the Peninsula*.

Having lost his role as a staff officer, Flashman finds himself commanding a company in an infantry battalion. In between cuckolding his soldiers and annoying his superiors, he finds himself at the heart of the two bloodiest actions of the war. With drama and disaster in equal measure, he provides a first-hand account of not only the horror of battle but also the bloody aftermath.

Hopes for a quieter life backfire horribly when he is sent behind enemy lines to help recover an important British prisoner, who also happens to be a hated rival. His adventures take him the length of Spain and all the way to Paris on one of the most audacious wartime journeys ever undertaken.

With the future of the French empire briefly placed in his quaking hands, Flashman dodges lovers, angry fathers, conspirators and ministers of state in a desperate effort to keep his cowardly carcass in one piece. It is a historical roller-coaster ride that brings together various extraordinary events, while also giving a disturbing insight into the creation of a French literary classic!

Flashman and Madison's War

This book finds Thomas, a British army officer, landing on the shores of the United States at the worst possible moment – just when the United States has declared war with Britain! Having already endured enough with his earlier adventures, he desperately wants to go home but finds himself drawn inexorably into this new conflict. He is soon dodging musket balls, arrows and tomahawks as he desperately  tries to keep his scalp intact and on his head.

It is an extraordinary tale of an almost forgotten war, with inspiring leaders, incompetent commanders, a future American president, terrifying warriors (and their equally intimidating women), brave sailors, trigger-happy madams and a girl in a wet dress who could have brought a city to a standstill. Flashman plays a central role and reveals that he was responsible for the disgrace of one British general, the capture of another and for one of the biggest debacles in British military history.

Flashman's Waterloo

The first six months of 1815 were a pivotal time in European history. As a result, countless books have been written by men who were there and by those who studied it afterwards. But despite this wealth of material there are still many unanswered questions including:

-Why did the man who promised to bring Napoleon back in an iron cage, instead join his old commander?

-Why was Wellington so convinced that the French would not attack when they did?

-Why was the French emperor ill during the height of the battle, leaving its management to the hot-headed Marshal Ney?

-What possessed Ney to launch a huge and disastrous cavalry charge in the middle of the battle?

-Why did the British Head of Intelligence always walk with a limp after the conflict?

The answer to all these questions in full or in part can be summed up in one word: Flashman.

This extraordinary tale is aligned with other historical accounts of the Waterloo campaign and reveals how Flashman's attempt to embrace the quiet diplomatic life backfires spectacularly. The memoir provides a unique insight into how Napoleon returned to power, the treachery and intrigues around his hundred-day rule and how ultimately he was robbed of victory. It includes the return of old friends and enemies from both sides of the conflict and is a fitting climax to Thomas Flashman's Napoleonic adventures.

Flashman and the Emperor

This seventh instalment in the memoirs of the Georgian rogue Thomas Flashman reveals that, despite his suffering through the Napoleonic Wars, he did not get to enjoy a quiet retirement. Indeed, middle age finds him acting just as disgracefully as in his youth, as old friends pull him unwittingly back into the fray.

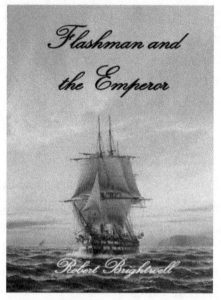

He re-joins his former comrade in arms, Thomas Cochrane, in what is intended to be a peaceful and profitable sojourn in South America. Instead, he finds himself enjoying drug-fuelled orgies in Rio, trying his hand at silver smuggling and escaping earthquakes in Chile before being reluctantly shanghaied into the Brazilian navy.

Sailing with Cochrane again, he joins the admiral in what must be one of the most extraordinary periods of his already legendary career. With a crew more interested in fighting each other than the enemy, they use Cochrane's courage, Flashman's cunning and an outrageous bluff to carve out nothing less than an empire which will stand the test of time.

CPSIA information can be obtained
at www.ICGtesting.com
Printed in the USA
LVHW041727231119
638280LV00003B/271/P